Ship of Shadows

STOLEN CROWNS
BOOK TWO

TEE HARLOWE

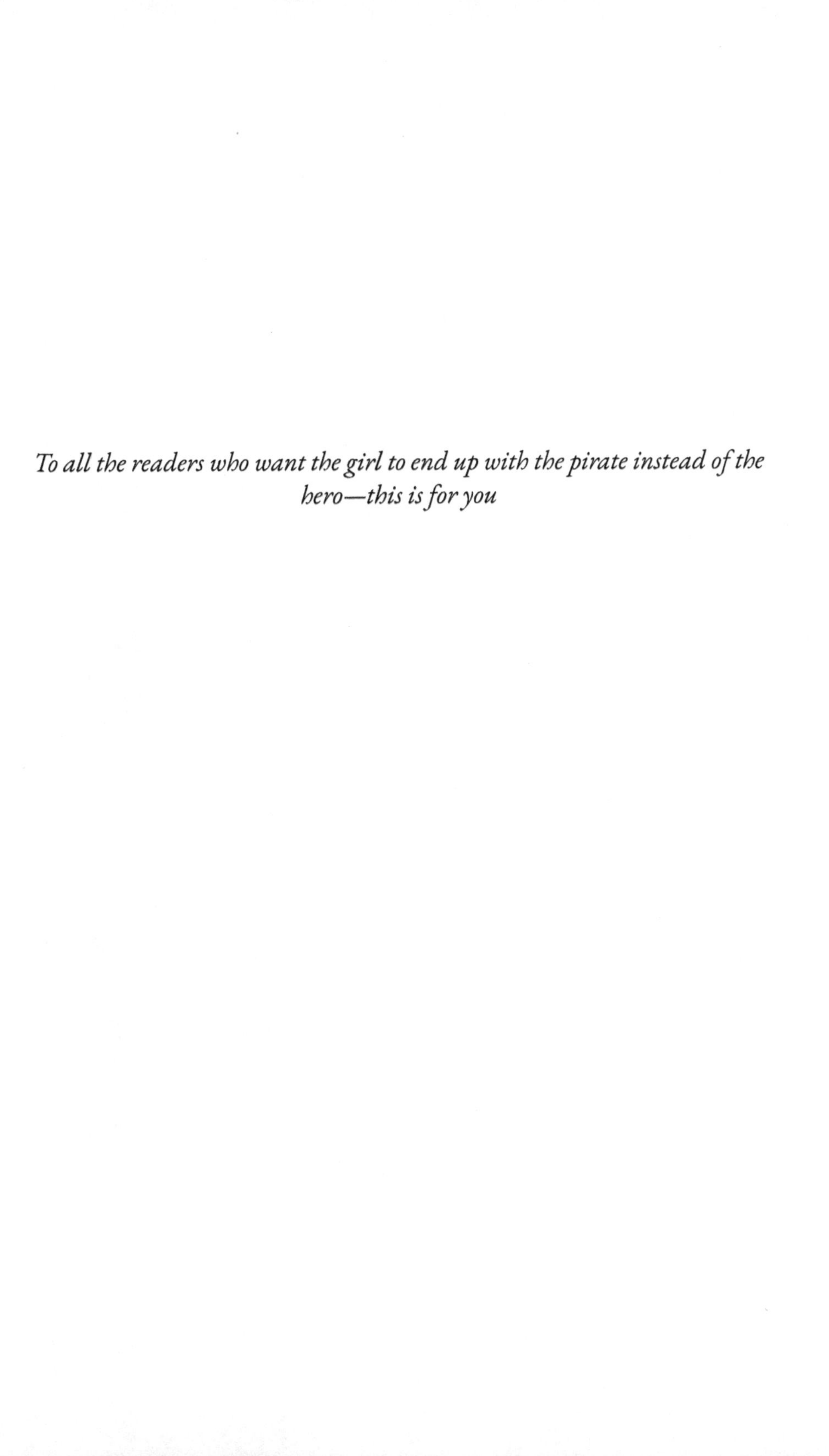

To all the readers who want the girl to end up with the pirate instead of the hero—this is for you

Introduction

If you'd like access to a free fantasy romance novella, plus exclusive content like bonus scenes, behind-the-scenes looks, and early sneak peeks at character art and cover reveals, then click here to subscribe to my newsletter.

STOLEN CROWNS
VALORIS: THE SKY COURT
THE SILVER SEAS
FYRIAD: THE FROST COURT
GLACIER MOUNTAINS
THE DEADLANDS
DRAGONSTONE MOUNA
MOSSWOOD FOREST
ELWEN: THE EARTH COURT
GILRA
THE FIRE
PYRE DESERT

Arathia
THE DARK SEAS
SORRENGARD:
THE SHADOW COURT
APOLIS:
THE WATER COURT

Part One

"Take care, lest an adventure is now offered you, which, if accepted, will plunge you in deepest woe."

Chapter One

I'd never seriously considered the merits of flinging myself off a cliff until today.

Now I was walking toward said cliff, stars twinkling above, sand squishing under my bare feet. A warm breeze flowed through the air, and my white chiffon fluttered, brushing against my skin.

It would be quite the scandal if anyone knew the princess of the water court was currently slinking around outside, alone and unprotected.

But that was the point. I wanted to be alone. This would likely be the last night I would ever be able to do something like this, and I was going to take advantage of it. A final reckless act before everything changed.

I could just hear my mother's voice in my head. *You've really let me down this time, Gabrielle.*

If she only knew the ways I'd actually let her down, but I was not thinking about that tonight. Not when I had more important things to do. Things like free-diving off cliffs.

The ocean waves rushed up over my feet, the water warm and inviting. I looked out over the inky black of the sea, a sheath of heavy fog hanging above it, the view murky.

High and jagged cliffs rose in the distance. In the night, they looked like monsters, snaggletoothed and ready to devour anyone who attempted to climb them. I remembered the stories I'd tell my brothers about them when we used to sneak out, the three of us, adventurous and carefree. But my brothers were never cowed like I expected them to as I described the stony jaws of death that would snatch them up should they come too close. They were as fearless as me.

Now I was alone. Carrying on the torch of stupidity for all three of us. If they were here, they'd no doubt be by my side, likely the only ones encouraging this foolish mission.

"You know, I'd love it if just once you'd include me in your hare-brained schemes," a voice said from behind me.

I jumped, turning to see Leoni standing there.

A look of amusement lined her face, her red-gold hair in a tight bun atop her head. She planted her hands on her wide hips, adorned by a golden belt that cinched her chiffon to her waist, a sword hanging at her side. "I knew you were careless, but attempting this, on the eve of the most important day of your life? You're being an idiot," she said in a singsong voice.

I crossed my arms. "You realize you're talking to your future queen?"

She cocked a brow. "Apologies. You're being an idiot, Your Majesty." She dipped into a curtsy.

I spun on my heel. "Well, this was a nice chat. Let's just pretend you didn't see me. None of this happened," I called behind me, continuing on my way down the shoreline.

"I know what you're doing," she shouted, "and I'm not going to let you."

The point of something sharp poked into my back. Spirits below. I sighed. "Is this really necessary?"

"Yes, because if anything happens to you, it will be my fault, and I will lose my job, and probably my head along with it."

"Wow, that's so sweet." I put a hand to my chest. "Glad to know you care so much about me."

That wasn't fair. Leoni had been my best friend since we were children. I knew she cared, and I also knew this job meant the world to her. She loved what she did—was my fiercest protector. That's why I'd recommended her for the position. But tonight, I didn't want her to be my captain of the guard; I just wanted her to be my friend.

I slowly turned. "Put down the sword, Oni. I'm not going to fight you."

As many times as we'd sparred and trained together, I wasn't in the mood for it tonight.

She eyed me warily and slowly lowered her weapon. The gold cuffs around her arms glinted in the moonlight as she relaxed her shoulders. "There's a reason you and your brothers never attempted this. Because it's stupid. It's dangerous. And it might get you killed."

I eyed the tall cliffs in the distance, and my heart squeezed. Yes, it was all of those things, but I had to do this. Leoni didn't get it. After tomorrow, everything would change. I wouldn't have the freedom I had now, wouldn't just have Leoni watching me. It would be everyone, all the time. This was truly the last day of my life I'd be able to do something so reckless, and I wanted to. Not just for myself, but for Mal and Lochlan.

Leoni's face softened. "Fine," she said.

I narrowed my eyes. "You're not going to stop me?"

"Would I be able to?"

I smiled. "Not likely."

She heaved a big breath. "Then let's get this over with. But if you die, I will find a way to bring you back just so I can wring your neck."

I believed it. She might have been half a foot shorter than me, but she'd bested me enough times in the sparring ring that she could injure me if she really wanted to. I blew her a kiss and continued my trek along the beach as Leoni grumbled something about me being a "pain in her ass" while she followed, her sandals squishing in the sand.

"I never got why you and your brothers wanted to do this, anyway," she said. "It's the Cliffs of Death. The name has death in it. Why would you want to jump from them into the Dark Seas?"

I laughed. "Because it's fun?"

"Fun?" Leoni echoed. "Fun is gossiping. Fun is sparring. Fun is splashing in the ocean. Not flinging yourself off a cliff."

I threw out my arms. "I don't know how to explain it, Oni. It's the thrill of it. The danger, the adventure."

The feeling of freedom, something I sorely lacked as princess of the water court.

"If you want danger, then go try Mistress Tessa's fish rolls." She shook her head, then mumbled, "Trust me, that's about as dangerous as it gets."

A smile quirked my lips. The fish rolls supposedly tasted amazing but also came with a great risk of food poisoning.

Leoni jabbed a finger at me. "You know, being captain of your guard has aged me at least ten years." She pointed to her hair. "I found a gray hair this morning. I'm twenty-eight, and I have gray hair. Yet look at you: thirty years old and hair as auburn as those pretty leaves in the earth court."

I ignored the comment about my hair. "And you're attributing that to me?" I asked. "It could just be bad genes, you know."

"No, it's definitely the stubborn princess whose ass I'm always saving."

"You know, at some point you need to learn to filter yourself. You're going to be the captain of the queen's guard now. That mouth will get you in trouble."

She huffed. "Just worry about yourself, okay? If your mother knew you were here, she'd have a heart attack. She'd kick my ass. Then she'd kick yours."

I lifted my chin. "If you're going to be negative about this, then I'd rather you go back to the castle."

We neared the cliffs, their sharp edges and ridges outlined under the bright moon.

"I'm not letting you do this alone."

I nudged her. "Thanks, Oni."

"Don't thank me." She nudged me back. "I still think this is stupid, but I also know you're as stubborn as the Seven Spirits and won't listen to reason."

"You know me well."

I flipped my braid over my shoulder as we came upon the curve of the shoreline that rounded the tall cliffs. Vicious waves rose high and then crashed down with a thundering force. Leoni winced.

No one ventured to this part of the water court, the wildest part, where the waves rolled untethered. That's why I loved it so much, why

Mal and Lochlan had loved it. It had been a respite from everyone, everything, we constantly had to deal with. My father's stern, watching eye, my mother's badgering. Out here, we could just be us, talk about our hopes and dreams. Pretend we could have things like hopes and dreams.

I swallowed. But that had been a different life.

My gaze trailed to a ship jutting out of the water near the shore. Well, ship was a generous term. It crested up on the rocks, holes battering the hull, planks sticking out at awkward angles. A shipwreck. Which was what generally happened to any vessels that came near this part of the water court.

"Are you just going to stand here all night? I'd like to get some sleep, so let's hurry this idiotic scheme along please." Leoni shooed me forward.

I gave a stiff nod, then began my climb, fingers and feet digging into the crevices and cracks. I'd climbed these cliffs so many times I could probably do it with my eyes closed.

But then Leoni might actually kill me.

I looked down as she stared up at me, sea water spraying us from the unrelenting waves crashing at the little cove.

"Are you coming?" I called.

"No, I'd like to not break all the bones in my body, thank you," she said.

I snorted a laugh and continued my climb, muscles stretching, hard rock cool and firm under my hands and feet. My breaths grew labored as I ascended, and sweat formed on my brow, trickling down the sides of my face. Finally, I made it to the top and pulled myself up, walking along the edge and to the point that jutted out over the sea.

"Took you long enough," Leoni called up.

I just shook my head, giving myself a moment to look out over the shimmering dark waves. Leoni was right. This was stupid.

I was going to do it anyway.

I inhaled a deep breath, bracing my legs and readying myself to jump, when my gaze caught on something in the distance. A ship. I could just see its outline through the fog.

"Oh, don't tell me you changed your mind," Leoni yelled over the roar of the ocean. "It's all good and fine if you don't want to jump, but

I'd appreciate this revelation much more if you'd had it before we made the trek out here."

I squinted at the dark form, sails billowing, ship gliding through the waters. No ships came to the Cliffs of Death. It was too violent, too dangerous to even attempt to dock a boat here. No one came here, except . . . *him.*

I stilled. But no. I'd told him to never return, that I never wanted to see his face again. Besides, he didn't have a ship anymore. My gaze flicked to the wrecked vessel below. I'd made sure of that.

I looked closer, recognizing the blue-and-green flag flapping in the wind. The colors of Apolis. I'd know that flag anywhere.

My father's ship—which hadn't been seen for six months. Six long months since he'd left to find my brothers. Six long months of guilt weighing on my shoulders for the role I'd played in their disappearance. My heart hammered in my chest. Had he found them? Was he back with all of them safe and sound? But why would he sail here? It didn't make sense.

"Hello?" Leoni shouted. "What has gotten into you?"

My eyes snapped to her round face, and I pointed, yelling back, "There's something out there."

She spun, facing the water, rising on her tiptoes and arching her neck. "I don't see anything," she called.

I looked back up. Nothing but fog rolled across the ocean.

I'd just seen it. It was there. It had to be. Unless I was imagining things, wishing it into existence. Because if my father had returned with my brothers, then everything would be okay. My life wouldn't have to so drastically change tomorrow.

I shook my head, still searching. Leoni was right. There was nothing, just the dark expanse of sea and thick gray mist.

Leoni turned back to me. "What did you think you saw?"

"I—my father's ship—I swear it was there."

Leoni planted her hands on her hips. "Your father is gone. He's not coming back. I know you miss him. I know you miss Mal and Lochlan, and I know you feel guilty over what happened to them—"

"Don't," I snapped, and suddenly the weight of everything crashed over me.

"Is that what all of this is about?" Leoni shouted.

I sighed and sunk down on the edge of the cliff, legs hanging over the side.

Leoni stepped toward the tall rock. "I know you think it's your fault—"

"It is my fault." I massaged my temples.

"This"—Leoni gestured to the cliff right as another wave crashed, shaking the rock underneath me—"isn't going to bring your brothers back."

I squeezed my eyes shut. She was right. What was I doing out here? What was I thinking? That I'd jump off the cliff and somehow feel closer to my brothers, feel like I was honoring them in some way? That I'd do this ridiculous stunt we always said we'd do and my life would magically be okay? Maybe part of me thought the sea would swallow me up—and my guilt along with it.

But none of those things would happen. Blood and water. I'd been so stupid. I started climbing down, Leoni silent until I hopped into the soft sand, facing her. Disappointment welled in me. This entire trip had been a waste of time. A silly fantasy that I'd thought was a good idea. This grief, this guilt, was twisting my mind.

She put a hand on my shoulder. "You can't keep blaming yourself for what happened to them—or to your father." I'd never stop, but she didn't understand. She couldn't understand. "C'mon, let's get back to the castle. Hopefully you can at least get a few hours' sleep."

Right. I'd need it.

Tomorrow I would be crowned queen of Apolis, and my life, as I knew it, would officially be over.

Chapter Two

I stood at the front of the throne room, filled to the brim with people from all the courts on the continent, leaders from the human lands, and even some of the seafolk, who rarely left their ocean dens to venture onto land. I supposed this was a special occasion, and we'd always had a kinship with the seafolk over any other court because of our shared water powers, our shared connection with the sea. I glanced out the huge windows lining our throne room to see a few more seafolk emerging from the ocean, their tails separating and turning into legs as they walked ashore. Scales covered their arms and snaked up their necks, sparkling under the bright sun and matching their even brighter hair: all shades of the rainbow, from green to orange to scorching red.

Despite their legs, you'd never mistake the seafolk for a human or an elemental. Not with those scales.

A few human guests bowed before my mother, and she nodded her head in return. Elementals and humans were harder to tell apart, our features almost identical—but today, in my throne room, it was an easy difference to tell. The humans looked nervous at being surrounded by so much magic and power. They shifted on their feet, eyes constantly moving from side to side. But the courts had created treaties long ago to ensure we had no conflict with the non-magical beings. We traded with the humans, welcomed them to our lands, and generally left their lands alone.

The bright sun, now high in the sky, lit the space with its golden hue, and the entire water court was on display from our castle windows. I loved my court, thought it was the most beautiful of all the courts on Arathia. A glittering river, fed by the sea, snaked its way through the town in a circle. Beige-colored shops and houses dotted the rocky terrain, all the buildings shoved close together and lining either side of the river. Narrow stone streets zigzagged through the buildings.

Despite our small size, if you didn't know our court well, it was easy to get lost in those streets. But always an adventure. Getting lost was the best way to discover new shops with delectable treats, lost treasures, and some of the finest bath salts and scrubs on the entire continent. From here, I could see my people in their small boats, paddling their way through the river, going about their day and waiting for my official presentation as their queen later today.

The throne that would soon be mine sat behind me, glimmering gold, the seat cushion a deep blue that reminded me of our sapphire sea. Steps led from the dais down to the white-tiled floors, where everyone stood, sandwiched between tall white columns, chattering and murmuring as they waited for the ceremony to begin. Pink flowers and blue coral decorated the columns, reminding our guests of the beauty of the sea.

Our borders had been closed ever since my brothers—and all the boys of Apolis—disappeared, but my mother had insisted we reopen them for this. She didn't want the other courts to think anything was amiss. I didn't blame her, not when all the courts of Arathia were so terrified of any kind of conflict.

Leoni leaned over from where she stood next to me. "Can you look a little less like you're walking to your death and more like you're about to be the queen of Apolis?"

Walking to my death. That felt accurate, actually. But I couldn't show that on my face. She was right. I needed to put on a better front. I cleared my throat and stretched a smile across my face.

All the foreigners would no doubt be wondering where the king and princes of the water court were. After I was crowned queen, we planned to tell them the truth of what happened. We'd avoided it for so long, waiting for my father and brothers to return, but it was clear that wasn't going to happen.

We just hoped the other courts wouldn't react badly to the news. We had the support of the earth court, at least. I searched the crowd for Queen Liliath, even though she wasn't here. It would be nice to see a friendly face, to see someone who understood what it was like for your court to be weakened.

She'd sent me a lovely note explaining why she couldn't come, and I understood. She'd just won back her own court from her stepmother, and she needed to be there to rebuild. She also was planning a wedding, one I'd been invited to attend.

Liliath had mentioned she was sending someone in her place to represent the earth court. My gaze landed on Driscoll, one of her closest friends. Like Leoni, he had no problem speaking his mind. He smiled and gave a wave, and I nodded in acknowledgement.

Leoni leaned over. "The queen is smiling so hard at you I think she's about to burst a blood vessel."

Leoni was right. My poor mother's smile looked so forced I was surprised her face didn't ache from the effort of it. She stood in the front, the crown on her head gleaming, aqua-blue jewels studding the points. When I was little, I'd spend hours staring at that crown, mesmerized by the way the jewels reflected all the colors of the sea. I'd trace the lines carved into the sides that looked like curling waves. I'd think about how heavy that crown might weigh on my own head.

Today, I'd find out.

Leoni nudged me. "Bloody waters, could you please just give the crowd a smile?"

Right. I kept forgetting. I plastered a smile on my face, hoping it looked genuine and not like, how did Leoni put it? Like I was walking to my death.

Leoni nodded and went back to scouring the room with her assessing blue eyes, hand on the sword hanging from her golden belt.

I blew out a breath and patted the dark blue skirts of my dress, which spread out on the ground and trailed behind me like a pool of water. Every detail today had been planned to remind us all of the beauty and power of the water court, to wow everyone so much that maybe they'd forget to be horrified when I told them why half our population was missing. I snorted. What an idiotic plan.

Blood and water. I wanted this day to end as soon as possible. Speaking of—I arched my neck, looking for the head priestess who would be overseeing the ceremony. We couldn't begin until she arrived, and I was more than ready to get this over with.

"Where is Priestess Amari?" I asked.

Leoni frowned.

My mother leaned over and whispered something to the captain of her personal guard, and my brows scrunched together as I read her lips: *Where is Priestess Amari?*

She was wondering the same thing. A rock settled in my stomach, hard and heavy. Priestess Amari was never late. In fact, she was known for whipping her acolytes for tardiness. She wouldn't arrive late to a dinner, let alone a coronation. My mother's tired gaze met mine, and she tugged at the loose gray curls that framed her face, the rest of her hair in an elaborate updo of braids, all twisted into a bun that sat atop her head. She wrung her hands together, and from here I could see the way they shook. She was as nervous for today as I was. And here I stood, thinking all about how this was affecting me.

My mother was doing what she thought best for her people, ushering in a new era of hope after she'd lost her husband and two sons. Yet my only concern had been me, me, me. Shame swept over me like the force of a wave.

Finally, the big golden doors burst open in the back of the room, Priestess Amari standing there in the golden robes that all priestesses of the water court wore, her long white hair hanging loose down her back. She didn't have her usual calm demeanor, but instead, her chest rose and fell with heavy breaths, her eyes wild.

The entire room fell silent as everyone turned toward her, no doubt expecting that the ceremony was about to begin.

"He's back," she said, her voice echoing around the cavernous room that had sunk into silence.

Leoni sucked in a sharp breath, and my mother looked like she was about to faint. I stepped forward.

"Who is back?" I asked in a calm, assured voice expected of a future queen.

"Your father," she burst out. "His ship has returned to Apolis."

Chapter Three

The room burst into chaos, everyone immediately running for the doors and following Priestess Amari to the docks, yelling out and shoving each other to get through and figure out what in the bloody waters was happening. Something I'd like to know, as well.

My mother actually did faint. Right into her guard's arms.

I instructed the guards to take the queen back to her room, then spun on my heel and marched in the opposite direction of the doors.

Leoni followed me up the steps of the dais and behind the massive throne toward a column that stood against the back wall, the head of a statue sitting on top. It was of my great-grandfather, his face so serious, lips in a thin line, eyes surveying the room. Lochlan had often joked that every time we used this secret passageway, his frown grew deeper.

"What are you doing?" Leoni asked.

I hated that I was about to reveal this to her. She'd likely have it closed up so I could never use it again. But this was an emergency, and I needed to get to the docks before everyone else.

I took a deep breath and looked behind me. No one was paying attention, everyone either looking out the windows or trying to shove their way out the doors.

I pushed the column, and it tipped diagonally, the statue's head tipping with it. A hole was dug into the white stone, just big enough for a person to get onto their hands and knees and crawl through the opening.

Leoni's mouth dropped open, and she planted her hands on her hips. "Are you kidding me right now? A secret passageway?"

I dove into the opening in the wall. "I don't have time to explain." I hadn't been in this tunnel in so long, not since my brothers were still here.

"When this is all said and done, I'm going to murder you," Leoni grumbled, following after me as I dropped onto my hands and knees. "Metaphorically. But you should still be scared."

"Go ahead and make it literal," I said. "It would solve all my problems."

She snorted behind me. "Where does this lead to?"

"You'll see," I told her as we crawled in darkness, the ground rough and pebbled under my hands.

"I can't believe you've kept this hidden from me all these years. What if part of the tunnel collapsed and you got stuck in here?" Leoni asked. "What if you got closed in? What if—"

"Well, none of those things happened," I gritted out, feeling my way ahead in the darkness. Dirt probably coated my face, my hands, my entire dress, at this point.

"This isn't going to fix things, you know," Leoni said from behind me.

"What are you talking about?" The ground rubbed against my knees, scraping at my skin. I'd need a salve for that later.

"I know what you're thinking." Leoni's sword clanged against the tunnel wall. "That if your father is back, if your brothers are back, things can return to how they were. But they can't. You're not just going to be able to run away from all this, not like you'd planned to."

Not like you'd planned to. Her words struck down my own, rendering me silent until I finally sputtered, "You knew?"

"Of course I knew," she scoffed.

I could just imagine the way she was rolling her eyes as she said it. I thought I'd been so careful with my planning. I'd spent months routing out my escape: the day, the time, the location. I hadn't told a soul, not even my brothers, who might've been the only ones who'd understood. I was afraid that if I told anyone, they'd stop me. I so badly wanted my freedom, and I'd been so selfish.

"Why didn't you say anything?" I asked. "Why not stop me?"

She sighed. "Because you were the happiest I'd ever seen you. And because I didn't want to take that from you. Not yet, anyway. I was never going to let you leave, but I didn't have it in me to dash your dreams, so I waited, and then . . ."

And then it all went to shit, and my brothers and all the boys disappeared, and my father went after them, and it was because of me. Because of him. I'd let myself fall for him, fall for his stupid promises of freedom, fall for his easy smile and charming words. Then he betrayed me and blew my life to pieces. And Leoni had known about every bit of it.

"How could you still want to be my friend?" I asked. "Protect me? I betrayed you. I betrayed everybody."

"No." Her voice was fierce. "He did. And if I ever see the pirate lord of the Dark Seas again, I will run my sword straight through him."

That made two of us. A light appeared ahead, squeezing through the round iron grate. We were almost out of the tunnel.

I'd confided in Leoni about my affair with the pirate lord, but not about my plan to run away with him. She hadn't approved of the relationship, of course. Warned me that he was not to be trusted. I didn't listen. She was right, in the end, but she'd never rubbed it in my face, never said the dreaded *I told you so.* Now she knew the full, ugly truth. Not only had I let that man into my heart, my bed, but I'd been planning to abandon my duty and leave with him.

"I don't deserve you," I said as I approached the opening of the tunnel.

"You definitely don't." I could hear the smile in her voice. "You were following your heart, okay? I can't blame you for that. And you shouldn't blame yourself either. If we're going to blame anyone, it's the pirate lord."

That was too easy of an out for me. I couldn't place all the blame on him. I was a grown woman, and I'd made my choices.

I reached into my hair, pulling out a pick and shoving it into the lock.

Leoni tsked behind me. "I thought I told you to get rid of that thing."

"I keep it just in case."

She muttered under her breath. "You're a princess. What kind of princess keeps a pick 'just in case'?"

"It comes in handy." I wiggled it this way and that until the lock finally clicked and the grate swung open. "Like right now, for instance."

I crawled out of the tunnel and jumped to my feet atop the rocky hill, the docks just below. Apolis spread out before me, taking my breath away like it always did. The rocks led down to the coastline, the sparkling sea spreading out beyond. The docks floated in front of a stone boardwalk, and steps from the boardwalk led down to the white-sand shore.

My heart stopped in my chest as I searched the water. There was my father's ship, sailing straight toward the docks, those green-and-blue sails billowing in the wind, sea swiping at the sides. Its name was scrawled across the side: *Pearl*. It was real. Spirits below, it was real.

Leoni jumped out of the tunnel and bumped into me, forcing me forward. "Oops, sorry," she said.

The roar of the crowd caught my attention as Priestess Amari led them toward the docks, all of them marching down the steep steps cut into the rocks that led from our castle.

"Let's go," I said.

I picked my way down the rocky hillside until my slippered feet hit the sand, and then I ran for the docks, sand flying in all directions as I rushed up the steps and across the boardwalk. I slowed as I approached the docks, watching the ship.

My heart pounded, blood thrumming in my veins at the sight of the vessel. I never thought I'd see my father again. Everything was going to be okay after all. After all the heartache, the suffering my people had gone through, their king was home, and we'd figure out the rest together. Maybe he'd found valuable information about how we could save our boys that had disappeared. My brothers.

Maybe he had them on his ship.

I lifted my skirts and ran across the wooden planks. Ocean water misted my face, the warm wind blowing my hair as more and more of it fell from the bun on my head. I swiped at my auburn strands and capped my eyes from the glare of the sun.

Leoni's sandaled feet pounded against the dock as she approached behind me. "Why does the ship look so empty?" she asked.

Why, indeed?

A cold dread quickly replaced my elation. Something wasn't right. The crowd grew closer, everyone yelling, shouting out as they stood on the sand next to the boardwalk. Furrowed brows and looks of confusion filled their faces. At this point, no one had any clue what was happening, and they'd be demanding an explanation. One I'd need to provide. I prayed to Spirit Water my father would soon appear to answer those questions.

I peered at the ship as it sailed closer, but it wasn't coming toward the docks like I expected. It was sailing right toward the shore—right toward all the people gathered.

Shit.

I waved my arms. "Move!" I called out as the ship barreled toward them, riding in on the rolling waves. "We have to do something." I closed my eyes and tugged at that invisible thread of magic inside of me, pulling at it and imagining it traveling through my veins, filling me with its power, until it snaked down my arms and to my fingers. I opened my eyes and stuck out my arms, pulling them toward the sky and commanding the water up, up, up.

It obeyed, rising into a tall wall of shimmering sea. Seaweed, fish, and other sea life floated in the wall like little decorative ornaments.

Others from the crowd began stepping up, their elemental magic flaring to life in their opened palms: a ball of fire, vines stretching out and slithering along the ground like snakes, ice shards floating in the air and ready to strike like daggers. The humans staggered back, the seafolk shooting glances at each other, no doubt wondering if they should jump back into the sea and swim away from all of this.

"No," I shouted, my panic rising, my magic wavering, as my concentration broke. Bits of the water wall fell away, splashing down into the sea. "Don't! We cannot risk hurting the king!"

Wariness overcame them, but Leoni ran to the boardwalk and down the stone steps. She motioned to the other guards, who all formed a line in front of those who summoned their magic. With wary glances at each other, they let their powers fade away, hands dropping to their sides.

The wall I'd created ran right along the shoreline, separating the crowd from the sea. It shimmered, transparent, the ship coming ever closer until it finally crashed through the water, a thunderous sound filling the air. The wall slowed it considerably and gave everyone a chance to back away toward the boardwalk as the ship flew through my magic and landed in the sand with a resounding crash. I ran down the dock and onto the boardwalk, staring in horror.

Wood splintered and shot out, some people ducking, others instinctively throwing up their magic. Fire sprang from one woman's hand, incinerating the wood before it hit her. People screamed, crouching down. Others shielded loved ones.

This was a nightmare.

Still, the crowd stayed, everyone curious to see the king who was about to emerge from that ship.

I stepped forward, readying myself to jump up and yank him out if need be, but it turned out I didn't have to.

He rose from the deck floor, standing up slowly, scratching his head through that thick black hair.

My mouth dropped open, and a collective gasp sounded from the crowd.

It wasn't my father at all.

It was him. Bastian Lore. The pirate lord of the Dark Seas.

Chapter Four

Bastian's cold, hard stare speared me, nothing like the man who'd spent months whispering sweet nothings into my ear. Worse, he didn't look well. Purple smudges stained the area under his eyes, his normally tanned face was pale, too pale, and he hunched like he was in so much pain he couldn't stand straight.

For a moment, the world faded away as I stared at him over the crowd, and he stared right back at me, his face bunched in a grimace. My heartbeat pounded in my ears. My fists curled at my sides, breaths coming in quick spurts.

Then everything came tumbling back into a stark reality. Yells exploded as the crowd surged forward, everyone talking all at once, some wondering who this man was, others already whispering his name: the pirate lord. His face was plastered on Wanted posters in every court across Arathia. At this point, he was a well-recognized man.

Just another reason it had been so foolish to dream of a future together.

Leoni and other guards tried to stop the crowd from rushing the ship. Bastian didn't move, just leaned against the bannister. He looked barely conscious.

"Do something, Princess Gabrielle!" Leoni shouted over the crowd, who was now calling for the pirate lord's head. I stood frozen on the boardwalk behind everyone, thankful they weren't looking at me and the horrified expression that was no doubt plastered to my face.

Lochlan had always teased that I was terrible at hiding my emotions.

"He's a criminal!" someone shouted.

"He's killed the king of Apolis," someone else yelled. "Why else would he be on the *Pearl*?"

"What in the bloody skies is going on?" someone else asked.

The crowd shoved forward, clamoring to get to my father's ship and yank Bastian from it.

It was mass hysteria.

I shook my head, snapping out of whatever trance his appearance had put me in. I rushed down the boardwalk steps and pushed through the crowd.

"Move," I yelled, shoving my way through until I stood in front of the rope ladder dangling down the side of the *Pearl*.

I climbed the ladder halfway up, then turned and held out my hand, summoning a sword made of water.

"Don't come any closer," I shouted, hanging from the rope with my sword pointing outward. "The pirate is in the water court's jurisdiction, and he will be dealt with accordingly."

A man with fiery red hair stepped forward, a scowl on his face. I recognized him from the frost court. "And how do we know we can trust you?" he asked, ice crackling over his hands. "Apparently your king is missing? And now his ship appears with the pirate lord steering it? What in the spirits below has been going on in the water court?"

At his words, yells once again erupted from the crowd. I was losing them, losing all the control. Blood and water. This day couldn't be any worse. I was supposed to be able to tell them what had happened on my terms.

Now it definitely seemed like we were hiding something.

"Why is the pirate lord on the king's ship?" another voice yelled.

That was a very good question. One I intended to find the answer to. I whipped around on the rope ladder, arching my neck to look up at Bastian. He hadn't moved, was still hunched over, and I could've sworn he let out a groan.

Fuck.

What was wrong with him? The Bastian I knew was fierce, ready to fight anyone and anything standing in his way, had a sharp word always ready at the tip of his tongue. It would almost make me feel better if he tried to fight me. Tried to do something other than just stand there.

I sighed. I couldn't worry about him. I didn't want to worry about him.

The crowd pushed against my guards, all of them with their water magic swirling, creating a barrier, ready to stop anyone who dared come too close to their princess. They could only hold the people for so long, though. Their magic wouldn't last forever, and they'd soon deplete their stores of it. I had to fix this.

"Kill him!" a young woman screamed from the middle of the crowd, a human. "He and his pirates raided our town, stole many of our goods. Kill him for his crimes!"

"We will take him back to the castle and let the queen decide his fate," I said firmly, my voice carrying over the cries for his head.

The man with the red hair crossed his arms. "None of us are leaving until we see that justice has been served and you explain what in the spirits below is going on."

Everyone nodded in agreement behind him.

Perfect. Just perfect.

We arrived back at the castle, Bastian in tow. The entire walk had been a blur. I kept my distance from him, but he could barely walk, the guards dragging him most of the way up the steep stairs. His head lolled. The queen might not even have to order his execution. He seemed nearly dead already.

I swallowed back any feelings that thought brought up, reminding myself of his betrayal.

Our castle sat at the top of the rocky hill, on a cliffside that jutted over the water. It gleamed white under blue skies. It was beautiful, from its intricate statues of mermaids that framed all the balconies to its golden peaks at the highest points to the stained-glass windows that glimmered like sea glass under the sun. Most would kill to call this their home, yet here I'd been, trying to run away from it. I didn't think the shame would ever leave me.

The guards kicked open the huge wooden doors and yanked Bastian across the threshold and toward the golden doors of the throne room. His black boots scraped along the white marble floors, making me wince.

The crowd marched behind us, silent now, no doubt eager for whatever punishment the queen would dole out. We needed their trust, needed them to understand that Apolis was strong. If anyone could make them believe that was true, it would be my mother. My mother at her best, which she hadn't been in a long, long time.

The throne room was empty, my mother still resting in her room. I'd have to send for a servant to fetch her. Hopefully she was awake by now, regaining her strength. My mother was strong, but even the strongest of women could only handle so much. She'd just heard her husband might be alive, returned to her, and now she was going to find out all over again he was gone. That instead of his ship delivering him back to Apolis, it had brought the pirate lord, whom she detested. Like most of Arathia.

We marched past the tall white columns of the throne room that stretched to the ceiling, where blue waves were painted.

Bastian was infamous across all the courts of Arathia, known for selling dangerous items on the black market, for stealing and looting and terrorizing anyone who dared to cross the Dark Seas.

He was also far too charming, gorgeous, quick witted, brave . . . At least, I thought he had been, until I learned of the truth about what he'd done—and it was so much worse than stealing some dangerous items.

His wavy black hair curled around his ears, head bobbing as the guards threw him onto the steps of the dais, and he landed with a sickening thud in front of the throne.

He rolled onto his back, eyes barely open. He groaned and propped himself up, his black leather pants and black boots smudged with dirt and sand. He lifted a hand to stroke his bearded jaw, his black eyebrows bunching in confusion as his gaze met mine.

"Well, hello, love," he slurred in that deep accent that I loved. "It's been a while."

I froze. I had no idea what was wrong with him, but he was clearly out of it, and I needed to shut him up.

"Do not speak to me like that," I said, stepping forward. "I am the princess of Apolis, and you will address me as such, or you'll lose your tongue."

Bastian chuckled darkly. "You won't cut out my tongue, not when you know firsthand all the things I can do with it."

Leoni stood next to me, her hand hovering over her sword. The crowd was silent behind us, drinking in our exchange.

"Did he just . . ." Leoni trailed off, at a loss for words for the first time in her life.

He did not just say that. He did not just remind me—and everyone in this room—of all the places his tongue had been on my body. All the ways he'd made me beg for that tongue. Fuck. Fuck. Fuck.

No one spoke. No one moved.

"Shut up," I whispered out the side of my mouth, a smile plastered to my face as I nodded back at the crowd in reassurance.

He gave a lazy smile, eyes glazed over. "Oh, so you want to play hard to get? You do know I like a good chase." He winked.

"Can he chase me?" someone whispered from the crowd, and I was almost certain it was Driscoll.

Someone shushed him. My face flamed.

"Let me shut him up," Leoni whispered. "Before he reveals too much."

I nodded at her. I didn't know what else to do. He'd already said too much, no doubt raised everyone's suspicions about my connection to him. If he said much more, they'd know of our entire relationship.

"Why are you here?" I asked as Leoni moved toward him.

His chin dipped toward his chest, then back up, and he blinked a few times. "I need your help, and you need mine."

"I don't need anything from you."

Leoni was almost to him.

"We both know that's not true. You want your brothers back, and I know how to get them."

I sucked in a sharp breath as Leoni stomped toward him, sword raised.

His eyes snapped to her. "Do your worst. It can't hurt more than the auburn-haired princess who broke my heart." He blatantly stared at me.

I tucked one of my loose curls behind my ear, self-conscious at the gazes burning into my back.

"Ended our relationship and told me she never wanted to see me again—"

Leoni reached him and knocked him over the head with her sword. He slumped down onto the stairs, but it was too late.

The damage had been done.

I slowly turned to see everyone staring, some with open mouths, others whispering to each other. Driscoll stood in the front, his gaze sharp, assessing. I wondered if he'd known about this. I'd told his queen in confidence after she'd shared her own troubles. No. Liliath wouldn't betray me like that. She'd kept my secret.

Bastian's words echoed in my mind. No longer a secret.

Hatred filled the eyes of everyone, but I could only focus on my people. On the betrayal shining in their eyes.

At first, no one in the water court had known where all our boys had gone or who had taken them, but the seafolk helped us track them. By the time we found out where they were—and whose ship they were on—it was already too late.

I'd been devastated when the seafolk returned with the truth: it had been the pirate lord, and he'd taken them to the shadow court, whom we hadn't heard from in over sixty years, not since they'd been banished to their island, exiled from Arathia for their own terrible crimes. No one knew how the pirate lord did it, including me. How in the span of a single night he'd managed to lure all our young boys to his ship and sail them away. Or why. Why the shadow court was once again at play and what they wanted. It had all been too much for my mother, my father, for me. My father and his men left shortly after that to rescue them— and never returned. We closed our borders, shut down the water court, and hid away. But we couldn't hide anymore.

Especially not now that everyone knew the ugly truth: that the princess of the water court had a relationship with one of the most wanted men in Arathia.

They hated me. I didn't blame them.

"Is it true?" a voice asked, and I closed my eyes as the crowd parted to reveal my mother standing there, crown still gleaming atop her head, her face pale, chin wobbling. "Is what he said true, Gabrielle?"

This could not get any worse. Leoni came to my side, her arm grazing mine, a reminder that I wasn't completely alone.

I swallowed, thinking through my options. I could lie. I could tell them Bastian was out of his mind, clearly mistaking me for someone else. But I was tired of the secrets, of the guilt.

"Don't," Leoni whispered, reaching a hand toward my arm.

I shook her off and stepped forward. "What he said is true."

My mother's eyes widened in horror.

"I had . . . a relationship with Bastian Lore, and then he betrayed me and took everything from us. I'm the reason our boys are gone. I'm the reason they're in the shadow court's possession. I'm the reason they're never coming home."

Chapter Five

"How could you, Gabrielle?" My mother paced back and forth in her private chambers, chambers that were filled with my furniture. I was supposed to officially move into the queen's chambers today, after the ceremony and celebration.

Now I'd gone and ruined that. The guards had taken Bastian away to the prison cells while he screamed at me to think about his offer.

"You know I can find them, love. If anyone can navigate the shadow court, it's me."

Meanwhile, everyone else screamed for an explanation, which my mother and I had finally been forced to give, divulging the full, horrifying truth to everybody about what had happened, and now they knew of my involvement, my guilt.

"This is truly the worst thing you've ever done," my mother said.

I winced. "I know it was stupid."

My mother stopped and stared at me where I sat on the chair tucked into the corner of the room. A breeze whispered through the open windows, fluttering the thin white curtains.

"Stupid?" my mother repeated. "Stupid is you and your brothers sneaking out for a midnight swim in the ocean. Stupid is sparring with Leoni without any armor. Stupid is staying up late drinking too much wine and gossiping with your ladies-in-waiting. Not falling in love with the most notorious pirate to ever sail the Dark Seas. This was not stupid, it was reckless, dangerous, selfish—"

"I never said I was in love." I curled my knees up to my chest, looking out the window to the endless ocean, wishing I was out there right now.

"How did you even meet him?" she asked. "How could you even entertain speaking to him?" She glared at me with those light brown eyes, the exact same shade as mine.

I thought back to the first time I'd met Bastian. I'd been on the northern shores, walking and collecting seashells when I'd seen him lounging on the beach, on my beach. I'd marched over to him, ready to question this stranger, but he'd blinked up at me, smiled that charming smile of his, and then we spent the rest of the day lying in the soft sand and talking. As the sun set, he'd confessed his true identity, and I wanted to hate him, but it had been too late. I'd already fallen for him, fallen for his wild, easy nature, the way he craved adventure as much as I did, the way he made me laugh, the way conversation just flowed between us as seamless as a river.

"And a human, Gabrielle," my mother continued. "What was your plan, exactly? Did you really think you could have a human by your side as king of the water court? That our people would accept someone with no magic? Would accept heirs with a diluted bloodline?"

I winced. I hadn't been planning on becoming queen, but I couldn't exactly confess that to my mother.

"Was it the sex?" she asked. "Is he hung like a—"

I straightened. "Mother!"

My mother had never been shy talking about sex, preparing me for what was to come when I took lovers, but I had no interest in speaking with her about this.

She threw out her arms. "I'm not blind. I always knew you liked your adventures, knew you could be reckless, knew you envied your brothers and their freedom. But I never thought . . . I never imagined . . . He steals dark magic and sells it to desperate people. Dark magic that is made in abhorrent ways."

I knew all too well how dark magic was made. Sorrengard, the shadow court, was full of it. Long ago, all seven elemental courts agreed to never use their magic for darker purposes. The shadow court could manipulate shadows, bend them to their will, but they also had the power to steal shadows, to rip away a person's shadow. That had been expressly forbidden. Somewhere along the way, the shadow court grew bitter about the restrictions on their powers. In secret, they'd begun kidnapping people, taking their shadows, and eventually it led to a war that had cost so much, in the end. That had been long ago, before I was born. They'd lost the war and been severely weakened, most of their people dead, including the king and queen. The rest had been exiled to their island, and they'd sunk into obscurity.

Until now.

I couldn't imagine what they wanted with our boys, why they'd targeted us specifically, and how Bastian was connected to it all. He'd only told me about the magical items he stole—not that he was kidnapping people and delivering them to the shadow court so they could steal their shadows.

Magic always had a cost, and the price depended on how much of the magic was being used and what the magic was being used for. Using shadow magic for dark purposes had a horrible price, it turned out. Every time a shadow person used their magic to rip someone's shadow from their body, a new item appeared on their island. Dangerous items with dark powers.

I'd never visited the shadow court, but I'd heard rumors that the island was full of these objects: tantalizing magic. Since Sorrengard's exile, many foolish individuals made the journey to the island, hoping to steal the items, either to use the magic themselves or sell it. Few of them ever returned, except the pirate lord, who'd somehow learned the secrets of the shadow court and capitalized on those secrets, creating a booming business from selling the dark magic. As usual, the other courts had ignored the dangers of the shadow court over the years, convinced Sorrengard was so weakened after their exile that we needn't worry about them.

Now they were at play again, and we could no longer brush them aside.

"What would your father say?" My mother was still speaking.

I sank deeper into my chair. I knew what he'd say, had thought about it many times since Bastian's betrayal. He'd lecture me about Spirit Water, how I'd let the spirit who granted us our powers down, how I hadn't lived in her image as I was expected to in all areas of life. My father was the most stringent of all the rulers on Arathia, expecting his court to live by ancient rules in ancient books written by ancient people who worshipped the same spirits as we did. His insistence on following some of these rituals and rites felt archaic, but my father was convinced that if he did everything right, he'd be rewarded by Spirit Water, that the water court would be rewarded. I still didn't know what that reward was, and it certainly hadn't been granted yet. Quite the opposite, given everything that had happened.

I shrank into myself against my mother's searing stare. "I'm sorry." I didn't know how many more times I could apologize. I'd probably spend the rest of my life apologizing for this.

She tugged the crown off her head, unentangling it from her gray strands, then set it on my navy blue dresser.

"The pirate lord." She rubbed her forehead. "You had a dalliance with the pirate every court has been trying to catch and imprison for years. Do you know how many dangerous items he's responsible for selling? The chaos that's ensued from his dark dealings?"

I knew it well. He'd told me about many of them, the lengths he'd gone to to steal them from the shadow court.

She looked so, so tired in this moment. The last month had been nice. I'd seen a renewed sense of hope in her, and I'd doused that hope with my actions.

She looked up at the gold-embossed ceiling. "This has caused a fury among the other courts. It will weaken their trust in us."

It was true. The courts hated conflict of any kind, terrified that if we used our powers for the wrong purpose, the Seven Spirits would rain down their displeasure and take away the magic they'd gifted our people so long ago.

"You have put our entire court in jeopardy," my mother said.

I came to a stand. "I fell in . . . to a relationship with the wrong man. I don't expect your forgiveness, but I am a grown woman, Mother. I don't need to be told I did wrong. I already know. I already shoulder the burden of our loved ones' disappearance. I will spend the rest of my life making it up to you, to this court."

"You can't." My mother's eyes shone with tears. "Don't you get it? They're gone, and there's nothing you can do to bring them back."

I thought about Bastian's words earlier, hating myself for letting him get to me. But what if he could help me . . . No. No. My mother was right. We had to move forward.

My mother sank onto her plush bed, the thick comforter a pristine white. "I can't do this. I can't be strong for us anymore. You have to earn back our people's trust." She gave a decisive nod. "He'll be executed tomorrow morning, at dawn, and you'll be the one to do it."

I stilled, heart stuttering. I'd had a chance to kill Bastian once, right after I'd found out about his betrayal, and I hadn't taken it. I hadn't been able to. Now my mother was telling me I not only had to kill him, but I had to do it in front of everyone?

My mother continued, "Then we'll crown you queen, going on with the coronation as planned. We must," she said. "We'll find you a good, dependable husband. Show everyone you're over the pirate lord and ready to lead our court into a new era. We won't give the other courts any reason to distrust us."

She couldn't be serious.

"What about Father's ship?" I asked. "Bastian was on that ship. He might at least know something about where Father is."

"No," she snapped, then her face softened. She walked forward and grabbed my hands. "I miss him as much as you do. He was the love of my life. But he's gone. He'd never have relinquished that ship. The *Pearl* was his pride and joy. If it's in someone else's possession, that's all the confirmation I need that he isn't coming back."

Spirits below, she was right, but that didn't mean we couldn't at least get answers.

"We cannot waste more resources trying to rescue the boys, your brothers. Look what happened to your father, to so many of our men. They went after those taken and paid the price. We can't lose any more of our people, not when the fate of Apolis hangs in the balance."

Her words were like a hand around my throat, slowly choking the life from me. For the last eight months, I'd stood back and watched my people suffer. And I'd done nothing. I convinced myself that doing nothing was the right thing, but now I wasn't so sure. I searched my mother's brown eyes, full of so much pain and loss. Wrinkles lined her face that hadn't been there just a year earlier. Her hair had lost so much of its luster. Her gown hung loose on her thin frame.

She needed this as much as our people did. She needed hope.

"Get a good night's rest." My mother cupped my cheek with her hand. "Tomorrow the pirate lord will die, and you will become queen of Apolis."

Chapter Six

I tossed and turned in bed that night, the events of the day rolling through my mind like endless waves.

Bastian. Bastian was here. Bastian was in prison. Bastian was going to die.

The covers tangled over my sticky body, misted in sweat from the combination of nerves and heat. I needed to go for a walk, to get out of the confinement of this room.

I grabbed a shawl and threw it over my thin nightgown, then put on my sandals and slipped from my room. I knew how to sneak out of the castle, had spent years doing it. I knew the guards' rotations, the right shadows to stick to, the doors that didn't creak, the empty hallways.

Soon enough, I was outside, breathing in the briny air. I inhaled deeply, descending the rocky terrain, paying no attention to where my legs carried me. I didn't care. I just wanted to be free.

Soon I came upon a statue of Spirit Water nestled in the rocks. The statue had been built long ago by our ancestors, and it was truly breathtaking. At least three times my height, she rose up, her hair like the ocean waves, the clothes on her body rippling like a waterfall. Her face was calm, and in her hand she held a trident, a powerful weapon she'd been rumored to wield. No one had been able to find this weapon, but my father had always been obsessed with it, convinced that finding it would bring glory to the water court. He'd gone out on multiple missions to find this mysterious trident but always came back empty handed.

Even if the trident didn't exist, I loved the lore behind it all, loved that this beautiful statue was here to honor Spirit Water and the powers she'd granted us.

A breeze blew my hair around my face, and I swiped the strands away. In the distance, ocean waves rolled in and out, the rush of them calming my frayed nerves.

I wandered past the statue, trying not to think about tomorrow and what I'd have to do. I hated Bastian Lore for what he'd done. That didn't mean I wanted to be the one to kill him.

It all felt like too much, happening too fast. I had accepted my fate. I had to be queen, a leader for the water court, but then Bastian sailed right onto our shores, and . . . and what? What had changed in the last few hours?

His words echoed in my mind again. He said he could help me. That I could help him. But what could I possibly do for him? I chewed at my bottom lip, feet stumbling over the rocks that led down to the shores. My brothers had poked fun at me for scaling these rocks instead of just using the stairs. Mal had been more practical, serious, about it— his usual nature. He spouted off all the reasons it was dangerous for me to stray from the stairs. Lochlan had just laughed and joked that of course I'd choose the more challenging pathway. But I liked the challenge of it, the journey of it, how I'd find random seashells or plants, how I could take a different path every time. It was never predictable, not like the stairs.

Stars twinkled in the sky above, the moon big and round, lighting my way as I mulled over Bastian's words, his proposition.

"Couldn't sleep?" a voice asked, and I whirled around to see Driscoll, the earth court ambassador, standing there. His dark skin gleamed in the moonlight. Soft brown trousers hugged his skinny, long legs. He wore a blue silk shirt that looked incredibly expensive with its gold buttons and embroidered cuffs. He stepped forward. "I wanted to thank you, by the way."

My brows bunched together. "Thank me for what?"

"Giving me such a good story to take back to the earth court. Queen

Liliath sent me here because it was supposed to be an easy, simple trip. Show up to the coronation, congratulate the new queen of Apolis, come home. Now I get to surprise her with the gossip of the century." He smirked.

"You don't hate me like everyone else?" I asked.

Driscoll ran a hand over his tight black curls, shorn close to his head. "For sleeping with the hot pirate lord who has that whole tall, dark, and handsome thing going on?" He shook his head. "If you hadn't snatched him up, I might have myself."

I snorted, and before I could help it, laughter bubbled out of me. This wasn't funny, but I was short on sleep and slightly delirious. "Now I get to thank you," I said.

Driscoll studied his manicured nails. "And why is that?"

"For making me smile for the first time in days." I paused. "Well, I was smiling during my coronation, but it was fake."

Driscoll's eyes widened. "That was supposed to be a smile? I thought you were constipated."

I rolled my eyes, but in truth, I was thankful for this small distraction.

"What's wrong?" Driscoll asked. "Other than the fact that you got completely humiliated today and might have possibly ruined your reputation?"

I gave him a look.

"Oh, right. Not helpful."

"I have to kill him tomorrow," I said softly, staring out at the sea.

"The hot pirate?" Driscoll sputtered. "The hot pirate has to die?"

"You know, he's also kind of evil." I turned toward Driscoll. "I think."

"The hot ones always are."

"Well, it doesn't matter. He said he could help rescue my brothers. But I can't trust him, and even if I could, I don't think there's any hope."

"Huh" was all Driscoll said.

I narrowed my gaze at him. "What does that mean?"

He shrugged. "Everyone told Liliath she'd never be able to defeat her stepmother. No one believed she could take back the earth court, restore our magic, rebuild. But she did it. She never gave up on us. I'd follow a leader like that anywhere."

His words struck me. Liliath and I had had that very argument when she'd been here just a few months ago. She'd told me not to give up on finding my brothers or my father, and I'd snapped at her, told her it was too late to save them.

Driscoll was right. Liliath had never given up on the earth court. Not when her stepmother murdered her father and stole the crown, not when the evil queen had Liliath imprisoned, not when Liliath had been kidnapped from her prison cell, dragged all over the continent. She never lost faith, and she defeated her stepmother, in the end. Just like Driscoll said. She'd saved everyone.

Maybe I had it wrong all along. Maybe I'd given up too easily. If there was a chance I could save my brothers, save everyone, didn't I have to take it?

Before I could change my mind, I made a sharp turn and stalked toward the prison cells, located underneath our castle.

"Uh," Driscoll said. "Where are you going, Princess Gabrielle?"

"To . . ." I thought of Driscoll's words. "Not give up."

Driscoll's boots scraped against the rocks behind me. "Wait, wait, wait. What are you planning on doing, exactly?"

I raised my chin, not sure if I should tell Driscoll. Then again, what was he going to do? Run to my mother in the middle of the night and tattle on me? Doubtful.

"I'm going to visit the pirate lord. To hear him out."

Driscoll jumped in front of me, his tall shadow stretching out in the moonlight. "Okay, no offense, but that sounds like a really stupid plan."

I planted my hands on my hips. "You're the one that just told me that whole story about Liliath not giving up on her court, that she fought for her people. What do you think I'm trying to do right now?"

His eyes widened. "That's what you got from my story? I didn't mean you should seek out the pirate lord, who's currently in prison, about to be executed for his crimes."

I shoved past him. "Sorry to disappoint you, but that's exactly what I'm doing."

Driscoll continued to follow me. "But you said he's evil."

"I said I think he's evil, and either way, now that I know he's evil, I can be on guard."

"Liliath is going to murder me," Driscoll muttered, then he adopted a nasally, high-pitched tone. *"Just go to the water court as my ambassador. Stay out of the way, don't cause any trouble, and, please, keep your mouth shut."*

"Was that supposed to be Queen Liliath?" I said over my shoulder.

He huffed loudly. "This is none of my business, this is none of my business, this is none of my business."

"You're right," I called. "It's not any of your business. You can go back to your room, pretend this conversation never happened, and Liliath won't have to know that your little speech inspired me to go visit my sworn enemy."

He groaned. "Oh, this is a disaster."

I sighed and stopped, turning to face him.

He slipped on a rock but caught himself and straightened. "Are you changing your mind?" he asked. "Why don't we go back to the castle and stay up all night gossiping." He waggled his eyebrows. "I know there's gotta be some good drama about the servants. I saw the way one of the maids was staring daggers at your lady-in-waiting. Let me guess: ex-best friends, one of them slept with the other one's boyfriend."

I raised an eyebrow. "You're the one who was just fawning over the pirate lord, and now you're acting like it's insane for me to go visit him."

"Excuse you." He scoffed. "I do not fawn. He's objectively hot, yes, but he's also objectively a murderer. Probably a sociopath too. So while I might have some forbidden fantasy about him tying me up and spanking me, I wouldn't act on it."

I stared at him for a moment, mouth open.

His eyes darted to the side. "I was kidding about the spanking. Kind of."

I shook my head. "Well, lucky for me, I'm not planning on letting him tie me up." Just the thought of that exhilarated me far more than I'd ever admit. "He will be behind bars, like all of our prisoners are, and I'll simply be questioning him. Is that good enough for you?"

Driscoll chewed on his bottom lip. "I suppose."

"Queen Liliath won't even know this conversation took place. She can't blame you for something she doesn't know happened."

Driscoll raised his hands. "Okay, okay fine. Well, I'm going back to my room and getting some sleep so I don't have eye bags tomorrow." He shuddered like eye bags might very well be the worst thing to happen to him.

"Great."

He gave a strained smile. "Fantastic."

I spun on my heel and walked toward the prison cells. Time to have a little chat with the pirate lord.

Chapter Seven

I marched up to the prison guard, who sat on a rickety wooden chair outside the open entrance to the prison that led underneath our castle. The gleaming white walls of my home rose high into the sky, its peaks seemingly touching the stars.

When the guard saw me, she stood at attention.

"Your Majesty." She bowed. "I swear I wasn't sleeping. Maybe I drifted off a little, but just for a moment, and then I—"

I held up my hand. "It's okay, Kalaris. Really, I'm not here to reprimand you." I cleared my throat. Here went nothing. "I just need to see one of the prisoners."

Kalaris stiffened at that, tugging at the golden rope tied around her white chiffon. "Oh?" she asked.

This was ridiculous. I was to be queen. I didn't have to explain myself like this. Worry that the guard might tell on me to my mother. So what if the guard did? I was interrogating a prisoner. Nothing wrong with that.

I raised my chin. "Yes, the pirate lord."

At that she audibly swallowed, her eyes darting around like just saying that name would summon him. "Your Majesty, I'm under strict orders from the queen to not let anyone see him."

"Yes," I said, an edge to my voice, "and now your crowned princess is telling you to step aside so I can speak with him." I paused. "For official water court business."

She eyed me warily.

"Oh, blood and water, Kalaris. What do you think is going to happen? I just have a few questions for the pirate lord before he's set to be executed tomorrow."

I held my breath as she stood in front of me, hand resting at the sword hanging by her side. She chewed her bottom lip for a moment before stepping aside.

"Thank you. I promise I'll call if I need anything."

I entered the dirty stone prison, floor covered in straw and feces from various rodents. Criminals leered at me from their cells, some sleeping, others staring like they wanted to wrap their hands around my throat and choke the life from me. They couldn't use their magic against me, not with the iron bars surrounding them, dulling their powers. All the prisons across Arathia had bars like these, ones that counteracted our elemental powers.

I avoided making eye contact, striding down the aisle between the cells on both sides. Moonlight stretched in through the barred windows, but other than that, darkness covered everything, as did the stench of urine, vomit, and—I sniffed the air, regretting it immediately—body odor.

I continued on, a few prisoners standing at their bars and rattling them.

"Come on, pretty princess, let's play," a bald man with blackened teeth said as he sneered at me.

He'd been caught with an item from the shadow court, a cloak with the power to make its wearer invisible. He'd been using it to steal valuable items from around our court. He was also missing six fingers—the price he paid every time he'd used the cloak's power. We'd finally caught him and thrown him in here.

He flicked out his tongue at me.

Spirits below, I hoped this was worth it.

Finally, I arrived to the very back of the prison, a single sconce hanging from the stone wall, flickering with a dim flame. And there he was.

My breath caught in my chest as I watched him. He lay on the straw-covered floor, eyes closed, chest rising and falling with shallow breaths. His skin was so pale, and the dark purple smudges under his eyes appeared worse than before. The top buttons of his black shirt were undone, exposing his chest, his long coat splayed out under him. I gasped. Blue lines stretched from the top of his chest all the way up to his neck. Even through the tattoos covering his chest, I could see them. Blood and water. How sick was Bastian?

"Come to get a peek at me?"

I jumped. I'd been so busy staring at his chest, I hadn't realized he'd awoken.

Now he slowly sat up, staring right back. "I'm not at my best right now, but I'd wager I'm still more handsome than anyone else in this prison."

He wasn't wrong, which was mostly infuriating.

He ran a hand through his thick black hair, the same way I'd run my own hands through those strands so many times during our year-long affair.

I stepped back. "What's wrong with you?"

He stretched his arms out wide. "Not doing so well, I'm afraid. I need to get to my ship. The ship you so kindly wrecked. Thank you for that, by the way."

I cocked my head. "How is getting to your ship going to help you with this?" I motioned toward the blue lines stretching over his skin.

"Ah, there's a special elixir aboard that can heal me."

I narrowed my eyes. "Is that why you came back here? For the elixir? Why in the spirits below would you sail my father's ship to our docks? Our very public docks?"

He cleared his throat. "Afraid I wasn't quite in my right mind. This sickness, it addles my brain sometimes, makes me confused, forget who I am and where I am. Believe me, I had no intention of alerting anyone to my presence."

"Well, you did." I lowered my voice, gaze flicking around the dark prison. "You also exposed our affair to my entire court."

He quirked an eyebrow. "Did I, now?"

I scowled at him. "Yes, you did. You humiliated me, Bastian. You—you"—I lowered my voice to a whisper—"talked about all the places your tongue has been on my body."

He let out a laugh that turned into a cough. "Sounds like some good old-fashioned dirty talk to me."

"During my coronation ceremony?"

"There's never a bad time for dirty talk, love."

"Don't you dare call me that." I turned my back to him. "I don't know why I came. This was a complete waste of time."

"You came because you know I spoke the truth. I can help get your brothers back."

I whipped around. "My brothers that you kidnapped?"

He stood, wincing with the movement. "I didn't kidnap them. The idiots got on my ship of their own accord."

I glared at him. "Don't you dare speak about my brothers like that. They are, were, brave and kind and selfless. The opposite of everything you are."

"Aye, I suppose you're right about that."

I wanted to walk away and turn my back on him, but he'd piqued my curiosity. "What do you mean you didn't kidnap them?"

He held up his hands, palms facing me. "I just came for the boys, and your brothers are certainly not boys."

They'd always be my baby brothers, but Bastian was right: Mal was twenty-four and Lochlan was twenty-eight. They hadn't been boys for a long time.

"I don't know how they did it, but your brothers somehow snuck onto my ship after we'd left with the boys."

Bastian was right. They were idiots. My heart splintered.

"They hid belowdecks." He swallowed. "I had no idea of their presence until it was too late. Until we got to Sorrengard, got the boys off the ship, and then your brothers stormed the island, trying to be heroes and save everyone, not understanding the price they'd pay once they entered that jungle."

My brothers liked to play hero. Despite being younger than me, they were always trying to protect me, looking out for my best interest. And I'd failed to do the same for them.

"So you just stole all the boys from my court, but not my brothers. That makes it so much better. Thank you for the clarification."

"Well, I'm always happy to help." He flourished his hands and did a bow.

"What do they want with our boys?" I asked. "What do they want with their shadows?"

Something was stirring in the shadow court, something dark, and they needed our boys for a reason. I just didn't know what.

"I don't ask questions." Bastian stared at his fingers like he was bored with the conversation. "I just follow orders."

"Whose orders?" I demanded.

Bastian's lips flattened into a thin line that told me he wasn't going to reveal anything.

"Did you lie to me our entire relationship?" I asked, trying to keep my voice from betraying my hurt.

His jaw ticked. "I never lied about anything, love."

"Right. You just withheld the fact that you were working with the shadow court, that you were trafficking people to their island so they can steal their shadows for who knows what purpose."

Bastian shrugged. "Well, looks like you got me all figured out. Good on you."

I started pacing. "Do you do this regularly? Kidnap people and take them to the shadow court? How do you do it? How did you take all of our boys in a single night?" The questions poured out of me, one after the other. Questions I'd had for so many months with no way to get answers.

He fingered the long silver chain around his neck, a small clock hanging from it. I squinted at it. He'd never worn that before. It must've been new.

He let go of the chain. "That's not what you came here to discuss."

I stopped pacing, facing him. "Why would I ever trust you again?"

"Because I'm your only option." He jabbed a thumb at himself. "I'm the only one who knows how to navigate that island, where to find your brothers."

It was clear Bastian wouldn't be answering my questions. And if he died tomorrow, I'd never get the answers I sought. At least not from him.

"What do you want in return?" I stepped forward, close enough that I could reach through the bars and touch him, trail my finger down his cheek. No, if I could reach him right now I'd be more likely to strangle him. "You'd never do anything out of the kindness of your heart."

He flicked a piece of dirt from his leather jacket. "You know me so well."

"Unfortunately."

He ignored that. "I'm sick. Something plagues me, and the elixir is only a temporary reprieve." He opened his shirt farther, revealing those muscled pecs, covered in a layer of dark curly hair. "See these blue lines?"

I nodded, unable to tear my eyes from the way they snaked across his skin, sickly and bulging, like veins.

"Once they reach my heart, I'm a goner."

The blue lines stretched dangerously close to the middle of his chest.

"The elixir is simply a bandage, not permanent, and I can't rely on it forever."

I hadn't known he was ill. He'd never shown any signs of it when we were together.

"Is it contagious?"

He shook his head. "I wouldn't have come near you if it were."

"Of course not. You'll kidnap half my court and send them to their doom, but you draw the line at infecting me with an illness. How considerate of you."

He clucked his tongue. "It's really very simple. I want it back."

I swallowed, still remembering that horrible day I'd woken up to find out the boys of our court, my brothers, were gone—and Bastian had been the reason. It hadn't taken long to create a plan: when Bastian came back to visit, I'd hurt him like he had me. I waited for him on the Cliffs of Death, and when his ship came into view, instead of letting it anchor out at sea, letting Bastian come ashore on one of his rowboats, I used my magic and reeled the ship in like a dangling fish. Bastian had been shouting at me, the crew panicking as the sea tossed the ship this way and that. Power had coursed through me as I brought the ship right toward the rocks that would damage it. But I didn't stop there. I'd seen the little vial of sparkling magic in Bastian's hand, felt its power. I figured it was just another piece of dark magic he'd stolen from Sorrengard. So I used my water magic to take it. Then from high up on those cliffs, I told the pirate lord he had exactly one hour to find a way off his wrecked ship and off the shores of Apolis before I called my guards upon him and his crew. That had been the last time I'd seen him. Until today.

Bastian paced back and forth. "That dust can solve this illness. I will help you get your brothers back, and if you're really nice, I'll tell you how I ended up on your father's ship."

My stomach balled into a thick knot. The pixie dust was going to be a problem. Mainly because Queen Liliath currently had it in her possession. In the earth court. Her husband-to-be had stolen it from us and used part of it for his own purposes. I'd managed to move past the betrayal, though I'd been furious when I first found out. I bit the inside of my cheek. But Bastian didn't have to know that. He'd withheld information from me, played me to his tune so he could betray me. I shouldn't feel bad about doing the same. Especially not if it meant I could save my brothers, undo all the damage I'd caused.

"I'll think about it," I said, still not sure working with him was a good idea.

"You'd better hurry, love. My offer has an expiration date."

I raised my brows. Did he know about his execution tomorrow?

"I won't be here for too long." He winked.

No, it sounded like . . . like he had a plan to escape. Of course he did.

"Like I said, I'll think about it." I looked him up and down. "You're not in much of a position to bargain here."

He smirked. "I could say the same for you."

"I have to kill you tomorrow, you know," I said.

He cocked his head. "Well, you can certainly try."

I was about to tell him this wasn't a game, but he coughed into his hand, and when he pulled it away, a crimson red stained his palm. I sucked in a sharp breath. "Bastian, what are you sick with, exactly?"

He gave me a smile. "Nothing you need to worry yourself about. That pixie dust is powerful, powerful enough to heal me for good."

His eyes clouded over, and a horrible hacking sound spit from his lungs. I moved forward to help him before remembering we were separated by bars.

He hunched over, his entire body shaking each time he coughed, blood and spittle flying from his mouth.

"Bastian," I said, but he didn't hear me.

He sank to his knees, those blue lines stretching just a little farther before he collapsed to the ground, his eyes closing and his body growing still.

My throat grew thick, and my heart lurched. I feared that he was dead. But no, the blue lines hadn't reached his heart yet. He was still breathing, and I didn't know how to feel about that.

I backed away, not wanting to leave him but knowing I had to. I hated that he still had this hold on me. After everything he'd done, I was worried about him. It made me feel weak, like I was under some spell. Maybe I was. At this point, nothing would surprise me. I backed farther away, then turned and ran until I reached the open doorway of the cells. The guard sat there, once again dozing off. It was only once I was outside in the silence of the night that I took in a deep lungful of the salty air.

I couldn't believe I'd ever let that man into my bed, into my heart. One thing was for certain: neither would ever happen again.

Chapter Eight

The next day, I stood outside and faced everyone whom I'd told the truth to yesterday, all their faces stony, their gazes full of suspicion, anger, betrayal. I didn't blame a single one of them.

I imagined what Mal and Lochlan would say if they were here. Lochlan would try and make a joke to lighten the mood. Mal would be displeased, but he'd try to get to the root of it. My sweet sensitive youngest brother would give me a chance to explain before judging. Spirits below, I wished they were here.

Everyone stared at me from the sandy beach where they crowded together as I stood on a wooden pier that jutted from the boardwalk, my mother and Priestess Amari next to me as the cerulean ocean rushed around the planks. The white and beige homes of the water court scattered across the rocky hillside behind us, and I imagined all the people peering from their windows to see the execution of the pirate lord.

Mist sprayed my face, and I closed my eyes for a moment, letting myself imagine it was just me and the water, no responsibilities, no Bastian, no execution. Just the wide open sea waiting for me.

My mother nudged me, and my eyes popped open as the guards led Bastian down the stairs that cut through that rocky hillside and led to the shore. Water cuffs looped around his hands, Leoni with a firm grip on his arm as she tugged him forward. She looked silly next to him, half his height, but if he tried anything, she'd have his ass on the ground. People often underestimated Leoni since she didn't look like the typical muscly tall guard, but that was their mistake.

The pirate lord looked no better today than he had yesterday, yet even with this illness wracking his body, he was still a formidable man. Tall, muscled, clad in black leather with his long trench coat flapping in the wind, a confidence oozing from him that made no sense given he was being led to his execution. I'd told Leoni to be on guard, that Bastian likely had something planned. I just didn't know what.

The pier wobbled under my feet as waves sloshed around us, clouds blocking out the sun. The day was gloomy and dreary, just like my mood.

Priestess Amari opened a heavy tome she carried, dust flying from the brittle pages. This book was a revered one, ancient as the continent itself, one that detailed the ways in which we should handle different aspects of life and death in the water court: births, burials, celebrations, and executions. Every court had one of these tomes, found long ago when our people first settled here, though most of the courts were more lax in their interpretation of it. My father, however, had insisted on reading it front to back, on knowing every single ritual we were supposed to perform. He'd often sent our priestesses and scholars to other courts to educate them on new findings. He'd always been frustrated with the other rulers not taking these ancient texts as seriously as he did.

I eyed the pages, which looked like so much as a gust of wind might break them. Priestess Amari had her scribes working night and day to copy the text so that we weren't at risk of losing it should anything happen to the book.

The wind whipped her long, white hair around her shoulders and face, but the priestess paid no mind as she flipped the pages of the book, looking for the ritual needed to ensure we performed the execution exactly as we were supposed to. She studied the words for a minute before snapping the book shut.

The guards parted the crowd, pulling Bastian forward and onto the dock, where they stopped, waiting for my mother's signal to bring him to us. My hands grew clammy at my sides, and I did my best to steady my breathing as I watched him. I'd stayed up all night thinking about his deal but ultimately decided against the offer. Regret crept over me like shadows, but I shook them away.

I caught sight of Driscoll's face in the crowd, and he gave me a nod. I thought about what he'd said the night before about Liliath, how she'd fought so hard for her people, her court. My brothers, my father, deserved the same kind of champion. Not someone who would just hide away and give up on them. I bit my lip. Was that what I was doing right now? If Bastian died, it felt like closing a chapter on them, writing them out of the story entirely. My heart stuttered at the thought.

Beside me the priestess spoke, one hand cradled under the heavy leather-bound book, the other hand placed on the cover. "Spirit Water," she mumbled under her breath, eyes closed, "we ask for your permission to use our powers of water to take the life of Bastian Lore, pirate lord of the Dark Seas. We do not ask this lightly, but only because he is a threat to our very existence, to the powers you've bestowed upon us. We are humble, we are your loyal servants, we are forever in your favor."

She knelt down and dipped her hands in the blue sea, then stood and walked the length of the dock to Bastian, flicking the water at his face, his arms, his chest, his legs. He flinched, just barely, but it was enough that I noticed.

My mother raised her hand in the air and beckoned the guards forward with their prisoner.

My gaze settled on the tome Priestess Amari carried. I always wondered what might happen if we simply didn't follow the words and actions of this book, didn't ask for Spirit Water's favor, but that kind of thinking was blasphemous. Normally, I loved to think about these rituals, how they were created, if the spirits cared, or even knew, if we followed these guides. But today, as an actual participant, I couldn't find it in myself to think about anything other than the fact that in a few moments, I was going to have to execute the pirate lord.

My hands shook at my sides, and I tried several times to swallow the growing lump in my throat to no avail.

Now, instead of just creeping over me, regret outright seized me. I wasn't sure I could do this. Oh, bloody fucking water. I couldn't let my mother, my court, down. I'd already done that on my coronation day, and this was my chance at redemption.

The guards stopped in front of us, Bastian standing just an arm's reach away, wind ruffling that thick black hair, making the edges of his black shirt flap in the wind. The blue lines were stark today. If I didn't kill him, this illness would. Unless I helped him. Got him to his ship so he could take the elixir. Revealed the location of the pixie dust. After everything that had happened, Liliath would give the remaining dust back to me, of that I was sure.

But it was all too late. I'd made my decision, and now there was no turning back.

Bastian Lore was going to die. And I was going to be the one to end him.

His eyes closed for a brief second as he swallowed—he must've been in immense pain. He breathed out slowly, then cracked his neck and opened his eyes. We were close enough that I could see the yellow flecks in that dark brown, and I remembered the way the colors of his eyes would shift in the morning light. How I'd wake up and roll my naked body on top of him, staring into his eyes, watching them change to a brighter color that reminded me of the leaves in Elwen when colder weather blew in.

"We've got to stop meeting like this, love." He shot me a wicked grin.

My mother stiffened beside me, and I glared at him.

"You will address my daughter as Your Majesty," my mother said, voice hard and cold.

"Oh, but I like 'love' so much better."

"Can you control him?" my mother whispered to me.

I wanted to dive into the ocean and let it swallow me whole. This man had no shame. Something I used to love about him, but in this moment, it made me want to throttle him.

"It's time," said the priestess, business as usual.

All the feeling left my body, and I inhaled a shaky breath while Bastian looked like he was out for a stroll along the beach. Maybe the sickness had addled his mind more than I'd realized. Last night, he'd made it sound like he had short spells where he was confused, but maybe he was confused all of the time. Like right now. When the idiot was smiling and calling me "love" like he wasn't about to get drowned in the sea. The very sea that he feared.

Leoni shoved Bastian forward, and I could smell that familiar scent of sea and sandalwood that he carried wherever he went, could practically taste the sea salt on his skin. I curled my fingers into my palms, summoning my magic. In just a few short seconds, the sea would rise and snatch Bastian away, pulling him to its depths and keeping him there for eternity.

I could do this. I had to do this. I stuck out an arm over the water. Slowly, I lifted my arm, commanding a tall wave to rise over us. I imagined what I wanted it to do, and it formed into a hand. A few in the crowd gasped, probably those from other courts who had never seen an execution done in the water court. Many of my people might never have seen something like this either. All the courts agreed we would do our best to only use our magic for good, never to kill or injure unless it was absolutely necessary. We didn't do executions very often, hadn't needed to since everyone in Arathia was so obsessed with keeping the peace, so afraid of the spirits and their wrath should we misuse the powers they granted us.

Bastian leaned over and whispered, "Meet me at the northern shore, at our place."

So I was right. He was out of his mind. Maybe it was better this way.

I closed my hand into a fist, and the water dipped down and grabbed Bastian. His cocky smile faltered, eyes flashing with stark fear as it yanked him from the dock and straight into the sea. And just like that, he was gone. I used all of my strength to keep myself from crumpling.

My mother's shoulders slumped in relief while the crowd broke out in a cheer.

I was going to be sick. I stared in shock, but Bastian had already disappeared from view through the clear waters; the only evidence that he was ever here were the little bubbles popping up on the ocean's surface.

"Well, I'm glad we took care of that," my mother said, voice brisk, like we'd just checked something off our to-do list. "We can carry on with your coronation later today and pretend like this entire incident never happened."

I was so tired of sweeping things away. It felt like that was everyone's plan on this spirits-damned continent. Smile and pretend everything was okay, and then it might be. Except that's not how it worked. It wasn't living in reality. Maybe if we'd reached out to the other courts sooner, they might have helped us get our boys back. Get Mal and Lochlan back. Maybe my father never would have left if we'd just asked for help.

Thoughts bounced through my mind, so scattered after what I'd just done.

Everyone began heading back toward the castle, shuffling in the sand and kicking it up behind them as they moved toward the stairs that shot up through the rocks.

The priestess strode away, and my mother stopped by my side and clapped a hand on my shoulder. "You did good, daughter. Now we can put the past behind us and look toward the future."

I couldn't tear my eyes from the water, from where Bastian's head had sunk below the surface. It didn't make sense how much I loathed him for what he'd done yet how much I was already grieving the loss of him. I hated these warring emotions inside of me. My mother's hand slipped away and the dock creaked as she walked back toward the castle.

"Princess Gabrielle?" a voice said, but it felt far away, distant.

The water was so still now. He was really gone.

"Is she okay?" another voice said.

"Does it look like she's okay?" the first voice snapped.

I peered closer to the water, walking to the edge of the dock.

"Well, you're snappy."

"And you're annoying. Who are you, by the way?"

Did I see something down there? A flash of black hair, pale skin?

"My name is Driscoll, thank you. Ambassador of the earth court."

"Great, thanks for the introduction. Now scurry along, Driscoll."

I shook my head. No. It was just a fish. What had I been thinking? That my magic had failed? Or that Bastian could somehow breathe underwater? Use some kind of magic to get himself out of this? But no, Bastian was human—his entire crew was as far as I knew.

"I just need to make sure she's okay, alright?" the voice said again.

"She's not your responsibility."

I snapped back to reality and turned to face Leoni and Driscoll, who would've been nose-to-nose if it weren't for the fact that Leoni barely reached his chest as she tipped her head up, glaring at him.

I brushed past them. "Will you two stop your bickering? I appreciate your concern, but I'm fine."

"Uh," Driscoll said, "I hate to point out the obvious, but you don't look fine. You look like you just got thrown off a horse, then it stomped all over you."

"Why would you say that?" Leoni asked. "What is wrong with you?"

"I don't know, okay?" Driscoll said. "My brain and mouth don't always connect."

She snorted. "Well, that's apparent."

I whirled around, and they almost ran right into me. "I'm fine. Really. If I don't look well it's because I got very little sleep last night, and I'm about to be crowned queen of a court that's falling apart. Now, if you'll excuse me, I'm going to take a walk. Both of you can head back to the castle, and I will see you for my coronation ceremony."

With that, I spun on my heel and stalked to the beach, already knowing exactly where I wanted to go.

Chapter Nine

"*Meet me at our place,*" he'd said.

Little did he know that before it had been our place, it had been my and my brothers' place. The wild northern shores. Where Mal and I would have long, deep conversations. Where Lochlan would go to escape the gaggle of women constantly vying for the attention of Arathia's most eligible bachelor. I didn't want to try and jump off a cliff again like I had two nights ago; all I wanted was peace and quiet.

The warm water washed up over my sandals, the ends of my blue chiffon wet and sticking to my ankles. I tugged at my long braid, wondering how in the bloody waters it felt like everything and nothing had changed all at the same time. This all was so eerily familiar: me going to the Cliffs of Death before my coronation, mourning the loss of my brothers and father, hating the pirate lord. Except . . . now a part of me grieved him, too, which also made me hate myself.

I'd done the right thing, so why did it still feel so wrong?

I stared at the cliffs. I didn't understand how I'd missed it—all the signs of his impending treachery.

When he'd first admitted he was the pirate lord, I'd been ready to run away despite my strong feelings for him. But Bastian had told me some sad story about how he stole items from the shadow court and sold them on the black market so that he could buy freedom for himself and his crew from some tyrannical boss who lorded over them—whom I'd never learned the identity of. He'd made me feel so sorry for him, so convinced he had no choice in the matter, that he wasn't the villain everyone in Arathia thought him to be.

I had been such a fool to believe him, to want to help him earn his freedom and be a better man.

Rain pattered down, and I looked up at the angry skies, clouds puckering. I arrived at the cove, the waves especially wild today with the wind and rain. They rose high, then barreled with a viciousness onto the little shore, battering against the cliffs. I stood to the side, avoiding their wrath, watching them with wonder as the Cliffs of Death towered high over me.

"Spirits below, this sand really gets everywhere, doesn't it?" a voice said. "I mean, it's in every crack in my body. Every. Crack. Just imagine."

"I don't want to imagine all the cracks in your body," another voice said, this one female.

Damnit. I sighed and turned to see Leoni and Driscoll hiding around the bend of the cliffs that rose up. "I told you two to leave me be."

They stepped out, both looking guilty.

Leoni planted her hands on her hips. "You're not jumping!"

Driscoll's brows drew together. "Jumping from where, exactly?"

"I'm just here to get some peace and quiet, which you both are determined to not let me have."

"To be fair, it did seem like you were having a mental breakdown," Driscoll said. "It was our duty to follow you."

Leoni shot him a glare. "It was my duty. You followed me despite me telling you to fuck off."

A thoughtful expression took over Driscoll's features. "Ah yes, I do vividly remember that part."

I pinched the bridge of my nose. "Now that we've established I'm not jumping off anything and I'm not having a breakdown, will you two leave? I will be back at the castle to get ready for my coronation shortly."

Leoni threw out her arms. "We have not established that you're not having a breakdown. Quite the opposite, actually."

The rain started coming down harder, plastering my chiffon to my skin.

"I actually agree with her," Driscoll said. "She's short and snappy like a tiny turtle, but she's right. You seem like you might be going a little . . ." He twirled his finger by his head.

I crossed my arms. "Well, I'm not. I'm going through a momentous life change, and as I've already explained, you both have nothing to worry about."

Leoni stepped forward. "I always have something to worry about when it comes to you."

My mouth dropped open. "Might I remind you that I'm the one in charge?"

She huffed. "Oh, please. You wouldn't know what to do without me."

That was true, but I was not admitting it right now.

"Can we wrap this up?" Driscoll asked, his fingers pinching his green silk shirt. "Wet doesn't look good on me."

Both Leoni and I glared at him.

"Right. I'll just . . ." He pointed and slipped away so he was no longer in hearing distance.

"Oni, please just give me what I'm asking for. I know it's your job to protect me, and I know you're worried about me."

Her gaze was focused on something behind me.

I continued, "But I promise, all I'm planning is to climb the cliffs and to take a few moments to gather my thoughts. This is my best thinking place, whether you . . . Are you even listening to me right now?"

She squinted, taking a few steps forward.

"What are you staring at?" I turned as she brushed past me, like someone in a trance.

"Gabrielle," she said, a warning edging her words.

"Yes?" I asked.

She pointed to the rocks cropping up in the shallow part of the water. "Wasn't there a ship there before? A ship you put there?"

My gaze followed the line of her finger. "Of course there's a ship . . ." I trailed off.

"Oh, fuck me," Leoni said.

"What?" Driscoll came running. "What happened? Are you two about to fight because full disclaimer: I'm not going to break it up. I cannot risk cracking a nail."

Blood and water. Bastian's ship—his ship that I'd wrecked on these very rocks eight months ago—was gone.

Chapter Ten

I blinked a few times to make sure I wasn't, in fact, losing my mind like Driscoll and Leoni had accused me of just moments before. But no, Leoni saw it too. As did Driscoll.

Driscoll held up a finger. "Okay, so let me get this straight. You fell in love with the pirate lord, then he betrayed you by stealing the boys of your court, as well as your brothers, so in retaliation you broke it off with him and wrecked his ship right on these rocks, and that same ship has now disappeared?" He flashed his hands in the air. "Poof. Just vanished from thin air?"

"You're a fast learner," Leoni chirped.

"Why does everyone keep assuming I was in love?" I asked, annoyance spiking.

"You just can't get enough of me, can you?" I tilted my head. I could've sworn I'd just heard Bastian speak, the accent so charming and seductive all at once.

Driscoll and Leoni stared in the direction of that voice, both of them with horrified looks on their faces.

I slowly turned, goose bumps rising up along my arms.

There he stood, leaning against the side of the cliff, looking back to his regular self: tanned skin, shiny, thick hair, black beard, and no more smudges under his eyes, blue lines gone from his chest.

Driscoll cleared his throat. "Does anyone else see the pirate lord standing there, looking all hot and smoldery?"

My mouth dropped open, all the blood draining from my face. Leoni blinked a few times like she couldn't believe her eyes.

"I'm going to guess the answer is yes," Driscoll said.

Bastian stepped forward, and all of us immediately moved back.

He spread his arms out. "Oh, come now, I don't bite." He shot a look at me. "Well, sometimes I do, but I recall you rather liked it."

"What are you—" I stopped. "How are you—"

I couldn't even form the words.

"What in the fuck?" Leoni asked.

Driscoll nodded. "What she said."

"This shouldn't be possible." I stepped forward. "I saw you die."

Bastian held up a finger. "Correction, you saw me go into the water."

I shook my head. "Stop with the games. For once in your life, just say what you mean. How did you survive, Bastian?"

He tsked. "You're feisty. I did always like that about you."

I crossed my arms and nodded at Leoni. "Arrest him."

"Gladly." Leoni flipped her palm up and a ball of water appeared. She brought the ball back, readying herself to fling it at the pirate lord and trap him.

He held out his hands. "Let's not be hasty. I wasn't the only one on your father's ship. My crew was there too. Sleeping in the cabin belowdecks. They didn't know how out of it I was, that I was sailing the ship straight toward the beach instead of here, where I was supposed to bring us. When the ship crashed, they awoke but stayed belowdecks, knowing if they emerged, they'd be arrested along with me."

I stepped back, my hand floating to my mouth. "That's why you weren't worried. You knew they'd come for you."

"Aye, I did."

Leoni still had her hand back, ball of water at the ready. "What happened next? Why is your ship gone? Where's your crew?"

He tugged on the lapels of his leather jacket. "They fixed it up, then staged a rescue after everyone had departed the beach. It's that simple, love."

"Do not call me that," I snapped.

"Old habits die hard, I suppose," he murmured, gazing at me, drinking me in.

I shifted, looking away.

"I don't buy it," Leoni whispered out the side of her mouth.

I wasn't sure. I hadn't wrecked the ship beyond repair—hadn't been able to. Not when it was such a magnificent vessel. Then again, the pirate lord and his crew were infamous for taking magical items from the shadow court. Maybe they'd used one of those magical items to repair the ship. I shuddered to think about the price they'd paid for it.

"Thank you for meeting me here, by the way," Bastian said.

Leoni and Driscoll gaped at me.

"You were meeting him here?" Leoni asked.

"No!" I cut a sharp look at Bastian. "Before he died—or didn't die—he told me to meet him at our place. I didn't think anything of it, believing he was out of his mind from an illness he's suffering from. I didn't come here to meet him, I swear it."

Bastian's gaze never left me. "Well, either way, you came. So what do you say, love?"

Driscoll wrinkled his nose. "Am I the only one having a hard time following this conversation?"

The rain began to fall harder, the sky rumbling with the promise of a storm.

"No, you're not. Because she is once again keeping secrets from me." Leoni let the ball of water disappear, glaring up at me, the bun on top of her head bobbing.

"I'm not keeping secrets from you, Oni. Bloody waters." I tugged at my braid. "I visited him in prison, okay?"

"What?" Leoni's screech was so loud everyone in Apolis probably heard it.

Okay, so I'd kept one tiny secret from her. "I just wanted to see if I could get information out of him."

Her gaze was murderous.

"He wanted to make a deal: I give him his pixie dust back, and he helps me rescue my brothers. I didn't take it, obviously. You saw me kill him."

"The question is"—Bastian stepped forward—"are you going to take it now?"

Both Leoni and Driscoll turned wide eyes on me.

"She's obviously not," Leoni replied.

Driscoll leaned over and said out the side of his mouth, "She looks like she might."

Bastian stayed silent, rain pelting him, his black hair now slick against his scalp, his shirt soaked, showing the outlines of his carved abdomen as his long coat whipped in the wind. Water slid down my face, and I blinked the drops out of my eyes.

"You can't be serious," Leoni said.

I turned to her and took hold of her shoulders. "I think I have to do this."

She shook her head. "No, I won't let you."

"I know you're looking out for me. It's what you've always done, and I love you for it. But this is my best chance at fixing everything."

Leoni's lips formed a thin line. "It's not just your problem to fix. This is not your weight to bear."

She still didn't get it.

"Besides"—she shot a look at Bastian and lowered her voice—"you don't have the pixie dust."

"He doesn't know that," I whispered back to her.

"Isn't it all gone?" she asked.

I shook my head. "I thought so, too, but Liliath wrote to me shortly after she defeated her stepmother and took back the earth court. She told me there was some dust left in the vial, asked if I wanted it returned." I'd never responded to a query so quickly. "I told her to keep it. To protect it."

I hadn't wanted anything to do with it anymore. Not when it was a constant reminder of the pirate lord.

I let go of Leoni's shoulders, but she grasped my arm, her hold tight. "What makes you think you can trust him?"

"I don't, but can't you see? That's the difference between before and now. I know I can't trust him."

"What about your mother?" Leoni asked. "Everyone? They're going to be waiting for you to return."

"You're going to tell them that I left to save our boys. You don't need to give any other details."

It was better if everyone thought the pirate lord still dead.

Leoni's blue eyes widened even more, and I gently shook my arm from her grip and marched up to Bastian, rain pelting down between us.

Leoni shouted behind me, but I ignored her protests as I stuck out my hand. "We've got a deal, Pirate Lord."

<h1 style="text-align:center">Chapter Eleven</h1>

I stalked through the sand, following Bastian. "Are we leaving now?" I shouted, then looked behind me at a stunned Leoni and Driscoll, whom I could barely see through the downpour.

"No," Bastian shouted over his shoulder, the wind carrying his words. "I thought we'd stick around, give your mother and your captain of the guard a chance to arrest me. Maybe you could even drown me again. That would be fun."

I glared at the back of his head. "I didn't even have a chance to say goodbye!"

"Not my problem," he said.

Cold-hearted bastard. I hated him. I hated myself for doing this. But it had to be done.

"So did you take your elixir, then?" I asked. He must have since he was back to his normal, infuriating self.

"Aye. I didn't know you cared so much."

"I don't. You're my only hope of saving my brothers." I looked behind me again but saw no signs of Leoni or Driscoll now that we'd rounded the tall Cliffs of Death. "Where is your ship?" I asked.

He pointed in the distance where the ship sat in the ocean, the waves rolling underneath it, rocking it this way and that.

"And how are we supposed to get to the ship?"

He stopped and turned. "Well, I do believe you have something called water magic, love. Maybe you can use it?"

Spirits below, had he always been so . . . sarcastic? Maybe I'd been so in love that I'd been blinded, not seeing the truth of his awful behavior. But no. I'd never have fallen for him had he treated me like this. Like I was his enemy all of a sudden, just some means to an end. That was fine with me. It was easier to hate him when he acted like this, and I very much preferred to hate him right now.

We arrived at the edge of the sand, water pounding the shore, clouds rolling above. In the distance, lightning flashed.

"We need to hurry," Bastian shouted. "Outrun the storm."

"I think it's a little late for that," I said right as a loud clap of thunder shook the ground.

"Wait!" Leoni and Driscoll ran to catch up, Driscoll clutching his side and gasping for air.

They stopped in front of us, and I swallowed back the tears forming at the thought of not seeing Leoni for however long it took to rescue my brothers. Leoni and I had been by each other's sides since we were little and barely able to walk.

"I'm going to miss you," I said.

"This is all very good and sweet." Bastian stepped between us. "Heartwarming, truly. But we don't have time for it."

I shoved him aside, staring at Leoni, using every bit of my strength to not let the tears fall.

"You idiot," she shouted. "You think I'm going to let you do this alone?"

My mouth dropped open. "You can't come with me."

"I agree," Bastian said. "So glad we settled that. Now let's get going."

Leoni cut him a glare, then turned her gaze to me. "I can and I will. This is your stupidest idea yet, and you've had some truly wretched ones."

I sighed. She wasn't going to back down, and in truth, I didn't want her to. "I could use a friend."

"How about two?" Driscoll stepped forward.

"Fuck me," Bastian muttered. "This is turning into a circus."

I shook my head. "No, you can't come. You need to return to the earth court. Liliath needs you."

He waved away my words. "She doesn't need me. That's the problem. She has no use for me." He fingered the round silver pin on his shirt that signified his role in the earth court. "Gave me some stupid role as ambassador because I have no skills. I mean, I'm very good looking, obviously, but I'm ready to be more than a pretty face. If I go on this journey and help you rescue your brothers, I'll finally be taken seriously."

"But you're going to miss her wedding. She's one of your closest friends. Surely you wouldn't miss such a momentous occasion?"

He tugged at the collar of his shirt. "This is just between us, but Liliath is already married."

"What?" I screeched, and Bastian stuck a finger in his ear, which I ignored.

"She and Penn wanted something private, personal, to them. So they had an intimate little ceremony a few weeks ago. I already saw her get married. This big one is just for show, a chance to assure all the courts that Elwen is no longer weak, that we're an asset to the rest of Arathia."

That was so damn romantic, and I loved that Liliath got the wedding she wanted. I sighed. "This is going to be dangerous, Driscoll."

He clapped his hands together. "Well, good thing I have all you fine people to protect me. Let's get going."

"Yes, please," Bastian said, annoyance lacing his words.

I looked at Leoni and nodded, then we both turned and stuck out our hands toward the waves.

"How are we getting to the ship, exactly?" Driscoll asked, letting out a nervous laugh.

Bastian eyed the water rising before us, throat bobbing before a mask of stone slipped over his face. If he was terrified, he was doing his best not to show it.

Leoni and I commanded the wave to lower down and slip under our feet, and it gently cushioned us as we were lifted into the air.

"Oh no, no, I don't like this." Driscoll's eyes shifted back and forth as we rose higher and higher.

It took all my concentration to keep us safe in the wave's grasp, the storm fighting for its attention. The wave tugged for control, wanting to break free, but I pulled it back under my command. Bastian's face had gone pale, his body rigid next to mine, and it felt cruel to be so delighted that this, at least, had been real—his fear of the ocean. I didn't know how the most notorious pirate to ever exist was scared of the sea, but in this moment, that fear etched itself into his tensed body.

The wave rode under us, water soaking through my clothes. I didn't think I could get any wetter, but it didn't bother me.

"Oh, not my boots," Driscoll whined, looking down at the soaked suede.

"Who wears suede in the water court?" Leoni asked, her hands still out as she helped command the wave to take us to Bastian's ship.

"Someone with a sense of style," Driscoll retorted.

"Will you both shut the bloody hell up?" Bastian asked.

For once, I agreed with the pirate.

"Someone's testy," Driscoll muttered under his breath.

Spirits below, I just wanted to get to the damn ship.

The storm whirled around us, water pounding at our wave, rain pounding down, wind pounding us. We were being battered at every angle. Finally, the ship appeared through the heavy curtain of rainfall, and I raised my hand, commanding the wave to spit us out right onto the slick deck where we landed.

We were here. We'd arrived at the pirate lord's ship, and I could only hope that I wouldn't come to regret this.

Part Two

"*Hook was not his true name. To reveal who he really was would, even at this date, set the country in a blaze.*"

$$Chapter\ Twelve$$

As soon as we landed Bastian started shouting orders to his crew in rapid fire. Everyone sprang to attention as the boat crested up on a wave and heaved down, water spilling over the sides. Driscoll, Leoni, and I flew backward, our bodies hitting the railing.

Bastian shouted, but I could barely hear him with the frenzy happening in front of us, feet pounding on the main deck, some crew members climbing the ratlines to the top of the mast, others running belowdecks, while Bastian stood at the helm, rain barraging him as he steered the ship. Lightning flashed behind him, illuminated his face, stark, all hard lines and sharp angles, his dark beard scraggly, which was so unlike him. His beard had always been neat and trimmed, but I supposed he'd been a bit busy the last few days.

"Does anyone else feel really useless right now?" Driscoll asked.

Leoni huffed and got to her feet just as another wave rammed the side of the ship and sent her straight onto her ass.

"Might as well get comfy," Driscoll said. "I don't think we're going anywhere."

We could try and use our magic to calm the waters, but my magic was weak from using it to get us to Bastian's ship, and controlling a storm like this wasn't an easy feat.

Bastian wrenched the wheel, steering the ship in the same direction as the wind blew. The white sails billowed above, the ship gaining speed, riding on the waves. The flag, a skull with a sword rammed through its eye sockets, flapped wildly.

Driscoll held his stomach. "Oh, I don't feel so good."

"This doesn't make us pirates, right?" Leoni tapped her chin. "Because pirates are criminals, and I cannot be labeled as a criminal. I'd lose my position as captain of the guard if anyone found out—"

"We're not pirates," I snapped. "We're on a rescue mission."

The rainfall slowly lightened to a drizzle, the sky still dark as we sailed through the storm. Crew members paid us no attention as they went about their duties like clockwork, none of them the least bit frazzled by the vicious winds and rain.

Leoni nodded her head toward Bastian. "What are you going to do when he finds out you don't have the pixie dust?" She gasped. "What do you think he's going to do to us?"

Driscoll's head snapped in our direction. "I'm sorry, what?" He leaned his head closer. "Did she just say you don't have the thing the pirate lord wants? The thing that you're using to bargain with him?" He stuffed his head between his knees. "Oh, blood and earth."

I stared straight ahead. "Luckily, I know who does have it and where it is. All I have to do is give Bastian the information he needs. Then we can go to the shadow court and get my brothers."

"Just your brothers?" Leoni whispered.

"Of course not. Once I figure out where they are, then we can also save our boys."

I wouldn't come home without every single one of them.

Driscoll raised his head. "And let me guess: the pirate lord isn't aware of that either?"

"He doesn't need to be," I replied.

"I think I'm going to be sick." Driscoll shoved his head between his knees again, roping his lanky arms around them.

That made two of us. I couldn't believe I was here. On Bastian's ship. Missing my own coronation.

I gasped.

"What?" Leoni straightened. "What's happened now?"

"You were supposed to tell my mother where I went. She's going to be worried sick—"

"I'll send a message," Leoni said, voice calm. She always had a solution. Thank the spirits for that. "I'll write to her, put it in a bottle, and let the sea deliver it."

My shoulders slumped in relief. That would work. "But don't tell her we're with Bastian. The fewer details she knows the better. Just tell her that we got a lead that we're following and we hope to be back home soon with all of our boys."

Leoni bit her lip but gave a curt nod. She hated lying, and it was going to be especially hard for her to lie to her queen. But this was a lie that needed to be told.

Leoni stayed silent as we sailed until the sky lightened from black to a murky gray, the rain finally stopping. Waves slapped against the ship, splashes of water plopping in front of us. From the helm, Bastian put two fingers in his mouth and let out a loud whistle.

"Everyone on the main deck," he bellowed.

There was a rush of movement as people congregated before us, eyes darting between us and Bastian. I couldn't imagine what they must think of these three bedraggled strangers Bastian had brought aboard. I wondered if they knew of his plan or if we were a surprise. As Bastian descended the steps of his ship, his crew stood at attention, a mixture of both men and women, about thirty in total if I had to guess. They didn't hesitate to follow his orders and stood ramrod straight. He must've been just as fearsome as all the rumors said.

I'd never seen this side of him, the pirate lord side. He'd had a commanding presence, sure, but he was never cruel or scary. Now I was realizing how wrong I'd been about him—or how much he'd misled me.

Bastian stepped down onto the main deck and beckoned for us. We obeyed, but when I tried to stand, my legs buckled, shaky and weak after all the power I'd used. I sank against the railing behind me while everyone now stared. More like glared. It felt downright hostile.

Bastian sighed. "This is Princess Gabrielle, her captain of the guard, and . . ." He gestured to Driscoll. "Well, a random man, whom, frankly, I don't know and don't wish to."

Driscoll scoffed.

Everyone continued to frown at us, and one of the crew growled.

"Introduction's over," Bastian yelled. "What in the bloody hells are you all doing standing around and staring? Get back to your positions or you'll walk the plank."

They all snapped out of their stupor and scuttled back to work. I'd never met any of Bastian's crew. He'd always snuck ashore while they anchored in the shallower parts of the water and stayed on the boat.

Our entire relationship was stolen moments. Secret trysts. A lie.

Once the crew members were out of earshot, Bastian gestured to a door next to the stairs. "We need to talk," he said.

A stubbornness rose up in me, and I stopped Driscoll from moving forward. Leoni, as always, waited for my lead. "I'm sorry, was that a command?"

Bastian shoved a hand through that thick black hair, still damp from the rain. "Ah, so we're doing this, are we?"

"Doing what? I just don't understand why you think you can command me. You're not my captain."

His jaw ticked. "I bloody well am while you're on my ship, and you better remember that."

"We can talk," I said.

A look of relief passed over Bastian's face. "Thank you."

He turned toward the door.

"If you ask nicely," I continued. He was not going to treat me like he had those crew members, like I was scum on the bottom of his boot.

He stopped, his shoulders bunching up by his ears.

Driscoll looked over to Leoni. "We're going to be shark food, aren't we?"

"I might prefer the sharks to this." Leoni gestured to Bastian's ship, to everyone shooting murderous glances our way.

Bastian slowly turned, locking eyes with me, his gaze never wavering from mine. I was tempted to break whatever staring game he was play-ing, but then I'd lose, and I refused to cower to the pirate lord. I was the one in control here, and he needed to realize it. I was princess of Apolis, and I would've been queen by now had Bastian not run my father's ship ashore and wrecked everything.

He stopped in front of me, so close I could feel his breath on my skin. We hadn't been this close for . . . well, for a long time ago. Those brown eyes flickered with something I didn't recognize.

"Please," he said through clenched teeth like the word was being pulled out of him.

My throat grew thick, palms sweaty. How many times had I said that single word to him? In very different situations than this one.

He cocked a brow and murmured, "Is that nice enough for you?"

I shoved past him.

"Oh . . . are we going now?" Driscoll asked.

"Yes, we're going," Leoni said, exasperated.

Bastian strode ahead of me and opened the door for us. It was time to reveal the truth about the pixie dust. I only hoped when Bastian found out we wouldn't be walking the plank after all.

Chapter Thirteen

We entered the captain's quarters. I stopped short inside, and Driscoll bumped into me. I quickly stepped out of the way to make room for everyone but couldn't help letting my gaze wander around the space.

I didn't know what I'd expected, but it wasn't this. The room was tidy, no clutter, not even a speck of dust. A desk stood against one wall, a map of Arathia, the Dark Seas, the human lands beyond, plastered to the wall over it. Pens and parchment lay across the desk, no doubt scattered from the recent storm. Windows lined another wall with a perfect view of the sea. He had his own private tub and toilet in the corner. I gulped. And there was his bed. Where he slept. Where he did . . . other things.

Suddenly, I was in a different place, a different time. We sat together in our favorite little cave, secluded and cut off from everyone else. He'd just taken me, rough, in the sand. Then again up against the smooth cave wall. Afterward, we'd lain in each other's arms while he'd stroked my hair and told me of the long nights at sea, nights where he'd do nothing but think of me while stroking himself. In that very bed with its simple straw-filled mattress and thin linen sheets.

Now I was thinking about his cock.

This had been a very, very bad idea.

"Princess?"

My gaze snapped from the bed to Driscoll.

I cleared my throat, hoping no one could see the flush crawling up my neck. "Yes?" I asked, voice far huskier than I'd meant it to be.

"Uh, well." Driscoll scratched his head. "The pirate lord asked you a question."

Bastian stared at me, those dark eyes simmering like he knew exactly what I'd been thinking about.

I bit the inside of my cheek, then straightened my shoulders. "My answer is no."

At this point, I just assumed that I'd disagree with whatever the pirate lord said.

"No, you're not okay sleeping belowdecks with the rest of the crew?" Bastian opened his arms wide. "Well, that leaves only one other place for you." He tipped his head toward his bed. "Well, there's also room in the quartermaster's cabin with Kara and Mia, but I don't know if they'll be so willing to share. Not like I am."

Damnit.

"Oh, I don't think so." Leoni stepped in front of me.

I placed a hand on her arm. "I simply misunderstood the question. Yes, sleeping belowdecks is fine."

He clapped his hands together. "Wonderful." He eyed my sapphire chiffon, still soaking wet and stuck to my skin, and . . . I looked down . . . showing my hard nipples. Perfect. "And when we next dock, we'll find you more appropriate attire for a pirate ship."

Driscoll raised his finger. "Question. Do we have a clothing budget? I prefer silk or velvet." He gestured to his body. "Wool just gets so itchy."

Bastian looked at me. "Is he always like this?"

I pinched the bridge of my nose. "Can we move on to more important topics? Like rescuing my brothers from the shadow court?"

"We're not rescuing anyone until I get my pixie dust, love."

"Stop calling me that," I said at the same time as Leoni said, "Stop calling her that."

I shook my head. "And what do you mean? That wasn't our deal!"

He leaned against his desk, those long legs stretching to the floor, one boot crossing over the other. His back rested right next to the gleaming gold spyglass, its handle brown and smooth. How many times had Bastian pulled that spyglass from his coat and pressed it to my eye, telling me to look up at the stars.

Second star to the right, he'd said. *That's our star.*

"We didn't exactly have time to hammer out the terms of our deal," Bastian was saying, "now did we?"

My fists curled as I shook the memory away. "We're getting my brothers first. Then you get the pixie dust."

"I'd love to sail straight to the shadow court and sweep your brothers away. But there's a few reasons why that can't happen. First of all, getting in and out of the shadow court with your brothers is going to take a lot of planning. Planning takes time. Not to mention, we're going to need their shadows, which have almost certainly been ripped from them. They cannot leave the island without them. I don't know where the shadows are kept. If I did, believe me, I'd have—"

He stopped himself and took a deep breath, and I wondered what he'd been about to say.

"We need time, is my point. Also, I don't know if you remember that I'm sick? I'm not getting any better without that dust."

My teeth clenched together. "You look fine to me."

"That's sweet of you." He flashed an arrogant grin. "But if I'm going to sneak you into the shadow court and steal from it, then I'm going to need to be at my best. So just tell me where you hid the pixie dust, and then we can be on our merry way."

Leoni and Driscoll shot each other nervous glances.

I straightened. Here went nothing. "I hid it a bit . . . far away."

Bastian cocked an eyebrow. "Define 'far away.'"

"In the earth court."

"Fucking hells." Bastian pounded a fist on the desk. "The fucking earth court? How did it end up there?"

"Liliath has it," I answered cooly.

His eyes bulged. "Liliath? As in Queen Liliath? The one who just defeated her stepmother and took her court back? That Liliath?"

"Yeah, she's pretty badass, isn't she?" Driscoll said, smiling in fondness. He must've missed her, just like I would've missed Leoni had I left her behind.

Bastian shot him a look that could incinerate a man on the spot.

Driscoll cleared his throat. "Right, not the best time to sing the praises of the woman who has the item you want and probably also hates your guts. Actually, she's my best friend, so I have it on good authority that she does, in fact, hate your guts."

That made Leoni let out a snort.

I wondered if I should reveal the other part of it: that not only did Liliath have the pixie dust, but that she'd used some of it. Well, her husband had. No, no, he couldn't know that part.

"How in the fuck are we going to get into the earth court and get the pixie dust from Queen Liliath?" Bastian threw out his arms. "That's going to take days, if not weeks."

Outside the window, the skies were still gray, the waters calm, sloshing up against the boat. I wanted to get out of this cabin and into the fresh air, inhale that salty sea scent I loved so much.

I took a deep breath. "Well, luckily for you, she's getting married in a week's time, and I just so happen to have an invitation to her wedding."

Driscoll raised a finger. "And did I not just mention I'm her best friend? Am I invisible? Can no one hear me speaking?"

Bastian snorted, attention fixed on me. "And you think you're just going to stroll into her wedding with the pirate lord of the Dark Seas on your arm?"

"What makes you think you'll be on my arm?" I asked through gritted teeth.

Bastian shook his head, a few strands of that black hair falling over his forehead. "You think I'm going to let you go alone? No, love. That's my pixie dust, and I'm going to get it myself. But I don't think Queen Liliath will exactly welcome the pirate who sold dark magic to her step-mother, the same dark magic that sent her court into ruin."

I thought about everything that had transpired between me and Liliath. How she'd shown up at my court just months ago, asking for asylum when really, all she and Penn had wanted, unbeknownst to me, was that pixie dust. She'd used me, lied to me, stolen it from me, brought an infamous criminal into my court and hid his identity—and yet, I'd forgiven her for it all.

"Yes," I said, "she will."

"Bollocks," Bastian spit out.

"I don't owe you an explanation," I snapped. "You either want the pixie dust or you don't. I'm not you, Bastian. I don't betray those I lo—"

I cut myself off as a small gasp escaped Leoni's mouth. Bastian's jaw clenched, and my face flushed. I might've stopped myself, but everyone had known what I was going to say, including the pirate lord. We'd never officially said it. I'd felt it in the way he'd looked at me, made love to me, spoken to me, but the words had always felt too scary to say out loud.

I agreed with Leoni. I'd rather walk the plank than deal with this.

Bastian looked away, showing off that exquisite bearded jawline, a jaw I somehow wanted to punch and trail my fingers across at the same time. "Fine," he said. "I'll trust you."

I stepped closer. "But I still don't trust you. So I'm going to need assurance that once I give you that pixie dust, you won't just drop me in the middle of the sea and sail away."

"Bloody hell." Bastian rubbed his jaw.

"Why should she trust you?" Leoni asked. "You kidnapped our boys and delivered them straight to the shadow court." She jabbed a finger at him. "You're a sad excuse for a pirate and a sad excuse for a man."

"Actually, I'm a rather good pirate," Bastian said, not even fazed by her insult, "but you're right about that second part." His voice lowered. "I'm a very bad man."

Driscoll let out a whimper, and I couldn't tell if he was afraid or turned on. Probably both, much like myself in this moment.

"We won't help you get the pixie dust back until you do as the princess said." Leoni's hands curled into fists. She wouldn't back down, even if I was tempted to, tempted to give in and get going, to trust Bastian even when my instincts told me not to.

"Fine." Bastian took a deep breath, then unhooked the silver chain with the clock from around his neck. It wasn't anything fancy. In fact, it looked like a piece of junk. But he touched it like it was a prized possession, something important. He looked physically pained as he unclasped it.

His hands shook as he walked forward and moved behind me. I stilled. He lifted my braid, still wet from the rain, and his hands brushed against the nape of my neck, his breath warm. I suppressed a shiver.

He fumbled with the clasp, the heat of his body behind me almost too much, his scent of sea salt and sandalwood enveloping me.

"Let me do it." Leoni shoved Bastian aside, cold dousing the flames building within me.

"Careful," he snapped. "It's old. It needs to be treated with care."

Driscoll wrinkled his nose at the tarnished piece of jewelry, and I could tell he was biting back some snarky comment about it. I didn't know why this meant anything to Bastian, but it clearly did, which was all that mattered.

I looked down and studied the clock, silver with small dots representing the time. "I'll keep it safe while it's in my care," I said to him.

He nodded, eyeing it like he was tempted to snatch it back. "So we have a deal, then?"

"Are you sure about this?" Leoni whispered from behind me.

"Yes," I said. "We have a deal."

"Then get yourselves ready to set sail." Bastian strode toward the door. "We have a wedding to attend."

Chapter Fourteen

After our deal was made and Bastian ordered the crew to change course toward Elwen, we were given a tour of the ship, which turned out to be very brief.

A stony-faced woman named Kara stood in front of us, little round earrings lining one ear, a red bandana tied around her brown hair. She cocked a pierced brow as she stared at us. Tattoos covered her arms and crept up her neck. She seemed so familiar, but I couldn't quite place my finger on what it was about her that I recognized. Surely we'd never met before.

"Quarterdeck." She pointed toward the stairs that led up to the helm, a huge mast rising into the air. "Forecastle deck." She pointed to the opposite end of the ship with another tall mast. "Main deck." She pointed down to where we currently stood, right next to the third and final mast. Long ratlines stretched across them and down to the decks, crew members climbing them. "And over there leads down to the crew cabin belowdecks, where you'll each get a bunk. Mealtimes are morning, midday, and evening, and you better not tarry because we're hungry, and we're not particularly keen to share, especially with those who aren't part of the crew."

Then, without another word she stalked away, mumbling what I thought was "complete waste of my time."

Driscoll turned to us. "Well, she was just a ray of sunshine."

Later, we were shown our bunks, which were so small, Driscoll's feet hung over the edge. In between the bunks were barrels of drinking and bathing water, boxes of dried and salted meats and crackers, and various other goods that I didn't pry into. The space was dingy and dark and had an odor of moldy water. Driscoll pinched his nose closed, and Leoni wrinkled hers. I would have felt bad that I'd dragged them into this, except I hadn't. They chose this after I'd loudly protested, so if they weren't happy, the fault lay on their shoulders.

Driscoll patted a heavy black cannon that sat next to his assigned bunk. "This isn't alarming at all."

Leoni climbed the rickety ladder, which was missing a rung, to her top bunk and plopped down on the sagging mattress. "I've always wanted to see one of those in action." She gestured to the other cannons that were nestled between the bunks. "You think they'll fire one off for us?"

Driscoll tugged at his collar. "Spirits below, I hope not. Are you a masochist or something?"

I put a hand on his shoulder. "We have to be prepared for anything, Driscoll."

He sank onto his bed, and a billow of dust rose that he swatted at. "I did not think this through."

After that, we ascended to the main deck, and I leaned against the railing of the ship, watching the way the water ebbed and flowed, the beauty of the undulating waves, the power of the sea. It never ceased to amaze me. Out here, I felt alive. Exhilarated. I couldn't say the same for my companions, who sat shoulder to shoulder against the railing, bickering about who should get the bottom bunk.

"I'm almost a foot shorter than you," Leoni said. "It's easier for you to reach the top."

"Yes, it's also easier for me to bang my head against the ceiling when I jolt awake in the middle of the night from an inevitable nightmare—probably one about this ship."

I tuned them out, thinking about what was to come and hoping I knew what I was doing.

I must've stood there for at least an hour, watching the clouds as they moved through the sky, Leoni and Driscoll finally falling into silence.

A bell rang out, and Kara's prediction was true. Everyone left their posts and raced to the galley down below, located right next to where we slept. When the three of us finally made it down the stairs, we had to pick our way through the crew members sitting in the narrow hallway, scooping their dinner from their bowls. We entered the galley, a long rectangular table overflowing with more crew members, sans Bastian.

One of the pirates, Ollie, I thought his name was, waved his hands in the air. "And then I jumped from the ledge of our ship to the enemy ship and jabbed my sword, fighting off three men at once." His red frizzy hair poofed out of his black bandana. Another crew member sat next to him, a man with a scarred face, scribbling down everything Ollie was saying.

"You mean you fell into them like a toppling tree," Kara said as she took a deep gulp from her cup. "Almost ran yourself through with your own sword. I had to jump in and save your arse."

Ollie tore off a small piece of bread and threw it at her. "It's a fine arse. Wanna see it?" He stood and made to pull his pants down when someone else grabbed him and shoved him back into his seat.

"Trust me when I say no one wants to see that hairy arse," someone yelled from the hallway.

The table roared with laughter as Ollie made a face and threw another piece of bread.

"Hey!" said a man with a tall white hat on his head. "You throw any more of that food I labored over, and I'll throw you overboard."

Ollie waved his hand dismissively, and the man, who I assumed was the cook, turned back to the stove where he stood.

"Where is the captain?" I asked, then immediately regretted the question as the laughter and chatter died down, everyone turning their stony gazes toward us.

"Eating in his quarters," one of the crewmen finally said, barely looking up from the bowl of mush that sat in front of him.

Driscoll strode over to the table and grimaced. "What is this fine delicacy, if I may ask?"

Leoni sniffed the air and wrinkled her nose.

"It's a new recipe I'm trying." The man wearing the white hat stood over a small fire hearth, which crackled with an uncomfortable heat. He looked over his shoulder as he pulled out a loaf of bread from the hearth while stirring a large pot that sat on its iron top. He threw the bread on the table, and everyone immediately began tearing into it.

A bald man looked up. "Cook here would own the finest restaurant on our continent if he wasn't trapped on this ship with us."

I didn't understand why Cook couldn't just leave, but maybe Bastian had somehow enslaved everyone here. They didn't seem like slaves, but at this point, nothing would surprise me.

"It . . . smells delightful." Driscoll's smile was strained.

Kara stood and held out her bowl, and the cook ladled more of the slop into it. She sidled back to the table, not even glancing at us as she spooned it into her mouth.

"Well, I guess we should eat," I said, feeling the weight of the tension in the room. "We need to keep up our strength."

"For what?" someone grumbled. "Being nothing but dead weight?"

Everyone else snickered. Leoni, Driscoll, and I shot each other questioning glances. It wasn't as if I thought we'd be best friends, but I didn't think we'd be so ill-received by Bastian's crew.

We inched by the wooden table and benches, then each grabbed a bowl.

"Oh." The cook lifted his hat and scratched his head, looking into the bubbling pot. "We're fresh out, I'm afraid."

My mouth dropped open, and I shot a glance at Kara, who cocked her pierced brow and gave me a look that said "told you so."

"But—" I pointed toward the mush and Driscoll elbowed me.

"Let's not argue with the pirates." He punched his fist across his stomach. "Thank you for your time. Since we're fresh out of . . . mush, I'm going to call it a night. Need my beauty sleep."

No one acknowledged him; they didn't acknowledge any of us. This journey was going to be worse than I thought.

"Breakfast'll be served when the sun rises tomorrow," the cook said. "Better come early if you want some."

"Good to know," Leoni grumbled.

With that, we left and made our way to the cabin. Leoni shot

Driscoll, who already lay in the bottom bunk, a glare as she climbed the
ladder to get to her bed. I dropped into mine, the mattress lumpy and
poking into my ribs, and despite my empty stomach, I fell into an imme-
diate sleep.

Chapter Fifteen

"Princess, Princess Gabrielle! Wake up," Driscoll whispered, voice frantic.

My heavy eyes blinked open to see Driscoll leaning over me. "What do you want?" I asked, groggy.

He frowned at me. "Wait, why am I talking to you? I need your captain of the guard. Even if she is the size of a gnome."

He scrambled up the ladder of their bunk, which sat across the narrow aisle from mine. "Wake up, Leoni! We have an emergency."

She sat up in bed, her long reddish-gold hair tangled and tumbling down past her shoulders, her chiffon from yesterday wrinkled and stained. "What in the bloody waters do you want?"

She sounded how I felt.

"Someone is trying to murder me, and I need you to defend me."

She blinked a few times. "Oh? That's all?" She lay back down and rolled over.

He let out a groan and shook her. "No, I'm serious."

She ignored him, her determination to sleep impressive.

I sighed, fully awake now. My limbs creaked as I stretched my arms overhead, smelling myself and almost gagging. I was going to bathe today. Hopefully. I didn't know if the ship had a tub anywhere other than in Bastian's quarters, but they must have. The other option was too horrifying.

Driscoll twisted around, still clinging to the ladder. "He keeps following me, and he called after me with this growly, low voice that just screamed 'I want to murder you.'"

Leoni huffed and sat up, finally giving up on slumber. "Who?"

Driscoll threw an arm out. "How am I supposed to know his name? Do you make it a habit of asking for someone's name when they're trying to kill you?"

Leoni rolled her eyes. "I make it a habit of not irritating anyone so much that they want to kill me."

I sent a cursory glance around the room. The empty room, which meant . . . we'd likely slept in too late and missed breakfast. Damnit. My stomach grumbled.

"So where is he now?" I asked Driscoll. "This murderer that's after you?"

"I don't know!" He looked around. "We have to be prepared." He twirled his hand in Leoni's direction. "So, prepare."

Just then the door to the bunk room banged open, a low growl coming from that direction, and we all froze.

I shot a look at Leoni. "I didn't think he was serious."

She shrugged. "It surprises you that someone wants to murder Driscoll?"

"Thank you," he said to her, then paused. "Hey!"

Boots clomped on the stairs, shadows encompassing the figure. Driscoll shrieked but didn't move, his gaze stuck on the stairs.

We all waited with bated breath as the figure stepped into the dim lighting, and I swallowed.

A man stood before us. No, no, that wasn't right. He towered over us. Scars covered his entire face, and his knuckles and hands were cracked, blackened with what looked like blood. His clothes were similar to all the pirates on this ship, leather boots, dark trousers, a linen shirt tucked into them, and a blue bandana tied around his head.

His gaze locked onto Driscoll, who let out a squeak and shriveled into himself.

The man took a few steps forward, and I stood, moving toward Driscoll, but the man reached him first.

"Oh . . ." Driscoll trailed off, unable to form words as his head slowly tipped up.

Leoni looked at me and mouthed, "What do I do?"

Fuck if I knew. *I* didn't even know what to do. I was a good fighter, but I wasn't sure I could take on this man, especially in my weakened state.

"Please don't butcher me into little pieces and throw me into the sea!" Driscoll said in a rush, throwing an arm over his eyes.

The man reached into the pocket of his trousers, and I readied myself to lunge forward and grab his arm, try and wrestle away whatever weapon he was about to pull out, but when he withdrew his hand, I paused in confusion.

He held out a little silver pin. Light caught on the round object, illuminating the trees carved into it and the circle of vines around the edge.

"I believe this is yours?" the man said, holding it out to Driscoll.

"You've got to be kidding me." Leoni cuffed Driscoll on the back of the head. "This is what you woke us up for?"

Driscoll stared at the object, then took it and pinned it to his green silk shirt. "Oh." He cleared his throat. "Thank you."

The man didn't have any eyebrows, puckered scars in the place of them, but I imagined if he did, he'd be furrowing them right about now. "Wait a minute, did you say butcher?" He reached into his shirt pocket and pulled out a kerchief, dotting his head. He stuffed the handkerchief back into his shirt. "The name's Bartholomew. Your pin was so beautiful. I didn't want you to lose it." He tilted his head. "Why did you think I was going to butcher you? I don't butcher anyone. I'm the one who writes all about the butchering."

"Yes, Driscoll," Leoni said, holding back her laughter, "why did you think he was going to butcher you?"

"Because . . ." Driscoll stated like it was obvious. "I mean . . ." He gestured to Bartholomew.

"Oh." The pirate's eyes widened as he looked down at himself. "You mean that I look like a man who could crush your head with my boot?"

"Yes, that," Driscoll said weakly, his dark skin looking clammy.

Bartholomew clapped him on the shoulder, and the force of it almost made Driscoll fall off the ladder. "No, you don't have to worry about that. I'm the bard. You might've heard of me?" He cleared his throat and flourished his hand in front of him. "Barty the Bard?"

We all stared at him blankly.

He began to hum, then broke out into song.

"What is happening?" Leoni asked.

"I don't know." Driscoll stared at the man in utter confusion as he belted out,

"The town is dark

The people aslumber

The Lost Boys are ready to plunder

They'll steal your goods

They'll take your wives

If you're not careful

They'll take your lives . . ."

He trailed off as we continued to stare.

Driscoll started clapping, his eyes darting from side to side like he wasn't sure if this was the right move.

Bartholomew scratched his head. "Really? You haven't heard of me? That's my most popular song. Sang it in every tavern across the Halios."

The collection of human lands.

"Well, we are elementals," I said. "So maybe that's why we haven't heard of you? We don't exactly travel to Halios much."

I'd been on a few diplomatic trips to meet various leaders, but the trips had been short and we certainly hadn't frequented any taverns.

I didn't want to hurt the poor man's feelings. He was so proud of his song.

"We have our own bards," Driscoll offered. "Crooning Crow?"

Barty swore. "That's a good name."

"Oh yes, I love him," Leoni said, and I shot her a warning glare. "Sorry." She scratched her head. "Um, your song was really good too?"

Bartholomew started pacing. "I never even thought about visiting Arathia. I have an entire untapped audience there."

Driscoll clapped his hands together. "Well, now that we know you're not going to cut me up into little pieces, maybe we can eat something?"

Bartholomew frowned. "Oh, you missed breakfast, unfortunately. You'll have to try again at midday."

Driscoll's shoulders slumped. "Ugh."

I studied Bartholomew in curiosity. "Why are you on this ship?" I shook my head. "I don't understand. You sing songs about the Lost Boys?"

"Aye," Bartholomew said. "Someone has to document their adventures, and who better than Barty the Bard?"

He broke out into song again.

"Is he going to do this all the time?" Driscoll whispered out the side of his mouth.

"His voice has a pleasant timbre," Leoni offered.

The door creaked open again, and a woman emerged, this one with cropped brown hair and a heart-shaped face, her bandana a bright yellow. Just like with Kara, I had the distinct feeling I knew her, but I couldn't figure out why. "Bartholomew, are you singing again? I told you that singing times are strictly after sundown."

She approached us as Bartholomew trailed off, then shoved his hand into his pocket and pulled out a little pocket journal and a pen. He started scribbling on it, the ink getting on his fingers. So not blood covering them, then.

The woman cleared her throat. "We have duties, you know." She shot us a look. "Especially with the extra people we now have on board."

Bartholomew tsked. "Mia, be nice."

She squeezed her eyes shut and pressed her lips together. "I'm sorry," she finally said. "That was rude. We weren't expecting your presence is all. It's a . . . distraction."

A distraction. I assumed she was talking about me. I'd wrecked their ship, had their captain arrested, tried to drown him. It had been stupid to think they'd just welcome us aboard.

"I'm Mia," the woman said, voice slightly less aggressive than before. "And he gets like this sometimes." She nodded toward Bartholomew, who was once again scribbling in his little journal. "Well, all the time. He gets an idea for a song, and then you've lost him. He's either writing songs or singing them. I don't know which is worse."

"Wait a minute." I pointed at Mia. "You're Kara." I shook my head. "I mean, without the tattoos and piercings."

They had the same face shape, the same eyes, the same nose.

"Yes, we're twins." Mia shifted. "What of it?"

"I just . . ." I couldn't figure out why they were so familiar to me.

Mia sighed and grabbed Bartholomew's arm. "Come on, we have work to do. Cap needs you, and you don't want to make him angry." She turned to us and her gaze flicked to the necklace hanging down between my breasts, Bastian's necklace. She frowned. "If you'll excuse us."

Despite only coming up to his shoulders, she managed to drag Bartholomew toward the stairs.

"But I wasn't finished writing," he whined. "I thought of a new song about a stowaway princess."

They exited the room, the door slamming behind them.

"She didn't like you very much." Driscoll studied his nails.

I stared at the door. "I don't think any of them like us." My jaw clenched. "But they're the ones who took our boys. If anything, we should be the ones who dislike them."

Leoni squinted at me, suspicious. "Why do you care if they like you? Or is it a certain pirate lord you're concerned about?"

"I don't care about the pirate lord," I said quickly. "About any of them." Once upon a time, I would have. Bastian had told me so much about his crew, Mia and Kara included.

"Barty was friendly, at least," Driscoll pointed out.

"Because he hoped we'd be his newest fans," I said. "He's already trying to write a song about us."

Leoni shook her head. "Let's just get up on the main deck and figure out how close we are to Elwen."

She and Driscoll started walking toward the stairs while I chewed at my bottom lip, still so certain I knew Kara and Mia. There were secrets lurking on this ship, and I intended to uncover them.

Chapter Sixteen

The next day, I emerged from belowdecks to see that the ship was sitting still in the ocean, pirates milling about, many of the crew napping on the main deck, others sitting and playing cards, some drinking what smelled like liquor.

"What's going on?" I asked Kara, staring at her tattoos, one of a skull that looked a lot like the skull on the flag of the ship. "Why aren't we moving?"

She rolled her eyes. "In case you didn't notice, Princess, we need wind to move. Unless you can make that happen, we're stuck."

She shoved past me and stomped away. Well, the animosity toward us hadn't calmed at all. I looked at the sky. I wasn't from Valoris, the sky court, so I didn't have the power to control the wind. I eyed the dark blue sea, its color dim under the cloudy skies. But I did have the power to move the water.

Mia stood by the helm, talking to a crew member whose hands gripped the wheel.

I approached them. "Can I speak with you?" I asked Mia.

She eyed me but nodded, following me to the end of the quarterdeck. "I'm busy, so I don't really have time to . . ."

She trailed off as I struck out my hands and commanded the ocean to carry us forward.

Her eyes widened as the ship lurched. "What are you doing?"

"Moving the ship," I said. "Is that helpful?"

"I—well, yes. Until the wind picks back up." She looked up at the sky. "Rain might be coming in, so I imagine the winds will pick up soon."

Crew members jolted as the ship moved, some scratching their heads in confusion.

Mia tugged at her short brown hair. "I thought your magic was depleted?"

I concentrated on keeping the ship moving. "Well, it was. After we use magic, it drains us temporarily, weakens us, but as we rest, it builds back up again."

The sails billowed above us as the ship moved faster.

I kept my hands out, the ocean pushing us along. "I won't be able to do this for long, but Leoni can help too."

She stared at the moving water in fascination. "So you can command water and also create it?" she asked.

"Something like that." I paused. "We can make water take on different forms, we can command it, manipulate it, and create it. But we try not to use our magic unless necessary. We don't use it frivolously."

At least we didn't in the water court. I couldn't speak for the other courts, for how strict they were with their use of magic.

Mia leaned against the railing, biting her cheek like it might be a betrayal to ask me these questions. I needed to get on someone's good side. Having allies on this ship would make our journey easier.

"I'll answer any questions you have," I offered, the ship still moving forward.

She glanced around, but no one was near us. She leaned closer. "Does manipulating water drain you faster than creating something from water?"

I lifted my head as a breeze formed from the ship's movement, fanning my face. "Yes, because sometimes the water doesn't want to do what we are asking it to. It fights us. When we create a water spear or water sword or a wall, that's easier to command. But creating something big or something that has a lot of moving parts might drain an elemental faster because of how much power it takes to control it." I cocked my head. "And some elementals are better at controlling the sea or rivers while some are more skilled at creating water."

Mia leaned her elbow on the railing, propping her chin in her hand. Her eyes crinkled in such a familiar way. Maybe if we became friends, I could ask if we'd met. "Are some elementals stronger than others? Royals or guards?"

I shook my head. "We're all given equal power, though some of us train harder, are more adept at fighting with our magic or using it for different purposes."

"And all the courts are like this?" Mia asked.

The ocean rolled under the boat, and the crew members darted glances at me, starting to catch on that I was the one doing this. For once, I got something other than glares sent my way. In fact, it seemed like some of them might actually be admiring me and my magic.

"Yes," I said. "But our magic tends to be weaker in other courts, giving them advantage over us. If I were to visit the fire court, my water magic wouldn't be as strong there. Whereas, if someone from the frost court came to Apolis, their magic would be weaker. It's why most elementals tend to stay in their own court. Some travel for trade or other reasons, but in general, we like to stay in our home territory."

Mia tapped her finger against her chin. "That makes sense," she said. "Is that why you all avoid conflict? Compared to our lands, the elementals always seem to be at peace."

I tipped my head. "That and the fact that we have peace treaties in place, trade agreements, alliances. Breaking any of those could mean severe consequences."

She slowly shook her head. "Then why would you ever have fallen for Bastian?"

The question took me off guard, and my magic faltered, the ship lurching. I stumbled, quickly sticking out my hands and regaining my balance.

Mia's face turned stony. "Surely you must've known the consequences of leaving your land behind. Leaving your people. Your magic weakened. Why would you tell him you'd give all that up? Unless you were just toying with him?"

My own anger flared at that accusation. "He's the one who betrayed me."

Her jaw locked, and she crossed her arms. Right then, a gust of wind blew past us.

"Wind!" someone yelled.

Mia straightened. "Thank you for your help, but I think we can take it from here." She stalked away.

I rubbed my arm muscles, sore and weak after that use of magic. The crew got to work as the wind picked up further, clouds darkening above.

So much for getting on someone's good side.

Chapter Seventeen

After three days at sea, I was growing tired of sitting around and watching the crew scurry about, doing their duties. I assumed Bastian had a talk with them because they'd finally left some food for us, but other than Bartholomew, most of them completely ignored our presence—other than to shoot glares our way. Just so we remembered how unwelcome we were.

Kara seemed to harbor the most hatred toward us. Toward me, specifically. Every chance she got, she'd sneer at me, shove me if I was in her way. I swore she'd even stuck out her leg and tripped me on purpose one time, though Leoni and Driscoll said they thought it was an accident.

I tugged at Bastian's necklace that hung around my neck, looking around the ship, at crew members up on the mast, managing the helm, cleaning the lines and canvas, swabbing the deck. I yearned to know more about how it all worked, how they kept this ship operating so smoothly.

I watched Bartholomew as he sat on the opposite side, scribbling in that journal he always seemed to carry. If anyone would be willing to tell me more about how this ship functioned so I could participate in some of the tasks, it would be him. Driscoll and Leoni were belowdecks napping, so I took the opportunity to meander over to Bartholomew and plopped down next to him.

"Working on your newest song?" I asked, and he paused, setting down his journal.

"Yes." He tapped a pen to his chin. "About a princess of the sea and the pirate who won her heart."

"Then stomped all over it," I muttered. "Don't leave out that part."

"Ah, well, every story has two sides."

I crossed my arms. "But let me guess, you're not going to tell me Bastian's side?"

"Not my story to tell," Bartholomew said.

"Right. You're a bard who tells everyone's stories except for the one person whose story I'd like to hear."

The crew wouldn't speak to me, but even if they would, I had a feeling they were under orders to not answer any questions about the shadow court or why they'd kidnapped our boys. Bastian remained tight lipped as ever and barely acknowledged me. It was like I had a disease he was afraid of catching, and whenever we happened to be in the same space, he'd brush past me without a word.

Bartholomew lifted his journal. "Well, some stories I have permission to tell and others I don't."

I nodded toward the booklet. "Do you have a favorite song?"

"Ah, that's a hard question to answer." He sat for a moment before snapping his fingers. "I don't have favorites, but my fans do. One of my most requested is a song about the time the crew were on the run in Gilraeth."

I raised a brow, surprised they'd ventured that deep into the continent, all the way to the fire court.

"They stumbled upon a cave full of treasure: glinting jewels, sparkling diamonds, enough gold that the weight of it would sink our very ship."

I had a feeling Bartholomew was exaggerating, but I supposed that was his job as a bard.

"They ran into the cave, stuffing their pockets with the expensive trinkets, not realizing they hadn't just stumbled upon treasure—they'd stumbled upon a dragon."

I sucked in a sharp breath. Dragons were native to Gilraeth and had been at war with the residents of the fire court for ages. I'd heard that Princess Seraphina had a special relationship with the dragons. Her coronation was in a month's time, and supposedly, the dragons would be there to show their support for the new queen. It was just gossip, but Princess Seraphina had always had a special place in her heart for the outcasts, for the misunderstood, and I had a feeling this was one rumor I could believe.

I leaned back on my elbows and looked up at the cloudy sky. Nothing but clouds since we'd gotten on this ship. I missed the sun on my face. "So what happened next?" I asked.

"Well, the dragon moved in front of the entrance to the cave, trapping the crew," Bartholomew said. "But our brave captain had a plan." Bartholomew leaned closer. "He used himself as bait, lured the dragon away from the entrance so his crew could escape."

If someone had asked me a year ago if that would've surprised me, I'd have said no. But now? Now I couldn't believe Bastian would do any such thing.

"It worked. The crew escaped the cave with the treasure, while Bastian fought the dragon himself."

"But that's impossible. It takes at least ten fire elementals to bring down a dragon. Bastian is human. How could he have survived that?"

Bartholomew raised a finger. "None of the fire people are as cunning as our captain. He baited the dragon into letting loose a stream of fire right as he leapt up over the dragon's head. The dragon blew the fire up toward the ceiling, and as Bastian slid down its back and tail, right out of the cave, rocks fell down from the force of the fire, trapping the dragon inside."

"That's quite a tale."

"It's a great song," Bartholomew said. "People go wild over it."

"So you just visit taverns when you dock?" I asked. "No one questions your connection to the Lost Boys?"

"Artists are exempt from persecution," Bartholomew said. "Many of us are here to tell important stories, to bring news to the people, to keep them informed and entertained. I don't pillage, plunder, attack. I simply observe and tell the tales. For that, I'm appreciated, not scorned."

There was a sadness in his voice I didn't understand.

"Do you not like your job?" I asked.

"I love it. I was never cut out to be a pirate, and Bastian knew that, I think." He gestured toward his face. "I tried my hand at it, and during an attack I ran away and hid behind a barrel on the ship. A barrel filled with alcohol. An enemy from the other ship shot at the barrel with an explosive and it blew up in my face."

I stared at him, horrified. "That's how you got those scars?"

He nodded. "After that, I felt useless. Didn't know my place anymore, didn't feel like I belonged. It was Bastian who disappeared one day when we docked and reappeared on the ship with a banjo and a pocketbook. Told me he was in need of a bard if I'd give it a shot. Turns out it was my calling. I've never looked back."

That left me stunned. "That was nice of Bastian." I nodded toward the booklet. "Is that the one he bought for you?"

Bartholomew chuckled. "Oh no, I worked my way through that one long ago."

"Wow, you must write a lot. Those journals are thick."

He cleared his throat. "Yes, I tend to be wordy."

"So why the sadness?" I laid a hand on his arm. "I sensed it when you were talking about singing in the taverns."

His shoulders slumped. "I suppose I feel trapped sometimes. I wish I could go where I wanted when I wanted, wish I could tell the stories I want to tell, not just about the Lost Boys."

"What's stopping you?" I asked. "Just leave."

"It's not that simple." He looked away.

I supposed maybe he felt he owed Bastian something for giving him this position on his ship. I was about to tell him he didn't owe the pirate anything when Bartholomew said, "I suspect you know what it's like to feel trapped."

I pushed a few stray wisps out of my eyes. "What do you mean?"

"When you and Bastian were together, he told us a little about you, about your predicament."

Bartholomew was full of surprises today. It didn't shock me that Bastian talked about me with his crew, but it was surprising he'd told them such specific things about me.

"Yes, that's true. I did—do—feel trapped sometimes. Trapped in a role I don't want."

"I see the way you light up on this ship," Bartholomew said. "Despite the circumstances you've seemed happy these last few days."

I was. And the weight of that guilt was so heavy it would sink me straight to the bottom of the ocean. Feeling happy here, of all places, felt like a betrayal to my mother, my brothers, my father—to everyone. I felt more alive on this pirate ship than I ever had in Apolis.

I didn't want to talk about it, think about it, so I steered the conversation in a different direction. "Can you tell me more about the ship? I'd like to help out some, pull my weight, but I don't know most of the terms you all use, the jobs necessary to sail this ship, keep it running."

Bartholomew's lips stretched into a smile. "Ah, I'm happy to tell you anything you want to know."

I shrugged helplessly. "Everything?"

Bartholomew laughed. "Well, Bastian is our captain."

I rolled my eyes. "I do know that much, at least."

"Mia is his quartermaster." He pointed to the opposite side of the stairs that were across the main deck. "She gets her own cabin and shares with Kara, since they're the only females on the ship."

"So what does the quartermaster do?" I asked.

"She makes sure Bastian's orders are carried out."

That surprised me. Mia was more soft spoken, whereas Kara was so commanding, a force to be reckoned with. I said as much to Bartholomew and he laughed.

"There's power in a gentle hand. The men respect Mia because she doesn't try to control them, to micromanage their every move. Kara would probably have someone walking the plank every other day."

He made a good point. "So what does Kara do?"

"Well, she's our carpenter." He nodded to her as she sat across the deck, carving out a piece of wood. "She helps keep damage to a minimum, keeps our ship afloat. She knows this vessel inside and out."

He pointed to a man who was walking toward Bastian's cabin with a long rolled piece of parchment. "That's our navigator there." He nodded toward the helm. "Our helmsman, though during storms or attacks, Bastian likes to take the helm."

I remembered that first night on the ship, Bastian at the wheel while the rain battered him.

Bartholomew pointed at a man whose name I thought was Ollie, his red hair frizzier than ever today. "Ollie, there, is our boatswain. He's in charge of getting supplies for us when on land. Making sure we have fresh water, that our food isn't spoiled, that we have the right amount of supplies for our upcoming journey."

This took so much organization, and it surprised me. I'd never known much about it. "I always thought pirates were just a bunch of criminals who got together and terrorized others," I said to Bartholomew. "This seems very . . . structured."

Bartholomew stroked his chin. "Well, it has to be for us to survive."

My eyes trailed back to Bastian's cabin, where the man had disappeared inside with what I assumed was a map. I loved looking at maps, at all the possibilities that lay before me, so many places to see, to explore. If I had the freedom to do so, that was. "So what is the navigator talking with Bastian about right now?" I asked.

"Oh, probably updating him on our route, talking about possible places to dock once we get to Elwen, places we can stop on the way to replenish supplies." Bartholomew lifted his bandana and scratched his head. "I think I overheard him telling Bastian yesterday that we could stop in Porth, which is where we found your father's ship."

I straightened at that, and Bartholomew must've realized his mistake immediately. "I didn't just say that."

"My father's ship?" I grasped his arm. "You found it in Porth?"

A human town. A well-known stopping place between Apolis and Elwen.

Bartholomew swallowed. "Well, yes, but—"

I stood. "When are we going to be passing Porth?"

Bartholomew paled. "I think around evening time tomorrow? But, Princess—"

I stalked toward Bastian's cabin.

"Where are you going?" Bartholomew called after me.

"To have a little chat with the pirate lord."

Chapter Eighteen

"Absolutely not," Bastian said while sitting at his desk, back to me. He hunched over, scribbling something on parchment with a pen.

The navigator looked between us before quickly leaving the cabin, most likely sensing this was a conversation he didn't need to be part of.

"Why?" I pressed. "Bartholomew said we have to stop for supplies, and it's on our way, so what's the problem?"

Bastian paused, setting down the pen and turning to me. "Because I don't have time for a side quest. Finding out what happened to your father was not part of our deal. I said I would tell you what happened, and that was it."

"So, then, what happened? You still haven't told me."

Bastian leaned back in his chair, stretching out a long leg. "Actually, I said I would tell you if you were nice."

"After what you did to me, to my court, you're lucky I haven't gutted you with a knife. That's about as nice as I'll get."

"Well, to be fair, you did try and drown me."

I shook my head. "Forget it. Talking with you is a waste of time, as usual." I turned to go.

"After you so kindly tricked me and wrecked my ship," he said, stopping me in my tracks, "my crew and I fled on abandoned rowboats we found littering that little cove on the northern shore. We were afraid your guards would be coming after us if we didn't make a quick exit. Since you so kindly stole the pixie dust, I planned on hiding out for a few days, then coming back for my ship and the dust. Except a storm hit us, carrying us far out to sea. I didn't have any of my supplies: no compass, no map, nothing. We got lost at sea, starving, parched, baking under the sun. From there we experienced months of setbacks trying to make our way back to Apolis. Everything you can think of: storms, attacks, getting lost, getting stranded, sickness. We almost didn't survive."

If he was trying to make me feel bad, it wasn't working. He'd deserved everything that had come his way. I turned, now fully invested in his tale.

He rubbed his jaw. "After months of bad luck, we finally washed up on Porth, on the jungle side, opposite of where the town is."

I stepped closer. "And that's where you found my father's ship?"

"Aye."

I shook my head. That didn't make sense. That was way off course if my father was trying to get to the shadow court. Or maybe he'd found a clue about how to help my brothers and it had led him to Porth. Even more reason why I needed to get to that island.

"We saw the ship, saw that it had been abandoned, and stole it." Bastian cleared his throat. "We had business to attend to before we could make it back to Apolis."

"Business." I crossed my arms. "Is that what you call stealing people's shadows?"

Bastian held my stare, not an ounce of shame in his blank expression. "Yes, that is what I call it." He stood and walked toward me, too close for comfort. "We got our bearings and finally made our way back to Apolis. And you know the rest."

I did. Every moment since he'd sailed back into my life was branded into my mind. "We need to stop in Porth," I said.

Bastian stepped closer, his fists tight at his sides. "I already told you, I found nothing at the site of your father's ship. No remains, no signs of anyone."

"Forgive me if I don't trust you. I want to investigate for myself."

His voice lowered. "And what is it going to take for you to trust me?" His fingers twitched, like he wanted to reach out and touch me.

My traitorous body wanted him to. I might have made up my mind about hating him, but my body hadn't caught up yet.

I glared at him. "Well, unless you have a way to turn back time and not kidnap a bunch of children from my court, I'd say quite a fucking lot."

His jaw locked. "My answer is no."

I surged forward so we were practically nose-to-nose. "You don't get to make that decision."

"Actually, as captain, I absolutely do." His lips were inches from mine, and I could almost taste the salt on them. "You were always so stubborn."

"Don't talk about me like you know me." My chest rose and fell with quick breaths.

He raised his brows. "I do know you." His gaze raked over my body. "Very well, actually."

I wouldn't let him toy with my emotions like this, flirt with me like he hadn't committed unimaginable atrocities, like I'd just forget his betrayal if he turned on his charms. "What?" I threw out my arms. "Because you fucked me? Told me some sad stories in a cave and got to hear my own sad stories in return? That doesn't mean you know me. You got glimpses of me, never the whole picture."

His voice dropped to a whisper. "Now I know that's not true." He lowered his lips to my ear. "You can tell yourself whatever you want, love, but I saw you, the real you. I saw your hopes, your dreams . . . and so much more."

I stepped away, putting distance between us while my heart hammered in my chest. I hated him. I hated the way my body still reacted to him, like muscle memory. "Stop," I said. "Just stop." My voice broke on that last word.

Bastian straightened, the fire in his eyes fading, and that stone-cold expression slipped over his face like he was coming out of a trance. He cleared his throat. "If we're done here, I have work to do." Without waiting for a reply, he spun on his heel and marched back to his desk.

I glared at the back of his head. If he wasn't going to stop the ship, then I'd find a way to get to Porth myself.

I MARCHED out of Bastian's cabin, fuming over our interaction. Leoni sat on the steps leading up to the helm, enjoying the cloudy but beautiful day at sea. Her hair was wound up in its usual tight bun, her chiffon still wrinkled and a complete mess from days before, which I was sure irritated her to no end. Leoni had a different uniform for every day of the week to ensure they were always sparkling clean and wrinkle free. She'd be so happy to get clean clothes. We all would.

The crew worked around the ship. I had no idea where Driscoll was. Probably trying to find a mirror so he could fix his hair.

"Oh no," Leoni said, looking up at me. "I recognize that look. It's your determined face. What happened?"

I sank down next to her and caught her up on everything she'd missed. "He said no," I told her. "That it wasn't part of our deal and we couldn't get distracted from our goal."

I left out the other parts, the way we'd been so dangerously close to each other.

"Can you believe it?" I asked.

"Yes, actually, I can. He's a terrible human being."

I took a deep breath. "I have to do something. If I have a chance to investigate this . . ."

Leoni chewed on the inside of her cheek.

"What?" I asked, nudging her. "Just say whatever you're thinking, Oni."

"I can't believe these words are coming out of my mouth, but I agree with him."

I stilled.

Leoni turned to me. "Oh, come on. Do you really think it's a good idea to pursue this right now? We're on the way to the earth court to get this pixie dust. We have to rescue your brothers." She lowered her voice. "All the boys of Apolis. And somehow, we have to work with the pirate lord to do it. Do you really think it's smart to add yet another thing to our agenda?"

"That thing is your king," I said, an edge to my voice.

Leoni winced. "I'm not saying it isn't important. I'm just saying that right now might not be the best time. Something happened to your father, something bad enough to wreck the *Pearl* and take him and all his men out—or cause them to abandon ship. What if it's still there, waiting for someone else to come? We can't afford to find out."

I worried at my bottom lip, hating the logic behind her words. Leoni had always been the logical one, the strategic one, the one who thought things through—sometimes to a fault. Meanwhile, I was the one who followed my gut. Also, sometimes to a fault. And right now, my instinct was telling me this was important.

Important enough for me to risk doing something stupid.

Something Leoni absolutely would not approve of.

I just didn't know what that stupid thing was yet.

I looked up to see Driscoll stomping toward us, his brows bunched in anger.

"What now?" Leoni murmured.

"Be nice," I said back to her.

"He has no filter!"

I tapped my chin. "Gee, who does that remind me of?"

She shoved me, and I laughed.

Driscoll stopped in front of us, hands on his hips. We both stared at him, waiting for whatever he had to say.

"Well?" he asked, tapping his foot.

"Well?" Leoni gestured for him to continue.

He huffed. "Aren't you going to ask what I'm so upset about?"

"Wasn't planning on it," Leoni said.

I flicked her. "What's wrong, Driscoll?"

He huffed. "I needed to relieve myself. Up until now I've been sneaking into the captain's cabin and using his toilet when he's gone." He flung a hand toward me. "But today, you were in there with him arguing loud enough for the whole ship to hear, and I couldn't wait any longer. So I asked one of the crew members where the toilet was. And now I've been completely humiliated."

Leoni looked at him, the corners of her mouth twitching. "Okay, you've got my attention."

Laughter bubbled out of me before I could stop it, then Driscoll shot me a glare. "Sorry," I said. "Um, how were you humiliated, exactly?"

"Well, let me show you."

He turned and stormed away.

Leoni looked at me. "I think that means we're supposed to follow."

We both got to our feet and followed Driscoll past the mast and to the other side of the ship, where five barrels sat in a corner. Tucked behind the barrels was an opening in the railing. Against the wall behind the opening lay a long plank. Driscoll edged around the barrels, then lifted the plank.

Well, he tried to lift the plank. He grunted loudly as we came to a stop behind him, struggling to even get it an inch off the ground.

"What does this have to do with needing a toilet?" Leoni asked.

Driscoll dropped the plank and straightened. "They told me I had to walk to the end of the plank to . . . you know. Told me to drop my pants and squat while balancing on this thing." He pointed down at the long piece of wood.

Leoni and I looked at each other and burst into laughter. Tears streamed down my face, and I couldn't stop, picturing Driscoll attempting to walk the plank and then squat at the end.

He gestured to Bartholomew, still mopping and humming away. "The bard said he was going to write a song about it. I'm going to be famous for trying to take a shit on the end of a plank!"

Leoni doubled over. "I can't believe . . ." She gasped, swiping at the tears on her face. "I can't believe you fell for that."

"I've never been on a pirate ship before." Driscoll planted his hands on his hips. "I don't know what kind of barbaric methods they use to go to the bathroom."

"Did you do it?" I asked between gasps.

"No, I didn't do it," Driscoll mimicked. "I got halfway across when the entire crew started laughing, and then I realized what was happening —and I still haven't found the toilet!"

Leoni rolled her eyes. She pointed up to the forecastle right behind the barrels. "It's up past there, on the bowsprit at the end of the ship."

He looked at the long bow of the ship that was below the forecastle and jutted in a sharp point. A toilet was cut into the bow, and I'd discovered a bathtub there as well, a barrel next to it with clean water for bathing.

Leoni twirled her hand. "Just hop down to the bow from the forecastle and do your business."

One of the crew members approached, a shorter man with bulging arms and a bald head. "Oh, already need to use the toilet again?" he asked with a smirk.

Ollie came up behind the man, guffawing. His frizzy red hair gleamed under the sun. "It was too easy."

Driscoll made a face at them as they continued past us, and Leoni and I burst into laughter again.

"You know what? Maybe I will walk the plank," Driscoll mumbled, heading toward the bow. "Won't have to deal with this lot anymore."

The laughter died on my lips as his words hit me. I stared at the opening in the railing. Walk the plank. I had a way off this ship. A way to get to land. I could walk the plank. I'd just solved my problem. And it might have been my craziest idea yet.

Chapter Nineteen

Bartholomew had said we'd be passing Porth around evening time the next day, so when that time finally came, I waited for the dinner bell, and sure enough the outline of the island appeared in the distance, trees rising up along the shoreline. The bell clanged, and everyone rushed to the kitchen. I stayed behind, telling Leoni I'd be down shortly. Once she was out of sight and everyone had disappeared, I was just about to put my plan in action, when Bartholomew appeared and cornered me. "Oh, good. A moment to get the princess alone."

I groaned inwardly. I didn't have time to talk with the bard. But I didn't want to be rude, so I plastered a smile on my face. "Hi, Bartholomew. Shouldn't you be eating with everyone else?"

I glanced at the island in the distance.

"Oh, I asked Mia to save me some grub."

"Perfect," I muttered, leaning against the railing behind me and trying to not keep glancing at the island. "How can I help you?"

He dug his pocketbook out of his trousers and slipped a pen from behind his ear. "I'll be the first to admit I never knew much about the Seven Spirits. I wasn't bestowed with their gifts, so I didn't see any reason to pay them attention, but now that you're on board with us, I'd love to learn more about these spirits you worship. I think I could write some great songs about them, possibly sing in taverns across Arathia, expand my audience, you know?"

That softened my annoyance. It was actually very sweet. I sent one more glance at Porth as we sailed along it, the ship going at a slower pace. Dinner would last for quite a while, and I still had time to enact my plan. "Of course I'll tell you anything you want to know."

"Oh great!" He opened his booklet and perched his pen to the paper as he stood in front of me. "Let's start at the beginning. How did you all get your powers?" He gestured. "Your ancestors and such."

I tapped my chin. "Well, all we have is the information that's been left for us. Journal entries, historical records, paintings, a few books. What we learned was that there was an Old World, full of elementals like us who had the same powers, worshipped the same spirits." A breeze ruffled my chiffon. "We believe the Seven Spirits appeared to them regularly, but eventually, something happened."

Bartholomew stopping writing in his journal, looking up at me. "Like what?"

"We don't know exactly, but we do know it was bad. Bad enough that everyone was wiped from existence, and the spirits disappeared. We've found countless excerpts from elementals of that time. It sounded terrifying."

Frost, fire, wind, water all raining down, the earth drying up completely. It had been a slow end for many of them.

"Whatever happened to them must've scared everyone else in the world enough that they stayed away. Arathia was abandoned for a long time, thousands of years, forgotten about—until my ancestors found the continent, wanting to flee from the human lands where chaos reigned."

"Sounds about right," Bartholomew said.

"They discovered a continent full of treasures, not gold or anything they could sell, but information. They found evidence of the existence of the Seven Spirits, the magic they'd bestowed upon the people of the Old World. They found temples and monuments, altars. And something amazing happened: they started manifesting the powers of the Seven Spirits: frost, earth, water, fire, wind, and shadow. They realized what a precious gift they'd been bestowed and didn't want to squander it like they'd started to discover those of the Old World had. So they created the courts, created rules and laws and treaties so that we'd live in a peaceful realm that didn't suffer from the wars and corruption of the human lands and of the past. They started recruiting people to come, following rituals they'd found in old tomes that asked for powers to be granted by the spirits. People came, settling into different courts. They completed the rituals, and powers appeared for them as well. Eventually, the rulers sealed those rituals away in hidden locations, deciding they'd populated the continent enough."

Bartholomew froze at that. "Are you saying anyone could become an elemental by completing some ritual?"

I tugged at the end of my braid, twisting it. "I don't know. That was hundreds and hundreds of years ago. Now, all of our powers are hereditary. I think the spirits granted the amount of power they wanted to, and I don't think a ritual would change that."

"So where are these spirits now? Why haven't they appeared to you?" Bartholomew asked, so engrossed in our conversation his journal now lay limp in his hand.

I shrugged. "We don't know. We continue to worship them, to use the magic they've given us in a respectful manner, in a way that honors them. We hope one day they'll reappear, but as to where they've gone, we don't have the answers. We do think that they became displeased with the way the people of the Old World were acting, how they'd become possessive of their powers, power hungry, even."

Bartholomew's face scrunched, his scars puckering. "You think the Seven Spirits killed everyone on purpose?"

"More or less."

He swore. "Those are some scary spirits."

"That's why we avoid conflict at any cost."

"But what about the Shadow War?" Bartholomew asked.

I was surprised he knew about that. It had happened sixty years ago, long before Bartholomew was born, and the humans didn't generally concern themselves with us.

Bartholomew cleared his throat. "I've heard about it in my line of business."

"Right." I sighed. "It was discovered that the shadow court had been kidnapping people, ripping their shadows from them in secret. Then they struck, attacking Shiraeth. The courts met, deliberating on what to do while the star court and all its people were being killed. The leaders were afraid waging war would bring the spirits' wrath down upon them. Eventually they decided it was necessary. The courts banded together to fight Sorrengard and banish them back to their island. But we couldn't do it before Sorrengard decimated Shiraeth, killed all the people of the star court. It was a tragedy, and all we've done since is ignore that it even happened."

After being destroyed, Shiraeth turned into the Deadlands, a place teeming with darkness and death. The courts walled off the Deadlands like it was just another thing to be forgotten about, like the star people had never existed at all. I'd heard their court had been a place of beauty. Silver and ethereal, from the trees to the water to the grass—everything glittered like stars.

"Then there's the shadow court." I picked at a loose thread in my chiffon. "Which clearly is more powerful than any of us believed. Our lands have been peaceful for so long by willful ignorance."

"Still, peace sounds nice," he said. "Better than our lands that are constantly ravaged by war and famine and greedy rulers."

"It's naive," I argued. "It sounds good in theory, but when you're that determined to keep the peace, you turn a blind eye to anything that's not what you want to see."

Bartholomew tapped his chin with his pen. "You think that's what you all have done? What the courts have done?"

I thought about my father, how determined he was to honor Spirit Water that he refused to see the cracks forming in his own court. The way I was deeply unhappy. I'd even confessed to him that I didn't want to rule, and he'd told me to never say that again. That I should be blessed I got this opportunity to be a queen. He was obsessed with Spirit Water, with honoring her and the gifts she gave to us, so obsessed that he neglected far too much.

"I know that's what we've done," I said. "The courts all have secrets." I thought about Liliath, how her own father kept so many secrets that led to his downfall, led to her stepmother usurping him. About the frost court, who were famously distant and rarely appeared in the other courts. "We bury our problems, determined to put on a brave face, but all we've done is isolate from each other because of this.

We're not a united front, and eventually the secrets are going to break us apart. It's not a matter of if. It's a matter of when."

"Wow." Bartholomew breathed out. "That's a lot."

"Even though I didn't want the responsibility of the crown, I did hope I could change things. I still do." I thought of Queen Liliath, of Princess Seraphina, who would become queen to the fire court soon. "A new era of rulers are emerging that think differently than our parents, our ancestors, did. Together, I believe we can change the trajectory of our future. That we can make the spirits proud while allowing for mistakes, for problem-solving."

"If anyone can do it, Princess, it's you," Bartholomew said. He tipped his head. "Thank you for being so willing to talk with me." He stood. "I'm going to eat now, and you better do the same."

I jumped, realizing I'd completely forgotten about my plan. Spirits below. I looked behind me, the island still in view. "I'll be down in a minute."

He disappeared. The cloudy sky had darkened while we spoke, and soon it would be nighttime. I'd better hurry if I wanted to do this. It was time to walk the plank.

Chapter Twenty

I strode toward that long plank in the corner and heaved it up, muscles straining and sweat building at the base of my neck. I took a deep breath and shoved the plank forward and out until it was hanging over the ocean, secured in the grooves of the cutout.

I'd never feared the ocean, not like the pirate lord did. I was a strong swimmer—and I had water magic, something that would prove very useful tonight. It wasn't a foolproof plan. Things could go wrong, of course. But it was a calm evening, no storms on the horizon, the best kind of weather for taking a dip in the ocean.

I stepped onto the plank and balanced my way across until I stood at the very edge. My heart thundered, and I couldn't imagine what it might be like to be here under duress, to know this might be the last breath you breathed as you stared into the dark depths of the sea. I shook my head. I was in control here. My father would remind me that as long as I had pure intentions, Spirit Water would be with me. Mal would tell me to really think this through before jumping. Lochlan would likely shove me in.

The ocean whisked by below, and I held out my hands, steadying the water so I could jump in safely. Once I made the leap, I'd direct the water to take me to Porth.

"What in the bloody hell?" Bastian said from behind, startling me. "You better not be about to do what I think you're about to do."

I whirled to see him standing on the main deck, fury rippling from him.

"You mean this?" I asked and stepped farther out on the plank.

Bastian jabbed a finger at the main deck. "Get back here right now."

"You could make me," I said, unable to help myself. Even better if he saw me jump. Then he'd know how determined I was to see this through. "Unless . . . you're afraid?"

He ground his teeth. "You bloody well know how I feel about the ocean."

I shrugged, taking another step backward. "I didn't know if that was a lie, along with everything else."

"I already told you—"

He stopped as I took another step. "Don't you dare jump. Don't you dare do it—"

Before he could finish, I launched myself into the water.

It hit me with the force of a thousand mallets, shocking my body still, immediately sucking me under, pushing me this way and that like I was a rag doll in a giant's grasp. It felt as if someone had tied a heavy weight to my foot, and I had no choice but to sink with it.

The saltwater burned down my throat, through my lungs, up my nose. I tried to reach for my magic, but that invisible weight was yanking me down, the water pinning my arms to my sides as it continued to apply pressure. Darkness spread across my vision as I struggled against the vortex that whirled around me. All sense of direction was now blotted out by black. I used all my strength to fight the water, to move my arms, my legs, my head—anything, but it wrapped around me in a tight bind.

I'd lived near the ocean all my life. We'd always warned visitors that if a wave sucked them in, to not fight it. Spirits below, in all the chaos, I'd forgotten my own advice.

I stilled, letting the ocean carry me where it wanted, respecting it instead of treating it as my enemy. Just like my father would instruct.

My lungs squeezed tight, chest seizing, and fear struck me. I needed air, and I had no idea which way was up or down. Everything was just dark. I struggled against the water's tightening hold, trying to pull at my magic, but I could barely move my arms or hands.

Suddenly, a body plunged down next to me, two hands grabbing me as the frenzy of water swirled up again. Arms wound around me, crushing me to a hard chest, and I knew instantly whose it was. A body imprinted into my memory whether I liked it or not. Bastian. His muscles tensed against me, and I realized he was gripping me so tight because he was terrified. The idiot had jumped in after me. What had he been thinking? He kicked out his strong legs, and we managed to rise just enough that the water's tight grip loosened.

Magic. I needed to summon my magic. Now. I stilled again, Bastian not moving either, sensing what I needed. I spoke to Spirit Water, just like my father taught me to do.

Calm, I thought to the water. *Let's work together, you and I. I am not your enemy. I am a part of you, and you are a part of me. Please, Spirit Water. I am seeking answers about your most loyal follower: my father. Help me in this quest.*

The water slowed its movement enough for me to summon it to do my bidding. I squeezed my eyes shut and pulled at the invisible thread inside of me, then moved my hand and commanded up, up, up. The water pushed us as black spots dotted my vision. The realization hit me that it might be too late. I couldn't go much longer without air. Bastian pressed his cheek against mine, a reminder that I wasn't alone. I gritted my teeth and jabbed my hand up again, the water listening and throwing us toward the surface with all its might.

Finally, the faint light of the evening sky sliced through the dark, and then we broke the surface, both of us gasping for air, riding on top of a wave. I sputtered and coughed, my throat burning, but I didn't even care. I was alive. We were alive.

I grasped at Bastian's necklace, relieved it still hung around my neck, the clock still ticking despite the water. I didn't have time to dwell on it, though.

"We did it," I gasped out, looking over to Bastian, whose face was deathly pale, eyes wild.

"I . . . can't . . . breathe," he got out, clutching at his chest.

"Bastian," I said slowly, "I think you're having a panic attack. Just hold on, okay?"

I looked around, the ship nowhere in sight. They could be miles away by now, no idea that we'd gone overboard.

The wave pushed us closer to the shoreline. Relief flooded me. At least we'd be safe on land. I lifted my hand and commanded the ocean to take us there. It obeyed, delivering us straight to the sandy shores while Bastian clutched onto me. Palm trees lined the coastline. The town must've been beyond the jungle on the other side of the island.

The wave dumped us onto the sand and receded. I landed with a soft thud and rolled over to see Bastian next to me, shaking.

"Okay, Pirate Lord. C'mon." I grabbed his arm and heaved him to his feet. "It's going to be okay. Let's just get somewhere warm and dry, and you'll be alright."

A cluster of palm trees swayed in the soft evening breeze straight ahead. "That'll be good enough," I said.

Bastian's legs faltered, and I roped his arm around my shoulders as we trudged through the sand, his heavy weight leaning against me.

"Not much farther," I grunted, my own legs shaking. My fight with the ocean and use of magic had depleted my energy, but after what I'd just experienced, I could make this short journey.

We finally made it to the trees and collapsed down, both of us leaning against the rough bark. I wanted to close my eyes and sleep, but I couldn't, not when Bastian needed me. I still hated him, but he'd jumped in after me, so I'd do this. I'd save the pirate lord one final time.

Chapter Twenty-One

I turned and took his shoulders. His face was still pale, those brown eyes so unfocused. "Bastian, I need for you to breathe, okay?" I paused. "Think about something, think about the way the breeze feels in your hair. The way the sand feels under your palms."

He still shook, and his breaths were shallow as he dug his hands into the sand. It wasn't working. Damnit.

"Okay, how about this?" I touched his face, letting my finger trail down his cheek. "Do you feel this?"

The shaking calmed, and he gave a small nod, his Adam's apple bobbing in his throat.

"How about this?" I drew a finger slowly down his chest, feeling his hard muscles. "Focus on my touch."

I hoped this worked. If it didn't, I was out of ideas. He didn't move, eyes shut tight. I continued to drag a finger over his chest, circling it across his damp skin.

Finally, he exhaled a long, deep breath, some of the color returning to his face. "So that's what it takes, huh?" he said weakly.

My shoulders slumped. "What what takes?" I asked.

"To get you to touch me." His eyes danced. "I just need to have a panic attack."

I shoved at him and sank back against the tree. "Shut up." I hesitated. "I've never seen you like that before. So . . ."

"Weak?" he asked, shooting me a sidelong glance. He took another shuddering breath, then leaned on the tree, shoulder touching mine.

I tucked a strand of hair behind my ear, braid now completely undone, blue ribbon somewhere at the bottom of the sea. "Weak is not a word I'd use to describe you."

He was silent for a moment, then he scrubbed a hand over his face. "Remember how I told you I got kidnapped by pirates at a young age? They're the reason I'm afraid of the sea."

I looked over at him, shocked by the admission. He'd never shared this in our time together, and I'd always figured it was too painful, whatever had happened to cause this fear. More painful than him getting kidnapped by pirates, torn from his parents when he was just fifteen years old, forced to watch them die and then forced into labor on one of those very ships. I remembered crying when he'd told me about it while we sat in one of our favorite spots, a little cave that was dark and secluded, where the water was still and calm, protected by big rocks that provided a barrier from the wild waves—and prying eyes.

"So that was all true?" I asked him. "What you told me about getting taken when pirates raided your home?"

He turned his head. "Aye. I told you I never lied to you, love."

"Don't call—" I started.

He waved away my words, already knowing what I was about to say. "Yes, yes. Do you want to hear the story or not?"

"Well, someone is feeling better," I pointed out, which earned me a look. "Okay." I mimicked locking my mouth closed and throwing away the key.

His lips twitched. "I spent years on that damned pirate ship until one day, I'd had enough. I'd grown six inches, put on muscle, and I wasn't scared of the pirates anymore. I was just fed up with being their slave."

The palm tree swayed above us, fronds rustling, coconuts jangling, and I hoped one wasn't about to fall right on top of our heads, though my mouth watered at the sight. Fresh coconut juice sounded divine right about now.

"So when we docked at our next port, I attempted to run away. I was caught, ended up punching one of the pirates in the face, and before I knew it, I was walking the plank. Years of being their slave had gotten me no lenience. One mistake and I was done for.”

I sucked in a sharp breath. I had water magic, and even with that power, I’d almost died jumping off that plank. I couldn’t imagine how a human with no magic could survive such a thing. I guessed that was the whole point.

“It was a stormy day at sea to make things worse. I could barely balance on the plank and ended up having to get onto my hands and knees to crawl. The wind howled. It was all I could hear: the wind and the ocean, both raging at me.”

His voice was so calm and steady, but his hands clenched tight at his sides like it was taking all his self-control to not tremble at the memory.

“I didn’t even get a chance to walk the plank. I clutched to it until a wave washed over me and pushed me off the damn thing. The sea sucked me down, spinning me this way and that, battering me until my body felt so weak and bruised, I wanted to die. Darkness cloaked everything in sight, and every time I tried to open my eyes, they stung so badly I had to close them right away.” He shook his head, little droplets of water shaking off with the movement. “I passed out, sure death was about to take me, but by some miracle, I awoke, washed up on an island I didn’t recognize.”

His eyes were distant, as if he was in another place, another time. “I scrambled onto the shore, which was lined by a jungle.” He gestured. “Much like this one. I ran deep into the trees, but no matter how far I got from the sea, I couldn’t shake away the images, the feeling, of the ocean and the power it held over me. I’d been ripped from my family, enslaved, but I’d never felt so powerless as I had in the ocean’s deadly grip. Suddenly I couldn’t breathe. It was like I was underwater, experiencing those terrifying events all over again.”

This wasn’t a lie. It couldn’t be. Not with the way his eyes shone with so much emotion, the way his body was so tense just telling this story.

Bastian swallowed. “Then I felt a hand on my shoulder. It was Barty.”

My eyebrows raised. “Bartholomew? The bard?”

“Aye. A bit younger. But he was telling me to breathe, to just breathe. Then he started singing. His calm voice snapped me out of whatever hold the memories had on me."

"So that's how you met him?" I'd never heard this story either.

Bastian had only told me that he'd found his crew after he escaped the pirates and that they'd banded together and become like a family over the years.

"Aye. He waited until I'd calmed down and then took me deeper into the jungle, where he and others lived, bedrolls spread out across the ground, fires roaring with food roasting. He introduced me to everyone. They called themselves the Lost Boys, all around my age, no one older than sixteen."

"So there were no girls?" I asked, thinking of Mia and Kara.

He shook his head. "No. Not then. They came later. The Lost Boys took me in, and we decided to start our own pirate crew, and you know the rest."

I nodded. I did. They stole a ship and sailed the seas, becoming the very thing Bastian abhorred. They spent years pirating, growing up, becoming men who were feared by everyone. Then they tried to steal from the wrong man. A powerful lord who caught them and threatened their lives. Bastian wanted to save his crew, so he'd made a deal with the lord: they'd pirate for him if he'd let them live.

Maybe that was why Bastian had taken all those boys to the shadow court. Maybe the shadow court paid the pirates for bringing people to the island, and in turn, Bastian gave a portion of the money to this lord who they worked for.

He'd told me early in our relationship not to ask questions about this mysterious lord. That he was working to earn his and his crew's freedom, but until he did, he wouldn't reveal any information, afraid I'd do something stupid and seek the lord out myself. He wasn't wrong. I'd wanted to. To stand up for Bastian if he wouldn't stand up for himself. Now, I didn't know what to think about it all.

The sky had turned black, stars strewn across, sparkling over us, and it reminded me of the many nights we'd lain together in the sand, looking up at the stars and making up the stories they told with their shapes. I still had so many questions, I still hated Bastian for what he'd done, but in this moment, I wanted to forget it all and pretend life was as simple as it felt when it was just me and him and a small cave.

I pointed up at the stars. "There's a bunny."

Surprise flashed in Bastian's eyes before his gaze turned upward. He paused, and for a moment, I thought he wouldn't play our game, but then he pulled that gold spyglass from his coat and pressed it to his eye.

"Look," he said and handed me the spyglass. I took it and pressed it to my eye, and he shifted closer, tilting it until it landed on a gleaming star that I'd recognize anywhere.

"Second star to the right," he said.

I swallowed. Our star. I handed the spyglass back to him, and he looked through it again, clearing his throat. "A bunny, huh?" He tsked. "But a snake is chasing it."

I laughed, seeing the pattern of stars that made up the snake he was referencing. "Mm, but the bunny is clever, and he knows that the snake is greedy. So he's leading it into the forest where even better prey is in abundance." I nodded toward a cluster of stars that looked like trees.

Bastian's eyes glittered. "I don't know about that, love. I think the snake enjoys the chase. I think the snake knows exactly what it wants, and it won't be deterred." He wasn't looking at the sky anymore.

Now we were playing a different kind of game.

I clenched my thighs together as heat flooded between them, unable to break whatever hold the pirate lord had over me. Except in this moment, he wasn't the pirate lord. He was just Bastian, and we were sitting in the sand, side by side, just like we always had.

He stared at me for a moment longer, then slowly leaned over, a question in his eyes. I didn't break the gaze, didn't move away from him, and his lips brushed against my jaw. A gasp escaped my mouth, and in a flash, Bastian had me pinned in the sand, his hard body pressed against mine, his even harder erection pushing against my thigh.

I opened my mouth, senses clouded over by the past, by want and need. So much need.

He dipped his hand down and ran it slowly up my inner thigh, bringing my chiffon up with it. His fingers worked their way between my legs and under my silk panties. I clutched the lapels of his leather jacket as he kissed my neck and rubbed my clit in slow, tantalizing circles.

"Bastian," I gasped.

He buried his face into my neck. "I've missed touching you so, so much."

His lips were soft and warm as they trailed kisses across my skin. I moved my hands up into his hair while his fingers made long strokes up and down my center. This felt so fucking good. After a long eight months of nothing but my own hand to satisfy my needs, feeling those rough fingers against me made my body sing in response.

I inhaled the scent of him, sea salt and sandalwood. Spirits below, I'd missed this. Missed the feel of his fingers stroking between my legs.

Waves of pleasure rolled through me, rising higher and higher with each circle his fingers made. Bastian dragged a finger down my center and plunged it inside me. Another gasp escaped my mouth.

"I don't think the rabbit is going to be able to escape the snake," he murmured against my neck, pumping his fingers in and out while I rocked with the movement.

"I don't think the rabbit wants to," I said back, barely able to get the words out.

He curled his fingers, hitting that spot he knew so well, and the waves in my body turned into an all-out storm, swirling inside of me until I had no control. My body tightened under Bastian's touch, and I took a shuddering breath as the storm came to a peak, pleasure rushing over me as I cried out, under his control now.

Finally, I wilted under him, limp and shuddering and completely satisfied.

We sat up, and as I regained my senses, the horror of what just happened immediately hit me. Blood and water, I couldn't believe I'd let him do that. I'd been so desperate to pretend we were still in the past that I'd let another sad story of his woo me. Shame overtook all the pleasure I'd felt just moments earlier.

I scuttled away, sand flying up as confusion flashed across Bastian's eyes, and hurt clouded his face.

"Why did you jump in after me?" I asked, voice raw with emotion. "Why did you tell me all of this?" I threw out an arm. "You refuse to answer any of my questions about the boys you took, why you would take them to the shadow court. This lord you work for. You're cold and distant on your ship, and then you open up and pretend to be vulnerable, pretend like you care about me? What is going on with you, Bastian?"

The playful smile, the teasing eyes, disappeared as Bastian straightened. "You were wrong about me, you know," he said quietly.

"What are you talking about?" I snapped.

"You said weak wasn't a word you'd use to describe me." His jaw ticked. "I'm a far weaker man than you realize." With that, he lay down and rolled over in the sand. "Let's get some sleep. With any luck, we'll be reunited with my crew tomorrow."

Chapter Twenty-Two

"Is she dead?" a voice said from over me, and either I was dreaming about Driscoll or Driscoll had somehow found me. The latter seemed more likely.

"No, she's not dead, you idiot." That would be Leoni.

"Captain!" another voice said.

Captain . . . Bastian. My eyes flew open as the events of the previous night flooded my mind. There stood Driscoll, Leoni, Bartholomew, and Mia, staring down at me—and Bastian, whom I was currently curled up against while his soft snores filled the air. My body must've instinctually made its way to his while we slept last night.

Traitor.

I elbowed him. Hard. He let out a grunt and shot up, eyes rimmed with red, hair messy and tangled, which should've looked bad, but instead it made him even sexier in a rumpled kind of way. Faint blue lines stretched from his neck, barely visible and small, almost just dots at this point. He must've forgotten to take his elixir.

Driscoll raised his eyebrows suggestively, and I made a "cut it out" face as I stood and cleared my throat.

Leoni crossed her arms. "What do we have here?"

Mia stepped forward, an edge to her voice. "Yes, what do we have here?"

My gaze bounced between Leoni and Mia. She seemed as annoyed with Bastian as Leoni was with me at finding us cuddling.

More than cuddling. Images of last night flashed through my mind, and I let out a shaky exhale. "I jumped off the plank to get to Porth so I could see the site where my father's ship was found."

Leoni's mouth dropped open.

"And what's your excuse, Cap?" Mia asked Bastian, tugging at her yellow bandana, her fiery gaze set on him.

Bastian placed his hands on his knees. "I—"

"He fell in after me," I cut him off. "He caught me getting ready to jump and tried to pull me back from the plank. We both got swept away, and I used my magic to get us safely to land. Simple as that."

The group glanced at each other like they didn't believe it was that simple at all. Bastian gave me a questioning look that I ignored. I didn't need Leoni hovering any more than she already was, and if she knew Bastian jumped in after me, she'd be hounding me, telling me not to fall for his charms again.

"How did you all find us?" I crossed my arms and used a commanding tone like they were the ones on trial here.

Bartholomew shifted on his feet. "We hoped you both made it to Porth since this is the nearest land for miles, so we docked and asked around early this morning. Some fisherman said they saw two people near the shore on the opposite side of the island, probably sleeping off some ale after a night at the tavern, but we decided to check it out anyway, and here we are. Everyone else is back in town, getting supplies."

I rushed into Leoni's arms and even roped Driscoll in for a hug. "Well, however you found us, I'm glad for it."

"Let's get back to the ship," Bastian said, and my head snapped to him.

"Absolutely not. We're here, and I'm going to the site where you found my father's ship."

A vein throbbed in Bastian's temple. "We don't have time for this. In case you're forgetting, we've got a wedding to attend."

"We have plenty of time for this. It won't take but a few hours. Unless you're hiding something?"

I let the challenge of my words hang in the air.

Bastian met my gaze, a challenge of his own flashing across his face.

"Well, I'm going." I turned and stalked from them. Sand rustled behind me, and calls for my name rang out. I didn't know where I was going, but this was a small island. I was bound to find something if I walked long enough.

"Princess Gabrielle!"

"Love, wait!"

"Gabrielle!"

I ignored it all. I didn't care about the pixie dust, the wedding, none of it. Right now, I just wanted answers. Some spirits-damned answers from someone. Anyone.

I marched along the tree line. If my father's ship was found abandoned, I doubted it would've been near town. Bastian had mentioned they'd found it on the opposite side of town, near the jungle. That meant I had to be close.

Bastian grabbed my arm. "Will you just wait one bloody minute?"

I wrenched my arm away. "Why? So you can keep more secrets from me? So you can lie to me more? I don't think so."

"Maybe you should listen to him," Leoni called from behind as everyone trudged through the sand.

I spun on my heel. Tears broke free, streaming down my face as I pawed at them and broke into a run to get away from Bastian, Leoni, Driscoll, the whole damn lot of them. I hated everything right now. I hated that Bastian still made me feel so much despite his betrayal. I hated that I felt like I had no control over anything. I hated that it had been eight months since I'd seen Lochlan or Mal, heard their laughs, done something stupid with them. I hated so much right now that I wasn't sure there was anything else left in my heart.

I tripped over something hard, stubbing my toe. It throbbed with pain.

"Fuck," I said.

I looked around for the object I'd just stumbled over when my gaze caught on something white and round in the sand. I swallowed, reaching for it.

"Gabrielle, stop!" Bastian yelled, but it was too late. With a shaky hand, I reached out just as Bastian jogged up by my side. "You don't want to see this."

I plucked the oval-like object from where it was buried, then turned it over and let out a screech as I dropped it. It was a skull, the empty sockets staring up at me, jaw hinged open.

My hand floated up to my mouth, and Driscoll and Leoni caught up to me, both of them grasping onto my arms. My gaze trailed from the skull to the edge of the island, a little rickety dock jutting out into the calm turquoise water.

White bones scattered across the sand. Blood and water. I'd stumbled onto a graveyard and . . . my stomach heaved. Suddenly I knew exactly why Bastian hadn't wanted me to see this. Why he'd told me to stay away. I knew in my gut who these bones belonged to.

So it was true. My father was dead. Now I needed to figure out exactly what had killed him.

Chapter Twenty-Three

I dropped to my knees, unable to tear my eyes from the mass graveyard.

"I'm so sorry," Leoni said quietly.

"Me too," Driscoll said.

They stood on either side of me. Tears rolled down my face, the droplets splattering to the sand as I stared. After all this time, I'd finally found out my father's fate. But that wasn't good enough. I swiped the tears away and stood.

"Where are you going now?" Leoni asked, her voice shaking.

I turned, eyes bleary, cheeks wet. "We have to give them a proper burial."

Bastian, Bartholomew, and Mia hung behind.

"You all can go," I said to the pirates. "Don't worry, I'm not running away. You're still going to get your precious pixie dust. But my father, all these men of Apolis, deserve to be one with the sea."

"I didn't know," Mia said quietly, rubbing her arm. "I didn't realize how important a burial at sea was for those from the water court."

I raised my chin. In order to get to Galaysia—the spirit world—one had to be joined in death with their elemental power. Every court had their own customs. In the sky court, they burned the bodies and let the ashes fly on the winds. In the earth court, they buried bodies in the soil.

In the fire court, they put the bodies on a pyre and set them on fire. The frost court was the most unique, freezing their dead, entombing them in ice. And in the water court, we put our fallen into a rowboat and let them drift off. Once they were far enough out, we used our powers to let the waves overtake the boat and sink it, and the body, to the bottom of the sea.

There were no bodies here to do that with. But we could gather the bones and put them to rest. That would be enough. It had to be enough.

My father would probably hate this compromise. He, out of everyone, deserved a proper burial. Every morning, he'd made a trek to the Temple of Water and prayed to Spirit Water, asked the spirit for strength, for clarity. He'd take me with him some mornings, and I'd kneel in the white-stone temple, columns holding up the ceiling, a statue of Spirit Water in all her glory at the front. We'd bow before her and stay like that as time ticked away. When I was little, I'd squirm and wonder when I'd be able to move again, but as I grew older, I appreciated the silence and stillness of the ritual. I hadn't visited the temple since my father left. It had reminded me too much of him.

At some point, Bastian, Bartholomew, and Mia had disappeared. They probably went back to town so they could drink and eat and fuck while they had a chance, while I was here, mourning the loss of my father all over again.

My jaw locked. It didn't matter.

I turned to Driscoll. "You can go too," I said. "You don't have to help with this."

His eyes softened and he ran a hand over his hair. "Of course I'm going to help. I know how important a proper burial is." He shrugged. "It's the only way to be united with the Seven Spirits. To finally greet them before you enter the spirit world. I wouldn't rob your people of that honor."

His words warmed my heart more than he probably realized. "Thank you," I said, trying to keep my voice steady as more tears dropped.

Leoni gestured to all the bones. Her own father had died when she was younger, so his wouldn't be among those scattered on this beach. "How are we going to do this?"

I twirled a strand of hair around a finger. "I think the best way would be to find a small rowboat of some sort and fill it with the bones, then set them adrift?"

Leoni gave a small nod. "So we just need to find a boat. Maybe we can trade for one in town?"

"Maybe," I said. "Or maybe there's one around here? Abandoned boats that people had no use for?"

Driscoll stepped forward. "I'll start looking."

He walked off through the sand, Leoni studying him as his figure grew smaller. "He's not so bad."

Despite the awful circumstances, that made me smile. "No, he's not."

Leoni and I started walking. "I'll go this way." I pointed. "You go that way, and let's meet back here when the tide has come in."

"Okay." She opened her mouth like she wanted to say something but closed it and turned.

I walked closer to the tree line, wanting to avoid stepping on any of the bones, eyes searching for signs of abandoned boats that we could use. We could collect the bones, one by one, and throw them into the sea, but that somehow felt wrong. Like we'd just be tossing them aside as if they meant nothing. They deserved better.

Not able to help myself, my gaze trailed to the graveyard of bones. Some were full skeletons, others were broken apart. I wanted to find my father, to say goodbye, but it would be impossible with nothing but bones left. What could have caused this? My father's entire crew just killed and scattered along the beach? It made no sense. My gaze flicked to the sea.

Unless . . . Bastian had somehow been involved.

He'd kidnapped the boys, so I couldn't put this past him either. Maybe that's why he hadn't wanted me to see it. Maybe there was a clue here that tied this atrocity to him and his Lost Boys.

But after hours of searching, I found no such clue.

I walked until my legs could no longer trudge through any more sand. Driscoll and I ran into each other and met back up with Leoni, who'd had no luck either. The tears started building again. I couldn't even do this one thing for my father and his men. So much was going wrong, and I had to wonder if anything would start going right at some point.

"Should we head to town, then?" Leoni asked.

My heart splintered at the thought of not being able to give them the sea burial they deserved. "I guess we have no other options."

Just then, Bastian's ship rounded the bend of the island, that skull flag billowing. The vessel sailed toward the single rickety dock that stuck out into the water.

"Is it time to go?" Leoni asked. "We still need to get clothes, to bathe."

"And maybe get some food other than salted meat and mush," Driscoll muttered.

Not to mention send these souls to sea. I spread my feet apart and planted them deeper in the sand as if readying myself for a fight. If Bastian was about to tell me we had to leave, I was going to drown him for good this time.

The ship arrived at the dock, and I squinted at two objects floating alongside it, long ropes tying them to the ship. Crew members hopped out, docking the ship, while Bastian climbed the rope ladder, along with the others, and jumped onto the dock. I realized what I was seeing floating in the water behind his ship: two smaller boats that they'd brought with them.

"How did you . . .?" I trailed off as Bastian approached.

"I know a thing or two about the courts and their customs. I've seen one of your water court burials from afar. Seen your priestess with her book, how you send your dead off." He gestured to the small boats. "We have a few rowboats stowed aboard. They're covered with tarp on the main deck, so you might not have noticed them. You're welcome to use them to send your people off."

I swallowed back the tears. I'd cried enough for one day. My eyes were swollen and puffy, my cheeks hot and sticky.

"Thank you," I said, and he just gave a curt nod.

Mia appeared next to him. She brought two fingers to her mouth and let out a loud whistle. "Let's get going," she yelled to the rest of the crew. "We have a lot of work to do!"

AFTER HOURS SPENT SEARCHING, we'd collected every last bone on the beach, all of them piled in the two boats. Everyone stood on the little dock as Leoni commanded the ocean to take the boats out to sea. It obeyed, carrying the smaller vessels.

My throat grew thick as I watched them float farther and farther away. I had to believe my father would be happy that he got a sendoff like this. He'd talked about how he didn't fear death, how death was just another form of life, a beginning, not an end. He'd always told me not to mourn his death but to celebrate his life. I would honor him by saving my brothers, by getting back to Apolis and throwing a huge celebration that showcased the man he'd been. The king he'd been.

I sniffled, wiping at the tears that never seemed to stop. Leoni sucked in a shuddering breath, and Driscoll wiped away a few stray tears of his own.

I would find out what had happened to my father and avenge his death. He might be at peace now, but I couldn't have peace until I knew why his life had ended in such a horrific way.

"I don't have the tome," I said to Leoni. "I don't know the words for the burial ritual."

She placed a hand on my shoulder. "It doesn't matter. They're at peace now. You did good."

Bartholomew stepped up, clearing his throat. "I can sing a song if you'd like. To honor the dead. It's one from our lands, but it's fitting, I think."

I gave him a soft smile and nodded, words stuck in my throat at the kind gesture.

Bartholomew opened his mouth and started singing, the song about a maiden who lost her life at sea. But it wasn't sad like I expected. It was full of hope, the words painting a picture about the woman who loved the ocean and how when she died the sea greeted her with gentle arms, a welcome smile, and whispers of comfort. It sounded so much like how my father viewed his relationship with death. It was perfect, and despite everything that had happened, I'd forever be grateful to Barty the Bard for this.

When the song ended Leoni took a deep breath as she grabbed my hand. "Are you ready?" she asked.

I straightened, then pushed out my hand and watched as the water obeyed and lifted up over the boats, crashing down and capsizing them. I watched until they both sank from view. It was done.

I turned to face Bastian, his entire crew. "Thank you," I said. "For understanding."

He held my gaze, giving the barest of nods.

I felt so empty, so raw, right now. I just wanted to lie in a bed, fall asleep, and close out the world, the pain. I'd already grieved my father twice. And now this felt like yet another punch to the gut, one so hard I could barely breathe.

Everyone began boarding the ship, climbing the rope ladder that flapped in the wind.

I scoured the beach one more time, making sure there was nothing we'd missed, when something caught my eye. A glimmer. I walked across the dock, jumping over a missing plank, feet dropping back into the soft sand.

The sun caught on a sparkle of gold, the object almost entirely covered.

"Princess Gabrielle, where are you going?" Driscoll shouted, but I ignored him, moving toward the object that lay near the jungle, gaining speed until I was in a full-on run.

I arrived in front of it and knelt down in the sand, digging frantically to unearth it. Finally, I'd dug enough that I could grasp onto its handle, and I pulled with all my might until it slipped from the sand.

I flew back with the force of the pull, landing on my ass with an oomph, the object clutched tight in my grip. Gasps sounded behind me from the dock. I shook my head slowly, looking down at the gleaming gold weapon that was almost as tall as Leoni. I sucked in a sharp breath. I'd seen this before. Heard about it from myths and stories passed down through generations, from sketches in historical texts. From my father. But I'd never actually believed we'd find it.

I stood, holding it up in wonder. The handle was long and solid gold, leading to the sharp points of the bottom. Power coursed through it, making my hands tingle.

"Blood and water," Leoni said as she arrived in front of me.

"What?" Driscoll called from the dock. "What is it?"

"A trident," I breathed out, unable to believe what I was seeing. "Spirit Water's golden trident."

Chapter Twenty-Four

After I'd discovered the trident on the beach, we'd boarded Bastian's ship and docked in town, and the first thing I'd demanded was that we find an inn where we could sleep for the night. The crew had cheered at that, silencing any protests Bastian had.

Of course he wouldn't care about our sleeping conditions. He had his own cabin, a bed, his own toilet and private bath. It was just a metal tub in his room, but still, it was better than the metal tub sitting across from the toilet on the bow of the ship—which smelled strongly of rotting fish and seaweed.

We'd spent the rest of the day exploring the little town on the water, cobblestone roads and shops shoved next to each other, tall and skinny with shingled roofs, palm trees sprouting up with fresh coconuts dangling and locals climbing the trees to pick them. The town was small, but it was a common stopping point for anyone traveling that far south on the Dark Seas, making it crowded and full of life.

We'd finally bought new clothes. Much to Driscoll's displeasure they were not silk. Just plain brown trousers and simple linen tunics. Since I had no gold on me, the pirate lord had paid for everything, and he hadn't even made a snarky comment about it.

"I'm surprised you're not just looting the place," I'd said to him, knowing it was immature and mean, but my emotions were still raw from what we'd done on the beach, from what had happened after that with my father's bones. So I'd acted like a brat as the pirate lord bought me new clothes. "Isn't stealing and pillaging kind of your thing?"

He'd ignored me, paying the shop owner and walking away without saying a word. I hadn't felt good about myself after lashing out like that, but I couldn't take the words back, couldn't even apologize, because Bastian had disappeared.

The rest of the afternoon had distracted me from the horrors of the morning as we wandered the town, bathed, changed, ate.

Now, as I entered the tavern with freshly braided hair and clean clothes, all the events from earlier came crashing back down with a vengeance: the bones, my father's death—the trident. I'd taken the object aboard the ship, which seemed like the safest place for it right now, but hadn't had a chance to ask Bastian about it yet. If it was what I thought it was, and it did belong to Spirit Water, then this was a huge discovery.

It was rumored that each of the Seven Spirits had their own powerful weapons scattered around the continent. These weapons were specially made for each spirit, forged with their powers. But none had ever been seen. We'd only read about them, seen sketches of them in various texts and historical records. Many of us had doubted if the objects really existed.

Of course it would be my father who found it. He'd never doubted the trident's existence, and he believed that finding it would bring us good luck. Oh, Father. I couldn't even imagine how elated he must've been to hold that weapon in his hands, only to then die. I needed to know why he wanted the trident, how it connected to my brothers.

It couldn't have been a coincidence that it was buried with the bones of my father and his men.

Tears welled in my eyes, but I held them back. I would not cry anymore today; I just wanted to enjoy a meal with my friends—and maybe a tankard of ale. I'd get my answers, but not in this moment.

Driscoll and Leoni already sat at a long table with some members of the crew. Others hadn't arrived yet, including Bastian. Much like me, everyone had a chance to bathe, and it had much improved their spirits, the table full of chatter, ale, and fresh bread and fish stew. Patrons in the tavern eyed the pirates warily, a tension thickening the already humid air.

Bartholomew stood on a small, raised stage, singing about the Lost Boys and a sea serpent they'd fought.

"Its eyes were dark and stormy
That gloomy night at sea
It rose tall as a mountain
Its breath shaking our ship like a leaf."

His voice faded in the background as I approached the table, overhearing Driscoll complaining that his clothes made him look like a peasant. I rolled my eyes as I sat down next to Mia.

"Here," she said and slid a tankard in front of me. "You look like you need it."

Kara glared at me from the end of the table before tearing her eyes away, each earring that lined her ear catching bits of light. I wondered how many years it had taken to acquire all those tattoos and piercings.

"Thank you," I replied to Mia, taking a deep drink of the amber liquid.

An ocean breeze whisked through the open windows, sand dusting the floor. The little tavern sat on the edge of the town, giving a full view of the shoreline, docks spread out along a long cobblestone boardwalk, ships bobbing in the calm waters. The sun sank over the ocean, the sky a creamy mixture of pink and orange. I took another sip, enjoying the view. I could rarely go out like this in Apolis. As my mother liked to remind me, queens didn't frequent taverns. If I wanted to drink, it would be wine at a feast, and only a few sips, at that. My brothers, however, got to go wherever they wanted, my mother and father letting them run wild while keeping a close eye on me at all times. I marveled at the feel of this: sitting, drinking, being out among people without judgment. These humans likely didn't even know who I was.

I'd love it if Mal and Lochlan were here right now, drinking, regaling the table with stories of their adventures. Mal was always the practical one, the one who got them out of trouble, while Lochlan was the one who usually got them into trouble. It made their stories that much more entertaining.

"I'm sorry about your father," Mia said.

"Thank you." I trailed my finger through a ring of condensation on the table. "But I don't want to think about that tonight."

Across from us, Leoni and Driscoll pointed discreetly at a couple sitting at a nearby table. The couple seemed to be in a heated argument, and my friends were speculating on what they could be bickering about.

"I think she's mad that he has a small penis and lied to her about it," Driscoll said, pinching his fingers to show his point.

Leoni laughed. "And he's angry because she told him size doesn't matter." Leoni burped, then banged her chest. "But of course it does."

I choked into my ale and waved my hand. "Sorry about them," I said to Mia.

"I'm a pirate." She huffed. "Trust me, I've heard worse."

Patrons gave wide berth to the table of pirates, and a few newcomers stopped in the door, seeing the pirates and immediately turning around and leaving. Bastian and his Lost Boys certainly had a reputation.

I took another sip of my drink. "So what's your story?" I asked Mia.

She wrinkled her nose. "What do you mean?"

"Well, I know how Bastian became a pirate, how he washed up on the shore of that island and met the Lost Boys. How they all banded together, but how did you get in with them? Bastian hasn't told me much about you or Kara."

Her eyes bulged. "He told you how he became a pirate?"

I reeled back. That seemed like a bit of an overreaction. "Well, yes. He told me a lot about his life during our time together. You don't have to talk about yourself if it makes you uncomfortable."

She tugged at her short brown hair, gelled into a cute pixie cut that framed her face so well. Her brown eyes flashed with a familiar look. There it was again. That sense that I knew her. "No, it's not that," she said slowly. "Bastian just doesn't talk to anyone about that time in his life, his, you know . . ."

"Fear of the ocean?" I asked.

She nodded, eyes darting around the tavern like she was afraid someone might overhear.

"Anyway," I said, "I don't want to talk about Bastian either."

She pursed her lips. "Do you need to make a list of topics we are allowed to talk about?"

I peered at her. "Why do you dislike me, exactly?" I waved my hand to the table. "Why does everyone dislike me so much?"

Her mouth went agape for a moment, then she closed it and paused like she was choosing her words carefully. "I don't dislike you," she said. "I'm wary of you and your friends."

"Why?"

"Because you're a threat to everyone I love," she snapped. "Your presence, your hold over Bastian, almost destroyed us once already."

I straightened at that, shock rolling through me. "What do you mean? Is this about your boss?"

"Um." She cleared her throat, hands twisting in her lap. "I just meant that Bastian was never the same after he met you. Started getting ideas about being a better pirate, being something we could never be. It put our business, even our lives, at stake. I've had a hard time forgiving him for that." Her voice quieted. "Though I suppose I really shouldn't blame you."

"Oh," I said, not expecting that answer at all. "Well," I said finally, "if it makes you feel any better, I hate myself, too, for falling for him."

She was quiet at that, contemplative. Then she took a deep gulp of her ale and said, "I grew up with Bastian, actually. In Aramis."

"Grew up with him?" That was a strange way to word it.

She gestured at her face. "I know he's got the black hair, and I've got the brown hair. He takes after Mother, while Kara and I take more after our father."

I spit out my drink. "Your mother? Your father? What, exactly, are you saying?"

Mia let out a heavy sigh. "I'm saying that I'm Bastian's sister."

Chapter Twenty-Five

I almost fell out of my chair. It made so much sense now.

"And Kara is our other sister. She's the youngest. By a minute. She's also the angriest, in case you didn't realize it." She nodded her head to the end of the table, where the other brunette sat. I didn't think my jaw could drop any lower. "After the pirates kidnapped Bastian and killed our parents, Kara and I fled, moving to other islands where we could find work. We tried to track Bastian over the years, keeping an eye on him as much as we could, getting glimpses of him whenever the ship he was on rolled into town. We wouldn't see him for two years, then suddenly that familiar ship with the bright yellow flag would sail to our docks, and he'd be half a foot taller. We survived on the streets, doing our best to stay alive, to figure out how to rescue him. Years later, when Kara and I were grown and running our own little business, we heard about a fearsome pirate and his crew called the Lost Boys. The more we heard about this pirate, the more it sounded like our brother. We sold everything and left town so we could track him. Eventually we found him and the Lost Boys and joined their crew. Bastian was so angry that we'd come after him. He hadn't wanted that life for us. But we had no one else. The rest is history."

I wrinkled my nose. That entire story—I couldn't believe Bastian had never told me about this. He'd also never told me where he was from. I hadn't heard of Aramis. Then again, there were many human towns I hadn't heard of. Aramis must've been a small coastal village.

Mia tucked a short brown strand behind her ear. "He finally got over us becoming pirates and got his head out of his ass enough to make me his quartermaster."

My head was still reeling from the revelation that Bastian had two sisters. No wonder they disliked me so much. They were protective of their brother, just like I was of mine. They viewed me as a threat. I wondered why he'd kept them from me. Maybe because he knew they hated me, and if I'd found out about them, I would've insisted on meeting them.

"Bastian probably won't be happy that I told you," Mia mumbled. "Then again, he's never happy these days, so what does it matter?"

"So why did you tell me?" I asked.

She looked up at the ceiling, made from palm tree fronds, all woven together. "I just thought you should know. And my brother can be such an idiot sometimes."

That was an understatement.

She raised her glass, and I clinked mine against it.

"Cheers to Bastian being an idiot," I said, then took a drink of the bitter ale.

She wiped her mouth. "What about your brothers? Are you close with them?" She winced. "Sorry if I shouldn't ask. I know Mal and Lochlan are a sore subject . . ."

"Stop asking about the damn playboy prince," Ollie yelled from across the table.

Mia's face flushed, and I stared at Ollie, shocked he knew about the playboy prince. I truly hated the nickname that Lochlan had somehow earned. Mr. Playboy Prince. The most famous bachelor on the continent of Arathia.

"I'm not asking about the playboy prince," Mia gritted out. "I'm making polite conversation."

Ollie smirked. "Mia here had a massive crush on him after she saw a painting we stole. There was that playboy prince standing at the helm of a ship, looking every bit the heartbreaker he's known as. Caught her staring at it quite a few times before we pawned it off."

I hid a smile behind my mug while Mia's face turned bright red, and she glared at Ollie.

"You better shut your mouth, Ollie, or I'll tell the entire table about the time you pissed your pants during a fight."

Ollie's lips flattened, and he flipped Mia off.

"I don't have a crush on your brother. I don't even know him. Obviously. I mean, I did see a painting of him, and he is . . ." She cleared her throat. "Well, he's gorgeous, objectively speaking . . ."

I put a hand on her arm. "It's okay. Lochlan has that effect on every female he meets. It's actually very obnoxious."

"The playboy prince," Mia said. "What a reputation."

"I hope he settles down." I realized how ridiculous that sounded given his current situation. "I don't think the bachelor life makes him happy." My brother avoided relationships, anything serious, really.

"Not everyone gets to settle down," Mia said, a sadness in her voice. "Get married, have children. It's not always in the cards. Maybe that's just not in Lochlan's future, and you have to be able to accept that."

"Right." I wrapped my hand around the tankard. "Is that something you want for yourself? I don't mean to pry," I said quickly.

Mia looked away. "I accepted my fate long ago. The day I boarded Bastian's ship was the day I became a pirate for life. I can't change that now."

It sounded so similar to the conversation I'd had with Bartholomew a few days earlier. He felt trapped too. Just another thing I didn't understand about these pirates.

One of the crewmen was now regaling the table with a tale about Bastian saving their ship from a pirate attack. A rival group that Bastian felled. The admiration in his voice rang out clear and loud.

"He showed them who was boss," the pirate was saying as everyone cheered. "Kept them from getting to the shadow court and stealing any of the magical objects."

Right. So he could keep his monopoly on them. How honorable.

Across the table, Leoni snorted into her ale at something Driscoll said, then burst into giggles.

"What are you all staring at?" Kara yelled loudly to a table of patrons. "If you know what's good for you"—she fingered the dagger strapped to her thigh—"I'd get back to your drinks and mind your business."

At that, their eyes snapped away.

"That happens a lot," Mia said.

The ale went down smooth as I took another sip. "How do you all not get arrested? You're the most well-known pirates on the Dark Seas."

I'd never thought about it before, how they went about their business, could travel to towns like this and drink and be so public . . . If they showed their faces to any court on Arathia, they'd be arrested. That was why Bastian had always docked on the northern shores in Apolis. He had places all over the continent he docked, secret meeting spots where he'd sell his goods.

"We have deals with all the human towns." She shrugged. "We humans are easily bought."

I gaped at her. "So you pay off the leaders and that allows you free rein?"

"Pretty much," she said, no shame in her voice.

This was a dirtier business than I'd ever imagined.

I peered at her with curiosity. "Do you know anything about that trident?"

She looked down at her hands, twisted together in her lap. "Not much. We'd heard rumors that the seafolk had a powerful object, powerful enough to fell an entire ship, sink it to the bottom of the sea, but we never saw any evidence of that. Now I wonder . . ." She trailed off. "Maybe they're in league with him—"

"Sister," Kara interrupted, and my gaze snapped to her as she stared down at Mia, eyes hard. "Ollie wants you to tell the story about the time you broke out of that prison using only the bandana on your head."

Mia looked at me. "That's a good tale. Excuse me." She stood and moved to the end of the table with Kara.

Him. She'd said maybe they were in league with him. That interruption by Kara hadn't been an accident. Mia had been about to reveal something Kara didn't want me to know. But what? I sighed. I was so tired of all the secrets.

The sky was dark now, the moon overhead, big and bright. Bastian was still noticeably absent while almost the entire crew filled the little tavern.

"He gets like this sometimes," Bartholomew said from behind me.

"Hm?" I asked, gaze focused on the window like I expected his large, leather-clad form to appear outside at any moment.

"Bastian," Bartholomew said, drawing my attention. "Moody, withdrawn. He goes to the beach and walks for hours. You won't see him tonight."

"I wasn't—"

"It's clear there's something between you two." He took a gulp of his drink. "Just don't break his heart again."

Right. Because the end of our relationship had been my fault.

I didn't know what to say to that. I cleared my throat. "I need to get some fresh air. If you'll excuse me."

Leoni and Driscoll were busy gossiping about yet another couple in the tavern, not paying any attention to me as I stood and slipped out the door and into the warm night air, already knowing exactly where I wanted to go.

Chapter Twenty-Six

The ship bobbed in the water, the night calm, the dark sky stretching endlessly over the dark sea. Bastian had locked the trident away in his cabin, claiming that was the safest spot for it. Bartholomew had said Bastian roamed the beach on nights like this when he was in a dark mood, which meant he wouldn't be in his cabin. I was going to get that trident, study it, and maybe find some clue as to why it was on the beach with my father. I just couldn't shake the feeling that none of this was a coincidence.

I walked across the dock and nodded to a woman sitting in a chair, a sword across her lap. She must've been the night guard, her job to make sure none of the docked ships got stolen. That seemed like a tall order for just one person, but I doubted anyone would attempt to steal the pirate lord's ship.

I pointed at it. "I'm just retiring for the night," I said and flashed her my red bracelet, the one that we all received when we docked as proof that we could board this ship. It was a clever system, I had to admit.

She nodded, and I made my way aboard, climbing up the rope ladder and hopping onto the main deck. The door to Bastian's cabin was closed, but I knew how to pick a lock. My brothers and I learned that trick early on in our lives when we wanted to escape the confines of our castle. I slipped a pick from my braided hair.

I crouched before the door, jamming the pick in the lock and deftly wiggling it until it clicked. The door swung open, moonlight slashing across the room.

The room that most definitely was not empty.

Bastian lay in bed naked, his hand moving up and down his large, thick cock, muscles constricting. All the breath left my body as I drank his sculpted body in, and a squeak escaped my mouth as Bastian shot up in bed, eyes wild.

"Fucking hell," he said, pulling the covers around his waist, bare chest still exposed and still as glorious as ever.

"What are you doing here?" I asked, remembering all too well what it had felt like when it was my own hand stroking him, my lips around his hard length, the way he'd murmur my name as he came in my mouth.

He pushed a hand through his hair. "What am I doing here? In my own bloody cabin, you mean?"

Right. I forgot about that part. I was the one breaking in.

He jumped up, giving me a view of that perfectly sculpted ass, right below his perfectly sculpted back that was covered in tattoos: a skull that reminded him of his mortality. A snake that reminded him enemies were everywhere. A moon that reminded him there was always light, even in the darkest of nights. Then there were the silly ones, the ones he got on a whim: a black cat for good luck, a fish he got when he was drunk, a heart he'd got after losing a bet to Barty the Bard. He yanked on his pants and whirled around, a fire in his eyes.

The tattoos wrapped around his chest, and my heart constricted as I thought about all the times I used to trace them, and he'd tell me their stories. What each and every one meant. Unlike his back, the tattoos that worked up his front painted a bigger picture: the sea foam, the coral and sea life, the bottom of a ship sitting atop it all, a thick rope dangling into the water. It was an ode to his first love: being a pirate.

"Well?" Bastian asked. "Would you like to explain yourself? I give you space, I stay as far away from you as I can, and yet you just cannot help yourself."

"I didn't ask for space," I said. "Did you not hear me picking your lock?" I threw my arm toward the open door.

"I was a little busy, in case you hadn't noticed," he said, lacing up his pants.

I could barely breathe, and at this point, I wasn't even sure air was what I needed.

He moved to stand in front of me, muscled chest heaving, eyes so full of passion, of want. "I'm trying to be so good," he whispered, "when all I want is to be so very bad."

I didn't move, letting his words, his breath, his scent, wash over me. Why was this so spirits-damned difficult? I hated him, so why couldn't I just say no? Why couldn't my body and my mind be on the same page, and why was my body always winning out? Despite myself, I took a step closer to him.

Wordlessly, I lifted my hand and let it trail down his chest. He stilled under my touch. Thick dark curls covered his pecs, his abs carved out by muscle. Blood and water, I missed touching him.

He closed his eyes, his entire body tensing.

"What were you thinking about?" I asked, voice low. "Just now, while in bed?"

My fingers dragged lower, closer to the waistline of his leather pants.

"What do you think?" he gritted out. "The only thing I think of night and day. The one thing I want that I cannot have."

I was weak, so weak, and I didn't care. "What if I told you that you can have me? Right now. You can throw me on that bed and do what you want with me. Or take me on the floor. Maybe bend me over your desk?" I wanted it all.

A muscle feathered in his jaw, and his eyes squeezed shut even tighter. "Love, you're not thinking straight. You lost your father today."

"I don't care." The words came out ragged and raw.

He raked a hand through his hair, eyes opening, clear now, that fire dimming. "I can't believe these fucking words are coming out of my mouth, but no. This cannot happen. The other night on the beach was a mistake."

I reeled back like I'd been slapped. His words a knife to my gut.

Fuck. My face flushed.

What was I doing? I'd just thrown myself at the pirate lord because I got a peek at his hard cock? I was losing it. Absolutely losing it.

Tears pricked my eyes as shame bubbled up. I felt so stupid. I crossed my arms over my chest as Bastian reached for me.

"Come here, love," he said, his voice so full of pity it broke something in me.

"No." I stepped back, out of reach. "I'm just here for the trident, okay? That's why I broke in. I want to see it."

He stroked his now-trimmed beard. He must've visited a barber on the island today. "How do you bloody know how to pick a lock?"

"Does it really surprise you that I do?" I asked.

"No," he murmured, "I suppose not."

I bit my lip. "Is the trident from the shadow court? Was it made from someone's shadow being ripped from them?"

He shook his head. "No, that object is not from Sorrengard."

So I'd been right. It had to belong to Spirit Water. Holy fuck. This could change everything. If the other courts knew about its existence, they'd surely want to find the objects associated with the other six spirits. Then again, this could be dangerous in the wrong hands. I didn't know what kind of power such an object could wield.

"Listen," Bastian said. "Let's leave it for tonight. You've had a long day. Now is not the time to investigate—"

"Why does it matter?" I snapped, glad to have a reason to snap, a reason to yell. "I found it. It was with my father's body. It belongs to the spirit of the water court. You don't get to just hide it away and pile it on top of all your other secrets."

I pushed past him and yanked the sheets off his bed. "Where is it?"

"Ah yes, I regularly sleep with hard metal rods in my bed."

I ignored him, lifting the mattress and searching underneath. It was nowhere in sight. I let the mattress drop back down with a thunk.

"You cannot be serious right now. You're going to have to put those sheets back on, you know."

I stalked to the other side of his cabin, pulling out his desk, my muscles straining with the effort.

"For fuck's sake," Bastian said. "Will you just stop? You're always so gods-damned stubborn."

I whirled. "Where is it, Bastian?"

He heaved a sigh and walked over to a ledge that jutted out from the wall. The windows spread over it gave a view of the black water sloshing lazily. He clicked open the ledge, and the top popped up, revealing a compartment underneath. He lifted the trident out.

"Do you know what it does?" he asked.

I thought back to everything I'd learned from my father, from his obsession with this weapon. "Spirit Water used it in times of need. Its power is the water element, same as mine, but much, much stronger. The weapons were used to kill, to protect, to defend, to silence someone for good. Maybe I should test it out on you."

I pointed it at his lips.

He looked away. "I think we already established how much you like my mouth."

Asshole.

I turned and left the cabin, trident in hand.

"What do you think you're doing?" he shouted after me.

"What does it look like?" I asked. "It's called leaving."

He followed me out. "I meant with the trident."

"Don't follow me." I flung a hand out. "Just go back to your cabin and finish whatever you were doing . . ." I trailed off, realizing exactly what he was doing before I interrupted.

He grimaced. "That ship has sailed, I'm afraid."

Right. When he became the rational one out of the two of us, when he turned my advances down.

"Just let me look at this thing in peace, okay?"

He crossed his arms over his muscled chest, still on display and still glorious. "What are you hoping to find, exactly?"

"Anything. Since you won't give me answers, I have to find them on my own."

"I don't have the answers. I don't bloody know what your father wanted with this trident. But I do know whatever it was couldn't have been good. This is powerful, ancient. We don't need whatever trouble it will bring. I say we hide it and forget about it."

I shook my head. "No. Not until I find out why my father had this. It could help us understand why he died."

Bastian rushed forward, taking hold of my shoulders, giving them a rough shake. "Will you just fucking stop? I'm so tired of you not listening, fighting against everything I say. I always knew you were reckless, that you liked to take risks, but you're taking it too far. Some secrets deserve to stay buried. Let this be one of them."

I shrugged out of his hold, stepping back. "Or maybe you're hiding something like you always are. You're using me. Just like I'm using you. So don't act like you want what's best for me, like you're trying to protect me. You hurt me worse than anyone ever could. You shattered me into a million pieces that I still haven't put back together. So if I'm being reckless right now, it's because I have to be in order to save my brothers. I refuse to let my father's death be in vain. If he died trying to save them, trying to find answers about how to save them, then I'm going to do everything in my power to finish what he started. You think I'm going to just rely on the word of a pirate?" I shook my head. "No. You lost the privilege of me listening to you when you betrayed me. So go back into your fucking cabin and just leave me alone."

Bastian swallowed, his mouth twitching like he wanted to say something. Finally, he gave a curt nod and turned, stalking back to his cabin and slamming the door behind him.

Chapter Twenty-Seven

I stood by some barrels, helping inventory supplies. After Bartholomew gave me a rundown of the ship and its main positions, I started offering to help where and when I could. A crew member nodded at me as he passed by. Nodded. Not glared or curled his lip or growled. But a nod. Working on the ship was earning me respect —and truth be told, I liked it. These tasks might be menial to the crew members, but it was nice to feel productive and have something to do to pass the time.

Bartholomew stood on the opposite side of the main deck. He strummed his banjo and sang a song about a time the pirates raided a village of women warriors, who they ended up bedding instead of pillaging. The crew roared with laughter at that, but imagining Bastian with another woman only darkened my mood. Some of the crew danced and whirled while Bartholomew sang, others sitting and drinking, others chatting. It would've been the perfect night if I wasn't still so angry at the pirate lord, who stood on the quarterdeck, back to me, gazing out at the sea.

We hadn't spoken at all today. I'd barely seen him, which was probably for the better. I also wasn't any closer to understanding why that trident had been on the beach with my father.

"Princess Gabrielle?" Driscoll cleared his throat.

I turned and he gestured to the steps and held out a cup of seafire. I supposed I could stop working for the day. Everyone else had. I set down the parchment and pen on a barrel, then accepted the cup and sat on the stairs.

Driscoll and Leoni dropped down on either side of me.

I looked between the two of them, Driscoll avoiding eye contact and Leoni's face set like she had a mission to accomplish.

"What is this?" I asked. "Why are you two acting so weird?"

They both looked away, which only made my suspicions grow.

Bartholomew finished his song and started another, this one about the Seven Spirits. He worked fast.

Mia and Kara approached.

"Can we get this over with?" Kara asked.

I shot confused glances around the group. "Get what over with? What is going on?"

Leoni scooted away so she could fully face me. "We need to talk."

The pirates dragged up crates that they sat on.

I set down my cup. "About what, exactly?"

Driscoll crossed his arms. "We're asking the questions here."

Leoni tipped her head toward Bastian, who remained oblivious to what was happening. "We saw you leaving Bastian's cabin last night and him following you out. Shirtless."

I scoffed. "That's what this is about?"

"Do you deny it?" Mia asked, her tone gentle.

Kara, predictably, just scowled at me, her brows furrowed, making her piercing pucker.

"Do I deny that you saw me coming out of Bastian's cabin? No, I do not. But nothing happened."

Over breakfast, I'd told Driscoll and Leoni about Bastian's sisters, what Mia had revealed of their childhood, but I might have left out our accidental rendezvous last night—and what Bastian had been doing when I stumbled in on him. Driscoll would likely have a stroke if he knew the truth.

"Oh, please." Driscoll shook his head. "I saw those abs, okay? It was like the man was made of freaking stone. There's no way you resisted that."

Well, he was right. It was Bastian who'd resisted me. My mood darkened. "I snuck into his cabin to get the trident, okay? I didn't realize he'd be in there. Sleeping."

Mia and Kara peered at me with suspicion in their eyes. I didn't know how I'd missed it before. The three of them were so similar, had the same crescent-shaped eyes, the same straight noses, high cheekbones. No wonder they'd felt so familiar to me.

"Well, that's the last time I'm telling you anything," I said to Leoni, annoyed I'd revealed anything to her and Driscoll.

Now they were all teaming up against me.

"And why isn't Bastian getting an intervention?" I asked.

Mia shot a glance at her brother, his back still to us. "We didn't include Bastian because he's been hiding away in his cabin all day."

I grabbed my cup of seafire and took a sip, making a face as the liquid burned its way down my throat.

"Okay," Driscoll said. "Maybe nothing happened between you two last night, but what about when we found you cuddling on the beach?"

"We fell asleep together," I said. "So what?"

Driscoll shook his finger. "Oh no. I know sex hair when I see it, and you both had the sex hair."

Kara glared at Driscoll. "Can you not mention sex hair and my brother in the same sentence?"

I massaged my temples. "I agree. Are we done now?"

"Spirits below." Leoni put a hand to her heart. "I didn't believe Driscoll, but he was right. Something happened between you two."

My hand tightened around my cup.

"How could you?" Hurt flashed in Leoni's eyes. "After what he did to our home?"

Shame crept its way up my throat, which grew thick with it. She was right, and I couldn't deny how wrong it had been.

"Bloody hell," Kara muttered while Mia just stared at Bastian, jaw locked.

I closed my eyes, wishing I was literally any other place in the world right now.

"Listen," I said, "yes, something happened between us on the beach, but it was just that one time. I don't need an intervention. I know it was wrong. Bastian knows it was wrong. Which is why nothing happened between us last night."

An image intruded my thoughts: Bastian's hand stroking up and down his cock, the way his face was flushed, his breathing heavy. The way moisture beaded at the tip. And all the while he'd been thinking about me.

"I told him she was bad for him from the beginning." Kara swiveled her head toward me. "What were you two thinking, pursuing this? Were you going to get married? Have children? Was Bastian going to be king of the water court?"

"They would make some cute babies," Driscoll said, and everyone turned to stare at him. "I'm just saying. Her cheekbones? His jaw?" He kissed his fingers. "Perfection."

Mia's nose wrinkled. "How would that work? Just out of curiosity?"

Driscoll raised a brow. "Making babies?"

Mia flushed. "No, the magic part of it. Would your children have your powers?"

I rubbed my temples, not wanting to talk about imaginary children with Bastian. Something I'd dreamt about at one point in my life. "The powers are there, but they're diluted. That's why if an elemental chooses to have children with a human, their children cannot live in the courts."

Some elementals did fall in love with humans and chose to live in the human lands, though they often hid their powers, afraid of being persecuted or hunted for them. It wasn't an easy life.

"That feels wrong," Mia said quietly.

It did. It always had.

"What about if two elementals from different courts have children?" Mia asked.

"In that case," Leoni said, "the children are born with the powers of the mother. We don't know why it happens, exactly, but it's the mother's genes that pass on. So the father must move to the mother's court if he wants to be with his children."

"Can we not talk about this anymore?" I didn't want to admit how many nights I'd thought of what our children might look like, what Bastian would be like as a father.

"I agree," Kara said, tugging at one of her many earrings. "We're getting off topic. I wanted to talk more about what idiots the princess and my brother are."

I slammed my cup down, liquid sloshing from it. "We agreed absolutely nothing is going to happen between us. Happy?"

Leoni stared straight ahead, her cheeks red. She was furious with me. I understood, because I was furious with myself.

Mia stood. "I need to go have a little chat with my brother."

Kara rolled up the sleeves of her tunic to reveal her many tattoos. "I'm coming too."

A vein throbbed over Mia's temple as she stomped away. She was usually the mild-mannered twin, but tonight she had murder on her mind.

They both stomped toward Bastian, shoving through other crew members. They reached him, making angry gestures as Bastian strode away and toward his cabin. They followed, the door slamming behind all of them.

Leoni swatted me. "I am so mad at you right now."

I sighed. "I know."

"Okay, but was it good?" Driscoll leaned forward, propping his chin in his hands. "You know, I won't be offended if you need to talk about it. Confess your sins. Get it off your chest."

"You need to get laid," I said.

"I do," he agreed. "It's been so long."

By now, the music had died down, the dancing stopped, as everyone had gathered into a circle, listening to one of the crew members telling a story about the Deadlands and the monsters they'd encountered while stuck there.

"Can we just go listen to tonight's story and forget about everything that happened?" I asked Leoni and Driscoll.

Leoni narrowed her eyes. "I am going to be watching you. Every step you take. Every interaction with the pirate lord will be monitored by either me or Driscoll."

Driscoll stood. "Oh, I don't know if you can trust me. I'm kind of starting to root for them."

Leoni just threw up her arms and stomped over to the circle. I followed, sitting on a crate near the mast. Driscoll settled by the railing, leaning against it. I tried to pay attention to the story, but my thoughts kept drifting toward a certain pirate. I wondered what his sisters were saying to him right now.

I was about to retire belowdecks when the ship rocked, everyone lurching to the floor from their seated positions.

"What in the bloody hell?" Bastian emerged from his cabin, Mia and Kara following him, the only ones still on their feet. The pirate lord ran to the railing and looked down. "Fucking fuck," he said and pulled the spyglass from his coat, looking through it at something in the distance. The ship jolted, its joints creaking.

Bastian stuffed the spyglass back into his coat and whirled around. "Get to your feet, sailors." Everyone immediately stood. "We're under attack."

Chapter Twenty-Eight

The main deck became a flurry of activity as some crew members ran belowdecks to man the cannons, while others stood at the railing, grabbing weapons and readying them for anyone who tried to board the ship. Bastian ran to the helm.

Leoni grabbed my arm and started pulling me toward Bastian's cabin.

"What are you doing?" I dug my feet into the ground and leaned back, but damn she was strong, her grip ironclad. "I'm not going to hide."

"I am." Driscoll rushed past us and ducked into Bastian's cabin as Leoni whirled on me.

"You are the princess of Apolis. I'm not letting you fight some battle on a pirate ship."

The ship rocked again, and I looked out at the dark sea, not seeing any other ships. Then who was attacking? The ship groaned from below, and I stumbled into Leoni, who held her ground.

The loud boom of a cannon reverberated through the air, vibrating the deck.

The attack wasn't coming from around us. It was coming from below, which could only mean . . . the seafolk were after us. I shoved past Leoni and ran up to Bastian, who stood at the helm.

"Do you have enemies everywhere?" I yelled over the sound of cannons firing and Bastian's crew shouting out as they jabbed what I now recognized as long javelins into the ocean.

"Not the time, love." Bastian kept a firm grip on the helm as the ship tipped dangerously.

I slid with the movement, my back hitting the railing.

"Get into my cabin," Bastian yelled. "Now!"

"We have to figure out why they're attacking," I said.

"Great plan. I'll just go and have a nice chat with them while they're trying to gouge out my eyes."

I ignored him. "Have you done something to them? Attacked them? Stolen from them? Stole one of them?"

"No, no, and no," Bastian gritted out.

I paused, mind reeling. The seafolk were notoriously private. They rarely ventured out, interacting with Apolis only because we shared the same magic, and that had earned us a begrudging respect from them. They stayed out of every conflict. They wouldn't attack for no reason.

I thought about what Mia had told me at the tavern the previous night. The rumors about the trident. I gasped and ran toward Bastian's cabin.

"And she finally listens," Bastian yelled after me. "Thank the bloody hells."

I rushed into the cabin, where Driscoll sat on the bed, biting his nails. "You princesses know how to stir up trouble. It doesn't matter if I'm with Liliath or you. You both attract danger."

I ran to the little ledge by Bastian's window, clicking open the compartment as a blast sounded outside. I had to get this trident before anyone got killed. If this belonged to them, they'd want it back, and that meant they could give me some answers about why it was on the beach with my father and his crew, why he might've wanted it.

"Are you about to go stab someone?" Driscoll wrinkled his nose. "Because that's a terrible idea."

I ran back out of the cabin.

"Nice chat," Driscoll shouted.

I bumped into Leoni, who launched balls of water at any seafolk who surfaced. "They're using their powers to control the water," she said. "I can't fight against all that magic. They're going to capsize us!"

A huge wave rolled over the deck, washing all of us away, and I swallowed a mouthful of it. My back slammed against the hard deck, a few of the crew members falling overboard, their cries echoing out.

"No," Bastian yelled. "Get the damn ropes and get our men back!"

I banged against my chest, coughing and sputtering out sea water. Leoni yanked me to my feet, both of us now soaked. "Get back in the cabin. We can't risk losing you!"

I held up the trident. "I think they're looking for this. If I offer it to them, maybe they'll stop attacking us."

Leoni shook her head. "Absolutely not. That's too risky. You don't even know if that's what they're looking for."

The boat rode up on a high wave, crashing back down as Leoni and I rolled backward, my body cracking against the deck for a second time.

"They're going to capsize us soon," I yelled, "and then we'll all be dead. This could be our only shot."

"So let me do it." Leoni stuck out her hand. "Let me offer up the trident."

I bit my lip. Knowing her, she'd just give it away without demanding information. No. It had to be me so I could ensure this was done the right way.

I ran to the railing, holding up the trident. "Is this what you want?" I screamed out in the void.

The water below stopped roiling, the waves slowing in their fury.

So I'd been right.

"Fucking hell, what is she doing now?" Bastian yelled down to Leoni.

"What she always does," Leoni said back. "Whatever she wants."

I held the trident up higher. Water lashed out at the ship, lancing the siding like a sword, punching a hole right near my legs.

"Not my ship." Bastian groaned. "Damnit."

"What are our orders, Cap?" a voice shouted behind me.

"Stand down," Bastian said, surprising me. I figured he'd order them to drag me away and lock me up. "Drop the damn anchor."

Water slithered up over the deck in the form of ropes, inching toward me, the seafolk using their magic to strike.

I had to hurry my plan along before they snatched me, and the trident, away. "We found this with my father's dead body." I swallowed.

"Not even a dead body. Just bones. He and his entire crew died, and I need to know why." I took a deep breath. "I'm Princess Gabrielle Aster of Apolis. My father was King Jaron Aster. We've always had a good relationship with the seafolk, and if you can help me understand why he's dead—" My voice broke. "We mean no harm. We don't intend to use the trident, and we'll be happy to turn it over, but please give me the answers I seek if you have them."

The water grew completely still, the boat no longer rocking, like maybe we'd imagined the entire attack. The crew shot each other uneasy glances.

Then I saw it. Heads emerging from the water. Their eyes were twice the size of ours, their noses and lips smaller, shimmering scales covering their necks and arms. Razor-sharp teeth poked out of their mouths. The hair on their heads were vibrant colors, and as they emerged from underwater it looked like a rainbow painting the dark sea.

The water washed up into a small wave that carried King Salazar. "Princess." He nodded, his white hair tied back. "You've found yourself with curious company."

"So I have," I said carefully.

He tugged at his long, braided beard. "We have what you seek, and as long as you promise to give us the trident, we will give you your answers."

Relief flooded me.

"Princess, are you sure about this?" Leoni asked from behind me.

"Love, think about what you're doing. That's a powerful weapon you hold in your hands," Bastian said, still at the helm.

I didn't turn to look at either of them. I didn't have to think about it. I stuck out the trident and said, "Now tell me what you know."

Chapter Twenty-Nine

King Salazar accepted the trident, silver scales stretching up onto his hand and shimmering in the moonlight. "I cannot give you any answers," he said once he held the trident.

Water appeared in my hand in the form of a spear, and I was ready to shove it right through his eye for lying to me like that.

"Easy, love." Bastian's hand curled around my arm, but I shook him off. I hadn't even heard the pirate approach, but now he stood at my side.

King Salazar held up his hands. "I cannot tell you what you need to know, but my daughter can." He raised the trident in the air as another wave brought up a seawoman. Her glimmering blue tail flapped, splashing water up onto the deck as she peered at me with her huge purple eyes and tucked a strand of her fire-red hair behind her ear. "As soon as I use this trident on her." He pointed the object at a little shell that hung on a piece of twine around her neck. It was white, unassuming.

She crossed her arms over her chest, a mixture of coral and seaweed woven together into a bra that stretched across her breasts.

My gaze snapped back to the sea king as I registered his words. "What are you talking about? That's powerful magic, ancient magic. You can't use it until we know more about it."

Anger flashed in his purple eyes. "I can, and I will."

Bastian swore, the rest of his crew standing behind him, silent and watching. "I knew this was a mistake," he said. "You're not using that trident, mate. I won't let you."

The sea king gripped it tighter, baring his sharp teeth. "It's my price to pay."

Bastian jabbed a finger at him. "You don't know what the price will be."

"Humans." The sea king scoffed. "No, I don't know the exact price, but it will be my price, and the cost will be worth it. I do not need magic explained to me by you, pirate."

A bored look passed over Bastian's face. "It seems that you do since I'm the one who has to remind you how bloody stupid this is."

The king raised his hand as if he might smite Bastian from the ship, but I stepped in between them.

I turned to the pirate. "He's right. If he wants to use it, that's his choice. Besides, it's not like the dark magic that comes from Sorrengard. This belonged to Spirit Water. We don't know if the cost will be deadly. We don't even know if there will be a cost. This is different from any magic we've ever encountered."

Bastian's jaw ticked. "And what if you're wrong and your life is the price?" He raised his brows. "Did you think of that, love?"

I squeezed my eyes shut. "Bastian, we've come too far to not get the information we seek. We can go round and round with what-ifs, but at the end of the day, I need answers, and this is the best way to get them. She is the best way."

Bastian stared at me with those dark eyes of his. It hadn't been that long ago that I'd made the very same argument to Liliath when she'd wanted to use the pixie dust for her own means. I'd told her it wasn't worth it, but now I realized how naive that was. She'd been trying to save her court, trying to do the same thing I was doing now. At the time, I couldn't imagine what would make anyone desperate enough to use magic that unpredictable. Now I realized I'd pay any price to save my home, my family, even if it meant giving my life.

Bastian threw out his arms. "Have her write the damn story out."

King Salazar growled. "Enough. She is my daughter, and I will free her voice." He pointed the trident at that seashell around her neck, and my breath caught in my chest.

"Her voice is stuck in there?" I asked.

Murmurs rose from the crew behind us.

King Salazar didn't answer. Water flowed from the forked end, spilling out and toward the sea princess. It surrounded her, swirling in circles, faster and faster and faster, so fast my eyes blurred. The water shot toward the shell and shattered it, a light floating from the broken remnants toward her mouth. Her eyes widened even bigger as she clutched her chest.

"Marian, are you okay?" King Salazar's brows scrunched together, the fear in his voice evident.

The light continued to pour into her mouth until it disappeared in a final flourish and she jerked. Everyone stood in silence, mouths agape, staring and waiting.

Finally, Marian let out a ragged breath. "I'm okay," she said, voice raspy.

Her father's shoulders slumped as he lurched forward and brought her into a tight hug. Tears pricked my eyes. Whatever the price, at least she'd gotten her voice back.

She pushed out of her father's arms and looked at me. "I'm so sorry your father is dead."

My heart clenched at the reminder. "Do you know why?"

She picked at a seashell that hung from her hair. "He was killed because of me."

I stepped back. "What?"

The water bubbled underneath her like a fountain, misting my face.

"It's time to tell the truth," her father said, voice stern. "What did you do to the shadow court to make them take your voice? I know you were visiting the island, but I don't know why."

Leoni sucked in a sharp breath behind me.

I didn't know Marian's exact age, but she looked to be no older than twenty. So young for such a burden to be placed on her.

"I went to the shadow court to find your brother's shadow," she whispered.

"My brother?" My brows furrowed. "Lochlan?" I asked.

Blood and water, almost every maiden on the continent wanted to marry him, but word of the playboy prince had also reached the sea princess? His charms truly knew no bounds.

She shook her head. "Maledonan."

I started at that. Mal. My youngest brother. Quiet, reserved, thoughtful Mal.

Tears spilled down her cheeks. "I just wanted to save him," she said between sobs.

"You loved him." I'd recognize the pain in her voice anywhere. I'd felt that same pain when Bastian had betrayed me. Blood and water, while I'd been having a secret affair with the pirate lord, my little brother had been having his own affair with the sea princess.

Relationships between elementals and seafolk weren't forbidden, exactly, but more frowned upon. The seafolk could sprout legs and walk on land, but they weren't like us. Their customs, their ways, were very different. Not to mention we had no idea what kind of offspring could be produced between the two species.

King Salazar's face turned a deep red. "The water prince?" he said. "You fell in love with an elemental?"

Marian crossed her arms over her coral top, defiance settling in the thin line of her lips. "I liked to watch him from afar. He was always going on adventures with you and Lochlan."

King Salazar let out a growl of displeasure.

Marian raised her chin. "He was joyful and lived his life to the fullest with no regrets. One day, I was watching him do something foolish. A dumb stunt riding a wave, using his magic. But he must've depleted his powers faster than he realized. He fell into the sea and hit his head on a rock. I saved him from drowning and stayed with him until he awoke. I'd never met anyone so handsome, so generous, so loving."

Bastian snorted, and I turned. He raised a brow while rubbing his jaw. "Reminds me of how we met."

I swallowed at the wistfulness in his voice.

No one else had moved an inch, everyone as shocked as I was at hearing this.

Marian took a deep breath while her father's frown deepened. "We were planning on announcing our relationship soon, telling our parents. And then he came." She jabbed a finger at Bastian. "He came for the boys."

My throat grew thick.

"Mal was with me that night," Marion continued, "in a little cove where we often met. He saw what was happening from afar and said he needed to get Lochlan, that they'd stop this. But they weren't fast enough. The ship left with the boys, and they had to use their water magic to catch up and sneak aboard."

Bastian swore softly.

"I followed the ship all the way to Sorrengard, where I saw the boys get carted off, marched onto the island like they were in some trance."

I shot a look at Bastian, whose jaw was locked.

"And then I saw Mal and Lochlan sneaking off the ship and going after them into the jungle." She sniffled. "They never returned."

My heart squeezed painfully. Bastian's hand curled around my elbow, steadying me. He was the last person I wanted any kind of comfort from right now. I wrenched my arm free.

"So they could be dead," Leoni said.

"No." Marian shook her head. "I said they never returned, not that I didn't see them again."

I rushed forward, hands gripping the railing so tight my knuckles turned white. "You've seen them?"

She nodded. "Their shadows are gone—all their shadows have been taken."

"But why?" I asked. "What does the shadow court want? To weaken us? To get revenge because of the Shadow War?"

"I don't know," she said. "The shadows swirl over the island like a dark cloud, hundreds of them. All trapped, just like the bodies they belong to. They protect the island, keep out intruders and keep those trying to escape trapped. They don't want to be reunited with their bodies, so catching them is difficult."

My hand floated to my mouth. How awful.

"The island is . . . odd," she said. "Mal and Lochlan had been reporting to me for a few months, and the situation seemed dire, so dire."

My heart dropped like a stone.

Marian's eyes welled with tears. "Your brothers never gave up hope, but it didn't seem like there was a way out. Not that any of us had found. I visited as often as I could, but it wasn't easy with . . ." She gestured to her father. "I couldn't come as much as I wanted to. I found out your father was planning an expedition to save Mal and Lochlan, so I went to him, told him everything I knew. I started working with him, planning. He was trying to find the trident. He believed that the key to helping your boys lay in Spirit Water."

Of course he did. My father would rely on his faith 'til the end.

King Salazar shook his head. "My daughter going behind my back like this. It's shameful."

Marian kept her eyes on me.

"How did you lose your voice?" I asked, willing her to keep going despite her father's disapproval.

"What did the shadow court do to you?" King Salazar demanded.

She looked down, her scaled hands twisted together. "It wasn't the shadow court that took my voice. It was the sea witch."

The seafolk behind her sucked in sharp breaths, and her father's face turned purple.

"What?" he asked, voice dangerously low.

I looked behind me to Leoni, who just shrugged. She didn't know this sea witch either.

"Who is the sea witch?" I asked, not knowing if I even wanted to know at this point. "And what does this have to do with my father? With Mal?"

Marian swallowed. "My aunt. My father's sister. She was the oldest, the crown was supposed to pass to her, but my grandparents bestowed it upon my father because they believed he'd be a better ruler. She's been disgruntled ever since, trying to find ways to hurt my father, so he banished her. She has followers, others who haven't been happy with the way my father has ruled. They were tailing me. They knew of my visits to the shadow court, knew of my affair with Mal. They'd been spying on me for months."

A vein throbbed in King Salazar's temple.

"They found me crying after a visit with Mal, told me to follow them and I could get the answers I seek."

My chest tightened.

"So I went."

"How could you—" King Salazar started, but I held out a hand.

"Let her speak."

He cut me a glare. .

Marian's voice shook. "They took me to my aunt. At first I told her I wouldn't make any deals with her. But she promised me that she would tell me the key to saving Mal if I made a deal. I told her I'd think about it."

"You didn't," King Salazar said.

"I'd do anything to save Mal," Marian snapped. "I went to your father, told him about this deal, and he didn't think I should take it. But he was no closer to figuring out how to get Mal and Lochlan off that island either. It was becoming more hopeless."

All this had been going on, and I'd had no idea. I'd been grieving, broken and lost, and my father had been scheming with the sea princess, searching for the trident. No wonder he'd been gone so long.

Marian shrugged, tears now spilling down her cheeks. "I didn't know what else to do. Your father said he'd gotten a lead on the trident's location that he was going to follow, but I just assumed it would be another dead end. We've been searching for that trident for centuries with no luck. I told your father I was going to take the deal, that it was a price worth paying. He said he'd have his ship waiting for me near the sea witch's lair, to come directly to him after I took the deal."

"Where was the sea witch's lair?" I asked, dread growing like a weed in my gut.

"Near the human island, Porth," Marian said. "I went to the sea witch and agreed to her terms. She said all I had to do was wear a necklace that she'd gotten from the shadow court." Marian fingered the broken shell around her neck. "She said I could ask it a question and it would give me an answer, but it would also demand a price. I know how shadow court magic works. I know how these items are created, that for every shadow ripped from a person's body, a new magical item appears. I also knew my aunt was doing this to hurt me. I didn't care. I planned to find out how to save Mal and go directly to your father and tell him. Even if the necklace took my life, I figured I'd get to your father first, be able to relay the information."

She paused, then, like this was almost too painful to speak about.

"I put on the necklace and asked it how to save Mal. It whispered to me, told me the key lay in the light. That shadows are afraid of light and in order to keep them at bay, we'd have to bring light to the island to save Mal's life."

"But we already know the shadows are afraid of light," I said, disappointment already welling up in me.

"This dark magic is full of riddles, just like my sister," King Salazar said, voice tight. "The necklace spoke the truth. If it says the light is the key, then it is. But it didn't give enough details to help. That's why if my daughter had come to me, I would've forbidden her from doing this."

Marian's face flushed, and I put a hand on her arm. "This isn't your fault. You are brave for what you did."

She sucked in a shuddering breath. "That's when my voice disappeared." She shook her head. "No, it was ripped from me. It felt like someone was physically pulling it up through my throat and out of my mouth. I couldn't take the necklace off, couldn't break it. I knew my voice was trapped inside. That was the price I paid for it answering my question."

I shuddered at that description, and King Salazar's eyes squeezed shut like it physically pained him to hear this.

Marian's hand floated to her throat. "It hurt worse than any other pain I've ever felt—like someone was dragging their sharp nails up through my throat, and once my voice was gone, a burning sensation was left in its wake. You have no idea how many times I've wanted to rip out my own throat just to not feel the pain anymore."

"I'm so sorry," I said.

"I swam to the surface in pain, and your father was waiting on his ship, holding the trident in his hand."

I gasped. He'd done it. He'd found it.

"He knew something was wrong right away. I gestured to the shell, and he was about to use the trident to break it when a wave hit his ship, and the trident fell straight into the sea."

"The sea witch," I guessed. "Why would she do that?"

"To keep your father from freeing my voice. She is so focused on the destruction of my family. It's all she wants. To weaken us, to hurt us. That's why she gave me that necklace. She knew that hurting me would be the ultimate way to hurt my father."

"So my father got caught in the crossfire of her vengeance," I said.

Marian looked down. "Yes. She capsized the ship. She and her followers used their magic to drown your father and his men. They tried to fight it, to use their own magic against her, but they were caught by surprise and they were outnumbered. They were also weak from using their magic to get that trident. Your father didn't even have a chance to tell me how he'd found it. I tried to save them, but the sea witch and her followers kept me from going after them. The witch and all her sea creatures descended on your father and his men, tearing them to pieces. I led her right to them." Her voice broke, and she sobbed.

What a brutal end for my father, and after he'd finally realized his dream of finding that trident.

"The trident was lost, your father and his men were dead, and I no longer had my voice, couldn't tell a soul what had happened. Couldn't write it either. I never returned to the shadow court to see Mal. I was so ashamed of what I'd done, how I'd caused your father's death."

Tears streamed down my cheeks as well, and Leoni and a few of the crew members sniffled behind me.

"It wasn't your fault," I said. "You made such a great sacrifice for my brother. Please don't blame yourself."

She spoke between sobs. "All their bones must've washed up on shore, along with that trident. I thought it lost to the sea. But then I saw it last night, on board this very ship. I couldn't believe it. I was sure I was seeing things at first."

Right. When I'd been waving it around like an idiot the previous night. Blood and water. We were lucky it was Marian who saw it and not her aunt.

"I went to my father, and he understood enough to follow me to your ship. Once he saw the trident, he knew what I wanted and that's when we attacked."

I squeezed her hand. "I understand. I'm just glad we could help you get your voice back."

Marian wiped the tears from her cheeks, her nails long and blue, dotted with little shells. "I do have information for you about the island. I've spent months studying the layout of it, and I know the best places to dock, to hide. I can at least give you that."

Bastian heaved a sigh.

"The pirate docks on the northern side, but that's the most visible part of the island. On the western part of the island, there's a pathway of narrow cliffs, dangerous to navigate, but if you can get through them, they'll provide the perfect cover for any ship." She took a breath. "On the eastern side is the marsh, surrounded by thick jungle and full of crocodiles. Dangerous for a different reason, but the foliage also provides good cover."

Crocodiles or sharp cliffs. Perfect.

Marian cleared her throat, wincing. It must've been getting harder for her to speak after so long not having her voice. "I've thought about it so much over the months, the necklace's comment about the light. I do think there's something to it. If you could find a way to trap the shadows with light, force them into a corner or something, then they could easily be captured."

I mulled over her words. That wasn't a bad idea.

"It's time for us to go," King Salazar said. "I have much to say to my daughter."

Bastian nodded to his crew, who started preparing the ship to once again set sail.

"Wait, what about the southern part of the island?" I asked, realizing she hadn't mentioned that.

"There's no cover there," Bastian said.

Marian nodded. "He'll see you. It's the perfect view from his—"

"Enough." Bastian's voice split the air like the crack of a whip.

My eyebrows furrowed together. "No, we're not done." I glared at Bastian, then turned back to Marian. "Who will see? Who are you talking about?"

Marian began coughing, the sound raspy and throttled.

Bastian stepped forward. "We're done here, Your Majesty. Thank you for the information."

Marian clutched at her throat, coughing hard. Her father put a protective arm around her. "Let's get you back home."

I looked at King Salazar. "Please, don't leave yet—"

"She's given you enough information," he said as he tugged his daughter away.

Bastian began shouting out orders to his crew as they hopped to attention and scurried to their posts. Leoni shot me a confused look.

"Please find Mal's shadow." Marian reached out for me. "Save him."

A determination settled in me as the ship started to move. "I will," I shouted to her above the rush of wind, watching as the seafolk became smaller and smaller, the ship gliding through the waters.

I looked up at Bastian, who stood at the helm, steering the ship. He'd cut Marian off, been so determined to sail away. She had been about to say something, something he didn't want me to know.

"So what did I miss?" Driscoll emerged from the cabin and clapped his hands together as Leoni and I both stared at him. "Did we kick some ass?" He rolled his eyes as Leoni glared at him. "Okay, I might've fallen asleep on the pirate lord's bed, which is far more comfortable than the sad excuse for beds we have to sleep on. You know, we should lobby for new mattresses, and some pillows while we're at it. What kind of barbarians don't sleep with pillows—"

"Driscoll," Leoni said. "Shut up."

Driscoll's mouth snapped shut, and for once, he didn't have a snarky comment in return.

Leoni chewed the inside of her cheek. "The pirate lord is hiding too much, keeping too many secrets. I don't like this, Princess."

I didn't either, but if I knew anything, it was that secrets didn't stay buried forever, and I had a feeling I was getting closer to unearthing whatever Bastian was hiding.

Chapter Thirty

We arrived at the earth court a few uneventful days later. I barely saw Bastian as he hid away in his cabin, and I kept myself busy by continuing to help the crew with their tasks, learning more about what it took to keep a pirate ship running.

Elwen spread out before us, a thick forest sprouting along the coastline, the trees tall and filled with dark green leaves. The air had gotten cooler as we'd traveled farther south, and I rubbed my arms against the chill of the wind.

Guards were stationed at the docks, their armor shining green with the earth court emblem: a tree carved into their chest plates. I hadn't seen Elwen when it had been in ruin, but Liliath had worked so hard to rebuild her court in such a short amount of time. Some of the trees were still barren, blackened with no leaves on them, but for the most part, this was the Elwen I remembered visiting so many times growing up. I hadn't expected it to be so . . . normal after the extensive damage that had been done. From the coast, it would be a few hours' ride to Liliath's castle, and my stomach flipped at the thought of asking Liliath for the pixie dust. Yes, she'd stolen it from me. Well, her husband had. But now I'd have to ask for it back, and that meant I'd need a good reason. One that she'd hopefully understand.

Bastian had insisted on taking down his flag, which was far too noticeable.

"I hope you know what you're doing," Leoni said as she came to a stand next to me.

"You and me both," I replied.

She'd been distant, too, barely speaking to me over the last few days.

"So remember," Driscoll said, approaching us, "if Liliath asks, I got kidnapped along with both of you by the pirates. No choice but to come along."

Leoni smoothed out her tunic as the ship slowly approached the docks. "Why would they kidnap you?"

"For my good looks and charms, obviously. And because I'm great company. Unlike some of us, shorty."

Unlike Leoni, Driscoll had been chattering nonstop since that attack by the seafolk.

"Why don't you want Queen Liliath to know the truth?" Leoni asked. "You're a grown man, Driscoll, and she's not your mother."

He scratched his jaw. "No, she's just my best friend and my queen, and it might hurt her feelings to know I chose to come with you all rather than return to Elwen and be her ambassador."

The docks came closer, busy with many ships arriving for the wedding from all over. I spotted the king and queen of the sky court swooping through the air, their white-feathered wings spanning wide and looking glorious with the sun splitting through them.

They had no heirs, and no one knew who would succeed them when they passed on. Traditionally, heirs always assumed the throne in the courts. It was up to each court when an heir could ascend, whether it was at a certain age or when the current ruler died. Either way, none of the courts had ever been faced with a situation where there was no heir to take over.

Just another issue the courts would have to address at some point.

I clapped Driscoll on the shoulder. "Why don't you just tell Liliath the truth? Tell her that you want to do this for yourself, that you want to be more than just an ambassador."

He scoffed. "Just tell her the truth? Just be honest? Just come out and say what's been bothering me?" He made a face. "That's the stupidest thing I've ever heard."

I turned my gaze back to the docks as we approached. The guards stuck out their hands, vines shooting from them that slithered toward our ship and pulled us in perfect line to exit onto the dock.

"Who goes there?" a guard shouted from down below.

I cleared my throat. "Princess Gabrielle Aster of the water court." I gestured to Leoni. "I'll be bringing my guard along with me."

"Guards," said a deep voice from behind, and I swore, cutting a look at Bastian as he smiled broadly. He raised two fingers in the air. "As in two." He gestured between himself and Leoni. "Both of us will be guarding Her Majesty."

The guard's brows furrowed as he looked from me to Bastian in confusion. I'd told Bastian that it would be risky if he came along, and he should stay back on the ship and let me handle this. I thought we'd been in agreement, especially after Kara and Mia chimed in, both on my side.

I sighed heavily. "Two guards," I said, and Leoni's head snapped in my direction, her gaze ablaze with fury.

Driscoll raised his finger. "And the ambassador to the earth court. You might know me? Driscoll Bayliss."

The guard gave him a blank stare. "Yeah, whatever." He tipped his head toward me, his tone softening. "Welcome to Elwen, Your Majesty."

Leoni, Bastian, Driscoll, and I exited the ship and were greeted by a woman who led us from the dock, across the beach, and toward a long line of horses. Other guests were mounting their horses, while members of the sky court flew above us and over the treetops.

"These two are yours," the woman said, pointing at a black horse and a brown one. She handed us a piece of paper. "And here's a map, though the horses are trained and know the way. It's a very straightforward journey."

I nodded, nerves in bundles at the thought of this entire endeavor. Especially after everything that had transpired with the seafolk, with the trident, which the sea king had taken. I trusted him with it. He was a fair man, a reasonable one, and he wouldn't misuse it. He promised to keep it safe, hidden, until the courts were ready to convene and figure out what to do with such a powerful object.

Bastian shoved his boot into the stirrup of the black horse and swung himself up. He held out his hand toward me. "Ready, love?"

I crossed my arms. "What makes you think I'm riding with you?"

"Well, shorty certainly won't," he said as Leoni was already mounting the brown horse. "And I don't think Driscoll would be interested either."

Driscoll shrugged. "I mean, I could be persuaded."

I raised an eyebrow.

Driscoll brushed past me. "Just want to see what all the fuss is about," he murmured.

Bastian narrowed his gaze at me. "You can't be serious."

I bit back a smile. "I think it's perfect. You two will get along great. Driscoll has many wonderful stories to tell to make the journey go faster."

"Bloody hell," Bastian mumbled as Driscoll swung himself up and settled in front of the pirate lord.

"He's got a strong grip," Driscoll said as Bastian just groaned.

Even Leoni was smiling as I joined her on our brown horse and we began our journey toward Queen Liliath's castle.

DRISCOLL LASTED all of thirty minutes before Bastian pushed him off the horse, making the ambassador yell out and startling our brown mare, who rose onto her haunches, whinnying and almost causing Leoni and me to fall off.

"You got my shirt covered in dirt," Driscoll whined from the ground.

"I can't do it," Bastian said. "I cannot listen to another minute of gossip from the earth court."

"That was grade-A gossip," Driscoll said, clearly offended.

I rolled my eyes, hopping off my horse.

"What are you doing?" Leoni hissed.

I gestured to Bastian. "Do you want to ride with him?"

Leoni stayed silent.

"That's what I thought. It's fine. It's a short journey to the castle." I stomped over to Bastian's horse, and he held out his hand, a gleam in his eyes as he helped me mount. His large, warm hand swallowed my own, and I had to work to not think about the ways that hand had touched me just days ago in Porth.

I settled in front of Bastian, and he brought his arms around me to grab the reins, his hard chest pressed up against my back. Warmth pooled between my legs, and I clenched my thighs tighter around the horse.

Behind us, Driscoll got onto the horse with Leoni, whose face was growing stonier by the minute.

Wisps of hair escaped my braid, falling over my forehead, but Bastian reached out and brushed them aside, his fingers trailing so softly over my skin. Maybe this had been a bad idea. Every damn movement the pirate lord made caused a reaction in my body.

The horses trotted in a line down a dirt road that cut through the forest, carrying humans and elementals alike, hundreds here for the big wedding. A mixture of blackened tree stumps and towering trees rose up on either side of us. The sun sliced through the canopies overhead, providing some warmth from the chilly air as we delved deeper into the forest.

A waterfall crashed down in the distance, barely visible through the thick leaves, but I could see the rocks surrounding the falls, covered with moss. Vines hung between trees in a heavy curtain with beautiful pink and purple flowers growing from them.

Everywhere I looked color sprang from the earth: scarlet-red rose bushes, wisteria hanging in droves from branches, a type of yellow flower I didn't recognize with a bright pink center. The sea would always be my favorite view, but I had to admit, I loved the lushness of Liliath's court. She and her people took a lot of pride in their home, and I could tell how hard they'd worked to rebuild it.

"Well, I certainly haven't won over your friend," Bastian said in my ear, and I looked to see Leoni gazing daggers at him.

"Hm." I put a finger to my chin. "I wonder why. Could it have anything to do with you kidnapping our boys and taking them to the shadow court? Or maybe it's how you're keeping secrets from us? Or maybe it's—"

"Alright, love, I get it."

I shifted, trying to put space between our bodies that were plastered together, but all I ended up doing was rubbing myself against the pirate lord.

"Bloody hells, could you stop doing that?" Bastian gritted out.

"I'm trying to get comfortable." I moved again.

"Well, can you do so without moving like . . . that? I only have so much control."

The low timbre of his voice trailed down my spine.

I took a steadying breath. "You have plenty of control if I remember correctly."

"You just sent your father's bones to sea. I was not going to take advantage of you."

"It's fine. It was for the best that nothing happened. Besides, you're the one who wanted me to ride with you."

"No, I didn't want Driscoll to ride with me. There's a difference."

"Oh, so I was the lesser of two evils?"

"Lesser of three, actually." He tipped his head toward Leoni.

I twisted to look at him. "You know, you're an ass."

"I've been called worse."

Our faces were inches apart, and I swallowed as I stared into those deep brown eyes, swirling like a storm. "She's just trying to protect me, you know. Same as your sisters are trying to protect you."

Bastian's gaze flicked from where they lingered on my lips up to my eyes. Surprise flashed across his face at my words.

I turned and looked straight ahead, needing to put space between our mouths. If he kept staring at me like that, I was going to be the one losing all control.

"When did you find out?" he asked quietly.

"You mean that you have two sisters you never told me about? A few days ago. At the tavern. Mia told me."

We passed under two branches that stretched over the path, making an archway, bright fuchsia flowers dripping from them like jewels.

He swore. "I should make her walk the plank."

"Somehow I think she'd just end up shoving you off of it."

He let out a laugh. "That she would." There was a fondness in his voice that warmed my heart. "She's fierce. Not quite as fierce as Kara. Mia has a softness about her, a vulnerability. Kara is like a hard wall, and no matter how much you try to break her down, she won't budge."

"Hmm, wonder who that reminds me of?"

Bastian snorted.

"They both remind me of you," I said finally. "Yes, you're an impenetrable wall, but you softened and eventually let me climb you."

Bastian choked before he finally said, "I let you climb a lot of things." I elbowed him right in the ribs, and he let out an oomph. "Oh, come on. You walked right into that one."

I smiled. I supposed I did. My thoughts turned to his sisters, his childhood. I tugged at the end of my braid. "You've kept so much from me. I wonder if I ever knew you at all."

He stayed quiet for a moment. "I didn't tell you about them because I was afraid."

That caught me off guard. "Afraid of what?"

"That they'd scare you off, ruin what we had. I—" He stopped. "When we were together, it was like we had our own little world. No Apolis, no Lost Boys. No princess. No pirate. No brothers. No sisters. Just Gabrielle and Bastian. I wanted to keep that world safe for as long as I could."

My name rolled off his tongue in that delicious accent I loved so much, and I wanted to capture that sound in my memory. "But that wasn't reality," I said. "We couldn't just hide out in a cave forever."

"I was going to try. I was going to keep you in that world for as long as I could, keep everyone else out so it was just you and me and our stories." His voice dropped low as his lips brushed against my ear. "And our bodies."

A shiver ran through me.

"And no harm could come to us as long as I protected that world we'd created together."

"That's why it was never going to work out between us." Branches stretched over us, beautiful gold and red leaves dotting them. "Because you never truly let me in. You didn't trust in us." My voice shook, and Bastian stiffened. "You didn't trust that we could overcome whatever came our way. You thought the only way we could survive was to ignore the problems around us instead of treating me like a partner who could help you solve them."

"Love," Bastian started, and a few others turned to look at us from their horses.

I lowered my voice. "I don't know why you took our boys, but maybe if you'd come to me first, told me about whatever predicament you'd gotten yourself in that required that big of a sacrifice, I could've helped you."

"You couldn't." His voice was flat now.

I was so tired of this. One minute he was the teasing, charming, seductive Bastian that I knew, and the next he was the cold-hearted pirate lord. It was like constant whiplash.

"You don't know that," I argued.

"I do. Everyone in my crew knew it. That's why I kept you from them. Why I distanced myself from them when we were together. Because I had to fucking protect you at all costs."

"Protect me from what?" I snapped and turned to look at him.

His jaw locked, face once again a mask of stone. "People are staring. Wouldn't want to draw attention to me."

The road wound out from the thick forest, and in the distance, Liliath's castle towered upward. Whereas my castle was bright and white, Liliath's was stone and wood, sitting atop a grassy hill, dripping with vines and flowers, bursting with green and color. A sparkling blue moat wound around the outside of Liliath's home. From here I could see the potted plants on every balcony, flowers I would never be able to name jutting up in bunches.

"Let's just focus on getting through this wedding," Bastian said, voice tight. "We'll get the pixie dust and get the bloody hells out of Elwen."

Chapter Thirty-One

Everyone filled the ball room later that night, the women wearing lavish dresses that sparkled, shimmered, and swished, the men wearing their finest trousers and button-down tunics, covered by tailored jackets.

Vines with purple flowers hung down the walls and stretched overhead, making it feel like we were in an enchanted forest and not Liliath's ballroom. A tree sprouted up in the middle of the room, stretching all the way to the vaulted ceiling, its branches spreading out wide, leaves dangling over the crowd of people. Glimmers of light sparkled from the tree and its massive branches, emitting a soft glow in the room.

A band sat on a raised stage, playing a lively tune that people danced to, everyone twirling and spinning around the thick base of the tree. I stood by a table filled with stuffed pears, flaky pastries, spiced meats, and savory tarts that made my mouth water. I nabbed a tart, munching on it and watching everyone enjoy this lovely evening.

The wedding had been beautiful, Liliath and Penn swearing their loyalty to each other, vines wrapping around their wrists and binding them in a sacred earth ceremony as an earth priestess presided over them.

I'd had to work hard not to look over at Bastian. Not to think about how once upon a time, I'd dreamed of my own wedding ceremony. With him.

I snorted at my foolishness and finished swallowing my tart, then took a gulp out of my goblet of wine. I hadn't seen Bastian since the ceremony ended. He wore a brimmed hat to cover his face so that no one would recognize him, but the hat made him a bit conspicuous since it wasn't exactly in fashion for males. I stopped myself from searching for him.

Leoni approached, her light blue dress flaring out at her thick waist, bodice tight and pushing her breasts up. She frowned, tugging up at the dress as it continued to slide down.

Going shopping had put her in a better mood. We hadn't addressed the tension between us, but she'd at least been acting more like her normal self since we arrived to Elwen.

"I look damn good," she said as she came to a stand by me. "Even if this dress is very impractical for fighting."

I laughed. "It's a dress, Oni. You're not supposed to fight in it. It's for much more enjoyable occasions."

"Says who?" She grabbed an olive and popped it in her mouth. "Fighting is enjoyable."

"So is dancing. You've caught the eye of many a suitor tonight." I raised my glass toward a few men ogling her, well, mainly her breasts.

"They can ogle all they want." She wiggled her fingers at them. "But I have a job to do."

I peered at her. As long as I'd known Leoni, she'd been single minded in her focus on becoming part of the royal guard. Despite everyone saying she wouldn't be right for the position, that she was too short, too plump, too slow, she worked hard to prove them wrong.

But sometimes I worried this job took over her entire life.

I nudged her. "Go have some fun, Oni. Dance, drink. Liliath has guards posted everywhere." I pointed to the guards lining the walls. "You can be off duty tonight. I'm not in danger."

She sniffed, raising her chin. I pushed her toward a gentleman who gave her a shy smile, his blond hair gelled back, his blue eyes twinkling.

"Go on," I said.

"Well, I guess one dance couldn't hurt." She lifted her skirts, striding toward him. He pressed a kiss to her hand as she curtsied, then he swept her up in his arms and whirled her around. From here, I could see the smile playing at her lips.

I should dance as well, but the one man I wanted to dance with was the one man I couldn't have.

Liliath and her husband Penn stood near the front of the room, and despite the flurry of activity around them, they held each other tight, swaying back and forth to their own rhythm. She laid her head against his chest, eyes closed like she was savoring the feel of him. They were beautiful together, and a pang shot through my heart. I was happy for my friend. Of course I was. But I couldn't help the jealousy that arose at what she had with her husband. Something I thought I'd had with Bastian.

"Well, look at you in that stunning dress," Driscoll said, approaching me. He wore black pants and a blue silk shirt and carried a goblet of wine. "Come on, do a twirl."

I gave him a look but obliged, spinning around as the skirt of my lilac dress lifted and fanned around me. The straps of the gown hung down around my biceps, exposing my collarbone and shoulders. I'd bought the dress in town earlier today when Driscoll had taken me and Leoni shopping so that we wouldn't look like "sea rats," as he put it, at the queen's wedding.

I stopped spinning. "And why aren't you dancing?" I asked Driscoll.

He looked at a man who stood across the room. His pale skin was flushed and dark, loose curls grazing his sharp cheekbones. He was handsome, and he spoke with a shorter man with a full red beard, both of them laughing together. "No dancing for me tonight, I'm afraid. My boyfriend, well ex-boyfriend, kind of ruined that for me."

"I didn't even know you had a boyfriend," I said.

Driscoll traced his finger around the rim of his goblet. "We broke up before your coronation. Mutual. Just weren't right for each other. It happens."

"Ah, I know what that feels like." I took a sip of my wine, thinking of the pirate lord. "How can something so good end up being so wrong?" I murmured.

"I don't think you're talking about me and my ex." Driscoll nudged me. "I'm going to hazard a crazy guess that it's the pirate lord occupying your thoughts."

I shifted from foot to foot. "Sorry. I shouldn't have made that about me."

"Oh no, I want to talk about you." Driscoll's eyes danced with delight. "The tension between you two on that horse." He fanned himself. "Whew. I needed an ice bucket."

I swatted at him. "Except it's like you said. We're not right for each other."

Driscoll raised a brow. "No, I said me and my ex weren't right for each other. Now you're projecting."

"Well, given that he betrayed me and kidnapped the boys of my court, I think that's a pretty good projection."

"Fair point." Driscoll sipped his wine. "But"—he tipped his cup toward Liliath and Penn, who still swayed together like they were the only ones in the crowded room—"Liliath was able to get past Penn's betrayal."

I snorted into my drink. "Bastian is not Penn. He doesn't steal from the rich and give to the poor. He kidnaps people and delivers them to the shadow court, and they're never seen again."

"But why does he do it?" I remained silent. Driscoll nodded his head toward me. "Exactly. Nothing about these Lost Boys screams evil to me. They're keeping secrets, yes, but I think we're missing something. Something big. You don't know the whole story."

"Are you suggesting there's a good reason for what he's done?"

Driscoll held up his hands. "I'm not saying that. I'm just saying it's worth finding out, isn't it?"

"Except he won't talk." I set down my drink on a nearby table. "He refuses to explain anything. He keeps secrets. Not just why he took the boys but how he's connected to the shadow court, my father's death. Everything."

Driscoll wrinkled his nose. "He didn't have anything to do with your father's death. You told me everything that sea princess said."

"No, but he tried to stop me from investigating it."

Driscoll looked at me like I was an idiot.

I crossed my arms. "What?"

"You know he was trying to protect you, right?"

His words struck me. "What are you talking about?"

A couple whirled by us, and Driscoll stepped forward to give them room. "I overheard some of the crew speaking about it, arguing about the whole thing and whether or not it was right what Bastian was doing.

Mia said he was just trying to protect you, to keep you from seeing something that would hurt you."

"Oh." I didn't know what else to say. It didn't make a difference ultimately. Maybe his feelings for me were real, but so what? That didn't prove he was good. Just that he had a heart. A rotten one.

"I'm just saying, it seems like whatever was between you and the pirate lord was . . . deep. Maybe there's still hope for you two, and if there isn't, then you deserve some closure. No offense, but you're kind of a mess when it comes to him."

I scoffed, then caught sight of a lone figure outside the window, out in the courtyard. So that's where he was. He lurked near one of the bubbling fountains.

"Go talk to him," Driscoll said. "I'll distract Leoni."

I narrowed my eyes at him. "Why are you doing this?"

"Maybe I'm a romantic." He sighed. "Maybe I . . . care. Liliath almost didn't get her happily ever after. If you have a chance at that with this pirate lord, even if it's a small one, I think you should take it."

I bit my bottom lip and shot a glance at Leoni, who was now dancing with a different man, not a care in the world. Closure. That would be nice. "Thank you," I whispered in Driscoll's ear before turning and strolling out the ballroom and toward the courtyard.

Chapter Thirty-Two

A stone path wound through the courtyard, lined by sculpted hedges, their edges so neat and crisp. The hedges created different pathways that all led to a fountain, which sat in the center of the space. Spirit Earth rose up in the middle of it, hair made of vines, arms made of tree bark, petals scattered across her skin like clothing. The water poured from a watering can that she held and flowed down into the stone fountain. Bastian sat on the edge, hat lying at his side, and I made my way to him, sinking down next to him.

"Did you do it?" he asked. "Get the pixie dust?"

"Bastian, it's Liliath's wedding day. I need to at least give her some time with her husband before I start demanding things."

"You know that pixie dust is mine, right?" He jumped to his feet, stalking toward the tall hedge maze. He disappeared into it.

I rose and followed him. "I'm aware."

He whirled, and I almost bumped into him. His gaze raked over my bare shoulders and down my dress like a slow caress.

"Yes?" I asked.

"I—" He paused. "I've never seen you in a dress before." He reached out a hand. "Never seen your hair curled like this."

It cascaded down my shoulders, twined with ribbons that matched my dress.

Just another reason why our relationship had been rooted in fantasies. Bastian never saw me in a dress because he'd never been able to attend a ball with me. Would've been arrested on sight.

My mood soured. "This was a mistake." I turned to go and Bastian gripped my arm.

"May I have this dance?"

I paused, his grip still firm. I shouldn't. Leoni would kill me. Mia and Kara would kill Bastian. There were a million reasons not to do this. Yet with his voice so soft, so vulnerable, I couldn't make myself care about a single one.

I slowly turned. "There's not any music."

"I don't need music. Just you in my arms."

His gaze bored into me, and I swallowed, letting him place his hand in the small of my back.

He stepped backward, and I followed his lead. "The pirate lord knows how to dance?"

His voice dropped low. "The pirate lord knows how to do many things. As you well remember."

A flush crept up my neck. "The dancing, Bastian. Let's focus on the dancing."

His eyes gleamed wickedly. "My mother taught me."

It was so odd to think about Bastian Lore, feared pirate lord of the Dark Seas, having a mother. But of course he did.

"She and my father used to dance every night when he'd get home from working at the docks. He'd sweep her up in his arms and whisk her around the room while my sisters and I watched." Bastian lifted our joined hands above his head and spun me around, then whirled me back into his arms, the whole exchange leaving me breathless.

"Okay, Bastian Lore," I said in a teasing tone. "You really do know how to dance."

He swayed me from side to side. "I always thought it was silly, truth be told. My dad dancing with my mom. Especially because he hated it. Had two left feet. Couldn't keep any kind of rhythm. I asked him why he did it one day, and he told me it was because it made her happy."

Pain reflected in his dark brown eyes.

"That's really sweet," I said.

"Aye."

"That must have been hard, losing your parents when those pirates raided your town."

"It was hard. One of the hardest things I've ever been through. Right before one of the pirates shoved a sword through his gut, my father told me to always look after my sisters, to protect them at any cost." Bastian swallowed. "And my mother, well, right before they slit her throat, she told me not to forget to dance."

Tears welled in my eyes. "She wanted you to remember the joys in life."

He nodded as his hand flexed against my back, the smallest movement, but I felt it to my core.

He dipped me down, never faltering with his tight grip on me, and I thought about Liliath and Penn, how close they'd held each other in that ballroom, the same way Bastian was holding me right now.

Against all odds, those two found their way to each other. Maybe Bastian and I could do the same. Maybe it was naive and foolish and wishful thinking, but I couldn't help but wonder . . . what if? What if there was an explanation for all of this?

"Bastian," I whispered as he pulled me upright again. "The wall you're putting up . . ."

He cocked his head. "Are you trying to tell me you want to climb me? Because I'm very amenable to that."

I gave him a small shove. "Please tell me what's going on. Tell me the truth about the boys you took, your connection with the shadow court."

His shoulders tensed under my hand.

"Before you say no, just listen. You've kept secrets from me for your own reasons, and part of me wants to hate you for it. But I can't because something in my gut is telling me there's still hope." I cupped his cheek with my hand, and he closed his eyes. "There's hope when you dance with me under the stars. There's hope when you dive into the sea to save me, even though you're terrified of the water. There's hope when you try to protect me from seeing my father's bones on a beach."

Bastian opened his eyes again. "Love—"

I came to a stop and drew his hand down to my chest, where my heart beat in a steady rhythm.

"It might be stupid, but I believe you're a good man. I don't believe you're this cold-hearted pirate everyone's made you out to be. That's not the Bastian I know. So if there's a reason why you had to do what you did, then tell me. Let me in, Bastian. You don't have to shoulder this burden all on your own. Let me help. Let me be your partner in this."

His chest heaved, and I could see the faint blue lines starting to spread down from his neck. His illness. We needed to get that pixie dust so it no longer plagued him.

"We can figure this out together," I continued. "Whatever it is. You just have to trust me."

He stared at where his hand was pressed, his fingers twitching against my bare skin. "It's not that simple," he said, voice quiet. "I—I've wanted to tell you so many times, but . . . I failed to protect my sisters. I failed to keep them away."

I covered his hand with mine. "What do you mean? They followed you. They tracked you. That wasn't your fault."

"Because I was weak," Bastian said. "Because I couldn't stay away. I let rumors grow about me, gossip spread, hoping they would come after me. Now they're stuck on my ship, living a life they don't want, constantly in danger."

"Bastian, they love you. Even if you hadn't made it easy for them to find you, they would've come after you. You can't blame yourself for that."

He rubbed his jaw. "I can't make that mistake again. Not with you. I won't."

I was losing him. I tightened my grip on his hand, pressing it deeper against my chest, willing him to feel my heart. "Trusting me isn't a mistake."

He dropped his forehead against mine, and we sank into a silence as I let him work through whatever he needed to in that moment. His breath was warm against my cheek, his sea-salt scent clinging to him.

"Okay," he finally said. "Bloody hells, I want to be strong, but . . ."

"Gabrielle!" an angry voice shouted out.

I whirled around to see Leoni and Driscoll standing in the opening of the hedge. But they weren't alone. A third figure stepped out of the shadows and into view: Queen Liliath. She was holding the vial of pixie dust. My stomach twisted. The empty vial.

Chapter Thirty-Three

Whatever connection we'd had broke in that instant. Bastian's hand dropped from my chest, and he gestured toward Liliath. "Your Majesty. I believe you have something that belongs to me."

Liliath stepped forward, her green eyes glittering, pale skin gleaming under the moonlight. As she walked toward us, her golden dress trailed on the ground behind her.

Driscoll sent an apologetic glance my way. "I tried."

Liliath held up the vial. "There's nothing left."

Bastian stood so still he could've been a statue.

"Bastian," I started, but he held up a hand, silencing me.

"Where is it?" he said, voice deadly. "Where's the dust?"

Liliath swallowed but didn't cower, her shoulders straight, her voice steady. "We used part of it, as I'm sure Gabrielle told you, to break the mirror my stepmother used to control our court."

His gaze snapped to me, lip curling. "That might've been important information to relay, love."

"And we disposed of the rest," Liliath finished. "Threw it into the sea so that it couldn't be used. We tend to be suspicious of dark magic as I'm sure you're aware."

Bastian's head tipped up. "Fuck me."

"What's going on?" Liliath asked, gaze flicking to me. "Why is he here? With you?"

"It's a long story," I said.

Bastian whirled on me, any semblance of the man I was just dancing with now gone.

"That was the one fucking thing I needed to save me, to save everyone on my gods-damned ship. I waited to use it, I waited because —" He let out a frustrated yell, and I stepped back. "Because I'm an idiot. A moron of the most colossal kind. I betrayed one of my closest friends to get that fucking dust." I had no idea who he was talking about. His voice became more agitated. "Bloody hells, I was stupid enough to actually believe I could be a different man." His voice darkened. "Whatever you and I had in that little cave on the edge of Apolis, you're right. It wasn't real. It was a fantasy, one that we can never realize."

Tears pricked my eyes. Leoni raised her hand, water swirling in front of her palm, and I shook my head.

"Let him speak." I worked to keep my voice steady and set my searing gaze on Bastian. "Go on. You were just telling me how everything between us was a lie?"

He shoved both hands through his hair and let out a scream that broke open something inside of me. I took a few tentative steps toward him and slowly reached for his hands.

"Bastian, let me in," I whispered.

Behind us, everyone's eyes widened, all of them rooted to their spots.

Bastian's muscles slowly loosened, some of the tension flowing out of him at my touch. I could get him back. It wasn't too late.

"You don't mean any of it. I know you don't." I paused. Now was my chance to ask. "Is it him?"

Bastian stilled. "Him?" he asked, a sharp edge to the word.

"Mia said something, that maybe the seafolk are in league with *him*, but she got interrupted and then Marian mentioned someone at the shadow court—"

Bastian stepped back. "Bloody hell." He looked at his leather boots, then he raised his head, and his eyes glittered dangerously. I'd lost him now. "We're done here." He turned to go.

"What are you talking about?" My fists curled at my sides. "We had a deal."

He whirled and threw out his arms. "And yet I don't have my fucking pixie dust, do I?"

"You promised you'd help rescue my brothers."

"Well, you didn't deliver on your end, so I'm not delivering on mine." He jabbed a finger toward his chest. "That's what kind of pirate I am. What kind of man I am."

"Bastian." My voice was pleading now. I'd get on my knees and beg him if I had to. "Please."

My words seemed to have no effect on him. "I'm not the good guy. Don't you get it? I'm not the man you want me to be, and I never will be. I was using you, love. I just needed the fucking dust. I wasn't going to help you rescue your brothers. I was going to get what I wanted and dump you at the next port."

The air left my lungs like I'd just been punched. "You don't mean that."

"I do." His jaw set in a hard line. "I'm leaving now. I'm going back to my ship, and you will never see me again. You'll never see your brothers again. Go back to Apolis, become queen, and forget about all of it. Forget about me."

My heart wrenched, but I refused to cry in front of him, to let him see the way his words were breaking me.

"You're a coward," I said.

He shook his head. "No. I'm worse." He surged forward and ripped his necklace from my neck. "I'm a monster."

"That's enough." Leoni stood behind Bastian, a sword of water aimed at his throat. "Leave. Now."

"Gladly," Bastian said.

An explosion rocked the sky above us, the ground shaking, leaves rattling in the hedges. The pirate lord threw his body over mine, and we tumbled to the ground. My back hit the hard stone, and I looked up to see fireworks exploding in the sky, brilliant colors popping and bursting, people cheering in the distance.

Driscoll grabbed Bastian and yanked him to his feet. "Get off of her!"

Bastian looked up, seeing the same fireworks everyone else did.

Right. Fireworks. For the wedding couple. Oh, spirits below. I was ruining Liliath's wedding.

"Just let him go," I said to Driscoll, who listened.

Bastian straightened his jacket, gave me one last contemptuous glance, and stalked past everyone and out of the courtyard.

"Should I have him arrested?" Liliath asked.

I should've said yes. Instead I stayed silent and held back the tears that threatened to erupt. This was Liliath's night, and I was not going to make it about me. "Let's get back to your celebration." I walked forward and linked my arm with hers.

"Gabrielle . . ." she started.

"Please," I said quietly.

She gave me a soft smile. "Okay, let's get back to my wedding, then."

We walked toward the castle, and I looked behind me, watching as the pirate lord walked away, and out of my life, for good.

Chapter Thirty-Four

I stayed in my room for the next two days.

I didn't want Bastian's words to hurt so much, but they did.

The bastard.

So instead of emerging from my assigned room at Liliath's castle, I hid away like a coward, ignoring all the knocking on my door, turning away servants and Driscoll and even Leoni.

So when a knock sounded at the door early that morning, I grabbed a fluffy pillow off my bed and hurled it toward the sound. "Go away, Driscoll. I don't want to hear any more dirty limericks. They're starting to get disturbing."

"It's me."

I sat up straighter in bed. Oh no. Things had gotten so bad they sent the queen to check on me. Whom I couldn't say no to. Yes, she was a friend, but she was also the ruler of Elwen, and I was staying in her castle. I couldn't deny her entry to my room.

"Can I come in?" Liliath said.

I rose from the bed, my bare feet padding against the cool wooden floors. I unlocked the door and opened it to see Liliath standing there, her black hair short and curling around her ears, which I still wasn't used to. As long as I'd known Liliath, her long hair had been her pride and joy, but the short cut suited her so well.

She set her green eyes on me and pursed her lips as she swept past me, the soft fabric of her light blue dress brushing against my arm.

"Well, this is . . . pleasant." She gestured to the closed drapes, the dark space, the clothes all over the floor. "Glad you're making yourself at home here." She walked toward the windows and threw open the curtains, sunlight barreling in. A view of green hills and tall trees spread out below. From here, I could even see the main town, spread out along a river. People darted in and out of shops, making their way along the cobblestone boardwalk with baskets hanging over their arms, full of eggs and bread and hard cheeses.

"That's better." Liliath spun and walked toward the four-poster bed, sinking down onto it and patting the space next to her.

I sat next to her, eyes still adjusting to the warm light that now bathed the room in its glow.

"You know," Liliath said. "When I was in the middle of a crisis, you're the one who made me feel better."

I scoffed. I hadn't known she was in a crisis at the time. She'd kept that from me. She'd kept a lot from me. "What could I have possibly done to help you?"

She swallowed. "You told me the truth about the pirate lord, how guilty you felt for falling for him. It made me feel less alone in my own guilt. It made me realize that none of us are perfect, Gabrielle. Though far too often, as rulers, we're expected to be. It's okay to not always be strong, to not always feel strong. Those are the moments that help us become who we're meant to be."

I dragged a toe in circles on the floor. "What if I don't want to become who I'm meant to be?"

"Then don't," Liliath said.

"It's not that simple." My hands twisted together in my lap. "I have to go back to Apolis as a failure. I have yet again let down my people, my mother, and now I'll be stepping into a role I don't even want."

With a broken heart on top of it.

"Who says?" Liliath grabbed me by the shoulders and gave me a shake. "You don't need the pirate lord to save your brothers."

"He knows the shadow court better than anyone. It's not about giving up, Liliath. It's about being realistic. I can't risk any more on some foolish journey I should've never taken in the first place." I looked up. "You know, I'm not even sure I did any of this for the right reasons. Part of me wonders if I just wanted one last adventure. That I was so desperate to delay becoming queen that I sailed away on a ship and pretended to be someone I'm not."

"And who is that?" Liliath tucked a black strand behind her ear.

"Normal?" I asked, and she laughed.

"You're many things, but normal definitely is not one of them."

I gave her a little shove.

Cracks webbed the walls, and roots hung from the ceiling. Dirt stains smattered various places on the walls and the ceiling. I'd kept it so dark in here that this was the first time I was noticing it. "Is this from your stepmother?" I pointed up. "From the damage she inflicted during her reign?"

Liliath nodded. "We're slowly rebuilding, but everything takes time."

I thought about that empty vial. "Why didn't you use the rest of the pixie dust to defeat your stepmother?"

"I didn't need to," she said simply. "She wanted to destroy me, and in return she promised she'd stop stealing everyone's magic. I didn't want to use dust and not know the price I'd have to pay when instead I could pay the price myself. It seemed fair after everything that had happened." Her gaze was stuck on a dark vine that slinked down the wall. "She destroyed herself in the end, and Penn and I realized it would be better to get rid of the dust and rid ourselves of the temptation to ever use it."

I didn't blame her.

"It's brave that you didn't give up. It's amazing how you saved your court." I turned toward the queen. "But I'm not you. My situation isn't the same. My father died trying to find my brothers. That could happen to me, and then I'd truly doom my court. I need to stop being selfish, to stop putting myself first."

"Or maybe that's exactly what you need to do. Driscoll and Leoni have told me a lot about what's happened over the last week, everything you've discovered. You know where to dock your ship, you know what the shadows are afraid of, you know that Mal and Lochlan are alive and okay." She paused. "Well, as okay as they can be."

"What's your point?" I twirled a long strand of hair around a finger.

"My point is that we have a library full of information, and our scholars have been working tirelessly to recover all the texts we have on the shadow court. I know Sorrengard is planning something, and I'm determined to be prepared." She gestured to the door. "Take a few days to research, to read, to gather information, and then decide if you want to go home to Apolis or go to the shadow court and save your brothers yourself."

That took me aback. "You don't think I should go home?"

She took a deep breath. "I don't think there's a right or wrong answer. I think the problem is that you can't commit either way. You're in Apolis, but your heart is elsewhere. Then you're finally free, and your mind is still back in Apolis, weighed down with guilt. Make a choice and then stop running from what you've left behind." She searched my face. "It's not a decision that has to be made right this minute. Like I said, we're uncovering more and more information about the shadow court every day, transcribing old texts from our ancestors, finding maps of the island. Maybe some of it might spark an idea, a plan. Or maybe it won't. Either way, you deserve peace with whatever decision you make. Don't go back to Apolis with your head hanging low." Her lips quirked. "Besides, Driscoll is already driving me crazy and he needs a distraction. Maybe helping you will be good for him."

I groaned. "I can't hear another one of his limericks."

She wrinkled her nose. "They're truly awful."

"He wants to make you proud, you know," I said.

"I can't believe he joined your voyage, that he boarded an actual pirate ship. I honestly can't picture it." Liliath let out a soft laugh.

"You know, shockingly, he's done okay. Other than the whining about his clothes getting wet, his hair getting wet, smelling like fish all the time, and the food tasting like dirt . . ."

"So basically . . . everything?" Liliath asked.

We burst into laughter. "Somehow he's made it work," I said when I'd finally caught my breath.

"Well, he doesn't have anything to prove. I just wish he understood that." Liliath stood, and I stood with her. She reached out and pulled me in for a hug. "I have a council meeting to get to, but just think about what I said?"

I nodded and watched as she walked toward the door, her words turning over in my mind.

Chapter Thirty-Five

The next day, I sat in the massive library, made out of the biggest tree I'd ever seen. It was such a unique space that I had trouble concentrating on any of the books sitting in front of me, instead letting my gaze constantly wander. Tufts of fluffy green moss sprouted in between the shelves and trellises of flowers hung down the walls. A skinny pair of spiral staircases swept upward to a second level, filled with even more shelves of books.

Tables filled the first level, bouquets bursting with bright colors sitting on each one as centerpieces. I reached out and let my finger trail across a flower petal. Blood and water, how did anyone get reading done here?

"Help has arrived!" Driscoll stood in the open circular entrance of the library, his arms spread out wide.

Leoni was just coming down the stairs with an armful of books. She walked toward me, dumping the books on the table. "This is everything I could find on the shadow court."

Driscoll approached and pulled out a chair. It scraped across the ground and he sank into it. "Did anyone hear that I arrived? I at least expected a few claps, maybe some cheers."

Leoni ignored him, flipping through the pages of the thick green book in front of her.

"Is shorty in a mood?" Driscoll pointed his thumb at her.

"You know I can hear you," she said.

Driscoll raised his eyebrows. "Oh, now you're speaking to me?"

"She's mad at me, not you," I told Driscoll.

After she'd caught me with Bastian out in the courtyard, she'd sunk back into her terse mood.

Leoni slammed her book shut. "Yes, I am mad at you. Thank you for finally acknowledging it."

I leaned back in my chair. "Out with it, then. Why hold back? Let your feelings go so we can move on."

Leoni pushed up the sleeves of her tunic. "Oh, you want me to let it go?"

Driscoll's gaze bounced between us. "Normally, I'd live for this sort of thing, but maybe not in the library."

Leoni jabbed a finger at me. "You snuck out to see the pirate lord and were dancing with him. His hand was in between your breasts. Were you about to have sex with him? Right there in the hedges?"

"What if I was?" I snapped. "How does it affect you that I'm having sex with the pirate lord? Which I'm not, by the way, nor have I since he broke my heart."

Driscoll's mouth hung open while Leoni fumed. Scholars who stood on the second floor frowned down at us.

"How does it affect me?" Leoni scoffed and stood. "How does it affect your captain of the guard?" She tapped her chin. "Hm, let's think about this for a moment. It's my job to protect you. To keep you safe. But you constantly put yourself in unsafe situations."

I stood as well, placing my palms flat on the table. "Oh, so you think I'm incapable of taking care of myself without you? I'm thirty years old, Oni, not a child."

"And yet, I'm constantly getting you out of the messes you make of your life. Including this one! I told you it was a bad idea. I told you not to do this."

I clenched my teeth so hard my jaw hurt. "And I told you not to come! You're the one who said none of this was my fault. That I was following my heart and you couldn't blame me for that."

Leoni threw her hands up in the air as a few scholars shushed us. "Yes, because back then you'd been naive to his schemes. But this time, you knew. You knew what he did, and still you go back to him again and again and again." Her face twisted into a grimace. "I can't understand that."

Driscoll traced a finger along the table. "In her defense, he is incredibly hot."

Tears welled in Leoni's eyes. "I think about our poor boys, scared and alone on that island."

"They're not alone," I said, voice shaking. "They have Mal and Lochlan looking after them. I know they're looking after them."

"Still, he did that. How could you allow him back into your . . ." she trailed off.

"Vagina?" Driscoll offered.

We both glared at him.

"I'm just going to read my book." He opened up one of the books Leoni had dropped on the table, eyes scanning the random page he flipped to.

"I don't know, okay?" I burst out. "I'm as horrified by my actions as you are, but . . . there's something there, Oni. I can't explain it. It's this gut feeling that there's a reason behind his actions."

"Yes, of course there is." The bun on Leoni's head bobbed as she nodded. "He's an evil psychopath."

"No, that's not what I mean." I bit my lip. "There's a spark of the Bastian I knew left in him, and I feel like he's trying to push that Bastian down, to hide him away. Like he's pretending to be this horrible pirate lord."

Leoni shook her head. "Because you want him to be that man. But he's not. He never will be. He told you so himself."

My heart twisted at her words. "I'm sorry," I said quietly. "For everything."

Leoni's gaze softened, and she huffed, then opened her arms wide. "Well, come here."

I rushed into her arms, resting my chin on her head.

"Wait, that's it?" Driscoll asked. "You guys have made up?" He flipped a few more pages. "Well, that was anticlimactic."

"Now let's get to work," I said, sniffling. "We need to find a way to rescue our boys."

She stiffened. "Is that why you asked me to find all these books?"

I gave a hesitant nod, not sure how she'd take that. "We don't need the pirate lord." I thought about what Liliath had said. "We can do this ourselves. Make a plan and go get them back."

I expected some pushback, but Leoni just nodded, sat down, and opened up a book. "Then let's get reading."

Relief swept through me. I would do this alone if I had to. But I was glad that wouldn't be the case. I sank into my chair and reached for one of the books.

"Finally," Driscoll said. "While you two were yammering on, I've been here reading this page about human towns that have been destroyed. Boring, yada, boring, boring, boring." He put a finger on the page. "Hyamia, Traymis, Rigahan, Karstan, Aramis, Polotzia, Ferio—"

"Wait, what did you say?" I straightened in my chair.

Driscoll rolled his eyes. "You're not going to make me read that again, are you?"

"What was the place you said that started with an *A*?"

He looked back at the page, finger trailing over the words. "Aramis?" he asked.

"Why does that sound so familiar?" I mulled over the name. "Someone told me about that town."

Leoni slowly closed her book. "Well, the only humans we've spent time with have been the Lost Boys, so it would probably be one of them."

My eyes widened as it came to me. "Mia," I said. "She said that's where she, Kara, and Bastian were from. When was it destroyed?" I asked Driscoll.

He sighed like my question was the biggest inconvenience possible. "Uh . . . about eighty years ago. Pirates raided the town and razed it to the ground, I guess." He wrinkled his nose. "Why do we have these records, anyway? What do the human lands have to do with us?"

I stared at the book while Leoni answered, "All the courts keep records like this. It's important to document big events like entire towns being destroyed."

"Eighty years." I shook my head. "How did Bastian, Mia, and Kara grow up in a town destroyed eighty years ago?"

Driscoll and Leoni looked at each other, both of them with furrowed brows and confused expressions that likely matched my own.

"But that's not possible," Leoni said. "Bastian looks to be thirty-five, at the oldest."

"He's thirty-three," I murmured, my mind unable to comprehend what I was hearing. "Maybe it's a mistake in the book? Or maybe there's more than one place called Aramis?"

"Well, then there'd be a record, right?" Leoni asked, voice unsure.

"Right." I shot a look at some of the scholars, still up on the second floor, shoving thick texts into the shelves. "Maybe we can ask one of them?"

"Well, that is their job." Driscoll stood. "I'll do it."

My heart pounded in my chest. "Okay, yes. Good plan. I'm sure we're somehow mistaken about this."

We weren't.

"There's no other human town named Aramis?" I asked as Driscoll stood over me.

"Nope. I asked them to check their records multiple times, which they were very huffy about, by the way." He slipped back into his chair.

Leoni's frown deepened. "What in the bloody waters is going on? How are the pirate lord and his sisters from a town that was destroyed eighty years ago? That's not possible."

I drummed my fingers on the pages of the book in front of me, which I'd barely had a chance to start reading.

"No one can live that long," Leoni said. "Unless he's using dark magic? But I can't even imagine the price he'd pay for such a thing."

"Or why he'd want to." Driscoll shuddered.

"It's not possible . . ." I trailed off as my gaze caught on a paragraph in the open book in front of me.

The shadow court has a dark history of taking people's shadows in secret, directly in violation of the treaties they signed with the other six courts of Arathia. Many believe they were stealing people's shadows for years in preparation for the Shadow War, in which they attacked Arathia, waging war on the other courts. Ultimately, the courts won and banished a

My heart pounded, blood rushing to my head. Dizziness overtook me, and I needed a moment to catch my breath.

"What's wrong?" Leoni leaned forward. "Are you okay?"

I blinked a few times, the realization slowly hitting me. "Bastian doesn't have a shadow," I said, then thought back to all my interactions with his crew. So many of them had mentioned feeling trapped. Mia, Bartholomew, even Cook had said something to that effect. "I don't think anyone on his crew has a shadow."

"That can't be," Leoni said. "They'd be trapped in Sorrengard, with everyone else who doesn't have a shadow."

My brows furrowed as I thought back to every conversation I'd had with Bastian, every hint, every vague statement. "I don't know. I don't have the answers, but I don't think I'm wrong about this."

My hand went to my chest as I felt for Bastian's necklace before remembering he'd taken it back.

Leoni and Driscoll both sat across from me with their mouths hanging open.

"It's the only explanation," I said. "That tyrannical lord Bastian told me about, maybe it's some ruler who's risen up in the shadow court and forces Bastian and his crew to do his bidding."

"Or her bidding," Driscoll said.

"This is all just conjecture," Leoni said. "We don't know that's what's happening here. Besides, how could we have missed that they don't have shadows? Surely we would have noticed something like that."

I thought back to our journey. "Except it's been cloudy almost the entire time."

She drummed her fingers on the table. "You and Bastian had a year-long affair."

"And we always met in a cave." His idea. Blood and water.

My thoughts trailed off once again, going in a thousand different directions. "Bastian's illness." I pounded my hands on the table, making Driscoll jump in his chair. "Did either of you notice any blue lines on the other crew members?"

"Wait a minute. I did notice that." Driscoll said. "Thought I was drunk out of my mind."

"Well, you were," Leoni said.

"It's all connected," I slammed my book shut. "It has to be."

"So?" Leoni sat back and crossed her arms. "Who cares what secrets the pirate lord harbors? This isn't even what we're supposed to be researching. We need to find out more about the shadow court, things we don't already know."

"The pirate lord knows the most about the shadow court."

"Are you kidding me?" Leoni asked.

Driscoll stretched out his hands. "Let's just calm down."

"We can't do this again! Did you hear Bastian the other night? He wants nothing to do with you. The deal is off, he said. And then he stalked away and out of your life forever."

"Well, after he tackled her to the ground," Driscoll said. "That was kind of romantic, even if it was just fireworks he was saving her from."

"That's it." I leaned forward. "He's trying to protect me. He's always been trying to protect me." Excitement thrummed in my veins. "He's keeping these secrets because he doesn't want me to get hurt. This lord, whoever took his shadow, I think he's a bigger threat than we realize. And finding out his identity is the key to saving my brothers, all the boys. I'm sure of it."

Leoni scowled. "If Bastian can't even get back his own shadow, then what help do you think he'll be?"

"I don't know," I said. "But we have to find out."

"Spirits below," Driscoll said. "It sounds like you want to go after the pirates."

I stood. "We have to."

"Why?" Leoni asked, exasperation filling her voice.

"Because I love him," I said. "Because I love him, and I'm not going to run from that. My gut is telling me that Bastian isn't bad. That there's an explanation for all of this. And now I'm even more sure of it. He's been pushing me away to protect me. Before you all interrupted us in those hedges, he was so close to telling me the truth." I shook my head, thinking about my conversation with Liliath. "I'll never forgive myself if I don't pursue this, if I don't find out the truth once and for all. Our boys, my brothers, my father, they deserve answers too." I spread my arms wide. "All those trapped people whose shadows have been taken do. The pirate lord is our best chance, I'm sure of it. Somewhere along the way, I think Bastian lost his drive, his purpose. I'm going to find him and remind him of it."

"Damn, that's romantic," Driscoll said. "Okay, you convinced me." He raised his hand. "I'm in."

"You're going to come with me?" I asked. "Back to the ship?"

"I don't think I've proven myself enough yet." He shrugged a shoulder. "I said I was going to help you save your brothers, and I'm going to see that through."

We both looked at Leoni, who threw her hands up in the air. "Of course I'm going to come. But you better be right about the pirate lord, or I swear, I will drag you from his ship and back to Apolis and have you chained to your bed."

"That's a little kinky," Driscoll said, and Leoni elbowed him, but I didn't miss the quirk to her lips.

"Deal," I said, then started walking toward the entrance to the library.

"Where are you going?" Leoni called.

"To pack," I yelled over my shoulder. "We have a pirate lord to find."

Part Three

"Second to the right, and straight on till morning."

Chapter Thirty-Six

"Fucking fuck fuck," Driscoll said, kicking the mast. "Ow!" He hopped on one leg. "Damnit!"

"How's it going, Driscoll?" I said from where I sat on the small boat Liliath had loaned us for our journey.

Leoni smirked.

"How's it going, Driscoll?" he mimicked as he yanked at the rope that ran up the length of the mast and connected to the sails. "Not well. You know, you two could offer to help."

"We did," I pointed out.

"Several times," Leoni said. "And you told us that you could handle it."

Driscoll grumbled something under his breath that sounded suspiciously like "pain in my ass."

The boat was much, much smaller than Bastian's ship, but with only three of us, it was all we could handle. We'd been on the boat for three days now and were close to Porth, where we hoped to dock and get information about the Lost Boys. I had no idea where they'd gone, and it was almost impossible to track them. So we'd had to rely on good old-fashioned maps. Driscoll finally managed to get the sails fully open, and now they billowed in the wind while Leoni managed the tiller, steering us as I searched the map.

Driscoll dropped down and opened one of the books we'd brought with us about the shadow court.

"We should be close to Porth." My finger traced along our route on the map. "We'll keep our ears open for any recent pirate sightings, and we'll discreetly ask those who come in contact with the most people." I ticked off my fingers. "Barmaids, innkeepers, dock workers. Someone will have had to heard of something."

"I hope so," Leoni said, looking down at the battered boat, wood splintering and peeling. "Because this little vessel is only going to take us so far, and we've been extremely lucky with mild weather. If a storm hits, we're done for."

"Shh." Driscoll looked up from his book. "Are you trying to tempt the spirits?"

"I'm being practical," Leoni said and pinned her gaze on me. "And once we do find Bastian, if you can't get him to open up and finally tell you the truth, then we're done with him for good."

My gaze strayed out to the calm sea, nothing but sapphire blue surrounding us. She was right, even if it was hard to hear. I couldn't keep chasing after Bastian, trying to force him to open up. I was coming into this armed with new information, but if he still wouldn't let me in, then that would be my answer that I needed to let him go. For good. I hoped I could get through to him now that I strongly suspected he and his crew didn't have their shadows, were bound to the shadow court in some way that I didn't understand.

"You know," Driscoll said, book open in his lap, "this isn't actually so bad. The open sea, the feel of the wind in my hair, the adventure of it all. I think I'm starting to like this."

"Really?" I asked. "Because just moments ago, you were cursing loud enough for all of Arathia to hear."

"I'm not letting you dampen my mood." Driscoll's gaze dropped to the book. "I am powerful. I am adventurous. Hear me roar—"

Leoni splashed him with water.

Driscoll stuck out his tongue at her and continued reading his book. "Hey, check this out. Did you know that a person is bound wherever their shadow gets taken from?"

I straightened. I hadn't known that. I'd thought everyone was stuck in the shadow court if their shadows got taken. This made even more sense, though. Bastian and his crew clearly weren't stuck in the shadow court.

Driscoll frowned. "And did you two know the pixies were created by the Seven Spirits to be their servants?" He kept reading. "The spirits used them for errands, to carry out punishments, to hand out gifts, to summon the people of the Old World to them. They even gave the pixies their dust so they could use magic if needed." He kept reading. "The pixies can use their dust for anything they wish." He glanced up at us. "Can you imagine? Just being able to do anything with your magic, not being limited to our elements?" He glanced back down, frowning. "But every time they use their dust, it takes years off their life. That was the price the spirits put on their magic. Wow. Mind. Blown."

Leoni wrinkled her nose. "I definitely knew all of that. Did you not pay any attention in your schooling?"

Driscoll snapped the book shut. "No. Who pays attention in school?"

Leoni nearly fainted at that.

Booms filled the air in the distance, sounds of yelling and clanging ringing out.

I frowned. "What is that?" I studied the map in my lap. "Are we closer to Porth than I realized?"

"If we are, something is going down, and I'm not sure I want to be part of it." Leoni arched her neck, and a gust of wind blew some of her gold-red hair from her bun.

"I vote we turn around," Driscoll said.

"What happened to 'hear me roar'?" Leoni asked.

"That was when it was just me and a boat and the ocean," Driscoll hissed. "Not something that sounds like a cannon shooting from a ship."

I perked up at that, and Driscoll eyed me. "Oh no, she has a look on her face. Like she's set her mind on something."

"What if it's Bastian's ship?" I asked. "I mean, how many ships have we seen on these seas that have cannons like that?"

Another boom rattled the air.

Driscoll looked up at the sky. "Why did I have to open my mouth?"

"Because that's what you do," Leoni said. "You open your mouth and inevitably something comes out that you regret."

"Is she always this mean?" Driscoll asked me.

"Believe it or not, it means she likes you."

He scoffed. "Well, in that case, she must really like me."

Leoni just smirked.

A loud crash split the air, and all our heads snapped up.

"So you're wanting me to go toward that sound?" Leoni asked.

I stood, shading my eyes and squinting. I could just make out two ships far in the distance.

"Yes," I said.

"Here we go," Leoni said. "You better hope we don't find ourselves in the middle of an attack."

"Well, if we do, we always have our magic," I said.

"Oh yes, that'll work well against cannons," Driscoll said. "I'll just grow a flower in my hand and hope that saves me."

I stepped forward, trying to make out the ships, to see if I could recognize either one. "You wanted adventure. You're about to get a lot of it."

Leoni steered us closer, and my heart leapt into my throat when I recognized that billowing sail with the skull, a sword shoved through its eye sockets. We'd found them. Blood and water, we'd found them.

My excitement was quickly doused when I noticed the other ship, cannons mounted, ready to shoot right at the Lost Boys. We'd found them, but it might've already been too late.

<h1 style="text-align:center">Chapter Thirty-Seven</h1>

I didn't stop to think, didn't even question myself as my legs bent. It felt like slow motion as Leoni's eyes widened and she reached for me while Driscoll yelled out "No" as I jumped into the water.

Unlike the last time I'd jumped from a ship into the sea, I was prepared. I summoned my magic, willed the water to lift me in its gentle grasp before it could suck me down. I lifted my hands, and the water rose under me into a wave that curled gently and pushed me toward the boats.

"Have you lost your mind?" Driscoll shouted after me while Leoni yelled, "Get back here right now!"

I stood on shaky legs and braced myself, hands out as I commanded the wave to take me to the Lost Boys.

"Prepare to fire!" a voice yelled from the ship opposite Bastian's.

"No," I said, urging the wave to go faster. I'd been gone for three days, and they'd already managed to get themselves into an all-out attack.

I had no doubt the Lost Boys could win, but at what cost? I didn't want to find out. I was close enough now that I could see Bastian standing with a sword pointed toward the enemy ship, his crew grabbing long planks and stretching them to the other ship, ready to go and fight. Mia stood beside Bastian, yelling something at him as he cut his hand through the air to silence her.

She turned her head and spotted me, her mouth dropping open. She pointed a shaky finger in my direction, and Bastian's head slowly turned, his eyes widening.

"Stop," I yelled, waving my arms as the wave brought me between the two ships. "Stop, please!"

The captain of the enemy ship looked down at me. "What in the bloody hell is this? Get out of the way," he said. "Or you'll get blasted to pieces."

I brought up my hands, telling the wave to push me higher, and the man's eyes widened, like he was just realizing I was using magic.

"She's an elemental," he said to his men.

"Yes, the princess of the water court, if you want to get specific," I said. "You sure you want to kill me and risk bringing down the wrath of the courts upon you?"

Given how ardently they wanted to avoid conflict, I wasn't at all sure the other courts would avenge my death, but he didn't need to know that.

"Fucking hell," he said, scratching his gray bearded jaw. "What are you doing here? Why is a princess of the water court interfering in human business?"

"Because I have a vested interest in the Lost Boys."

I shot a look behind me to catch the murderous gaze in Bastian's eyes, while the rest of the crew stood behind him, gaping at me.

"Why are you attacking them?" I asked. "What did they do to you?"

"They took my son," he growled.

That stopped me. "W-what?"

"They kidnapped him and are keeping him aboard. We've heard the rumors. We know their dealings with the shadow court. That anyone they take there is never seen again." He stepped forward. "I just want my son back."

I raised my chin. "And if I can get your son? Will you stop this attack?"

He eyed me warily and glanced at the cannons pointed toward his ship. "You have one hour. One hour we attack and get my son back."

Bastian knew what he was doing. He was a skilled captain, and I doubted he or his crew were in danger. But I didn't want to see any blood spilled, including from the men on this ship.

Leoni and Driscoll waved at me from the distance.

"What are you doing?" Leoni shouted, voice echoing over the water.

"I'll get your son back," I said to the captain. "One hour."

He gave a stiff nod. I turned and thrust out my hands, the tall wave delivering me straight to Bastian's ship and spitting me out at his feet.

"You've got to be fucking kidding me," Bastian said.

Mia helped me to my feet. "You shouldn't have come back," she whispered.

I shook her off and straightened. "We need to talk," I said to Bastian.

"You need to get off my ship." His eyes blazed. "Now."

I stood my ground. "I'm not leaving until we have a chat. You can throw me off, but I'll come back again and again and again."

He raked a hand through his hair. "You are a fucking pain in my ass, you know."

"Is that a yes?" I asked.

The vein above his temple throbbed as he gestured toward his cabin. "Inside. Now," he growled and spun on his heel, not waiting for me.

Mia's face paled as she stared after her brother, his black trench coat flapping behind him. "I hope you know what you're doing, Princess."

I took a deep breath and followed him. I hoped so too.

Chapter Thirty-Eight

I closed the door to his cabin as Bastian settled against his desk and crossed his muscled arms over his chest. "Well?" he asked in a flat tone.

"I'm going to rescue my brothers with or without you."

"You can't rescue your brothers without me," he gritted out. "It's a suicide mission."

"See, I don't think so." I took a few steps forward. "I think you want me to believe it's a suicide mission."

"Why would I want you to believe that?"

"Because you don't want me to get hurt," I said softly, and his jaw ticked for just a second, but it was enough to give me the courage to go on. "I think you're protecting me from the shadow court, a specific person in the shadow court, if I'm correct."

A mischievous grin overtook his lips. "Or maybe I'm just as much of an asshole as everyone says I am."

"But everyone doesn't say that," I said. "See that's the other thing. You're the most feared pirates on the Dark Seas. Yet in our time together, I haven't seen you pillage, attack, raid, anyone. I think your bard spins quite the tales about you, tales that bolster your fearsome reputation."

Bastian quirked a brow. "Barty's not that creative. And I've been on my best behavior." His eyes dipped down to between my legs. "Well, mostly."

I wouldn't let him use his charms to distract me. Not this time. I ignored the heat that pooled where his gaze was set, forging on. "I see the way your crew respects you, cares for you. They're not cold-blooded killers. Mia? Kara?"

"I told you that it's my fault they're here. I try to spare them from as much as I can."

I took another step toward him. "But you couldn't keep them from losing their shadows along with the rest of you. That's what happened, right? They came to find you and their shadows got taken too. That's how they became trapped on this ship."

He stilled; the only movement was his chest as it rose and fell. "That's not possible, love."

"Well, then let's go check." I gestured outside. "It's a sunny day. Let's just see if you have a shadow."

He clenched his teeth, then straightened. "Fine." He spread out his arms. "You figured it out. We don't have our shadows. Haven't had them for sixty years."

My brows drew together. "Since the Shadow War?"

"That's right. And I don't have to explain a damn thing to you."

"Don't you get it?" I swiped some hair from my eyes. "You can't stop me from going to the shadow court. My best chance at survival, at saving my brothers, is you. If you won't help, then I'll go alone. It's your choice, Bastian. But I'll tell you this: I will not work with you until you tell me the entire truth about your past, about why you took our boys. Everything, Bastian. If you're not willing to do that, then I'll march back to our little boat and sail away to Sorrengard with Driscoll and Leoni."

He looked up at the ceiling, Adam's apple bobbing as he swallowed. "You're the bane of my existence. You know that?" He finally let out a long breath and gestured toward the bed. "Might as well sit and get comfy, then. It's a long tale. And, love? There's no going back."

With a confidence I didn't particularly feel, I strode toward the bed and sank down onto the edge. "I'm listening."

"Everything I told you about my childhood, finding the crew, my sisters, it was all true. But I left out a few key details. My age being one."

I tilted my head. "How old are you?"

"Ninety-five," he said. "I was fifteen when those pirates destroyed Aramis and killed my parents."

My mouth dropped open. I'd suspected as much but hearing him confirm it was something else. "How did it happen?" I asked.

"Remember when I told you about getting washed up on that island, finding the Lost Boys?"

I nodded.

"Well, we banded together, and we stole ourselves a ship. We began pirating, becoming exactly what I'd always abhorred. People feared us. It felt good. We pillaged, we raided, we drank, and we grew older and older. We kept on like that for over ten years. Rulers of the Dark Seas. Eventually, I wanted more. I'd heard rumors about the shadow court, that it was a place full of dark magic, mysterious items that had power. I'd also heard that no one who went there to steal those items came back out alive."

I tugged the end of my braid. "You were seduced by the challenge of it." I knew that feeling all too well.

"Aye. We all were, my whole crew. We'd grown arrogant, foolish. Reckless." He fingered the silver chain around his neck. "We didn't even plan. Just sat around drinking one night and someone mentioned the Shadow War, that it had severely weakened the shadow court. We decided that would be the best time to strike. That was that. We sailed to the island, anchored our boat offshore. The island was . . ." He trailed off, his eyes growing distant like he was back there again. "Beautiful. Tall palm trees, turquoise water. Black glittering sand."

I wrinkled my nose. "Where were all the people? The shadow people?"

"They live on a different part of the island, in the mountains. I've never seen any of them."

A chill skittered down my spine at that.

"We thought we'd found a paradise, and as we delved deeper into the jungle, we came across items scattered about. You could feel the power seeping from them. We were beyond excited. Couldn't believe we'd found the magic. We grabbed a few items and tried to leave. And that's when they attacked."

"Who?" I asked, pulse spiking.

"The shadows. They came down upon us, lifting some of us in the air and tossing us like rag dolls. They were so fast, like lightning. It was impossible to fight against them, but we did put up a good fight. We had torches and quickly figured out the shadows don't like the light. We were able to keep them at bay until it started raining. Jungle and all. I gather that happens quite often. Our fires went out and they descended."

"That's terrifying," I said.

"All I remember were the screams, and then nothing. I awoke in the jungle, these beings hovering over me and my men, skin tinted green, wings translucent and shimmering, teeth sharp. Pixies. I'd never heard of them, but I soon learned they wanted to talk, to make a deal on behalf of their boss."

My throat grew dry. "And who was their boss?"

"The shadow king."

Just the name caused the gooseflesh on my arms to rise. "The shadow king?"

But the shadow king had been killed during the Shadow War. Unless a new one had risen . . .

I opened my mouth to ask a question, but Bastian cut me off. "Before you ask, I don't know who he is, love."

"What were the terms of the deal?" I rubbed my arms, cold despite the humid air.

"Do you know how bodies get trapped? Why they can't age? Why they can't leave the island?"

I thought about what Driscoll had revealed from the books he'd read and nodded.

"The deal was simple," Bastian said. "This shadow king needed help collecting shadows." He held up his hand to stop me from asking the obvious question. "I don't know why. All I know was that he'd heard of us, and when we stumbled on his island, he knew he could use us. So we had a choice: let him take our shadows and bind ourselves to our ship, to him, or try our luck escaping the island, fighting through the shadows and the pixies. Wasn't much of a choice, I'm afraid." Bastian started pacing now, coat whipping behind him. "Truth be told, it didn't sound so bad. We wouldn't age, we'd be able to keep doing what we loved, and he was giving us free rein to take whatever magical items we wanted and sell them, use them, he didn't care."

"But what did he want in return?" A stone had settled in my stomach.

"Shadows," Bastian said simply. "We were to bring him a boy every month, any boy. He didn't care. All we had to do was drop them off on the island, and he'd take care of the rest."

My hand floated to my mouth. "So you've been doing this for . . . sixty years? Kidnapping children? Children, Bastian?"

His face was grim. "Yes. And I didn't say I kidnapped them."

I crossed my arms, waiting for an explanation.

"The shadow king told us to take orphans, boys that didn't matter, that no one would go looking for. Probably because he didn't want anyone to catch on to what he was doing." He took a deep breath. "The boys, they've created a home of sorts from what my friend has told me. A community, a place where they're happy on the island."

"Your friend?" I asked. "Is this the friend you mentioned who you betrayed? The one who gave you the dust?"

He nodded.

"Well your friend can't be correct," I said.

"It's what Goji says."

"How did you ever become friends with a pixie?"

"We started talking when I'd visit Sorrengard. Me on one side of the jungle, her on the other. She's the one who brings us the magical items that fill the jungle. We can't enter the jungle, what with all the shadows guarding it. So she throws the items onto the beach for us."

I couldn't believe he'd made friends with a pixie. We'd have to get more into that later.

"We did what the shadow king asked," Bastian said. "We looked for boys who had nothing, no one, to rely on. But we never kidnapped them. We told them the truth and gave them a choice. Some said no, but many said yes. Why wouldn't they? They had to fight for their lives every day, and we were offering them a place where they could be fed, clothed, never having to worry about anything again, and they'd get to meet other boys just like them."

I couldn't believe what I was hearing. "And through all of this you've never questioned what the shadow king wants? What does Goji say about these boys? How are they faring?"

He shrugged. "I told you, she said they're happy. That they've created a home, a life, for themselves. I don't even know if they are aware of the shadow king."

"Then what does he want?" My frustration at the lack of answers was growing.

Bastian let out an exasperated sigh. "I don't know, love. I've only seen the shadow king thrice in the sixty years since we made the deal. I can't even confirm it's the same person. Maybe he produces an heir, and that heir is raised to take over, to be the new shadow king. He has a castle at the top of the mountains that runs along the northern coast. It's walled off. It's where I assume those that are still part of the shadow court live. No one goes there, save for the pixies that are closest to the king, including Goji."

I tapped my chin. "You've seen him three times, you said. Tell me about that."

Bastian stopped, once again tugging at the chain around his neck. "The first was when he took our shadows. We all boarded our ship. And the shadow king appeared. He didn't look like us, not human or elemental. He was made of wisps and darkness, golden eyes sparking, the form of a man but not a man." Bastian shook his head. "He reached out to each one of us and gripped our shadows, ripping them away. A searing pain blasted through my body, like I was being split in two. Then it was over, and my shadow was flying off to the island, gone."

I peered at him. "What was the second time?"

"I think that's enough for now." Bastian strode to his desk and placed his hands on it, back to me.

I stood, walking to him. "What was the second time, Bastian?"

He spun suddenly, so close to me now, those brown eyes boring into me. "When he ordered me to take the boys of Apolis," Bastian finally said.

The ground rocked under my feet.

He scrubbed a hand down his face. "It was a punishment."

"For what?" I asked.

He gave me a look like it was the most obvious thing in the world. "For falling in love with you."

I stepped back, unsure I'd heard him right.

"I spent years on this ship, taking shadows, selling dark magic, and not caring a bit about any of it. I drank, I fought, I had dalliances, but I never truly lived." He reached out a hand and cupped my cheek. "Not until I met a feisty auburn-haired princess who saved me that day on the beach. I listened to your stories, your hopes, your dreams. You had this hunger for life that I hadn't had in over sixty years. You wanted to see the world, to experience so much, and for the first time in so long, I wanted those experiences too. I wanted them with you."

I couldn't speak, could barely breathe after that confession.

"From that day on, I thought I could be better. I decided I'd do everything in my power to get our shadows back, to break the shadow king's hold on us so that I could be with you in a way you deserved. For the entire year we were seeing each other, I didn't collect a single shadow, and I traveled all over the gods-damned world trying to find answers, a way that I could get my shadow back and break this fucking deal I made. It finally came from an unexpected source: Goji. She offered her pixie dust. I said no, knowing that it takes years from her life. There had to be another way. I'd boarded my ship to leave when the shadow king paid a visit." Bastian's throat bobbed. "He knew about you, knew about us, knew that I'd been neglecting my duties. He told me I was going to sail straight to Apolis that night and take all the boys. He didn't care how I did it, how I made it happen, but he said if I didn't return by morning, he'd kill my sisters by snuffing out their shadows."

I let out a gasp.

Bastian raked a hand through his hair. "I didn't know what else to do, love. So I asked Goji to get me an item, a magical one." He lifted the necklace that hung around his neck. "This clock. It lures whomever you tell it to."

"How?" I eyed it warily.

"Tick tock. Tick tock. Tick tock." Bastian dropped it and it thudded against his chest. "I sailed to Apolis, told the clock whom to summon, and it was that simple. It started ticking. The boys came. I took them to Sorrengard and dropped them off. They marched off into the jungle to be greeted by the boys who live there. That's when your brothers appeared and went after them before I could stop them. Goji found me, out of my mind with worry, and forced me to take the vial of dust."

Tears pricked my eyes, my heart so raw from hearing Bastian's story, I wasn't sure I could speak.

"Why would she give you the dust?" My voice shook with the single question.

He looked away. "Because I promised I'd help her escape the island. Pixies aren't bound to Sorrengard, but it's almost impossible to leave because of the shadows swirling around like a constant cloud. Goji wanted freedom, much like myself. We understood each other in that regard. She gave me the dust, which has the power to break dark magic. If we broke that binding, our shadows would come, and we could finally leave the damn ship without getting sick."

"The illness." I reached out and traced a finger down his chest as if I were tracing those blue lines, and he shuddered. "That was the illness. So there was never any elixir?"

He shook his head. "The minute we leave the place we're bound to, the illness starts, and it's slow, but it will kill you if you don't get back to where you're bound. That's why even if the boys escape the shadows, the island, they can't leave."

"So what happened with the pixie dust?" I shook my head. "You had it. Why didn't you take it right then and there?"

"I knew you were going to find out what I'd done. That was the shadow king's entire plan. He wanted to break us apart, for me to do something so horrendous you'd never forgive me, and I'd return to being his silent little sheep, doing his bidding. I didn't want to play his game anymore. I knew the seafolk had trailed us, were reporting everything back to you. I was afraid you wouldn't believe my side of it unless you saw the magic at work. I wanted you to see the pixie dust, to see the shadows return to us. So I decided to wait until we got back to Apolis to use it. I promised Goji we'd be back for her after it was all said and done, though she wasn't happy about it."

And then I'd gone and ruined all of that. Wrecked the ship, stole the dust, and told Bastian he needed to leave or the guards would be on him.

"Why didn't you tell me?" I shoved him. "Why didn't you explain everything when you saw me?"

His eyes shone with tears. "Because when I saw you, saw the pain I'd caused you, I'd given up, love. I'd realized it was a losing battle. That even if I somehow freed myself and my crew, the shadow king could come after you, hurt you, as a punishment for me breaking free. I realized it was selfish to dream of a life with you, selfish to have ever gotten involved with you in the first place. I needed you to hate me so that you'd leave me alone, and the shadow king would leave you alone in return. If I truly loved you, I had to let you go."

Tears streamed down my face. "Bastian . . ." I started, still so many questions, but I'd also gotten a lot of answers. More than I could have hoped for. And it broke my damn heart. I stepped forward and grabbed his hands. "I'm here now. You don't have to sacrifice yourself for me."

"Don't," he said as I brought his hands up to my lips and kissed his knuckles.

"I'm not going anywhere," I said.

"That's what I'm afraid of," he whispered before he let out a ragged breath. "I don't want the shadow king to find out about you. To use you against me so I'll keep doing his bidding. Look what he already took to hurt me. He can do so much more."

"So can I," I said. "He's going to regret striking out against Apolis. I'm going to make him regret it."

Bastian stroked my cheek with his hand. "My fierce princess."

I met his gaze, desire curling around me. "My fearsome pirate."

The world melted away, then, and it was just me and Bastian.

He dipped his head down, a question in his eyes, and I answered, tipping my head up. He brushed his lips against mine. The kiss started out slow, his mouth probing mine open. My hands winding up through his hair. His arms coming around my back and pressing me to him. Kissing him again after so long apart felt like a dream. It felt like coming home.

I moaned into him, and Bastian kissed me harder, nipping at my bottom lip, tongue sweeping across my mouth. This felt so fucking good. It was like taking a breath after being starved of air. His fingers trailed down my back. Heat skittered over me in the wake of his touch.

"I need more," I said, grabbing fistfuls of his shirt. "So much more."

The floor underneath us rumbled, and yells erupted outside Bastian's cabin right as the door banged open. We both sprang apart.

Mia stood there, glowering at us as sun haloed her. We both shielded our eyes for a moment, reality dousing the heat that had flooded between my legs. "If you two are done here, we're being attacked, in case you've forgotten?"

"Oh, blood and water." I had forgotten. Bastian and that tongue of his made me forget a lot of things.

Now, it all came back to me, and I sent an accusing look Bastian's way. "I thought you didn't kidnap boys?"

He looked sheepish. "One, we were desperate. And two, it's well known that young Cormac hates his father. He wanted to come with us."

"Well, little Cormac is going to have to work things out with his dad." I ran out of the cabin and past Mia.

"Where are you going?" Bastian yelled.

"To give back the damn boy you took," I said over my shoulder. "Just stay in there while I handle it, and then we're going to continue exactly where we left off."

Chapter Thirty-Nine

We didn't get to continue where we'd left off, and quite frankly, the absence of Bastian's tongue in my mouth was making me murderous.

I leaned against the railing of the ship, watching the blue waters whiz past as we sailed ever closer to Sorrengard, closer to my brothers. It would be a few weeks yet until our arrival, and I couldn't tell if I wanted to speed this ship up or slow it down.

"Approach slowly," Driscoll whispered from behind me. "Don't make any sudden noises or movements. Be gentle and use a soft tone when speaking to her."

"What is she, a wild animal?"

"I'm telling you, I've seen scorned women many a time, and I know how to treat them."

I held back a snort. Scorned. That about summed it up. After I'd saved Bastian, saved all the Lost Boys, from an attack and returned that boy to his father, Bastian had been all business. That familiar stone mask had slipped over his face, and he once again shut down. I thought we'd progressed past this, that once Bastian had opened up with the full truth, things would be different. But no. He'd spent those last few days hiding out in his damn cabin, avoiding me. Again.

"And I'm her best friend. I know what she needs."

"You both know I can hear you, right?" I asked, not bothering to turn around.

"You didn't listen," Driscoll said. "I told you to use a soft voice."

Leoni joined me at the railing. "How's it going?" Her tone was hesitant, like Driscoll was right and I was some wild animal she'd scare if she said the wrong thing or made the wrong move.

"I'm fine," I said. "I got what I wanted: the pirate lord's help saving my brothers. And the truth along with it."

I'd told Leoni and Driscoll the long, sordid tale, and they'd been just as horrified as I was.

"I don't think that's all you want from the pirate lord." Driscoll stood on my other side now, waggling his eyebrows.

"It doesn't matter what I want."

A pod of dolphins swam in the water alongside the ship, their gray bodies so sleek and majestic. I could spend all day watching them, standing here, just taking in the beauty of it all.

"I told you talking to her was a bad idea," Driscoll said over my head to Leoni.

"You need to snap out of it," Leoni said. "We're going to Sorrengard. We're entering this mysterious island run by a mysterious shadow king whom we know nothing about. Shadows will be attacking us. Pixies will be attacking us, and through it all, we somehow have to reunite the boys with their shadows."

"Well, when you put it like that, sounds like a walk on the beach," Driscoll muttered.

Leoni tapped her chin. "One part of the story I still don't understand is why the shadow king wants boys."

"Boys are malleable," Driscoll said. "Think about it. If he was kidnapping grown men and women, they'd be storming his castle, constantly trying to escape, constantly trying to get answers about what he was doing. They'd plot against him. They wouldn't just bow down."

"Wow," I said. "That's a really good point."

"It is," Leoni agreed. "He's smart. Taking orphans who have nothing to lose, who will see the shadow court as a paradise instead of a prison. But why not any girls?"

We all fell into silence at that, none of us having any answers.

I sunk my head into my arms and let out a groan. "What was I thinking?" I said. "Why did I ever think this would be a good idea?"

"Because you're reckless," Leoni answered.

"Thanks," I said.

"But also brave. You're attempting what no one has before."

I lifted my head and looked up at the blue sky.

"Listen," Driscoll said. "It's clear Bastian is obsessed with you. And I'm sorry he blue-balled you."

A crew member passed us, frowning as he overhead Driscoll.

He kept walking, and Driscoll yelled after him, "Metaphorically speaking! She doesn't have actual balls."

"Why don't you just talk to him?" Leoni asked.

My fingers curled around the railing. "You mean for the hundredth time? You want me to go to him and once again beg him to what? Love me back?"

Leoni let out an exasperated sigh. "I meant maybe ask him why he's avoiding you."

I threw up my arms. "I'm tired of being the one who has to go to him. He knows how I feel. And I know how he feels. He's being stubborn and hardheaded and a complete idiot."

"He's trying to protect you," a voice said from behind us.

I turned to see Mia standing there, that yellow bandana tied around her head.

"We'll give you guys a moment." Leoni clapped her hand on my shoulder and nodded her head at Driscoll, who stayed rooted to his spot, gaze bouncing between me and Mia. "Driscoll," Leoni snapped.

"Oh, fine. You ruin all my fun." He followed Leoni as they walked toward the other side of the ship while Mia stepped up next to me.

"I know he's protecting me," I said. "But I'm a grown woman. I don't need protecting, and I'm tired of chasing after him. A woman can only be rejected so many times."

Mia turned, leaning her back against the railing, elbows perched on it. "You know, I tried to hate you. When Bastian first told me about you, I couldn't believe what I was hearing. My big brother, the formidable pirate lord, had fallen for some princess?" She peered at me. "But I get it.

You're two sides of the same coin. You both crave adventure, you both live for danger and excitement, and you both carry so much guilt, so much responsibility, on your shoulders. Bastian is at war with himself," Mia said softly. "He blames himself for me and Kara getting trapped on this ship with him. He blames himself for making that deal with you, for involving you in this and sucking you into his world."

My brows furrowed. "How did your shadows get taken?"

She took a breath. "Kara and I tracked him to Sorrengard. It's where we found his ship. He was delivering some boy to the shadow court. We were horrified when we found out, tried to go after the boy, save him from what was about to happen. And we did. We got him before he crossed through that jungle. We gave him our boat to escape, but we didn't realize how we'd fucked over Bastian and his crew in the process. We boarded Bastian's ship, ready to tell him the truth, but the shadow king had already found out what we'd done. I think the pixies might have told him."

That was the third time. Bastian had said he'd seen the shadow king three times, but he never told me about that final encounter.

Mia gazed up at the sky as a flock of birds flew overhead. "As punishment, the shadow king took our shadows, and that was it. We couldn't leave the ship. Bastian didn't speak to us for a month. We thought he was angry the entire time, but it turned out he was ashamed."

"Oh, Bastian," I said.

Mia placed a hand on my arm. "Go easy on him. I know his moods are difficult to withstand sometimes, but he carries the weight of every soul on this ship, of so many souls on that island. He's tried to do the best he could, only taking boys who wanted to go. He sells the dark magic so we don't have to pillage and plunder. He guards the island so others can't come and get their shadows taken, attacks any ships who come near it and makes them turn around."

I straightened. I'd never realized any of that. I stared at his cabin, door closed, Bastian inside hiding away. "Thank you for telling me all of that, but I can't keep putting myself out there. If I haven't changed Bastian's mind so far, then nothing will at this point. He's made up his mind about us, and I just have to accept it."

Mia opened her mouth like she wanted to say something but just nodded and walked away.

From inside his cabin, Bastian yelled out, "Will someone get me a bloody pen that works?"

At least I wasn't the only one feeling murderous. That was, at least, one thing Bastian and I shared at the moment.

Chapter Forty

I stared down at the plank that lay against the wall. Bartholomew stood next to me, also staring at it.

"What am I supposed to do again?" I asked.

Driscoll, Leoni, and I had been sitting on the main deck, poring over the books we'd brought. So far, we hadn't learned much more about the shadow court, certainly nothing that could prepare us for what was to come. We still hadn't had any official meetings, no plans made.

Mia claimed that's exactly what the pirate lord was doing in his cabin: looking at maps, reading through the books we'd brought with us. At some point, he had to discuss the plan with me, with everyone who would be stepping foot on the island. My gaze narrowed in on his cabin door, anger whipping through me. He was acting like a child about this. He'd been the one to make the decision, so why was he acting like it was he who'd been rejected?

Bartholomew had interrupted our reading session and asked me for help with the plank, but it looked just fine to me. When I told him that, he laughed.

"Well, we won't know until someone walks out onto it."

My eyes bulged. "Excuse me? The plank is damaged and you want me to get on it?"

Bartholomew frowned. "It's not damaged. I fixed it. Well, I think I did. We'll find out once you're on it. You have water magic. Out of any of us, this should be the least dangerous task for you."

"I almost died last time. I would have if it hadn't been for . . ."

The man I was currently refusing to name. Out of principle. If he could act immature about this, then so could I.

Bartholomew's gaze softened. "Young love. Ah, I miss it."

"We're not exactly young, Bartholomew, and whatever is between us —it isn't love."

Amusement flashed across his face, and I noticed the ship slowing significantly.

"Who in the bloody hells took my map?" Bastian roared from inside the cabin, making me wince. Something had to change. He couldn't keep on like this with these foul moods and temper tantrums. He'd made poor Cook cry the other night when he'd tasted his newest creation and dumped it in the sea.

To be fair, even the fish wouldn't go near it, but still.

"See?" Bartholomew gestured to the crew members tugging on the lines and reeling up the sails. "We're slowing down so there's no risk involved."

I narrowed my gaze at him. "Why are you doing this? You're not in charge of repairs."

He glanced over his shoulder to Kara. "Our carpenter is currently occupied, and she just asked that we take care of this."

He heaved the plank over the water as crew members worked to shorten the sails, and the ship slowed even further. I supposed he was right. If anyone should do this, it would be me. With the ship slowing down and the calm day at sea, this wouldn't be a risk for me, not like it might be for other crew members. I had asked to be included, to pitch in. I rolled up the sleeves of my tunic. I shouldn't complain about being asked to do just that.

Bartholomew secured the plank in the grooves of the cutout, and I took a deep breath, remembering how this had turned out the last time I'd walked the plank. I shook away my fears. This was clearly a different situation.

I stepped out on the board as it creaked under my feet. "So what am I looking for, exactly?" I asked over my shoulder.

Before Bartholomew could answer, a voice said, "You've got to be fucking kidding me."

I turned to see Bastian standing there, staring at me with anger swirling in his eyes.

I planted my hands on my hips. "Oh, so the captain finally graces us with his presence."

"Get off the damn plank."

A stubbornness rose in me. He didn't even know what I was doing on here. He probably had no idea what was going on with his own ship since he'd spent so long hiding in his cabin, hiding from me.

"I feel like staying out here a little longer, actually." Crew members began to emerge on the main deck, converging around Bastian, watching the exchange between us.

"Do not make me come after you and drag your ass back onto this ship." Bastian took a step forward. "You will regret it."

"That didn't go so well for you last time."

"Damnit, love. Just listen to me."

I raised my chin in the air. "No."

He let out a groan of frustration. "Then you leave me no choice."

He stomped toward me. Oh fuck. He had been serious. He was actually coming after me. I backed away toward the edge.

"What are you doing, you idiot?" I asked.

He kept hold of my gaze, stepping up onto the board.

"Bastian, stop!" The plank wobbled under my feet, making my balance unsteady. "You're going to make us both fall in!"

"Now!" Mia yelled from the crowd right when Bastian reached me and grabbed my arm.

We both froze, staring at everyone in complete confusion.

"Now what?" I asked just as Leoni stepped forward and stuck out her hands, summoning a wave to come over us.

"What do you think you're doing?" I asked, heart beating wildly.

The wave dipped down and plucked both of us up, its grasp firm.

"Let us down right now." Bastian's voice was deadly.

Mia stepped in front of Leoni. "Not until you two work your shit out. We're tired of the moods, the tantrums, the avoidance. I don't care what history you have with her." She pointed at me, and I flinched. "Get it the fuck together because you have a crew depending on you, and we cannot have our captain falling apart."

The wave rushed toward a small island that stretched out in the water, a cluster of tall rock formations with small caves on one end, a few scattered palm trees on another. It was about the same size as Bastian's ship.

"You've got to be kidding me," Bastian muttered.

"When can we come back?" I shouted.

"When you can be on the same ship without flinching every time you see one another!" Mia yelled back, and the ship erupted in cheers.

"They're gone," someone said.

"Finally, we get a break," another voice chimed in.

I hadn't realized we'd been that bad. I glared at Bastian. Well, he'd been that bad. I wasn't the problem here.

The wave rode us farther away from the ship. Driscoll smiled and waved like we were taking a vacation. Leoni stared at us with determination in the set of her shoulders. The water washed us up onto the little sandbar as the ship sailed away. I grunted, sitting up and looking next to me at Bastian. Unbelievable. They'd left us. I was officially alone with the pirate lord.

Chapter Forty-One

We both struggled to our feet, sand covering us, crusting our hair and faces. The sun burned the top of my head, and I groaned.

"We need to get some shelter." I squeezed the water from my hair, which was now undone and tumbling down my back.

Bastian dug the spyglass out of his drenched coat and looked through it out at the sea. "Damnit. They're bloody leaving us. Sailing away to who knows where."

"Yes, Bastian, did you not hear anything they said? They clearly planned this. Now can we please get out of the sun?"

He stuffed the spyglass back into his coat, shedding it and gesturing toward the cluster of caves. "After you."

I rolled my eyes at him and stalked away.

"Oh, that's really mature," he called after me.

"Mature." I whirled around so he almost ran into me. "You want to talk about mature? You are a grown man who kissed me and then hid away for the last week."

I couldn't even look at him. I spun on my heel and continued toward the little caves on the edge of the island.

We ducked into a small one, the ground smooth, the walls and ceiling glittering and dark.

Bastian's heavy boots thumped on the ground behind me, but I didn't turn, suddenly feeling so, so tired. I crossed my arms and rubbed them, wet and cold now that we stood in the shade.

"We wouldn't be in this mess if you weren't such an idiot," I said over my shoulder.

"An idiot?" Anger laced his words. "No, we wouldn't be in this mess if you would've just listened to me. I told you to not come after me. But of course you do the exact opposite of what I say."

My fists clenched tight, nails biting into my palms as I turned. "You are not in charge of me. And as I already explained, you're my best shot at saving my brothers, so no, I didn't listen. I didn't stay away."

I failed to mention the other reason I came after him—it wasn't just that I didn't stay away. I couldn't stay away. Not from him. But I would not be admitting that right now, not when his gaze was so full of ire and wrath.

Water dripped from my hair to the ground, and my clothes were plastered to me. "The crew isn't letting us back on the ship until we fix things between us. So I suggest you start apologizing."

His jaw ticked. "And what am I apologizing for?"

I wanted to tear out my hair. "Have you not listened to a word I've said?"

"It's hard to listen when all you're doing is screeching at me."

My mouth dropped open, and I stepped closer. "I meant what I said in that hedge. You're a coward, Bastian Lore. You're not just hiding from me now. You've always hid. You hid parts of yourself from me the entire year we were together."

He flinched.

"And now, even when I know the full truth of your actions, you still hide."

"Because I'm trying to protect you," he burst out. "Why can't you understand? I never should've bloody offered you that deal in Apolis. I didn't mean to. It slipped out when the guards were dragging me away from you. Because I was afraid I'd never see you again. So I yelled that I could help you find your brothers, knowing you would come find me, knowing you would take the deal. I didn't expect you to try and drown me first, but . . ."

He stepped closer, every inch of his body coiled tight. Water droplets clung to his hair, and his wet shirt stuck to his skin, almost transparent, showing the hard ridges of his body, the outline of the tattoos underneath.

"Now you know." Bastian spread out his arms. "I didn't sail to Apolis expecting to see you. We were supposed to get my ship, fix it, and find the dust—without you. That's why my crew was so angry with me, so distant from you. I was weak." His lip snarled. "I just couldn't resist you. Not even if resisting was what I needed to do to keep you safe."

"Bastian—" I started, but he cut me off.

"Don't. Don't try and justify my actions or make them okay. I've put you in danger by telling you the truth, by not being strong enough to push you away one more time."

"I would've kept coming back," I said.

He looked up at the ceiling, throat thick with tension. "It's impossible, this thing between you and me. I can't be king of your court. You can't abandon your duty. So once again I'm trying to protect you by keeping you away. I'm trying to do my best after I've so royally fucked up this entire thing."

We truly were two sides of the same coin—just like Mia had said. We both had responsibility and we both felt trapped because of it, neither of us fully able to commit to the lives we led.

"Don't you get it? I'm not worth saving." Bastian pressed his hands to his chest. "I'm a sinking ship, and if I let you aboard, you'll drown with me."

"I'm already drowning!" My voice broke, and Bastian's nostrils flared. "Don't *you* get it? That's all I've been doing since you left me. I don't need you to protect me, Bastian. I don't need you to sacrifice for me. I just need you."

His chest rose and fell as his gaze bored into me, heated with something other than anger for once.

"Ever since you sailed back into my life, I can't let you go." I took a step closer, and he didn't move, body so still he could've been a statue. "But I also can't keep doing this." I gestured between us. "You can't keep pulling away. It hurts too damn much."

Water trickled down his face, his hands balled into fists at his sides.

I took another step forward and recognized that heated desire swirling in his brown eyes. Yet he still didn't move.

"Bastian?" I asked, uncertainty lacing my voice. "Are you going to say anything?"

"Bloody hell." He surged forward, gripping my face in his hands, his lips crashing into mine.

I stilled at first, but then his tongue pushed into my mouth, his hands dropping and sliding up inside my tunic, and I could barely form a thought. His fingers danced up my stomach, and I let out a moan, wanting that touch everywhere across my body.

"I've missed the feel of you," Bastian murmured. "Missed getting to explore every inch of you with my hands." His voice dropped as he rubbed his nose against my neck. "With my mouth."

"Bastian," I groaned.

He pushed me against the cave wall, lips locked to mine, tongue sweeping inside my mouth. His hard length pressed into my stomach, and I wasn't sure I'd ever needed something so badly as I did Bastian Lore.

He pulled at my tunic. "Let's get this off of you before I rip it right from your body."

Frankly, I didn't care how it came off—as long as it did. I laughed and stretched it over my head.

He stepped back like I was a piece of art to admire. His eyes darkened as he drank me in, that gaze searing over me. He placed his hands on either side of my waist, his touch scorching against my skin. "You're so fucking beautiful. You know that? I've lived ninety-five years, seen almost every corner of this world, and not a gods-damned thing compares to you."

His words lit a fire in me. My body ached for this man in a way it never had before, but I had to make my feelings clear and to know his in return. Before we went any further, I needed to know he wouldn't push me away again. I inhaled a shaky breath and pushed Bastian to arm's length. Confusion flashed across his face, his hands dropping from my waist.

"We can't do this," I said. "Not if you can't commit to me. You know that, right? I want you, but whatever comes our way, I need to know that whether it's a shadow king or a crown or a spirits-damned sea serpent, we'll face it together. You have to make a choice, Bastian."

He stared at me for what felt like an eternity before he finally said, "Okay, then."

My stomach twisted into a knot. This was it, when he'd tell me to let him go, and I'd finally have to.

His gaze softened as he hooked a finger inside my waistband and tugged me to him. "I choose you, Gabrielle Aster." His fingernail scraped along the skin under my waistband, and an aching need pulsed between my legs. "I will choose you every day for the rest of my life." His voice dropped low and his finger trailed down. "Which will hopefully be a long life because there is so very much I want to do to you."

"Oh?" I asked as he drew that finger down to my clit and stroked it. Spirits below. I arched against him and let out a gasp. "Like what?" I said, breathless.

He chuckled, a low sound that rumbled through me. "I'm a man of action." He brushed his lips against my jaw. "I think it would be better if I showed you."

He brought his hand back up and tugged my trousers down. I held his stare, kicking them off, along with my silk panties, now completely bare before him.

A feral look overtook him as his gaze raked over my body.

"Yes," I agreed, still unable to catch my breath as that ache between my legs grew to a throb. "I think the time is past for talking."

I grasped the bottom of his wet shirt and peeled it off of him, revealing his hard abs and tattoo-covered chest. Driscoll hadn't lied. It was like he was made from stone. Carved by the spirits themselves. I ran my hands over his broad shoulders, the thick black curls of hair on his chest, down to his muscled abdomen. I admired every sculpted inch.

"Keep touching me like that," he murmured, "and I won't have any control left."

"I was hoping to hear that," I said as I grabbed his trousers and yanked them down.

His hard cock, veined and thick, bobbed, the tip glistening and ready for me.

He kicked off his trousers, then let out a low growl and backed me against the wall for a second time. I thudded against it. He lifted my arms and pinned them over my head, his lips roaming over my jaw, my neck, down to my breasts. He took a nipple in his mouth, and I let out a gasp as his tongue flicked it.

Want crashed through me as fierce as the wild northern waves of Apolis.

I tilted my pelvis toward him, needing him inside of me. "Bastian," I rasped.

He chuckled and sucked harder on my nipple, then lifted one of my legs, hooking it around his waist. He raised his head, eyes gleaming with an untethered wildness. I shuddered as he pressed himself against my entrance, his cock rubbing against it and shooting sparks of pleasure through me.

It was just a taste of what was to come, and I wanted so much more.

He grazed my leg with his fingers, his gaze hooded as it dripped over me.

"You're mine," he said. "I will always choose you, love."

"That's good to know." I shot him a wicked grin. "Because now I can do things like this."

I reached down and stroked his cock, giving it a few long, slow pumps, and he let out a shuddering breath. I loved having this effect on him, knowing that I could make him come undone with just a touch.

"Now show me," I said. "Show me that you're choosing me."

All restraint gone, he cupped my ass and lifted me higher before plunging into me. We both let out gasps at the feel of being joined together again after so long apart. He thrust up into me again, and I rocked my hips with the movement to match his rhythm.

With each thrust he buried himself deeper inside of me. I dug my fingers into his back, clinging to him, wanting this feeling to last forever. Spirits below, how had I gone without him for so long? Never again.

I groaned out and buried my face in his neck as he pumped in and out with a frenzied need. Waves of pleasure rolled through my body, and I bucked against him, angling myself so he could go even deeper. Pulses of heat webbed out, spreading to my thighs, my lower stomach. This man would be my undoing. I gripped him tighter, moaning his name.

He captured my moans with his mouth. We were nothing but teeth and tongues and lips. His body was so hard and unrelenting, and I could feel the muscles constricting as he kept me pinned against the wall. My pirate lord.

My body spasmed as he rocked against me, thrusting so hard now, every slap of his pelvis bringing me to new heights of pleasure.

I cried out into his mouth. The way he rocked into me felt so fucking good.

"That's it," Bastian said. "Let the storm come, my love."

Not just love. My love.

The word swept me up, and my body shattered around him. His cock pulsed inside me as he came at the same time. We clung tight to each other, nothing but our breaths and gasps filling the cave.

I collapsed against him, skin sticky with sweat and sea water.

He pressed a gentle kiss into my forehead and slipped from me, releasing my leg that he'd held up around his waist.

"I love you." I placed my hands on his chest and looked up at him.

My declaration shouldn't have felt so powerful, so shocking. I knew how he felt about me, and he knew how I felt in return. Everyone did. But we'd never said the words aloud. They always felt too dangerous, too taboo.

The corners of his eyes crinkled, and he stroked my hair. "You consume me." He searched my face. "Love isn't a strong enough word to describe it. What I feel for you isn't love—it's magic. It must be for how deeply you're ingrained into every facet of my being."

"Bastian," I said, voice wobbling. "You can't just say things like that."

He pressed a gentle finger to my lips. "I pushed you away so many times. I made you think horrible things about me. Why did you come after me again and again and again? Why didn't you give up?"

I wound my arms around his neck, still needing to feel our bodies pressed together. "Because I'm tired of running. I run from everything in my life. I don't commit to anything, not fully. But when it comes to you, I don't want to run." I hesitated, biting my lip. "Did you mean what you said? Are we done pretending now? Pretending that we're going to stay away from each other? That this isn't worth fighting for?"

Bastian didn't move. "I did. Of course I did. But . . . how can you possibly see a future with me? I'm a trapped man. And you will not become a trapped woman. Not under my watch."

"We will fight to free you." He opened his mouth to protest, but I cut him off. "Bastian, you are worth it."

"You're to be queen," he said, voice grave. "I'm a pirate. Your people would never accept me. Your mother—"

"I'll fight for that too."

He scoffed. "For me to be king? Are you mad?"

"I am not running anymore," I responded, voice hard. I walked to where my panties and trousers lay and began pulling them on.

He studied me for a moment before dipping his head. "Alright, then. No more running." He raked a hand through his hair. "But, love, you have to promise you won't compromise this mission. We will fight to free my shadow, but not this time around. This mission is about freeing your brothers, nothing else."

I bit my lip, knowing full well that was not what this mission was about.

Before I could say anything, he crossed the length of the cave and stopped in front of me, grabbing my hand before I could lace my trousers. "What do you think you're doing?" he asked, voice low.

That familiar desire prickled between my legs. "Well, I was getting dressed," I said.

"You thought we were done?" His eyes glittered. "After nearly a year apart? Oh, love, I'm just getting started."

"What were you thinking?" I asked, suddenly feeling breathless all over again.

He leaned his head down and whispered into my ear, "That we have a lot of catching up to do and not a moment to waste. Now take off those trousers before I rip them off."

I gazed at him from underneath my lashes. "Is that a command, Captain?"

He shot me a wicked grin and said, "Aye, I believe it is," then closed his mouth over mine as he lowered me to the ground.

Chapter Forty-Two

"You know," Driscoll said as he, Leoni, and I swabbed the deck, "if I'd known that sleeping with the hot pirate lord would get me a permanent spot in his nice, soft bed, I'd have tried harder to seduce him. Ever since you two got back from your little escapade on that island, you've spent every night together."

Driscoll was right. Since Bastian and I had returned from the island, we'd spent every night—and some afternoons—tangled in the sheets of his bed. Well, a few times were spent bent over his desk and up against the wall, and one time on the floor when we didn't quite make it to the bed. My body was deliciously sore, sated, yet somehow insatiable. Now that I had him again, I could not get enough of Bastian Lore. I suspected I'd never get enough.

I swished the mop across the planks, a streak of water in its trail.

"No offense," Leoni said to Driscoll, "but I don't think you're his type."

Driscoll pushed his mop forward. "Really? And here I thought I looked so much like the auburn-haired water princess."

He framed his angular face.

I just laughed. As soon as we got back onto the ship, I'd reprimanded Leoni for that stunt she and everyone else had pulled, then thanked her, and I might've divulged what happened to her and

Driscoll, who'd drank in every detail. That man needed to get laid—and soon.

"Bastian only has eyes for Gabrielle," Leoni said, "so if you're planning to seduce him now, it might be a little too late. You could offer that pirate lord all the treasure in the world, and he wouldn't trade it for her."

My heart swelled because it was true. I was his and he was mine, and the thought buoyed me more than I'd ever thought it could.

Driscoll made a gagging sound. "First Penn and Liliath. Now Bastian and Gabrielle. I can't escape from all this romance."

"You and me both," Leoni muttered.

I studied her and she pushed her mop back and forth. She'd been happy for Bastian and me, but I could still sense something was wrong. I just didn't know what or how to even approach it.

Driscoll swiped a hand over his brow. "Bloody earth, it's hot out here."

"It's going to get hotter," I said. "Sorrengard is a jungle, you know. Humid and wet and sticky."

"Perfect," Driscoll said with mock cheer. "You know, I much preferred this ship when I got to sit around and do nothing. We really should've voted before you volunteered yourself, Leoni, and me to chip in."

"I thought you wanted to be of use," I pointed out.

Driscoll stopped, straightening. "No, I said I wanted to prove myself. By slaying a dragon or saving a princess and her brothers. Not mopping a pirate ship."

We'd managed to earn the respect of almost everyone on this ship by pulling our weight, helping out when and wherever we could.

I eyed Bastian's tattooed sister, who sat working near us. Except one person. Bastian said she'd come around, that she was just protective over him, but I hadn't gotten so much as a smile from Kara, not even now that her brother and I had worked through our issues.

"Do you think you can handle the rest of this?" I gestured to the main deck.

Driscoll's lips flattened. "If you're sneaking away for a little afternoon session with your pirate, then I don't think so."

Leoni smirked.

I made a face at him. "No, I just want to talk to his sister." I tipped my head in Kara's direction.

Driscoll continued mopping. "Go ahead. Try and win over the snarly pirate. Good luck," he muttered.

"Thank you." I walked over to Kara and crouched down next to her as she ignored me. "Need some help?" I offered.

"No," she answered, voice curt.

I sat down next to her anyway, stretching out my legs in front of me, back against the railing. "I wouldn't like me either," I said.

She held the wood piece in front of her, cutting it into a circle with a knife. She grunted in response.

"Listen." I picked at my shirt. "Is there any way you can put your feelings aside and we can be cordial to each other? We have a big mission coming up, and we all need to be in sync."

"Right. The mission where my brother puts his, and everyone's, life at risk for you. Again."

My mouth dropped open. "Okay, then," I said.

Kara continued to cut the piece of wood, then held it up to the hole in the hull. It was still too big, and she growled in frustration and continued cutting. I peered at the hole, then at some spare piece of cloth laying in a pile nearby, buried underneath a coil of line. I reached down and snatched the cloth, then stretched it over the hole.

"May I?" I asked Kara, gesturing to her knife.

She eyed me warily and nodded. I used the knife to cut the cloth while it was against the hole until I had a perfect match. I handed the piece to Kara. "Here. Might be easier now to get the wood piece to match."

She stared at the cloth, then looked up to me, then down at the cloth again. "That was smart," she said. "I don't know why I never thought of that."

I shrugged and settled back down. "Sometimes when we do things a certain way, it's hard to break patterns." Kara put the cloth over the wood and started shaving off more of it. "I don't want any of you to risk your lives for us," I said. "I just want my brothers back, and I want them to have the best chance at survival. That's your brother. He knows the shadow court better than anyone. You all do. I don't know who else to turn to." I shrugged. "You know, you remind me a bit of my younger brother, Mal."

She scoffed as she fitted the wood piece to the hole. "The prince?" she asked.

"Yeah." I looked at her wistfully. "He's quieter, more serious than me or Lochlan. He doesn't always speak his mind. He stews in his thoughts a lot."

"Sounds like a real joy to be around. Thanks." She picked up another piece of wood, a longer strip that she laid across the now-plugged hole.

"But he's loyal to a fault. He loves fiercely. And he protects those he loves with everything he has."

Kara's hand faltered on the slab of wood, and I reached up to help her steady it. "Damnit. Mia said you're hard to hate. She was right. As usual."

I laughed. "I want you to understand that I'm not just going to try and free my brothers. I'm going to try and free you all too."

Kara's head snapped up at that. "Does Bastian know that?"

I thought about our conversation just days earlier in that cave, how he'd told me not to even think about trying to get his shadow.

"Of course not." I rolled my eyes. "He'd no doubt put a stop to that plan."

"So why are you telling me?" She cocked her pierced brow. "I'm not going to keep your secrets."

"Because I think you want freedom."

"I love being a pirate," Kara said.

"Not for yourself." I drew my knees up to my chest. "For your sister and your brother. Loyal to a fault, remember?"

She closed her eyes for a second. "Mia would make an amazing wife, a mother. It's her dream to have children. And Bastian." She snorted. "Well, his dream is you."

Tears welled in my eyes at hearing her say that.

She gave a resigned sigh. "So how do you think I can help you?"

I took a deep breath. "I need you to distract Bastian so I can go after your shadows. I want to find them."

Kara's eyes widened. "He'll kill me. You know that, right?"

"But you can do it. You can make up some emergency or get into a fight with one of the crew members. Something that will distract Bastian just long enough for me to slip away."

"Why not ask one of your friends to do this? Why me?"

I bit my lip. "I don't know if I even want them to come onto the island."

A few crew members passed by and we quieted until they were out of earshot.

"Driscoll isn't trained for this kind of thing," I whispered. "And Leoni is too protective. She won't let me out of her sight once we're on that island, and she most definitely won't let me risk my life for you all. Mia is too nice to help me with this, but you . . . you will do anything for Bastian, anything for Mia, and this will be your best chance at helping them."

Sunlight glinted off the silver rings piercing the outer part of her ear. "Why would you risk your life for us?"

I thought about Bastian, how long he'd been trapped.

"Because you all are doing the same for my brothers, for my people. Once my brothers are safe, I'll know that the future of Apolis is secure. I can take a risk for you just like you're doing the same for me."

Kara finished securing the slab over the plugged hole, and she let her head thunk against the siding. "Fucking hell. Okay," she said. "Okay. I'll give you your distraction, but you better make it worth it, Princess. I hope you know what you're doing."

Before I could respond, Driscoll swaggered over, a smile on his face. "You know, I think the crew is really starting to come around. They just told me about this amazing eye cream that gets rid of all your wrinkles."

"An eye cream?" I asked doubtfully.

Driscoll squinted at me and tilted his head. "You could probably use some yourself."

Kara leaned against the railing. "And what is this magical cream called?"

"Seaman's cream. I haven't seen any yet, but if I can keep up this rapport with them, I think they'll show me how to get some."

Kara and I shot glances at each other.

"Seaman?" I echoed.

"Seaman," Driscoll said.

"Sea-man," I said even slower.

Kara rolled her eyes. "Just give him a minute."

Driscoll huffed. "Do you need to clean out your ears? Seaman. Sea man. Seeeaaamannn—" He paused, frowning. "Wait a minute. Semen? Oh, that's just disgusting." He turned and yelled at some of the crew members who stood on the opposite side of the ship. "You all are barbarians!"

They burst into laughter.

"Let me know when you want some of that cream," one of them yelled back, making Driscoll's face turn as red as a lobster.

They'd delighted in pranking Driscoll lately, but honestly, he made it so easy.

I looked around at this crew I'd grown to care about. I had to save them. I had to save everyone. Even if it meant going against Bastian's wishes.

Chapter Forty-Three

Bastian and I lay together in his bed, the dark night spread out beyond his windows. The moon shone bright tonight, its glow bathing the room in a silver hue.

He trailed his fingers up and down my back as I nestled my head onto his bare chest.

"Are you ready for tomorrow?" I asked.

"No," he said honestly. "I'm glad Marian gave us some guidance, but that doesn't change how difficult this is going to be. The shadows can do terrifying things to those who try to escape them."

I shifted against him. "So can we. No one has beat this shadow king because no one has tried. From what you told me people sneak onto the island to steal magical items. Has anyone actually tried to rescue a loved one? You told me yourself you chose boys who didn't have families, who no one would miss."

Bastian's chest rose and fell under my head with deep breaths, his heart thumping in a steady rhythm. "Listen, you need to steel yourself for the possibility that your brothers might not want to come home."

I propped my head up on my elbow. "What are you talking about? Of course they'll want to come home."

"I told you that the shadow court isn't what it seems. You don't understand—"

"Then make me understand."

He hesitated. "It's a paradise of sorts for the boys."

I scoffed, remembering him telling me something similar before, but I still couldn't believe it.

"Think about it, love. These boys came from the streets. From horrible situations: abuse, starvation, neglect, injury. At the shadow court they have free rein of the jungle. They've banded together to create a family. They're fed, they're taken care of, they're happy."

"It's a false happiness," I argued. "They don't have their shadows. They're too young to understand what they're missing, that their lives have been robbed from them."

Bastian tipped his head. "That may be, but it's the truth of it."

Except our boys weren't missing a community. They came from loving, good homes. Surely they'd want to return. I glanced at Bastian, and guilt rose up at keeping my full plan from him. I still hadn't told him that I planned to rescue all the boys, not just my brothers. That I planned to rescue him and his crew. He was so damn stubborn, and he wouldn't want to put me in any more danger than I was already in.

"Well," I said, "my brothers are not little boys, and they didn't come from a horrible situation. They're not going to be tricked into not wanting to leave."

"I'm just trying to protect you."

His words softened my sharp edges. "I don't need protecting. Are you ever going to learn?"

He rolled me over, his chest pressing against my breasts, his cock growing stiff. "No. Not when it comes to you. I'll never stop protecting you, no matter the cost."

He'd already proven that.

I trailed a finger down his cheek. "I suppose I can live with that."

He leaned down and kissed me tenderly. His hand stroked my waist, and he moved it up and down in gentle lines. Heat stirred between my legs, and I positioned myself so his hard length pressed right against my entrance.

He moaned into my mouth, slowly rubbing his cock up and down my slit while kissing me deeply. I slid my hands down his back, enjoying the feel of him, and in one deep thrust he entered me, filling me, making me feel so complete in this moment.

We rocked slowly together, kissing and touching and savoring every second of this. Tomorrow everything would change, and I wasn't sure I was ready for it. Part of me wished I could stay in this little cabin with Bastian forever, just us and the sea.

He started moving faster now, needing a release, and I bucked under him as he ground into my pelvis. My breathing grew heavy as pressure built in my core. He kissed me harder, and I threaded my fingers into his hair as we came together, both of us crying out.

He collapsed over me.

I trailed my fingers up and down his sweat-sheened back, completely and utterly content. I could not get enough of this man. This pirate who had somehow managed to steal my heart in a way I never expected. He pressed his lips to my forehead and rolled next to me, and I nestled into his side.

"I love you. You know that, right?" He looked at me with a grave expression that I didn't quite understand.

"Of course I do." I hesitated. "I love you too."

He closed his eyes, his breathing growing heavy while I watched him, memorizing every line of his face. Those full lips. That dark beard that covered his strong jaw. I got up from the bed, my feet pressing against the cool floor as I walked over to the candle where it flickered, right next to Bastian's spyglass. I leaned down and blew it out.

Outside the little cabin, chatter and music floated through the air. The entire crew seemed to have this sense that tonight was the last night before everything changed, either for better or worse. I tiptoed back to the bed, and slipped under the covers, then turned over, staring into the darkness, the pirate lord's words rolling over in my mind.

I love you, he'd said.

But it hadn't sounded like a sweet sentiment. It hadn't sounded like a declaration. It had sounded like a goodbye.

Chapter Forty-Four

The island of Sorrengard appeared in the distance, a ring of dark fog surrounding its tall, thick trees. It was larger than I'd expected, bigger than any of the human islands that were scattered through the Dark Seas. The black-sand beaches spread around the jungle, ominous and foreboding. A mountain rose up on the back of the island, green and shrouded in mist. We'd decided to anchor near the crocodile-infested swamps, deciding that would ultimately be easier than navigating through narrow cliffs, and then having to ascend those cliffs to get onto the island. Not to mention if we needed a quick escape, it wouldn't be easy to get back to the ship.

So crocodiles it was.

My hands trembled as I clutched the railing, staring at the island. My brothers were there. Right now. They were alive. I was going to see Mal and Lochlan soon. The thought made me want to jump off the ship and let the water take me there instead of waiting to arrive.

Kara came to a stand next to me. "Are you ready for this?" she asked, then lowered her voice. "You sure you want to go through with it?"

I looked behind me to Bastian's cabin, then back to the island. "I'm sure."

"Then you'd better be ready," she said. "Don't waste the opportunity I give you. No hesitating, no looking back. You're going to need to be fully committed."

I thought about freeing Bastian, giving him his shadow back so he could finally live out the life he was meant to. A life with me by his side.

"I am fully committed. You don't need to worry about that."

She nodded and slipped away as the ship slowed.

So many secrets I was keeping from Bastian. It was nice that he wanted to protect me, but who was going to protect him? I curled my fingers tighter, digging them into the railing as Sorrengard came closer, and we veered to the right toward the eastern side. Hopefully Marian's information was true, and the marsh would provide us the cover we needed to stay undetected. We planned to anchor the ship in the sun, where shadows couldn't reach us, which meant we'd have to use Bastian's smaller boats to get us to the marsh and past the crocodiles. We'd capsized two of them when we gave my father and his men their burial at sea. That left us with three boats to use.

Now that we were closer to the island, I could see how thick the jungle was. Trees and vines twisted together in tangles and knots. We'd need to bring swords to cut through all the bramble and brush. I squinted at the dark fog hanging under the cover of the trees and realized it wasn't fog I was seeing—it was the shadows.

They swirled, their forms translucent and wispy, eyes glowing red. I shuddered, thinking about how Lochlan's and Mal's shadows could be up there right now, staring down at me. The shadows were varied, some tall and lanky, some stout and short, while others appeared bulkier, bigger. That would at least make identifying Mal's and Lochlan's shadows—and the pirates' shadows—easier. Theirs would be the fully grown ones.

We sailed past the looming jungle and out toward the shallow waters, where sun shone down. Thankfully it was a sunny day, but this was a jungle island, and storm clouds could come in at any moment. We had to hope the sun stayed out and gave us a good chance at escape so the shadows couldn't follow us. I wondered just how many shadows were on this island, how many boys were trapped. Bastian had been ferrying boys over for sixty years now, but before that, I wondered how many had been kidnapped. The ship slowed, and my stomach lurched. A lump grew in my throat at the sight of the marsh that lay ahead. I could just make out green heads rising from the water. The crocodiles. Spirits below, there were so many.

Thin reeds and tufts of green sat on the marshy water, and round lily pads rested on the surface. This was going to be hard to navigate, even with my water magic.

I'd thought so much about what would happen once we got on the island, I hadn't considered the danger of actually getting to it. Why did everything have to be so difficult?

I turned away, needing a moment to catch my breath. If Mal were here, he'd be going through our plan one more time, rattling off our strategy, checklist in hand. Lochlan would predictably be making jokes to lighten the tension and calm my nerves. They'd both be up for this challenge. They'd face it head-on. I would do the same. If that were me in that jungle, they wouldn't hesitate to cross that marsh.

The ship finally came to a stop, and a flurry of activity erupted as the crew worked to lower the anchor. My gaze caught on three rowboats being lowered into the water from where they were stored on the bow. Bastian had told me each rowboat could carry fifteen men, more than enough room for all of us. I searched through all the activity for Leoni and Driscoll but didn't see them anywhere. Come to think of it, I hadn't seen them since breakfast that morning. Driscoll was staying behind to guard the ship, but Leoni had insisted on coming with me.

Bastian appeared outside his cabin, his gaze set on me. A sheathed sword hung from his belt. The top of his shirt was open and flapping in the wind, his long coat billowing behind him. He looked magnificent, every bit the feared pirate lord of the Dark Seas.

A clang sounded behind me, and I whirled around to see a few crew members emerging from belowdecks, carrying a large cage.

"What is this for?" I asked as Bastian approached.

"To protect you," he said.

My brows furrowed as Ollie unlocked it and opened the door.

"Me?" I asked. "How is this going to protect me?"

Bastian took a step forward, that stone mask slipping over his face. He reached out a hand. "Do you trust me?" he asked.

"Of course I do." I slowly placed my hand in his, and he reeled me to him, whispering in my ear, "Then you'll know I'm doing this for your own good."

He pushed me into the cage, and Ollie quickly locked it behind me.

Shock rippled through me, and for a moment, I couldn't move. Then I snapped out of my stupor and grabbed the cage bars, rattling them. "Bastian!" I yelled.

He didn't look back as he grabbed onto a rope ladder and disappeared over the side of his ship, the crew members following his lead.

"Bastian!" I screamed. "Don't you dare leave me on this ship! Those are my brothers out there! Bastian!"

He was already gone. I reached for my magic, but as hard as I pulled at it, I couldn't get it to surface. Then I realized what kind of prison they'd trapped me in. Iron. The cage was made of iron. I felt for the pick in my hair before remembering how Bastian had removed it last night and put it on his desk. The pirate lord had truly thought through every detail. Unbelievable.

Of course he wasn't going to let me onto that island. He'd spent almost a year away from me, getting sicker by the day, just to protect me from the shadow king. The idiot was still trying to protect me.

I groaned and my head thunked against the bars.

Bastian's intentions might have been pure, but he'd been wrong to trap me like this. I would find a way out of this cage and onto that island. No matter the cost.

Chapter Forty-Five

"Excuse you, get your dirty paws off my shirt!"

I looked up to see a few of the crew members dragging a bound Driscoll and Leoni toward us, both of them with iron cuffs around their wrists.

They sat my friends down, linking their cuffs to chains connected to the floor of the ship before departing and joining the waiting rowboats. There went any hope of either of them rescuing me.

"I don't really know if Bastian thought this through," Leoni said and gestured to the cups of water sitting next to her and Driscoll.

I had my own water in my cage.

"What if they're gone longer than he expects?" she asked. "What if we die on this stupid pirate ship from dehydration?"

I let my head thunk against the back of the cage.

"You two really do deserve each other," Leoni said.

"What is that supposed to mean?" I asked.

"He's just as reckless as you. He acts without thinking."

"Technically, he was thinking with his heart," Driscoll said. "It's kind of romantic in a twisted sort of way."

"You have to help me get out of here," I said quietly.

"Why? So you can run off to the island and save your brothers?"

Leoni asked. "Go ahead with your plan to try and make Bastian king?" She snorted. "Or you'll run away again and become some pirate queen?"

I cut a sharp look at her. "Why are you acting like this? I told you everything Bastian said. He's under the shadow king's control. He's not the villain we thought he was."

"I'm not blaming him. I'm blaming you." Leoni turned her head, jaw set.

Driscoll's wide eyes bounced between us.

"For what?" I threw out my hands. "How could I have predicted he'd do this? What was I supposed to do? Read his mind? Tell the future? Sorry, my water magic doesn't quite allow for that kind of power."

"You could have listened to me in the first place," Leoni said. "Now our entire plan is ruined, and you're no doubt plotting to do something stupid and reckless that will no doubt put us all in danger, and I'll have to once again save your ass."

I had no idea where this was coming from. The anger was there, but it felt off, like I was missing something. "So let me get this straight. You're upset about having to do your job? Do I need to remind you that you're my captain of the guard?"

"This is way above my pay grade!" Leoni said. "You act without thinking. You know, this little journey, it's been the first time in a long time I've been able to do things for myself. Drink at a tavern. Dance with someone." She snorted. "Which didn't last long because, as usual, you did something reckless, and I had to come save you."

"You didn't save me from anything," I snapped, thinking of that meeting with Bastian in the hedges.

Leoni just scoffed.

"It's not my fault you don't have a life."

"Yes it is!" she burst out. "I can't have a life because you're constantly making bad choices. One after another. You don't think of anyone but yourself."

"Leoni," Driscoll said, voice quiet.

Her chest heaved, her eyes rimmed red like she was about to cry. That made two of us.

"I didn't know you felt that way." I clutched the bars of my cage. "I mean, I knew you thought I was reckless, but I didn't know I prevented you from having any semblance of a life." I refused to cry. "Let me relieve you of your duties, then. You're no longer my captain of the guard."

"Princess Gabrielle," Driscoll started, but I held up my hand.

"When we get back to Apolis, you can do whatever you please, live the life you've always wanted to live. One where you don't have to worry about me."

Regret shone in Leoni's eyes, and I looked away.

"If we get back to Apolis," she mumbled.

I was about to retort when a figure jumped on board, and I had to squint against the sun to see who it was. My mouth dropped open. Kara. She stalked toward us.

"What are you doing here?" I asked. "Where's Bastian?"

"They got to the island after a little skirmish with the crocodiles, but he's fine," she said. "We decided to split up and meet back at the shore after we'd scouted out the area. Instead of going my route, I got on the rowboat and came back here to get you."

"Why?"

"Because you're as stubborn and stupid as he is." Kara knelt down and began picking the lock. "And I have a feeling you're just hardheaded enough that you might actually find our shadows and reunite us with them." The cage clicked open. "You're our only hope at this point, and I'm not forsaking that because my brother doesn't understand just how strong, how determined, you are."

I stepped out of the cage, and Kara stuck out a hand to help me to my feet.

"Are you ready to go save your brothers?" she asked.

Driscoll laughed nervously. "Um, you're going to unlock us first, right?"

Leoni's head was turned, and she refused to meet my eyes. I nodded at Kara. "You two stay here," I said. "No need to risk your shadows or your lives. It'll be good to have at least two people guarding the ship."

"Totally fine by me," Driscoll said as Kara unlocked his cuffs, then Leoni's.

"C'mon." Kara strode toward the railing. "We need to go."

I turned to say something to Leoni, but she still wouldn't meet my gaze. I sighed, closed my mouth, and followed Kara off the ship without saying goodbye. It was time to go to the shadow court.

Chapter Forty-Six

The rowboat heaved on top of the choppy waves, and water slapped at the sides of the vessel. I stuck out my hands to calm the waters around us as we approached the marsh. Bumpy green heads popped out of the water, looking bigger and bigger the closer we got. I didn't want to hurt the crocodiles. After all, they weren't doing anything wrong. If they snapped at us or attacked, it was because it was in their nature to do so.

Still, the thought of those massive jaws rising from the water and snatching me up sent shivers down my spine.

"So how did you get past the crocs the first time around?" I asked.

"Mostly luck." Kara rowed the boat toward the marsh. "One of them nearly bit off Bastian's hand, but I managed to stab at it with a sword and keep it at bay."

Our boat pushed through big lily pads, frogs sitting on them, staring at us with their black eyes.

"That doesn't sound so bad." I glanced down at her side. "And where is your sword?"

"The crocodile ate it," she said.

My eyes widened. "That sounds worse."

"And there's not thirty of us this time," she said. "It's just you and me and your water magic. So what can you do with it, Princess?"

I heaved a sigh. The boat rocked under us, and we both flew to the side.

"Was that the ocean?" I asked, knowing full well I was still using my powers to keep it calm.

Kara continued to row. "What do you think?"

"Right," I said as a massive crocodile lunged up from the water, jaws snapping at us, body thrashing as it swiped a massive leg through the air. Its claws scratched against our boat, its teeth nearly as long as my pinky. It landed with a crash on top of Kara.

"Use your magic!" Kara screamed as the beast hinged its jaws open, pinning her to the boat. She lay flat on her back, kicking at it wildly.

I thrust my hands out as the croc's teeth swiped dangerously close to Kara's face, and she grunted, straining her legs against its stomach, which seemed to have no effect on the animal.

I moved my palms higher, asking Spirit Water to aid me in this moment. Water curled upward behind the crocodile, dipping down and gripping it tightly. It thrashed, eyes wild, as the water gripped it tighter and yanked it back. Kara and I both slumped, breathing heavily.

"That wasn't so bad," I said as she shot me a glare.

"That's easy for you to say when you weren't about to be that croc's breakfast."

I nodded toward the oars. "Let's just keep going."

She looked around at all the bumpy, scaled heads peeking out of the water and grabbed the oars.

"Maybe I should save my magic for them. Do you think you can row us the rest of the way? The water's pretty calm here anyway."

"Yes, just focus on the crocodiles." Her eyes darted to the beasts as she started rowing.

The boat ran over the tall, brown reeds sticking out of the marsh, and we navigated around the big tufts of moss and spindly bushes that sat atop the surface.

"You're doing great," I said, keeping my hands out, ready to shoot my magic toward any threat that popped out.

Kara continued to row, her entire body tense. I didn't blame her. She'd been very close to getting her head bitten off. That kind of thing tended to stay imprinted in one's memory.

A crocodile lunged from the water as we passed it, and I shot a stream of water right in its eyes. It let out a screech and dipped back down.

"Good, just keep doing that," Kara said.

"Are you afraid?" I asked.

"I've been through much worse than crocodiles."

"No." I shook my head. "Of your brother knowing you betrayed him."

"Like I said"—her muscles bunched as she heaved the oars through the water—"I've faced much worse."

I couldn't imagine the things she'd faced in the last sixty years being aboard Bastian's pirate ship. Actually, since she joined the Lost Boys later, I didn't know how many years she'd been on this ship.

"He can't stay mad at me, at us," Kara finally said. "He's always had a soft spot for his little sisters, even though we're not so little anymore. Plus, he feels so much guilt over our shadows getting taken that he tends to forgive us pretty easily. I think he's afraid we'll grow to hate him, resent him eventually. So he tries to keep the peace as much as possible." She peered at me. "Except when it came to you. That was the one time he was willing to fight us."

"Oh," I said.

A long green body shifted in the water next to us, and I curled my hand into a fist, commanding the water to pull the creature down.

"You're good for him," Kara said. "We all knew it. But we also feared it. We'd seen how the shadow king descended upon me and Mia when we'd saved that little boy. He took our shadows as punishment. We couldn't imagine what he'd do if Bastian outright rebelled against him, refused to bring him more shadows. It made us angry. It made us hate you. But the truth is you make Bastian do something he's never done before."

"And what's that?" I asked.

"Hope," she said simply. "Hope is scary, but it's also powerful."

"Thank you," I said quietly. I smiled. "You know, I think I'm growing on you."

"Let's not push it," she said.

While we'd been talking, we'd gotten closer to the edge of the island. We could probably get out of the boat and slosh our way through the water, but I would not be stepping foot out of this vessel while the crocodiles lurked beneath the surface of the water. No, we needed to get as close to the land as we could.

Our boat rocked upward, Kara's eyes bulging as she let go of the oars and gripped the sides to keep from falling out. I tried to use my magic, but I didn't even know how to use it in this situation. I couldn't see where the attack was coming from. Kara's end of the boat rose higher, slanting more as crocodiles emerged, wading toward us.

"Do something," Kara said. "You're going to get eaten, and Bastian will never forgive me for that."

"I'm holding onto the boat," I said back. "I can't use my magic unless I let go."

The boat fell a bit, crashing down on whatever was underneath us, but then Kara's end once again started rising higher. It would soon be vertical and Kara and I would fall right into the crocodile-infested water.

"I'm going to let go," I said.

"How are you going to use your magic against so many crocodiles at once?"

The boat rose even higher.

"I'll figure that out as I go."

"That's your plan," Kara shouted, bracing her feet against one of the ridges on the bottom of the vessel.

"It's all I got," I shouted, glancing behind me at an emerging croc-odile's open mouth, waiting for me to fall right into it. I squeezed my eyes shut and took a breath, then counted.

One.

Two.

Three.

I let go of the boat, a cold sweat forming at the base of my neck. I immediately stuck out my hands, summoning the water to yank the crocodile down.

The only problem was I fell down with it. My body plunked straight into the cold water, nothing like the warm waters near Apolis.

My view became murky green, and reeds and other plants tickled my skin. Something nipped at my feet, and I yelped, sucking in a lungful of the water.

I kicked my legs, striking my hands out to push the water, to make it keep whatever was lurking in its depth at bay. I could only use my magic for one thing, and I had to choose: either use it to get myself back to the surface or to trap the crocodiles. Either way, my chances at surviving weren't looking good. I only hoped Kara made it to the island. Her best chance at getting there would be if I used my magic to trap the crocodiles.

So that's what I'd do. Decision made, I thrust my hands out, curling my fingers as water continued to swirl around me. *Down*, I commanded. *Keep us all trapped. Don't let anything rise to the surface.*

All I had to do was give Kara enough time. Hopefully she'd take it.

My lungs squeezed painfully. I couldn't see anything through the slimy green that surrounded me, but I felt the crocodiles closing in, their bodies brushing against mine. Right now they were likely distracted by the magic keeping them from being able to break the surface, but soon, they'd turn their attention onto me.

Spots dotted my vision, and my lungs burned, begging for air.

My magic faltered, and my limbs grew limp. Something swished by me, but I was too weak to be afraid.

Suddenly, a hand gripped my arm, tugging me up. I broke the surface, and Kara yanked me onto the boat.

I gasped, the air cleansing my lungs while I coughed and sputtered. Kara banged on my back.

"Now use your magic to push us toward the land," she yelled. "The oars are gone. So I need you to give one last push. Can you do it?"

I could barely see straight, my vision still clouded by dots, but I nodded anyway.

"They're coming," Kara said. "Your magic only held them back for so long. But we have a clear shot. Just get us to the land."

I slumped over, taking a shuddering breath.

"Come on, Princess," Kara shouted. "You can do this."

I pushed my hands forward. *Land, take us to the land.*

Nothing happened at first, and Kara swore. Then the water rippled, and our boat lurched forward toward the island until it shoved up onto the marshy land with a resounding crash. Wood splintered, flying out, and the boat cracked under us.

"Well there goes our ride back to the ship," Kara said, slumping down. "But we made it." She shot me a grin. "Well done."

I nodded, breathing heavily, body completely spent. I hoped we didn't need my magic again because I wouldn't be able to use it. Just as we'd stepped from the boat, a shout rang out in the distance.

"Bloody hell," a voice yelled.

Kara and I looked at each other and both straightened.

"Bastian," she breathed.

He yelled again, and fear laced his voice.

We didn't waste any time, both of us running in the direction of the screams. We'd gotten past the crocodiles, and now the real danger lay ahead.

Part Four

"*. . . and the sun went away, and shadows stole across the the water, turning it cold.*"

Chapter Forty-Seven

Thick jungle surrounded us, slowing our movements as we made our way deeper into the belly of Sorrengard. We had no weapons, so we were forced to use our hands and legs to push and punch our way through the thick tangle of brush and trees and vines.

Glittering magical items lay on the ground, hung from trees, were buried in bushes, tangled in thorny vines. They were everywhere. Power seeped from them, and I could understand the temptation to take one, to use its magic. I ducked under a cup that hung from a branch and wondered what it had the power to do.

"You feel it, right?" Kara asked. "That power?"

I nodded, a chill creeping over me at the sight of all this dark magic.

I grabbed onto a thick ropey vine, yanking so I could step over it, only to feel a sharp pain slice across my hand. A strip of crimson welled in my palm, and I looked back at the vine, realizing tiny thorns covered it.

"Don't touch that," I warned Kara, who'd just come up behind me.

Another scream echoed through the jungle. It had to be Bastian and his crew. Blood and water, I hoped the shadows hadn't already descended upon them. But the books claimed the shadows weren't a danger unless one was trying to escape the jungle.

I looked up at the swirling darkness hovering under the canopies. Shadows zoomed over us, a whoosh following their movements as they dove through branches, slipped under vines, and wrapped around trees. But they didn't bother us, didn't even seem to notice our presence. So what was causing those screams?

Kara had gotten onto her belly, scooting under the heavy curtain of vines and inching past a long black staff that shimmered. I sighed and followed her. At this point, mud caked my wet clothes. The humid air pushed down on us, and my clothes stuck to my body with a mixture of sweat and swamp water. We emerged on the other side, and continued deeper into the jungle. The thick canopies provided cover from the sun, which must've been why it was so easy for the shadows to survive here. The jungle of the shadow court provided them with the perfect cover to thrive, to guard the island so no one could escape.

"Do you think we're almost there?" I asked Kara.

Her gaze turned dark. "The island is bigger than it appears, the jungle hard to navigate. All that to say, I have no idea."

Perfect. The jungle veered upward, so steep we had to dig our hands into the moist ground and claw our way up. At this point, sweat slicked my hair to my face and trickled down the sides of my temples. We both breathed heavily, slowly working our way up, and I hoped this was the right direction. I was just about to collapse from exhaustion when another yell rang through the air, a clang of metal and heavy grunting following it.

Kara and I looked at each other and climbed faster, grabbing onto tree roots and pulling our way up the hill until we crested the top. I wanted to collapse and not get up for a very, very long time, but Bastian's distinct accent echoed through the jungle as he yelled, "Stop, damnit. I can explain!"

We raced toward that voice until we came upon a clearing, the canopies opening up, the sun shining down right onto Bastian . . . and my brother hovering over him with a sword to his throat.

I'd recognize that mop of curly auburn hair anywhere.

"You have to do something." Kara nudged me. "He'll kill him."

"Stay back," Bastian ordered his crew, throat bobbing. His sword was sheathed at his side. "You're not to hurt the brothers."

Everyone hovered around the edge of the clearing, watching as

Lochlan's large frame straddled Bastian, and he pointed the sword deeper into the pirate lord's throat, a prick of blood welling and trickling down.

"Stop," I yelled, the sound strangled and hoarse. "Don't hurt him!"

Lochlan froze, the snarl on his face melting into confusion. He slowly straightened, letting his sword drop by his side. "Gabby?" he said, that deep timbre of his voice so comforting.

"Loch." I let out a sob and broke into a run. He stood, and I barreled into him as his arms came around me and crushed me in a bear hug.

"What are you doing here?" He pushed me back, gaze searching me for injuries. "Did he hurt you? I'll kill him if he's laid a single finger on —" He paused, those thick auburn brows bunching. "Wait, why did you tell me not to hurt him?"

Bastian came to a stand, straightening his leather coat and cracking his neck.

"He's here to help us get your shadows back," I said.

"Help us?" Lochlan rubbed his jaw, thick and strong like my father's. "The pirate lord of the Dark Seas, the one who is working with the shadow court, is here to help us?"

"It's a long story." I looked around. "Is there somewhere we can go to talk?"

Lochlan let go of my shoulders and stepped back, crossing his muscled arms against his broad chest. He took after my father with his massive height and build. Suspicion clouded his eyes. "Just you. The pirates stay here."

"Lochlan . . ." I started, but Bastian gently grasped my arm.

"It's okay, love," he said. "We'll stay. You take the time you need with your brothers."

"Where is Mal?" I asked, and Lochlan nodded his head behind him.

"He's gathering firewood for our camp."

"Can you just give us a moment?" I glanced back at Bastian. "I promise I'll explain everything. I need to have a word with the pirate lord first."

Lochlan hesitated.

"Please, Loch?" I could hear the whine in my voice.

Finally, he nodded, backing away. "I'll get Mal and be back in a few minutes." He looked at Bastian. "And I will not hesitate to use this"—he lifted his sword—"if he tries anything."

"I don't doubt it," Bastian said as Lochlan stalked away and disappeared into the trees.

I turned toward Bastian, saw the anger etched across his face. I'd ruined his plans by leaving the ship, but I'd also saved his ass. I couldn't believe he'd thought this was a good idea. "What were you thinking? You idiot." I gave him a shove, and he didn't attempt to fight back. "You left me on that ship." I pointed a finger at him. "You knew how important this was to me, and you were just going to leave me behind? Again?"

Mia crossed her arms. "We told him it was a bad idea."

Other crew members nodded in agreement.

His jaw ticked. "I didn't exactly have a choice in leaving the first time."

"There's always a choice, Bastian, so stop making excuses." I stepped forward. "I almost died trying to get past the crocodiles. Your sister almost died. You almost died because you thought it would be a good idea to find my brothers by yourself. And you just expected they'd trust you? I told you that we work together."

He shoved a hand through his hair. "I know. I know, but I didn't want to risk your shadow getting taken. I was going to complete the mission and keep you safe while doing it. Win win."

I stepped forward. "No more secrets, Bastian."

He cocked a brow. "Oh, you want to talk secrets?"

"This might not be the place to do this," Mia said from behind Bastian, but he held my gaze, ignoring his sister.

"How about you planning on rescuing the whole lot of boys?"

I winced.

Bastian raised a finger. "But not just the boys. You were also planning on getting our shadows back. After I expressly told you no such thing was to happen."

I shot an accusing look at Kara, but she looked as dumbfounded as I felt.

"I know you, love." Bastian hooked a finger under my chin. "Why do you think I left you on that ship? I knew you were going to try something stupid, and I couldn't let you take that risk. Not for me."

"Well, you don't get to make that decision," I said. "You promised me in that cave . . ." I trailed off, thinking of all the things we did in that cave after he made that promise to me.

He smirked like he knew exactly what I was thinking about. "I suppose we call it even, then? You lied to me. I lied to you." He spread his arms. "All our secrets are laid bare."

"They really are perfect for each other," Kara muttered.

"It's romantic," Bartholomew said.

"I hope so," I said, "because I can't take any more of this."

I'd already fought with my best friend. I couldn't handle a fight with my pirate as well. My heart ached as I thought of Leoni, back on that ship, not here to guard me. At least she was safe.

Kara stepped forward. "She's a grown woman, Bastian. She can make her own decisions, and if you don't let her do this for us, then it's going to be your downfall."

He glared over at his sister. "Oh, you're on her side now? I thought you didn't like her. Told me she was dangerous."

Kara lifted her chin, sun glancing off her eyebrow ring. "I changed my mind. I'm allowed to do that, you know."

He rubbed his temples and muttered, "women" under his breath.

I took his hands in mine. "Moving forward we work together."

His thumb rubbed small circles around my hand. "I'm sorry."

I leaned up and pressed a kiss to his mouth. "I forgive you."

His mouth pushed firmly against mine in response, but suddenly I was being yanked back by a strong hand.

"Get off of my sister," Lochlan growled at the pirate, who stepped back, hands raised. Lochlan ran a hand through his auburn curls. "What in the fuck, Gabby?"

I winced. "Can we please go somewhere and talk? You, me, and Mal?"

Lochlan glared at the pirate, then turned his piercing gaze on me. "You're clearly not in your right mind."

Bastian rolled his eyes. "You know, I am quite likable once you get to know me."

Lochlan set his jaw, and I sighed. "Please take me to Mal," I begged. "What I'm about to tell you will change everything, I promise."

Lochlan stared at me for a long minute with those blue eyes, bright and searing like my father's had been. He looked so much like him, except his hair wasn't yet graying at the temples. Finally, he jerked his head toward the trees and stomped off.

"Well, that went well," Bastian muttered from behind me.

I ignored the pirate and followed my brother into the jungle. This wasn't the reunion I'd expected, but hopefully after I explained everything, Lochlan and Mal would be willing to work with the pirate lord and his crew. If not, I had no idea how we were going to pull this rescue mission off.

Chapter Forty-Eight

Mal stood in front of a crashing waterfall that pooled down into clear water. It bubbled over stones of all colors, making it look like someone had pulled a rainbow from the sky and splashed it across the rocks. Sun sliced through the clouds above, but as Lochlan and I approached Mal, I still felt the presence of shadows lurking in the dark cover of the trees.

Items scattered across the bottom of the pool: a red ring, a spear, a fishing pole. So many objects with so much power, it was dizzying.

Tears pricked my eyes as we got closer, and I broke into a run, crashing into Mal and holding him tight.

"What are you doing here?" he said. "Gabby, why did you come?"

"Just shut up and hug me," I said between sobs.

He quieted, his arms tightening. I pushed him at arm's length and studied my younger brother, his short black hair. My siblings and I were a mishmash of my parents: Mal inheriting my mother's dark hair, while Loch and I inherited my father's auburn hair. While I had my mother's brown eyes, Lochlan and Mal had my father's blue eyes, stark and bright. Mal and I had slighter, leaner builds like our mother. Lochlan took after our father, towering over us, broad chested and thick with muscle. It didn't hurt that he also had my father's strong jaw and crooked nose, which gave him a rugged kind of beauty that not many men could pull off. That was no doubt how he'd earned the playboy prince nickname, how he'd somehow become the most eligible bachelor on the continent of Arathia—and even in some of the human lands.

Lochlan strode forward and slung his arms around both my and Mal's shoulders. "Well, look at that. A family reunion."

Mal shot Lochlan a look of annoyance and shoved his arm off. He sat down on a large rock that crested the edge of the water. "What are you doing here?" His gaze flicked toward the ground. "Is your shadow—"

"I have my shadow." I gestured to it, the sun highlighting it as it stretched over the water.

Mal let out an exhale of relief.

"What about you two? How did you get your shadows taken? Have you seen him? Where are the boys? Are they okay?"

Lochlan raised a thick brow. "I think we might be the ones who need to ask the questions here." He looked at Mal. "Go ahead. Ask her who she's here with. You're gonna love her answer."

In usual Lochlan fashion, he was treating this like some entertaining game. It hadn't been so entertaining when he was threatening to shove a sword through Bastian's throat.

Mal's brows furrowed together, and he ran a hand over his black hair. "What is he talking about? Who are you here with? Father?"

I winced. They didn't know. I supposed that made sense. Marian had said she never returned after she'd lost her voice, so ashamed over her role in my father's death.

"I have a lot to catch you up on, it seems," I said.

Mal's face fell, and Lochlan tensed.

"So who are you here with if not Father?" Mal asked.

Might as well get this over with. "The pirate lord."

Mal shot to his feet. "He kidnapped you too?"

"Oh no, brother." Lochlan clapped one hand on Mal's shoulder. "Not kidnapped."

Mal looked between us. "Then what? What am I missing here?"

I gestured to the rocks. "Both of you sit your asses down, shut your mouths, and let me speak. I'll tell you everything, and when I'm done, you'll understand why I'm here."

MAL AND LOCHLAN both sat on the rocks in a stunned silence as I finished my story.

"You're in love with the pirate lord?" Mal asked.

I let out an exasperated sigh. "That's what you got from my story? I've been talking for thirty minutes, and that's what you're choosing to ask about? Did you not hear anything I said? He doesn't have his shadow. He's under the shadow king's command. He's ninety-five years old."

Lochlan leaned back onto his hands. "I think we got it, Gabby. It's just..."

"It's bullshit," Mal said.

Lochlan winced. "I was going to say it's a shock, but little brother here doesn't mince words."

I pinned my gaze on Mal. "Oh, you want to talk about bullshit? How about your secret relationship with the sea princess?"

Mal stiffened. "How do you know about Marian?"

I'd left out that part of the story, just focusing on Bastian and his backstory with the shadow king, explaining why he'd taken the boys in the first place and the deal we'd made.

"We helped her get her voice back," I said, then told them the story of Father and the trident, how he ultimately lost his life because of how he'd tried to help Marian. How Marian had been too ashamed to show her face here again.

"Father's truly gone?" Mal asked.

He and Lochlan both wiped tears from their eyes.

"The bastard finally did it," Lochlan said. "How many times growing up did we hear him tell us one day he'd find the trident and—"

"Bring glory to us all," we finished in unison.

We burst out into laughter, which turned into some more tears.

Mal shook his head. "Father knew about Marian. She never told me she planned to go find him, to tell him where we were."

"He already knew," I said. "The seafolk followed Bastian's ship and reported back to us. Everyone in Apolis knew where you were, where our boys were. We just didn't know how to get you back. Especially after Father left with all our men and then disappeared."

"How is Mother?" Lochlan asked.

"How do you think?" Overhead, clouds moved across the sun, blocking out its rays, and shadows crept out, whooshing down into the water, splashing and flying in circles, paying us no mind.

"You get used to it." Lochlan gave a half shrug.

Mal crossed his arms. "No you don't."

I tore my gaze from the shadows. "She's devastated. She lost her husband, her sons, her court is falling apart. And then I left, which she didn't exactly know about," I admitted.

Mal's head snapped up. "You didn't . . ."

Lochlan barked out a laugh. "Of course she did." He elbowed Mal, whose lips had flattened into a thin line. "How many times growing up did Gabby sneak out or plan some dangerous adventure without Mother's or Father's knowledge?"

Mal cut him a sharp look. "This is a little different, Loch."

"Okay," I said, not wanting to focus on myself any longer. "I've told you my tale. How I got here, how I'm in cahoots with the pirate lord."

"I'd say it's a little more than cahoots after I saw you two making out," Lochlan grumbled.

Mal's eyes bugged. "Making out?" He grimaced.

"We were not making out." I glared at Lochlan. "Will you shut up and just tell me what's going on here? Where are our boys? Are they okay? How did your shadows get taken?"

Lochlan cleared his throat. "Ours isn't as interesting as a tale. Mal and I hid belowdecks for days, sneaking out when everyone awoke and emptied the little bunk room, getting into the barrels for water and food. The boys were all on the main deck, in some kind of trance from what we could tell. None of them tried to leave, jump ship, fight back, nothing."

Because of the clock Bastian had used.

"When we finally docked, Mal and I didn't know where we were yet. We knew the pirate lord had taken the boys, but not why. We decided it would be best to wait until the boys were on the island, then we could sneak onto land, gather them, and make a plan to get the bloody waters out of there.”

Mal snorted. “That was one of our more idiotic plans.”

“The whole thing was an idiotic plan,” I snapped. “The moment you saw that ship full of our boys, you should’ve come to me, to Mother, to Father. We could’ve figured it out together instead of you two trying to play hero.”

Mal’s cheeks flushed while Lochlan just smirked. “You have to admit, I make a pretty good hero.”

Mal’s nostrils flared. “We didn’t know your boyfriend was kidnapping our boys to take them to the shadow court.”

Lochlan laid a hand on his arm, and Mal took a deep breath.

“Anyway,” Lochlan said. “We snuck onto the island, watched the pirate lord march the boys to the jungle, and we followed them. While we hid away in the trees, we felt this heavy presence looming over us, and that’s when we saw the shadows and put two and two together. The pirate lord had brought us to the shadow court. The pirates left, and we immediately gathered the boys, who were coming out of their trance, confused and scared.”

The image made my heart break. All the other boys Bastian had taken had a choice, a false one, but still a choice. They’d known what they were walking into. Ours hadn’t.

Lochlan shook his head. “We tried to leave, but the shadows swirled around us, darting down and attempting to snatch the boys. We couldn’t make it past the tree line.”

“They guard it,” I murmured.

Mal nodded. “We’ve spent months scouting out the island, trying to find some kind of break in that wall, but there is none. There’s no way out.”

“So how did your shadows get taken?” I asked.

Mal and Lochlan looked at each other as the sun came out again overhead, the shadows hissing and darting back toward the cover of the jungle.

“They descended upon us in a swarm,” Mal said gravely. “These figures with translucent, ragged wings, dust shaking from them each time their wings flapped. The dust made us all fall into a deep sleep.”

The pixies.

"When we awoke, our shadows were gone, our water magic gone, and we knew we were trapped. We've been trying to figure out a way off this damn island ever since."

"Have you ever seen him?" I asked.

"The shadow king?" Lochlan said. "No. But we've learned about him from the pixies. They work with him, have an alliance of sorts."

Bastian had already told me as much.

"Can I see them?" I asked. "Our boys? How are they? Are they terrified?"

I was sure they missed their home, their families. Thank the spirits my brothers had been here to watch over them.

Mal and Lochlan exchanged glances again, some kind of secret conversation passing between them.

"What?" I asked. "What is it?"

Mal stood. "It's better that we show you."

"We have to get Bastian and his crew," I said.

Mal's shoulders tensed.

"They're on our side, Mal."

"Why not?" Lochlan asked. "I already gave the pirate lord a good welcome. If he makes us mad, I'll just push him off one of the many cliffs on the island," he said cheerfully, but Mal didn't laugh.

"Loch," I said, a warning in my voice. "Be nice. Just get to know him. You might actually get along."

"Lochlan gets along with everyone." Mal brushed past me and marched into the jungle. "The real test will be if he can get along with me."

"Good luck with that," Lochlan whispered into my ear, a grin on his face.

The scoundrel was enjoying this far too much.

I sighed and followed them away from the waterfall. This was certainly going to be interesting.

Chapter Forty-Nine

I walked with my brothers, Bastian and his crew behind us. I shot a glance at the pirate lord, and he sent a wink my way, making me smile as I turned forward.

We made our way through the jungle, the hilly terrain thick with foliage sprouting everywhere. We carefully picked our way through the smattering of knotted trees, hanging vines, and bushes ripe with thorns and berries that Lochlan warned were poisonous.

I stepped over a large black helmet.

"Have you been tempted to use any of these items?" I asked Lochlan.

He shook his head. "For whatever reason, without our shadows we can't use this magic. I'm surprised how many people come to this island and take these items." His gaze darkened. "Most don't make it back out, not with the shadows trained to keep everyone in." He shuddered. "I saw one woman ripped to shreds by the shadows when she attempted to run out to the shoreline."

I ducked under a black arrow that stuck out of a tree.

Lochlan nodded his head at the arrow. "Should we test one out on the pirate lord and see if I can make it work?"

I elbowed him. "Are you going to be nice to him?"

"I don't think he responds well to nice." Lochlan slung an arm around my shoulders. "Besides, he seems like the type of guy who can take whatever I throw at him."

Mal just snorted.

"What?" I asked.

"Nothing," he said. "It all makes sense now. Why you were so distant those months before we disappeared. Why you never had time for us, why you shut us out. You were hiding him, your relationship with him."

"Of course I was." I spread out my arms. "Look how you're reacting, even though you know the truth of the situation. That he's as trapped as you are."

"Except we didn't resort to kidnapping," Mal retorted.

"You would have if it was the only way to save me or Lochlan or Marian."

Mal stiffened at that. "I would've found another way." He stalked ahead.

I wished Leoni were here. Wished we hadn't fought on that ship. I needed her right now, and her reassurance.

"He just misses Marian," Lochlan said. "He's been worried sick. He thought maybe the shadows got her, or her father found out and forbade her from seeing him."

I didn't think now was the right time to reveal that her father had not been happy to learn of her relationship with Mal. They'd have a steep hill to climb—if we ever got him out of here.

"So he's taking out his anger on me?"

"Well, on the pirate lord, if you want to get technical," Lochlan said. I elbowed him and he laughed. "It's good to see you, Gabby."

I nestled into his hug. "It's good to see you too, Loch."

We continued to walk through the jungle, shadows constantly whooshing over us, and each time one did, cold crept through me. I rubbed my arms despite the humid heat.

"You'll get used to that too." Lochlan tipped his head up. "The cold."

"Have you seen your shadow?" I followed his gaze to the shadows, all of them smaller, slighter, clearly young boys.

"Once." He shoved a hand through his hair. "It didn't go well when

I tried to catch it. Damn thing nearly threw me out of a tree. That's the other thing they don't like. When you try to catch them."

"We have a plan," I said. "We can discuss it when you and Mal are ready. After we've settled and had a chance to scout the area ourselves."

Lochlan didn't respond. "We're almost there." He pointed ahead to where Mal walked.

Two thick trees, both nearly as wide as Bastian's ship and as tall as his masts, rose up, and thick wisteria hung down like a curtain between them.

Mal swept the wisteria aside, and held it for us as we walked through. Once I was on the other side, I gasped.

The canopies above had been cut away, the clouds parted, sun streaming down onto grassy beds. Huge trees surrounded the massive clearing with ropes dangling from them. My gaze trailed upward to the branches, planks connecting the trees like some sort of system for travel. Little huts made of sticks filled the area, mixed with bigger canvas tents. A pathway wound through the huts and tents, and I could see through it to the center of the area, where a fire roared. And everywhere I looked, there were boys. Shirtless and running, covered in dirt, playing tag, fighting with wooden swords, walking across the planks, climbing the trees. Other boys danced around the fire. None of them looked older than twelve, at the most. It was like they'd created their own little city within the shadow court.

"What is this place?" I breathed, staring at it all with wonder.

"Welcome to Neverland," Lochlan said.

"Neverland?" I echoed. "What does that mean?"

He shrugged. "The boys named it."

"Our boys?"

Lochlan shook his head, the sun highlighting the gold in his auburn curls. "The older boys, the ones who have been here the longest. They found this place, made it their home."

"I can see that," I said as we walked along the dirt path that was carved through the bright green grass. Tents and huts stood on either side of us, and I peered inside to see bedrolls, journals, pens. "Where do they get all these supplies?" I asked Lochlan.

He nodded his head back toward Bastian. "Ask the pirate lord."

"What do you mean?" I said.

"You know, your story made a lot of sense. The boys kept telling us that the pirate wasn't a bad guy, that he rescued them from terrible lives and brought them here to this paradise. They said every time a new boy arrives, he comes bearing supplies, courtesy of the pirate." Lochlan scratched his head. "We just kind of figured he'd manipulated them somehow, lied to them."

Bastian hadn't told me that part. My heart squeezed. In an impossible situation, he'd done what he could. It wasn't enough. It couldn't be enough, but it was good and pure. It was the kind of man he'd always told me he wanted to be. Except he already was that man. That's why I'd fallen in love with him.

I looked back at the pirate, who walked with his sisters, all of them gazing around in wonder as well.

"Princess Gabrielle." A little body slammed into my legs, arms winding around them.

I looked down to see a thick mop of blond hair. "Benji!" The florist's son. I knelt down and hugged him tight.

"Are you going to live with us now?" Benji asked when I released him from my hold.

"No, Benji." I gently grasped his shoulders. "I'm here to take you home."

His bottom lip wobbled. "But I don't want to go home. I like it here!"

With that, he ran away and toward a group of boys who were wrestling on the ground, laughing and squealing.

I stared at them in confusion, then glanced at Lochlan. Bastian had tried to warn me about this, but I hadn't believed him. I hadn't believed our boys would like it here. Prefer it over their own home.

My body tensed. "They don't want to leave, do they?"

"Why would they?" Lochlan gestured around. "Look at this place. They have free rein. They have friends, they get to stay young forever." He shrugged. "Sounds kind of nice."

I shoved him. "We are supposed to be convincing them to leave, not stay here." I looked around. "How many boys are there?"

He looked around. "If I had to guess, about five hundred or so?"

Little boys rushed past us with their wooden sword. "Hi, Princess!" a few of them said like it was just every day their crowned princess waltzed into the shadow court.

We kept walking toward the central area with the big fire. "But that doesn't make sense. Bastian said he's been doing this for sixty years. There should be way more."

Lochlan shoved his hands into his pockets. "Some boys do want to leave. Some boys get their shadows and manage to escape. Other boys get sick. Other boys try to leave and aren't successful. Many have . . ."

He didn't have to finish that last part. I understood.

"Right," I said.

"Not all the boys get along. Some are bullied, some don't feel at home. Mal and I have been working to do conflict management, teach them better coping skills. They don't entirely trust us. Many of them have become wary of adults."

"What does he want with them?" I asked, more confused than ever. "Just to use their shadows, but for what? What is the point of all this?"

"No one knows," Lochlan said. "The boys have created this space for themselves. Most of them have never even seen the shadow king. They don't really care much about him." He pointed upward. "They cut the branches so sun would shine through. They made this place into a home for themselves."

"Mm," I said.

A boar sat on a spit over the fire, roasting, a few boys rotating it. "How do they get food?"

"They hunt. Another thing they taught themselves. These boys are resourceful. It doesn't hurt that the pirate lord has given them countless supplies over the years. Hunting tools, pots, pans, clothes, shoes, needles and thread, tents. It's amazing."

Mal stood in the distance with a group of boys who were jumping on his back, tugging on his sleeves, laughing and playing while Mal faked being a monster.

I laughed.

"He's done a lot too," Lochlan said, nodding at Mal. "He's taught the boys about structure, organization. They did well, but they didn't have a lot of routines in place, didn't have specific roles. Mal's worked with them to implement that. He's mentored some of them into being quite the leaders."

"He's good at planning." My youngest brother flipped a boy over his head. "At leading." I looked up at Lochlan. "You think he'll come around?"

Lochlan roped me into him and planted a kiss on the top of my head. "Of course he will. C'mon, let me show you where you all can sleep."

Chapter Fifty

Fires dotted the campsite that night, and Bartholomew entertained all the boys with his songs about the shadow court. He stood, strumming his banjo and singing, the fire illuminating the puckered scars across his face.

"He woke up covered in mud
The trees around him silent and still
He was determined to escape the jungle prison
So he spent his days roaming the land
Searching for his shadow
He stumbled upon it on a night so fine
And caught it in his grasp
But the slippery shadow darted away
Leaving the boy all alone
Every time he tried
It escaped through his grasp
Until he finally got a bright idea
That shadow would be his at last
He pounced on it and sewed its foot
Right to the bottom of his shoe
He escaped the island
And lived to tell the tale

His shadow and his body reunited once again."

The boys erupted into cheers, hooting and hollering. I wondered where Bartholomew had gotten the idea for that song. It was another catchy one.

After that, everyone retired to their tents. Mal and Lochlan both gave me hugs. Bastian nodded at me. He'd kept his distance, sensing the tension between me and Mal, and I appreciated it. But I also missed him. I watched until the last boy disappeared and the camp was silent and still.

Stars twinkled in the sky above, and shadows swirled like storm clouds under the cover of night. They paid me no mind, but I hated the cold that crept over the area with their presence, the feeling of darkness, like they were tugging at my own shadow to join them.

I wouldn't be able to sleep, not with all the thoughts rolling through my head.

I made my way past all the tents and huts, past the little clearing and to a shimmering silver pool, moonlight reflecting off of it. I needed to bathe and I certainly couldn't do so during the day with all these boys running rampant. Lochlan had given me clean clothes, ones that typically fit the older boys but just so happened to work for me as well. He'd given his and Mal's extra clean clothes to some of the pirates to change into and had ordered boys to launder everyone's clothes, something else he and Mal had implemented. Apparently the boys hadn't worried too much about bathing or cleaning their clothes, and Mal and Lochlan had quickly changed that.

I looked behind me at the silent camp. No wonder the boys were so strict about being in their tents and huts at night. They didn't want the shadows leering over them. Shadows bounced against the tents and huts, unable to figure out how to get in. It must've been hard to sleep through such a thing. Then again, I remembered when Mal and Lochlan were that young. They'd been able to sleep through anything, including storms and each other's snoring.

The water was cool against my skin, enveloping me as I waded in and dipped under, hoping what Lochlan said was true and none of the boys would emerge from their little shelters.

I surfaced, water trickling down my face.

"Care for some company?"

Bastian stood at the edge of the pool, shirtless, that perfect muscled chest gleaming under the moonlight.

"I didn't mean to wake you," I said.

"I'm mad you didn't wake me. You think I'd miss out on you naked in a pool?" He arched an eyebrow.

I pointed a finger at him. "If you're going to join me, then you better behave yourself, pirate. In case you've forgotten, we're in a camp full of young, impressionable boys."

He smirked and undid the laces of his trousers, pulling them down, his cock bobbing and as glorious as ever. "I'll do my best. Pirate's honor."

He stepped into the water, and I licked my lips as he lowered that massive body of his into the pool.

We hadn't gotten a chance to talk in depth yet.

He swam toward me, a gleam in his eyes.

"I know that look," I said. "Put that look away."

His eyes danced. "I don't know what you're talking about."

I clenched my thighs together as desire prickled between them. "Stop it." I splashed him in the face.

Water droplets clung to his thick dark eyelashes and the ends of his hair.

"Oh, you're going to pay for that."

He grabbed me and slammed me to his chest, pressing kisses down my jawline.

"I don't think I'm paying for anything," I said, breathless.

He slowly trailed a finger along my cheek, then brought his hand to the top of my head and shoved me under the water. I kicked at him, and when I surfaced, he was laughing.

"Truce?" I said. "I did come out here for a purpose, you know."

"Let me help." He swam to the edge of the pool, grabbing a bar of soap.

"Bastian," I warned.

"I'm just going to wash your hair, love. Nothing else."

I eyed him warily as he approached. He stopped in front of me and gently turned me in the water so my back was pressed to his. His hands threaded through my hair as he began to massage my scalp with the soap.

"How are you feeling?" he asked, drawing me into his chest.

I closed my eyes and savored the gentle touch of his hands. "I don't know. I'm relieved none of the boys are hurt, that they seem to be happy. But our job is going to be so much harder when they don't even want to leave." I gestured up to the shadows whirling above us like a tornado. "And how are we supposed to reunite these shadows with their owners. Look how many of them there are. What about all the other boys that are here? We're just going to leave them?"

Bastian's fingers faltered. "Some of these boys have been here for decades. What are we going to do? Return them to a home that might not even exist anymore? To a life on the streets where no one cares about them? I understand this isn't the most ideal place, but it's theirs. I agree we need to rescue your boys, take them back to their families, their home, but the rest of them—it's far more complicated."

He stopped massaging my head and cupped water in his hands, pouring it over my head. His hands worked their way down to my shoulders, digging into my tense muscles.

"Relax," he whispered.

"Relax," I scoffed. "How can I relax when we're up against so much? How am I going to convince our boys to leave? What are we supposed to do? Kidnap them again? Take them against their will?"

He dug his fingers deeper, and I let out a moan.

"We'll talk to them, remind them of what they're missing at home. Remind them of all the things they've forgotten. And as for the other boys . . ."

"Maybe we can make a new home for them," I said. "A place where they have their shadows but have the freedom and community they have here."

"Where?" Bastian asked. "We can't just create a place like that and expect them to be safe."

"I don't know." I shook my head. "I'll think on it more."

Bastian took the bar of soap and scrubbed it across my back. "It will take time, love. Time we don't have right now. Focus on the mission at hand. And remember our priority is not me or my crew."

I turned abruptly at that. "It is all of us. It is my brothers, my boys, and my crew."

Bastian's lip kicked up. "Your crew, huh?"

I shrugged. "They're growing on me. And we're leaving this place. All of us. Together."

Doubt lined his features.

I lifted a hand and brushed the hair from his forehead. "What is it?"

"I know we're in this together. But I still don't know what's going to happen once we leave here. How we're going to make this work." He swallowed. "I can't help but hate that I'm the reason you want to give up your crown, that you resent your duty. If I weren't here, if our paths had never crossed . . ."

"No . . . that's not . . ." I shook my head, unable to explain. "I don't regret you. I will never regret you."

"Okay, then," Bastian said after a moment as a shadow swooped down over him.

The breeze rustled the trees above, and Bastian looked up, letting out a low whistle. "Well, will you look at that?" He pointed upward.

My gaze trailed the direction he pointed, and a little gasp escaped my mouth. There it was, sparkling in the sky. Second star to the right. Our star.

I kissed him, slow, deep, savoring the taste of him, that scent of salt and sandalwood wrapping around me.

"And you said I was the one who needed to behave," he murmured into my mouth.

I drew away from him, giving the star one last look before I exited the little pool.

We dried off and dressed, then walked back to our tent, no more shadows accosting us, though they surrounded us, bouncing against the huts and tents relentlessly, hissing and letting out the occasional shriek.

Tomorrow we'd somehow have to convince my brothers and all the boys of our plan, a plan that was only half formed. At this point, it didn't seem like the shadows were going to be our biggest adversaries.

Chapter Fifty-One

Bastian, Lochlan, Mal, and I sat around a rough sketch of the island that Mal had drawn using a stick in the dirt.

Lochlan pointed with a stick to the middle part of the map. "So we're here." He moved the stick over toward the western part of the island, near the cliff side. "This is where most of the pixies reside." He dragged the stick up the coastline, where little triangles represented the mountains. "This is the shadow court, where the shadow king and his people live."

"The people that you've never seen?" I asked.

"Correct," Lochlan mumbled. "Not without trying, though. Mal and I have scouted out this entire island. It took hours to trek up that damn mountain to the tall walls surrounding the shadow court. They're built of stone, and Mal and I had to scale a tree to get ourselves up there."

"A tree?" I asked in disbelief.

"Well, how else were we going to do it?" Mal asked.

"I'm just surprised," I said gently, hoping to lessen the tension between us. "Trees are not exactly in abundance in the water court."

Mal had still been grumpy with me this morning, and I desperately wanted us to move past this so things could return to the way they'd been before Bastian, before they'd disappeared, before everything.

"So what happened next?" Bastian asked.

Mia and Kara approached and crouched on either side of him, both of them studying the map.

"We got up the tree and shadows swarmed us, knocked us down. Almost broke my arm," Lochlan said. "Instead, all I broke was Mal's fall." He jabbed a finger in our younger brother's direction.

Mal rolled his eyes.

"Did you see anything when you were up there?" Kara asked, scratching at her brow.

"Not much," Lochlan admitted. "The tops of what looked like thatched roofs, dirt roads, banana trees. And the castle, dark and at the top of the mountain."

Mal shifted. "We tried to go back, but every time, the shadows wouldn't let us near. It's like they're also trained to guard that place."

"What are these shadow people planning? Why don't they ever leave the confines of those walls?" My gaze traveled around the circle. "Do you think they're trapped as well? That the shadow king is keeping them hostage?"

Lochlan spread out his hands. "Your guess is as good as mine. The boys know nothing about this shadow king. The pixies work for him, with him . . . spirits if I know."

I shot a look at Bastian, and he raised his hands in the air. "Goji and I didn't discuss the shadow king or these shadow people. She didn't know much about him either. Apparently he's not much of a talker."

"Who's Goji?" Lochlan asked, brows furrowed.

"It's a long story," I said. "Do the pixies visit regularly?"

Lochlan shook his head. "They come by to collect the new arrivals. They use their dust to knock them unconscious, then fly them to the shadow king. He takes their shadows, and the pixies return the boys the next day. Sometimes when they come, they'll bring the boys food or supplies."

"How does he know when a new boy arrives?" I ask. "Do the shadows communicate with him?"

Lochlan opened his mouth.

"If you say I don't know one more time," I warned.

"It's not his fault," Mal snapped. "Ask your pirate lord about it. He's the one who's been working for the guy for sixty years."

"Fair point," Bastian said, not letting Mal rile him. "Unfortunately, like I just said, this shadow king isn't much of a talker. Just likes to rip our shadows away and not much else."

"What is your problem?" Kara asked my younger brother.

Bastian and I locked eyes. The last thing we needed was a fight to break out between Kara and Mal.

"Maybe we can take a break, continue this conversation later," Mia said.

"No." Bastian's gaze locked on Mal. "Let's settle this. You don't like me, mate. I don't blame you. Yes, I've been working for the shadow king for sixty years. He has our shadows, and I have no choice unless I want my crew, my sisters, to die. I took your boys because he commanded to me to, a show of faith after he found out about my relationship with your sister, whom I love very much."

Mal crossed his arms. "Tell me something new, pirate lord. Gabby has already told us all of this."

"You want to know something new? Your sister doesn't need protecting," Bastian said. "I have two of my own, and I know firsthand how hard it is to stop trying to save them. But they don't need us to rescue them. These women? They can save themselves. The best we can do is get out of their way and support them so we don't lose them. I had to learn that the hard way."

Mia and Kara both looked at Bastian, their faces softening at his words.

Mal's eyebrows furrowed. "What do you mean by that? That you had to learn the hard way?"

Bastian glanced at me. "I pushed your sister away to save her. I broke her heart, made her think I was a villain. I withheld parts of myself from her. It didn't matter. In the end, she was still going to do what it took to save you two, to save me. We both could've saved ourselves a lot of trouble if I'd just trusted that she doesn't need me to be her protector. She's the hero of her own story, not me." He grabbed my hand, and I squeezed it. "She doesn't need you to protect her either. Believe me, she will kick my ass if need be."

Mal swallowed. "I'm glad you recognize that."

"But do you?" Bastian asked.

Mal's eyes flicked to me for a second. He cleared his throat and pointed at the map. "Let's get back to it."

I caught Bastian's gaze and mouthed, "Thank you." He nodded, shooting me a wink that made Kara roll her eyes.

"So do you have a plan?" Lochlan asked.

I thought of what Marian had told us about the necklace, its prophecy. "We want to use the light to trap the shadows. Make them gather in one spot and then reunite them with their bodies. According to the necklace, the light is the key."

Lochlan sat back on his heels, frowning down as Mal stroked his jaw thoughtfully.

"That's not a bad plan," Mal said.

"We just have to pick the right location," Lochlan added. "One where the shadows can't escape back into the darkness."

"If we have enough light, we might not even need that confined of a space," Mia said. "We need torches and fire, and then we can create a pathway that leads the shadows straight to our boys."

"The shadows are all over the island," Lochlan said. "Not just in one location. A funnel like that isn't going to work."

I bit back my frustration. "Well, then we'll keep brainstorming," I said. "We can build on this plan and create a better one by working together."

Mal nodded and locked eyes with Bastian. "Together," he echoed.

Trees rustled around us, shaking with intensity. The chatter and laughter of the camp died down as the boys froze, all eyes turning to the hanging vines that protected their home.

Mia slowly stood, drawing a dagger from her boot. "What's going on?"

Bastian's hand went to the sword sheathed at his side.

"That's the pixies," Mal said, concern lacing his voice.

Kara's brows drew together. "But the pixies only come when there's a new shadow to take."

Lochlan's throat bobbed. "There's only one person here who has their shadow." He met my gaze. "And they've come to collect."

Chapter Fifty-Two

The vines trembled, all the boys standing there with bated breath, their eyes stuck on the entrance. A few younger boys shook, and the older boys stepped up to place their hands on their shoulders. Outside the entrance, a hiss filled the air, so loud I had to cover my ears.

Lochlan took a hand off one ear. "It's the shadows," he yelled. "They do this every time the pixies come here. I don't think they like them."

The vines parted and a stream of pixies flew through, their wings fluttering. I gasped. I'd never seen pixies before in person. I'd heard of them, of course, seen pictures of them in books, read about their kind—though like the seafolk, they were secretive, more withdrawn from society. It was amazing to know the Seven Spirits created them.

They were stunning. Just like Bastian had said, their wings were translucent, shimmering with sparkling glitter. Their hair was similar to elemental and human hair in color and texture, and it varied between them. Their skin glowed under the sunlight, a light green. The males wore no shirts, chests bare, while the females wore what might be akin to a bra with their stomachs showing and short skirts with tattered edges hanging down past their thighs. They landed on the various planks stretching between the trees high above. Some planted down on the ground, while others perched in branches.

A female stepped forward, her blond hair hanging down to her shoulders, straight and with a glow to it. Everything about these creatures glowed. Dust wafted from her wings into the air.

"Hello, pirate." She nodded toward Bastian.

She spoke with a beautiful lilt to her words, her accent so charming.

He winced. "Hello, Goji. Nice to see you again."

"I could think of a lot of words to describe this meeting, but nice is not one of them."

Goji. So this was Bastian's friend. The one he'd betrayed. Well, this wasn't going to go well for me.

Goji's green eyes, bright like emeralds, settled on me. "Hello, dear. You're going to have to come with us."

"No." Lochlan and Mal stepped up on either side of me.

"Goji," Bastian growled. "Not her. Do this for me."

She scoffed. "For you? No, I think not."

I heard the rasp of a sword being unsheathed from behind me. "Then I suppose I'll have to fight you."

He couldn't. They'd kill him. He would let himself be torn apart for me. Of course he would.

She rolled her eyes. "You're always so stupid when it comes to her, aren't you?"

I held out my hand to Bastian. The last thing we needed was a bloodbath. I would never forgive myself if any of these boys got caught in the crossfire.

"I'll go," I said.

"Absolutely not," Lochlan said at the same time as Bastian said, "Fuck if you are."

"What happened to me being able to protect myself?" Bastian met my gaze, pain flashing in those eyes. "This is my choice, Bastian. I won't let you fight my battle. Trust me. Please."

His jaw tightened.

"You don't know what you're doing," Mal said.

"I don't have a choice." I gently unclasped his hand from my arm. "And neither do you."

Goji raised her hand, and a few pixies fluttered forward, grabbing both my arms. I felt my feet lift off the ground, my stomach shooting up to my throat.

"You'll get used to it," one of the boys shouted from below as I rose higher in the sky.

"Goji, keep her safe!" Bastian yelled.

I looked back one last time as the pixies flew me over the trees, and everyone disappeared behind the canopies.

My eyes grew heavy, and my head lolled against my chest as I fell into darkness.

"WAKE UP," a voice said. "Oh, don't tell me my dust was that strong. Wake up, woman."

My eyes felt so heavy, my head like a stone.

Cold water splashed against my face, and I jolted upright. A figure stood over me, a halo of sun around them that streamed through the trees. My vision went sideways, and my head thumped against the ground again.

"Here," the voice said with that beautiful accent. "Drink this."

They tipped my head up, and I sipped a warm liquid that made my vision clear, my head less foggy. I blinked a few times at my surroundings. Goji stood in front of me at the edge of the jungle. She set the cup down. Through the thick foliage, turquoise water lapped gently at the shoreline, and tall trees and shrubs surrounded the water. Rock formations jutted up in the distance, blocking any view of the sea beyond this little lagoon. I wanted to get up and run through the trees and into the warm sun, but shadows lurked above us in the canopies, no doubt waiting to strike should we try to escape.

Escape. The pixies. Goji.

I shot to my feet. "What's going on? Where are the rest of the pixies?"

Goji smiled, looking completely at ease. "Don't worry, dear. They think I'm taking you to the shadow king to have your shadow extracted. That's usually my job."

I stepped back. "But . . . you're not?"

Goji peered at me. "You're the one, eh? The princess the pirate lord would sacrifice the world for." She said it so flippantly.

"I—" I sputtered. "Well—I—yes, I suppose that's one way of putting it."

She scoffed. "With the way he talked about you? It's the only way of putting it. He's an idiot, but I suppose we often are when it comes to love, eh?"

"He spoke about you." I rubbed my arms. "You were a good friend to him, and it's my fault your pixie dust is gone. I stole it from him. He didn't betray you."

She tutted. "No, he just acted like a fool. When I gave him that dust, I told him to use it right away, to break the binding, to get his and his crew's shadows back. But he insisted he had to wait to use the dust so that you'd believe him. That he'd come back for me. He sacrificed everything for you. That's what he does. He sacrifices. He puts everyone else first."

It was true, but I'd never thought of it like that until now. It broke my heart that Bastian feared I wouldn't believe him, so much so that he didn't use the dust when he could have.

A shadow swooped down over our heads, almost brushing against my scalp. I ducked, then slowly straightened. "Why can't you just leave?" I asked Goji. "Why do you need Bastian's help? Our help? If it's so bad here, run away."

She snorted. "Just run away. As if that's a simple thing when there are shadows keeping everyone trapped."

My gaze flitted to the canopies above. "Even the pixies?"

She gestured to them. "They have their orders. To guard, to protect. They cannot differentiate boys from pixies. They're not that intelligent."

I gestured to the dust floating in the air, little motes of color illuminated in the slivers of sun. "Why not use your magic?"

She peered at me. "Do you know anything about pixie dust?"

"I know that giving it is a sacrifice, that its use takes years off your life."

"And do you know why?"

I nodded. "The Seven Spirits. It was their way of putting a check on the magic they gave you when they created you."

Goji looked impressed. "Exactly. They couldn't have servants more powerful than themselves. We can live as long as we want if we never use our magic. Every time we use our pixie dust, it takes time off our lives. Just a little. So using our magic here and there isn't so much of a sacrifice, but a lot of magic?" She widened her eyes in emphasis.

"Is that why you can't give Bastian another vial of dust?" I asked.

"That and—" She flapped her wings, gesturing to the dust floating from them. "Do you know how long it takes to collect our own dust? It took me months just to get enough for that one small vial."

"So why work with the shadow king, then?" I asked. "Why help him? Why help any of the shadow people?"

Goji's eyes flashed. "The shadow people?" She frowned. "You elementals don't know much about the pixies or this island, do you?"

"That's because you've never shared much with us. You've kept to yourselves."

"For good reason," Goji said, then she gestured to the trees, which shook as the shadows slithered around the branches. "Come. We must get you back, and you must leave Sorrengard immediately. The shadow king will take your shadow if he finds you."

She turned and her feet lifted off the ground as she fluttered through the trees. I stumbled after her. "Why are you helping me?"

"I'm not helping you." She flew higher, over a branch. "If I let the shadow king take your shadow, then the pirate lord will never agree to help me, no matter our previous deal. I want to leave this place behind, and I can't do it by myself. Believe me, I've tried."

I stepped over a moss-covered log, my boot landing in the squishy mud. "Why? Isn't this your home?"

She sighed. "After the spirits disappeared so long ago, the pixies almost went extinct without them to protect us. Humans were attempting to kidnap us, trying to shake our dust from us, killing us for our magic. We settled here, hoping to remain hidden. When the shadow king came to Sorrengard after the Shadow War, he promised to protect this island, to let us have free rein as long as we let him collect his shadows. We knew the price. It would be hard for anyone to leave, but we didn't particularly care. Why would we leave when the outside world was so dangerous to us?"

I mulled over her words as we began to ascend a hill. So we were right. This shadow king had risen after the war.

A stitch formed in my side as I dug my fingers into the soft dirt, pulling myself upward. I grabbed onto what I thought was a root in the ground, but when my hand brushed against hard metal, I realized I'd grasped onto something that looked like a bolt. I gasped and let it go, staring at the glittering object.

"How did you and Bastian become friends?"

Her voice grew wistful. "I'd watch him through the trees every month when he came, bringing a different boy for the shadow king. He fascinated me, this commanding pirate of a fearsome crew. One day, I said hello through the tree line. We started talking. We became friends. He told me of his adventures at sea. I told him of my long life as a pixie. He painted a picture of the world. For the first time ever, I wanted to see it, to leave my home. The more we spoke, the more this place began to feel like a prison. We both felt trapped in our own way, I suppose. We understood each other."

"So that's why you wanted to leave," I said through heavy breaths. "To see the world?"

I finally got to the top of the hill and hoped we were close to the boys' camp. Shadows swooped down, closer than they'd ever come before.

"We need to hurry." Her emerald eyes flicked to the shadows. She turned and lifted through the air again, and I quickened my pace. "I can't stay here anymore," she said finally. "I need to let go. I need to start over."

Pain filled her voice, and I didn't want to pry. "So you're just going to leave your life behind?"

"I'm going to do what I need to," she said softly. "To save myself."

"Save yourself from what?" I hurried to catch up as she flew under vines hanging from a tree.

"Him," she said simply.

I was having a hard time following the conversation, putting the pieces together.

How she worded it made it sound like she felt threatened . . . but her tone . . . it didn't sound like she was afraid. I recognized that tone. Recognized that sadness in her voice. I'd felt the exact same after that fight with Bastian at the earth court. Him, she'd said. The shadow king. That must've been who she was talking about. But she wasn't afraid of him. She was . . . "You love him," I said. "You're in love with the shadow king."

She stiffened when I said it. "It doesn't matter." A sadness filled her voice as she continued to fly through the air. "I need to leave. I need a fresh start. This place reminds me too much of him."

I couldn't even begin to imagine how a pixie fell in love with the shadow king.

"I'm sorry," I said. "I'm sorry you have to feel that kind of pain."

"That is life," she said.

"Do you know what he's planning?" I reached up and grabbed her arm. She jolted and looked down at me. "Please, if you know why the shadow king is doing this, you have to tell me."

She shook her arm away and scowled at me. "I do not know his secrets any more than you do. That is part of our bargain with him. He protects us; we bring him the boys. We don't ask questions. But I can tell you he's powerful. I suggest you leave and forget the shadow king."

That wasn't going to happen. The shadow king had started something, and we were going to finish it.

A low hiss filled the jungle, and Goji's eyes snapped to the shadows, who were creeping closer. "The shadow king must know something is wrong. The shadows react to his moods."

"Can they communicate with him?" I asked.

She shook her head. "No, but they're connected in a sense. He won't know you're planning to escape. But he was expecting us, and we're not at his castle. So he's agitated." She gestured to a shadow who flew toward me, swiping at me with its wispy hand. "Meaning they're agitated. We need to get to safety."

"Where is the camp?" I ducked as a shadow swooped down.

"Just there." She pointed to the hanging vines. "Run. I must go back to the shadow king. I'll tell him you escaped and that I'm looking for you so he won't suspect anything is amiss. I will come tomorrow at dawn. Be ready with whatever you're planning."

Dawn tomorrow. That was far sooner than we'd expected.

"The shadows are going to be hard to catch," she said. "It can take days for a shadow to bind back with its body, so you need to be prepared to catch them and trap them until the binding is complete." She shoved me forward. "Now run."

I listened, pumping my arms and legs as I flew through the jungle. I didn't dare look back. Shadows darted in front of me, jabbing at me, and one reached out and touched me. I cried out in pain, a cut appearing on my arm from the shadow's touch. I tried to run into the small slices of sun that filtered through the canopies, keeping the shadows at bay, but there was far more darkness than light in this jungle.

My heart pounded as shadows closed in on me. Darkness started to creep in like I was stuck in a gray fog, and it was harder to see what direction I needed to go. I looked all around me but couldn't see anything, no trees, no Goji, no camp. Goose bumps prickled along my arms as the shadows hissed and whooshed all around me. One of them reached a hand out, swiping at my face, and a searing pain sliced across my cheek. I touched it, my fingers coated with blood. I froze for a moment, losing all sense of direction. These shadows might very well kill me because of the shadow king's current mood.

Then I heard it, not far from me: a laugh. I knew that sound. Lochlan.

With a final burst, I leapt in that direction, and shoved through the wispy shadows, through the vines of the camp. I landed with a crash in the sun-filled clearing. I lay in a heap on the ground, letting the sun fill me, pulse still racing from that effort. Arms wound around me, lifting me, crushing me to a hard chest.

I curled into Bastian as he cradled me.

"You're safe," he whispered. "You're safe now."

Tears pricked my eyes. I wasn't safe. None of us were. And if we didn't figure out how to get out of here by tomorrow morning, none of us would ever be again.

Chapter Fifty-Three

"Fuck," Lochlan said, echoing what we were all feeling after I told them everything that happened with me and Goji.

Mia wrinkled her nose. "Goji? In love with the shadow king?"

Bastian scratched his jaw. "I think you misunderstood, love. She would've told me something like that. She didn't even hardly know him."

"I'm telling you, that's what she said. That's why she wants to leave so badly."

Bastian still looked doubtful.

"And we have to do it by tomorrow morning." Mal paced inside the tent where we all stood.

The rest of the crew was outside, playing with the boys, helping them make weapons, cleaning, cooking, while we tried to create a final plan.

Bastian, Mia, Kara, Mal, and I stood in Lochlan's tent now, all of us looking at a new sketch he'd made of the island, this time on a piece of parchment, which was much easier to read than a picture in the dirt.

Mal's hands bunched at his sides. "We need more time to solidify this plan. I know that necklace told Marian we have to use the light, that it's the key to saving us, but I'm not sure light alone will be enough."

"Goji should've just let the shadow king take Gabrielle's shadow," Kara said. "Then he wouldn't be agitated, wouldn't have any reason to worry about someone escaping him."

"Goji made her choice," I said. "And I promised her we'd help her escape."

"Oh, great. Another person we somehow have to save." Kara threw up her arms. "This is going splendidly."

Bastian squeezed my hand under the table. He hadn't let go of me since he'd found me on the ground just inside the entrance to the camp. I didn't know if he'd ever let go of me again.

"This isn't helping." I directed my words at Kara, who just glared at the map. "We need to focus. We don't have a lot of time, so let's figure this out. The shadows are all over the island, right?"

Lochlan nodded as Mal still paced behind him.

Bastian cleared his throat. "You said that the shadows take days to bind to a person?"

I nodded, and he swore.

"I didn't know that was how it worked," Lochlan said. "I thought you grabbed your shadow and poof, you were reunited."

"Apparently not," I mumbled, staring at the map with furrowed brows. "Can we get to the shadow king?" I pointed to his castle on the map.

"That's far too risky," Bastian said. "We don't know what kinds of powers he holds, how to get into his castle. We don't have time to do that kind of reconnaissance. And from what Goji told you, it sounds like there's much we don't understand about this king, how long he's been here, where his shadow people are."

Damnit. He was right.

Mal's lips flattened into a thin line, his hands behind his back.

Right then, a little boy burst through the tent, falling with a heap on the ground in front of us. He was only four years old. One of the priestess's boys. It broke my heart that I might not be able to save him after all.

"Sorry, Princess." He bowed, such a look of contrition on his face that I couldn't help the laugh that escaped my mouth.

"Arlon, what in the Dark Seas are you doing?" I asked as I knelt down to help him stand.

He looked down at his bare, dirty feet. "We're playing treasure hunt," he muttered, face red.

Everyone was smiling now, none of us able to help it.

"Are you winning?" I asked, then whispered in a playful tone, "Has anyone actually found their treasure?"

Arlon looked up, excitement lighting his face. "We find the treasure all the time, but capturing it is the hard part."

Lochlan ruffled Arlon's thick black hair. "Run along, boy. The adults are talking, okay?"

"Wait." His words were so specific. Capture. He'd said capture. "What's this treasure you're hunting?"

He was practically vibrating now, bouncing on the balls of his feet. "The wispies," he said. "Haven't you seen them? They're all over the island. We try and capture them, but it's hard. They always get away. They're slippery." He donned a thoughtful expression. "Kind of like snakes. Our goal is to find our wispy. The one that belongs to us."

We all exchanged looks, every one us thinking the same thing.

Mal swallowed. "Arlon, will you go get Hammond please?"

Arlon nodded. "Yes, Prince Maledonan."

He ran from the tent and returned a few minutes later with an older boy whom I didn't recognize. Freckles dotted the boy's face, his hair orange and unruly.

"What's going on?" Hammond asked, staying near the entrance to the tent like he was ready to run if he didn't like our answer.

Mal stepped forward. "This treasure hunt game you all are playing . . . What are you trying to capture, exactly?"

"Our shadows," Hammond said like we were idiots.

We all gaped at him.

Bastian was the one who finally found his voice. "How do you know where your shadows are?"

Hammond and Arlon both shrunk away from the pirate lord.

"It's okay," Mal said. "You can tell us."

"Don't you feel it?" Hammond asked, his eyebrows bunched.

Lochlan scratched his head. "Feel what?"

"Your shadow." Hammond studied him. "It calls to you, and when you get closer to it, you feel a pull. It's like a rope is attached between you. My shadow is always in the same place, a cave near the cliffs."

Mal and Lochlan looked at each other, stunned, then back at the boys.

"That's what that is?" Lochlan's blue eyes widened. "I thought it was just some weird shadow court thing."

"Blood and water," Mal muttered.

"The wispies," Arlon said with glee, then his face turned into a pout. "I just wish they weren't so slippery. Mine never lets me grab it for very long before it flies away."

A plan began forming in my head as I mulled over Goji's words.

"You two can get back to your game," Lochlan said, and Hammond ushered Arlon out of the tent, the flap closing behind them.

Bastian's arm came around my waist. "What are you thinking, love?"

I met his gaze. "Have you felt it? That pull?"

"Maybe," he said. "But we're never on the island, near our shadows, long enough for me to." He brushed a stray strand of hair out of my eyes, and I leaned into him, into that touch.

Lochlan cleared his throat. "Are they always like this?" he asked.

"You mean obsessed with each other?" Kara asked.

"Yes," Mia said.

We both looked up at everyone else, and I just rolled my eyes.

"How does the game work?" I asked. "This treasure hunt they go on?"

Lochlan crossed his arms. "They break out into teams and the goal is for each team to capture the treasure. That's what they always called it. The team that comes back with their treasure are the ones who win the game."

My eyes bugged out of my head. "So they go out in teams and have to capture one of their shadows and bring it back to camp?"

Mal stroked his jaw. "Blood and water, we're idiots. The winning team always came back with a bag, the treasure inside. Lochlan and I just thought it was some silly relic in the bag. But it was a shadow. A damn shadow."

"And they what?" Mia tapped the table. "Just set it free?"

Lochlan groaned. "I guess. They don't care about getting their shadows back. In fact, most of them don't want them back. They want to stay here, stay young and free forever."

"This is perfect." Excitement thrummed inside of me. "Don't you see? They've been training to capture their own shadows. Some of them for years. They know where their shadows are. They can go get them."

"And what, stuff them in a bag?" Mal said. "How are we going to capture two hundred shadows and get them on Bastian's ship?"

My excitement burst like a bubble. I hadn't thought of that part.

Kara braced her hands on the table. "They're shadows. Surely we can stuff a ton of them into a bag."

"But every time you open the bag, there's risk the others will escape," I said. "I don't think that will work."

Bastian's arms tensed around me.

"There has to be something we're missing." I bit the inside of my cheek. "A key to all of this. We're so close to figuring it out."

"Too bad we don't have those books with us," Bastian said. "They're back on the ship."

Outside, Bartholomew strummed his banjo, the camp quieting as he began to sing.

I straightened, remembering the song he sang last night. "Was that song true?" I asked. "The one that Bartholomew sang about the boy who sewed the shadow to his feet so it couldn't escape him?"

Mal and Lochlan froze, and Mia and Kara gave each other unsure looks.

"I don't know," Bastian said. "Bartholomew tends to stretch the truth quite a lot in his songs."

"No," Mia said slowly. "That one is true. Bartholomew told me he witnessed it himself. Before Kara and I joined the crew."

"That's it," I breathed.

Lochlan cocked a brow. "We're going to sew our shadows to ourselves?"

"Yes," I said. "It's perfect. We have so much thread and needles from the supplies Bastian has brought over the years. Thread and needles that haven't been used because spirit knows none of these boys can sew. It won't take a lot. We give each boy a small piece of thread, and a needle. Send them out in teams and tell them the game."

Mal's eyes widened. "A treasure hunt. We send them on a treasure hunt."

I nodded. "We tell them the objective: capture their shadows, sew them to their shoes, and get to the marsh. And they'll win a prize."

"Their freedom," Lochlan mumbled.

"That's just crazy enough that it might work," Kara said, surprising me. She shot me a small smile.

I couldn't believe it. We had an actual plan. "We can use light to corral the shadows. Make them carry torches."

"How are we going to make sure the boys succeed?" Mal asked. "I won't leave any behind."

I frowned.

"We'll help." The tent flap opened, Hammond standing there.

Mal raised his brows, and Hammond flushed. "The boys like to eavesdrop," Mal said. "We've had many conversations about why that's not appropriate."

The tips of Hammond's ears turned bright red. "They're not meant to be here, those boys from Apolis." Hammond nodded his head toward the camp. "They cry in their sleep, you know. They cry out for their mothers and fathers. They cry for their magic. If they have good families waiting for them, they deserve to go home. The rest of us can help. We'll break into teams. We'll make sure they get their shadows sewn on."

I stepped out of Bastian's arms. "What about you?" I asked. "We can't just leave you here."

Hammond stepped back. "I've been here for . . . a long time. I don't have a home to go back to. Never had a home in the first place."

I swallowed back tears. "But if we could find a place for you, a place where you all could go and grow into men and live on your terms, would you want that?"

"Gabrielle," Bastian said behind me, but I ignored him, stepping closer to Hammond.

His eyes shifted. "Grow up?" he said.

I nodded. "Maybe meet a woman, or man, get married, have kids if you want, or do something else."

"That could be nice," Hammond said cautiously.

"Then we'll come back for you." I held out my hand, and he hesitated before reaching out and shaking it. "We'll come back when that place is real. And we'll save you too."

I turned to look at Bastian, who just threw up his hands. "She's the boss."

Kara leaned forward, elbows resting on the table. "Then we have our plan."

Mal moved toward the entrance. "I'll tell the boys. Prepare them."

"We leave at dawn," I called after him.

At that, everyone filed out of the tent until it was just me and Bastian.

"Are you ready for this?" he asked. "You need to be prepared that we might not be able to find our own shadows—"

"No," I said. "We will get your shadow, Bastian. And we will get off this island. Together. Please don't play hero tomorrow." I cupped his face. "That's not who I need you to be."

He placed his hand over mine. "Then who do you need me to be if not your hero?"

A grin spread across my face. "I need you to be what you're best at. The pirate lord of the Dark Seas."

Chapter Fifty-Four

We awoke before the sun rose, Bastian and his crew standing with Mal, Lochlan, and me, all of us huddled near a fire that crackled. The shadows' red eyes glowed in the dark, little pinpricks of crimson surrounding us.

Mal stepped forward. "You all have your assigned boys. Two hundred and eight in total. So each of us is responsible for six boys. You make sure those six are at the meeting place by the marsh before we board the ship. Hopefully once Lochlan and I have our shadows back, we can help Gabrielle and use our water magic to bring the ship closer and get everyone safely boarded."

"It looks like you all have a plan," Goji said, stepping into the glow of the fire.

Bastian stilled, then surged forward and brought her in for a hug. "Thank you for bringing her back to me."

"I didn't do it for you," Goji said.

"I still owe you," Bastian responded.

"Just get me off this blessed island, and we'll be even, pirate."

He nodded, then nudged her. "I can do that."

Her wings fluttered, dust floating from them, and she shot him a smile. I hoped she'd forgive him and they could be friends again.

Mal dismissed us, and we went from tent to tent, rousing the sleepy boys, telling them to get ready for our big treasure hunt. The boys hadn't been excited about the game until Mal told them that the prize would be their magic. That they'd get to use their magic again and board a pirate ship that would take them home to their mothers and fathers. It was like a light switch went off in their brains, and suddenly the camp had been a frenzy of excitement as the boys chattered about the game.

Once we'd gotten the boys up, dressed, and fed, we assembled our teams.

My six boys rounded up with me in the center. I crouched to the ground, and they sat around me. "You all are going to do great today," I said. "You'll have a leader with you." I nodded to the older boy who stood next to me. "He'll help your team in the treasure hunt. Your goal is to find all of your shadows, then sew them to your shoe."

One of the little boys held up his foot. "Do I have to wear this?" He wrinkled his nose, and I smiled.

"Yes. It's the only way to win the treasure hunt." My palms grew clammy the closer we got to leaving this place. "Now remember, once you get your shadows, then your team leader will bring you to the marsh. Don't forget to carry your torches. Each group will have two to ward off the other shadows."

"The wispies," another young boy said.

I bopped him on the nose. "Exactly."

One boy with blond hair and wide green eyes said, "When I get my magic back, can I make a big wave?"

I gave him my most confident smile. "Absolutely."

He squealed and clapped his hands together.

I blew out a shaky breath and stood. "Now remember, other wispies might try to stop you, to keep you from reaching the marsh, but part of the game is evading them with your light. Okay?"

The boys nodded, all of them with solemn looks on their faces. I fished out my roll of thread and began breaking off pieces, giving one to each boy. I gave a needle to the team leader.

Around me, Lochlan, Mal, Bastian, and his crew were all having similar conversations with their teams of boys. Soon, everyone finished, and the boys rose to their feet.

"Here's extra thread." I gave the leftover pieces to the team leaders. "In case you need it."

"Thank you," one of them said.

I grabbed his arm. "I don't even know your name, but *thank you*. From the bottom of my heart. You're saving these boys' lives."

He swallowed and nodded, and I let him go as he led his team out from the clearing and into the jungle. All the boys filtered out until the adults were the only ones left.

Bastian stepped forward. "Now we need to find our shadows. Break up, go out in small teams, and work together. It should feel like a rope is attached to you. Once you get that feeling, it means your shadow is near. You don't bloody leave this island without it. Once we get to the marsh, make sure your boys are there with their shadows. Understood?"

Everyone nodded.

I turned to Mal and Lochlan. "Do you both remember where you felt that pull? What part of the island?"

Lochlan tipped his head. "Near the castle."

"Same for me," Mal said.

A chill skittered down my spine. "Be careful." I threw myself at them and they both wrapped their arms around me.

Lochlan let go of me and clapped his hand on my shoulder. "Go get your pirate's shadow, and let's get the bloody waters out of this place."

With that, my brothers disappeared through the vines, Bastian's crew slowly filing out behind them. Mia and Kara hugged Bastian tight.

"You find your shadows," he said. "Do you hear me? Do not worry about me or anyone else. Get your shadows and get to the marsh."

Mia's eyes filled with tears while Kara cracked her neck. "Understood," she said.

She and Mia walked off together.

I turned to face Bastian. "Do you have any idea where your shadow might be?"

"I wish I could tell you yes, but I have no idea, love."

"Then let's get going. We have a long day ahead of us and no time to waste."

I stalked ahead, but Bastian grabbed my hand and reeled me to him. I crashed into his body as his arms wound tight around my back and he pressed his lips to mine. His mouth coaxed mine open, and he kissed me hard.

I pushed him away, breaking the kiss. "Stop acting like this is a goodbye."

A shadowed look passed over his face. "Gabrielle—"

"Let's get going."

With that, I whirled around and marched through the vines and out into the jungle.

Chapter Fifty-Five

The jungle teemed with shadows, the moon still out, slivers of its light peeking through the canopy above. Bastian carried the torch next to me, and we walked side by side in silence.

"Do you feel anything?" I asked.

"Not since the last time you asked," he said. "Which was two minutes ago."

I picked at my nails. "I'm sorry. I'm just anxious. I want everyone on that ship safe and bound for Apolis."

"I know, love. I want that too." He leaned over and pressed a kiss to my head.

"You two are so adorable," Goji said from behind us.

I jumped and put a hand to my chest. "You scared me."

"What are you doing here, Goji? Go to the marsh and wait for us."

She fluttered ahead. "And here I thought you might want my help. I'm hurt, Bastian."

"I want you to be safe," he said from next to me, raising the torch.

The firelight illuminated his strong jaw, covered with a thick, dark beard. I wished we'd had more time to plan, more time to prepare the boys, to teach them how to sew instead of the haphazard lesson we'd had to give last night. I wished I could've made love to Bastian in our tent instead of spending all night tossing and turning, worrying about what was to come. No. Bastian and I would have plenty more nights together.

I refused to believe otherwise. My gaze flicked to Goji's fluttering wings. We needed all the help we could get.

"We accept your offer."

Bastian's jaw ticked. "Am I ever going to get a say in anything?"

"Not likely." I stalked ahead toward Goji. "What do you know?"

"I know a lot, it turns out. Like where the pirate's shadow is."

My mouth dropped open. "Why didn't you tell us that before?"

She smiled, mischief lining her features. "I like the element of surprise. Besides, I didn't want the pirate lord to do something stupid like go after it without us."

My stomach turned itself into knots. "And why is that?"

"Because his shadow is in an abandoned ship that wrecked ashore and is filled with other shadows who like to lurk there. Many of them part of Bastian's crew, I suspect."

Her eyes danced like this was a game.

"Well, that doesn't sound so bad." I glanced up at Bastian, whose gaze stayed on Goji.

"What's the catch, Goji?"

Her eyes widened innocently. "There's no catch. I swear it." Her head tilted to the side. "Other than that it's right next to where the pixies live."

Bastian swore.

Goji raised her hands. "That's why I'm here, though. To help keep you undetected."

Bastian raised his brows. "No games, Goji. Not now."

She fluttered forward until she was almost nose-to-nose with Bastian. All the teasing left her face, now grave. "I'm not playing games, Bastian. Not when it comes to your life—or mine." She pushed past him, flying ahead into the darkness. "Let's go," she called behind her.

Bastian made to move, and I snatched his arm. "Are you sure we can trust her?" I liked Goji, but I didn't know her well enough to be willing to put Bastian's life in her hands.

He pressed a kiss to my forehead. "We can trust her. Besides, at this point, we don't have many other options."

I threaded my hand with his, and he raised the torch in the air, shadows scattering away as we followed Goji to find Bastian's shadow.

WE ARRIVED at the ship an hour later. The sun was just rising over the horizon. Its rays slipped through the trees in slivers, and shadows danced over the light, keeping to the dark.

The bow of the ship jutted up into the air, and vines crept up its side, wrapping around it. Trees poked out the broken windows. It was like the jungle was slowly eating the vessel. Holes battered the hull, like cannons had been shot through it at some point. And half the ship was missing. My gaze roved over the area, and I realized the other half wasn't missing. It was on the other side of the tree line. I could just see its outline through the thick foliage. It sat perched on rocks that the ocean battered against.

We stopped at Goji's side, her feet lowering to the ground next to Bastian. "Of course the pirate's shadow would find the one ship on the island." She nudged him. "Once a pirate, always a pirate, eh?"

Bastian's lips quirked as he looked at her. "You know me well, Goji." He stroked his jaw. "I can't believe you found my shadow."

Goji straightened, tone turning brisk. "It was pure luck. Happened upon it one day and recognized it. Figured it might be good to keep an eye on it in case you ever wanted it back."

Bastian snorted. "I never thought I'd find a way to get it back without your dust." He grabbed Goji's arm before she could move forward. "Goji, I'm sorry. I should've listened to you. About the dust. I should've used it when I had the chance to break the bond, to get my shadow back. It was selfish of me to wait like that, especially when it was your freedom at stake. When you sacrificed so much to give it to me."

Goji's eyes softened, and I felt like maybe I should give them a moment to talk. I backed away a few steps.

Bastian's head snapped to me. "Don't you dare go anywhere."

I froze as he turned back to Goji. "Will you ever forgive me? Will we ever be friends again like we once were?"

Goji cleared her throat. "It's fine, pirate. I understand why you did what you did. Now let's get your shadow back before anyone finds out we're here and alerts the shadow king."

We picked our way over tree roots that rose up and snaked across the ground. When we got to the ship, I peeked inside to see glowing red eyes looking back at me. I jumped back into Bastian's chest. A chuckle rumbled through him and vibrated through me.

I elbowed him, and he let out a grunt. "Stay out here," he said. "Goji and I will go in."

"Absolutely not. You idiot."

Goji barked out a laugh as I climbed in through the broken window. Bastian sighed and followed me, holding out the torch. The shadows flew toward the ceiling, melting into the dark corners and crevices of the space. Goji entered, those wings fluttering. Cobwebs reached from wall to wall, insects flitting about, rats scuttling away and through holes.

The entire space smelled like mold and rotting corpses. I coughed and covered my nose.

"It's there." Bastian pointed to a shadow hiding behind crates. His eyebrows furrowed. "I can feel it. Exactly like the boys said. Incredible," he murmured.

I swallowed. "So we flood it out using light. You grab it, and then I'll sew it to you."

Bastian took a deep breath. "This should be interesting."

I wondered how everyone else was faring right now. I hoped my brothers had found their shadows. I rose to my tiptoes and kissed Bastian's cheek.

"Go get 'em."

"I love when you talk dirty to me," he said.

Goji rolled her eyes. "Just get the damn shadow, pirate."

She shot the balls of light forward, and I grabbed the torch from Bastian, slipping to the other side of the crates to help funnel it. The shadow hissed and lunged forward. It barreled toward Bastian, and I sucked in a breath at its speed. He lunged for it and grasped onto its arm.

"Do you have it?" I yelled.

He grunted and fell to the ground, wrestling the shadow.

"It's strong," he said. "Bloody hell."

I ran to Goji and handed her the torch, then approached Bastian and his shadow. He pinned it to the ground, but the shadow squirmed under him.

"Keep your hold on it," I said.

"Easier said than done . . ." Bastian said as the shadow swiped at him, a fresh scratch on his neck.

My hand went to the scratch on my face that I'd gotten just yesterday from a shadow. It still hurt. Bastian flipped the shadow over, his weight bearing down on it as it hissed and flailed.

I snatched its foot and dug the thread and needle from my pocket. The ship lurched under us, making me lose my balance—and my grasp on the shadow.

"What was that?" I asked.

"Nothing good," Goji said. "I'll go check it out. You two hurry."

She fluttered away, and I grasped onto the shadow's foot again, stretching it against Bastian's boot. "The sole is so thick," I muttered.

Bastian jerked as the shadow punched him. "That's going to leave a mark. Tell me, will you still love me if I'm missing a limb?"

I ignored him, pushing the needle through the shadow and into Bastian's boot.

The ship creaked and rumbled, and my head snapped up. "What is going on out there?"

"Just worry about what's going on in here." Bastian let out a groan as the shadow lifted its knee into his groin. "I might not be able to give you children anymore," he gasped out. "I hope that's not a problem."

I focused my attention back on his boot, now prodding the needle through the sole and attaching the shadow as quickly as I could.

Bastian's foot wrenched out of my grasp as the shadow darted toward the ceiling, lifting Bastian upside down. "You've got to be fucking kidding me," he yelled.

The ship rocked to its side, and I flew with it, my body slamming against the wall with a crack.

"Are you alright?" Bastian said, all concern for himself fleeing. "I knew this was a bad idea. You should've never worried about getting my shadow back."

I gritted my teeth and shoved out my hand, water unfurling from my palm and shooting toward Bastian. It roped around his ankle and pulled him to the ground, the shadow having no choice but to follow.

Bastian grunted as he attempted to grasp onto his flailing shadow and get it under control. "You know, I wouldn't object to you using that little trick to tie me up in other situations."

He strained, pulling the shadow down and once again pinning it to the ground as I slowly came to a stand, wincing at the pain in my back and ignoring the pirate.

"We have to hurry. Something is happening outside, and it isn't good."

Two figures burst into the space through the closed doors on the other ends, which were now sideways after the ship had been rocked to its side.

I raised my hands, ready to shoot my water magic at whoever stood there.

"What is going on?" Mia asked, stepping forward.

I finished sewing the shadow to Bastian, who stood and grabbed the lapels of his coat, tugging and adjusting them.

"Do you have your shadows?" I asked as wood splintered, flying toward us. Bastian tackled me to the ground, the sharp pieces shooting over our heads.

"Can't have you getting impaled after I finally got my shadow back," he murmured into my ear. "I'm still very interested in the ways you can use water to—"

"Are we interrupting something?" Kara asked.

I gave Bastian a quick kiss and pushed him off of me as we came to our feet.

"I feel it." Kara's eyes widened. "I can feel my shadow."

Mia stepped forward, holding a torch. "Me too."

We all turned toward the two other shadows hiding in the dark corner, behind a large cobweb.

"Well, I'm out." Mia stepped back. "I don't do spiders."

The ship groaned, more wood cracking.

"What is happening outside?" I asked.

Kara looked toward the crack. "We came in on the other side, so I can't say for sure, but I think the pixies are here."

Blood and water.

"Goji must be fighting them," I said. "Get your shadows and meet us out there. We'll help her ward them off."

"Bloody hell, it never ends," Bastian muttered.

The window we'd entered through was now pressed into the ground, so we made our way toward the doors. Bastian pushed them open and we crawled through. I sent one look back at Kara and Mia, who both inched toward their shadows, then climbed my way through the opening to fight off the pixies and get the bloody waters out of here.

Chapter Fifty-Six

Sun blinded me as I stepped out onto the tilted main deck. We were so close to the shore, but we needed to get to the marsh, and that was inaccessible by way of the beach. We'd have to trek through the jungle to get there.

I shaded my eyes just as a ball of pixie dust came flying at my head. Bastian grabbed my arm and reeled me to his chest.

"I like this whole working as a team thing," he whispered into my ear. "You saving my ass, me saving yours . . ."

I looked over his shoulder at the chaos around us. Pixies fluttered through the air, shooting balls of their shimmering dust toward the ship, the balls like cannons, bursting when they hit the ship, cracking it and shaking it.

"To be fair, it's a very nice ass. One I have many plans for once we get off this bloody—"

"Bastian, duck!" I yelled, and we both crouched down as more magic shot over us. The pixies must've been fighting us on orders from the shadow king. They wouldn't use this magic unless they absolutely had to.

Bastian shielded my body with his own.

"We have to help Goji," I said.

"I know." He pressed a kiss to my forehead. "So let's get to it, then."

He stood and jumped from the tilted ship to the ground.

I held out my hand, letting my water flow from it and shoot toward a pixie above me. The water hit her square in the chest and she fell toward the ground with a thwack.

Meanwhile Bastian climbed a tree, balancing his way across a branch and fighting through the pixies who lunged at him. He stabbed one with his sword, balancing on his feet as he then spun and sliced down another one. A ball of magic flew at his feet and he jumped, landing back on the tree and wobbling before catching his balance. I'd never actually seen him fight before, but he was amazing. I supposed when you were ninety-five years old, you had a lot of time to learn how to be a master swordsman.

"Love, I know I'm handsome, but there's an angry-looking pixie coming your way, so maybe focus on that?" Bastian yelled as he ducked to avoid getting hit with magic.

I startled, jumping to attention right as a pixie descended upon me. Instinctively, I threw up a water shield, and the pixie slammed into it. Then I used the shield to ram straight up into the pixie's chin, and they shot into the air before dropping to the ground.

Above us, Goji shot out her magic at the pixies. I couldn't imagine what made her turn on her own kind. Yes, she loved the shadow king, but how did that love outweigh her loyalty toward her own? I glanced at Bastian again as he now fought against three pixies. He thrust his sword toward one of them while kicking out his back leg and jamming it into another's chest, then he slammed his head into the other pixie. They littered the ground now, but still, more came. We wouldn't be able to sustain this. They'd kill us, or more likely, capture us and take us to the shadow king so he could dole out whatever punishment he pleased.

We had to get out of here. I needed a distraction. Maybe a big burst of magic. It would drain me, though.

I bit my lip as a ball of magic flew at my stomach. I whirled to avoid it, then shot out my hand. Water speared through the air and straight toward a pixie.

Using an enormous amount of magic could be dangerous since we'd likely need my magic to help us cross that damn marsh. Bastian sheathed his sword, then hopped down, grasping on to the tree branch with his hands and dropping to the ground. He landed in a crouch as more pixies descended upon him.

Then again, we wouldn't make it to the marsh if I didn't do something now.

Kara and Mia burst through the ship's doors, and slid down the deck to the ground. I breathed in relief as their shadows stretched behind them.

"They've got their shadows too," a pixie yelled, pointing. "He won't be happy about this."

This was getting out of control.

"Goji," I called to the pixie up in the air. "We have to retreat. I'm going to use my magic to outrun them. On the count of three, you go."

"The hell you are!" Bastian growled after running his sword through a pixie right as magic swiped against his cheek, leaving yet another cut.

Kara and Mia joined in the fighting, but more pixies emerged from the jungle. My body grew cold. This would very well be the end if I didn't act.

"She's right," Mia shouted. "We can't keep them at bay for much longer, not when there's so many."

Bastian stopped fighting and locked eyes with me.

"Trust me," I said.

His hand tightened around his sword, and he gave a nod.

"One," I said.

Bastian kicked a pixie away.

"Two."

Goji blasted her magic and started flying backward.

"Three!"

Mia, Kara, and Bastian ran, and Goji flew through the air, all of them getting behind me as I pulled at that thread inside of me, calling for my magic to aid me. It wasn't as strong, here, so far away from my home, but it was enough. The water flowed through my veins and out the palms of my hands, a wall of it forming and holding off the pixies as everyone ran. I strained, stretching the wall so high it touched the canopies, so wide it stretched to the tree line. The pixies threw their magic at it, but they couldn't break it.

My muscles shook with the effort, and I turned and ran, my entire body feeling like it was being pulled in two different directions as I held that wall behind me. Bastian glanced behind him, slowing, but I shook my head.

"I'm coming," I yelled. "Just keep going, and don't you dare stop!"

Mia and Kara sprinted ahead of him, and Goji flew above him, her gaze darting down to Bastian and then to me.

Kara cried out ahead and faltered, and it looked like she'd twisted her ankle. Mia ran to her sister and grabbed her arm. "Help us, Bastian," she yelled to her brother.

His brows furrowed. "Don't you do anything stupid, you hear me?" he said to me.

I shook, the strain of keeping that wall up weakening me. "I promise," I said back. "Go help your sister."

He gave me one last look, then swore and ran toward Kara. She put both arms around their necks and they continued on.

My magic quaked inside of me, that thread I pulled at so close to snapping. I wouldn't be able to hold the wall much longer, but we'd at least gotten a head start.

With a final effort, I pushed the wall forward, and looked behind me to see it crash into the pixies, knocking many of them from the air, whooshing over them like a wave. Some threw up their magic to shield themselves, while others pushed through the wave. I was so weak now, I could barely walk, let alone run.

The marsh wasn't far from here, and if I squinted, I could see the tree line where we'd be able to escape if we could get through the shadows—and then we'd face the crocodiles. Suddenly, it all seemed so impossible, and I fell to my knees under the weight of this mission.

The pixies began moving forward again, and I turned and crawled on my knees, digging my fingers into the dirt, pulling myself forward with slow, painful movements. My joints ached, and my head pounded after that use of magic. I grunted, pulling myself forward again. I could no longer see Bastian, trees blocking him from my sight—and me from his.

A blast of magic lit my peripheral vision, and I winced. This was it, then. I would die here.

"Go!" a voice shouted from above me.

I looked up to see Goji hovering over me, a new wall shielding me: her pixie dust. She couldn't use that much power. She'd told me herself that once one's pixie dust was drained, their life was forfeit. The wall stretched longer and taller than my water shield had, and the green from Goji's skin was slowly turning white, her face paling, her body shaking, her dust flowing into that wall, literally draining her before my eyes.

"Goji, no!" I slowly came to a stand. "You can't do this. You'll die."

"Some things are worth dying for," she said through heavy breaths.

"I don't understand." Tears welled in my eyes. I hadn't spent a lot of time with Goji, but I knew how much she meant to Bastian. "What could be worth this kind of sacrifice?"

"You, better than anyone, should understand," she said.

I stared at her, hearing her voice in my head. *He's an idiot, but I suppose we often are when it comes to love.*

My eyes widened as tears ran down Goji's cheeks. "It's Bastian. It's Bastian who you love."

The pixies battered Goji's wall with their magic, bursts of it blowing through.

"That's why you've done everything you have. Why you rescued me, why you're helping us. You just wanted to save Bastian. You never expected to leave here, not this time. It was a lie." My heart squeezed tight. "Goji . . ."

"Do not let my sacrifice be in vain. He is not complete without you. It will break him if you do not survive, and I don't want to see my pirate broken. Not when I worked so hard to put him back together, but I couldn't. I wasn't you."

I stumbled back as tears spilled down my cheeks.

Her body shook as her dust continued to flow from her. "He disappeared for a year, and I thought he was dead. I realized then that I loved him. I vowed if he ever came back to the island, I'd give him my magic, free him and he could free me in return. I'd tell him how I felt, and we could be together. He finally returned, but something had changed."

He'd met me.

"I hoped I could give him the dust, that maybe we still had a chance, but once he took that dust and refused to use it, said he needed to see you first, I knew. I knew he loved you more than anything. But I couldn't change how I felt about him."

She grunted, sweat trickling down the sides of her face, plastering her blond hair to her head.

"I'll never be able to thank you," I said with a shaky voice as the pixies on the other side of the wall started to break Goji's magic, cracks forming.

"Love him. Help him become the man he always dreamed of being. The man you made him want to be. That will be enough."

More cracks webbed in her wall as pixies shot their magic at it. I turned and summoned all the strength I had to run. My legs and arms felt like tentacles, my lungs like a wrung-out rag, but still I ran, and I didn't look back.

Goji yelled out behind me, a flash lighting up my peripherals.

Pain seared through every part of me, and I couldn't stop crying, couldn't stop thinking about Goji's sacrifice, how much she must've loved Bastian to do something like that.

I turned my head to glance behind me and slammed into a hard wall. I screamed.

"Shhh, love, it's me. Kara and Mia are at the tree line, waiting for us. But the shadows are there, and our torches are not enough light to scare them away. Hey." He cupped my cheeks, forcing me to look at him. "What's wrong? Where's Goji?"

"She—" I couldn't get the words out. "She—" I sobbed.

"Okay, okay. It's alright. Here's what we're going to do." He lifted me and cradled my body into his chest as he ran toward the tree line. I looked over his shoulder and didn't see any pixies, but they'd be coming soon. Goji wouldn't last much longer using so much magic.

As the tree line came into view, so did Lochlan and Mal—and many of the boys. So many boys. I sniffled, wiping away my tears. We'd gotten this far. We could do this. We had to do this.

Lochlan and Mal came toward us, grabbing me from Bastian's arms.

"What happened?" Mal said, bringing me into his arms protectively.

I sniffled. "It's a long story, but the pixies are going to be here soon, and we need to find a way out."

Shadows swooped down over us, hissing and swiping at anyone who dared get too close to the tree line. The marsh was right there. We just needed to find a way through.

"Can you use your magic?" I asked Lochlan and Mal.

"It's weak," Lochlan said, "after so long of not having my shadow, not being able to use it, it's going to take practice to master it again."

More and more boys ran to us, emerging from the trees and the foliage, coming in all different directions. Bastian's crew came, too, everyone converging, waiting for us to save them like we said we would.

Like I said I would. "Torches!" I shouted. "Bring your torches." But many of the torches were no longer lit, and a strong wind blew through the trees. Wait, no. Not from through the trees. It was coming from the shadows.

"They can blow out fire?" I said.

Lochlan scratched his head. "Apparently so."

In the distance, I could see the shimmer of pixies, flying toward us. Goji's wall had broken. She was dead, and it was going to be all for nothing.

The remaining fire on the torches flickered out, the shadows closing in around us. More boys filtered into the area, but it no longer mattered because we didn't have a way out.

The necklace had said the light would save us. So why wasn't this working? I fell to my knees and pounded the ground in frustration.

The crew and the older boys surrounded the boys of Apolis, and shadows began plucking those too close to the tree line and throwing them. A few hit trees with sickening crunches, others screamed as the shadows ripped them apart.

"No," I said, my voice breaking.

Bastian watched with horror as shadows ravaged his crew. Still, the remaining boys and crew members stood their ground, protecting the younger boys. Protecting our boys.

All of a sudden, the trees parted, a blinding path of light shining into the jungle. The shadows screeched, scattering away.

"Take that, bitches!" a voice yelled, and I collapsed to my knees in relief.

Driscoll. He stood there, his hands held high as he parted the trees and allowed the sun through. Allowed a clear pathway.

"We figured it out," he yelled, smiling. "The necklace said the light is the key. So here I am, bringing in the light."

"Go!" I yelled at the boys and they began running out, sticking to the path of light that Driscoll had created.

"Who in the bloody waters is that?" Mal asked.

"Don't worry about it," I said, watching as boys ran past us and out into the sun, their shadows stretching along the bank of the marsh.

Leoni stood on the other side, and I wished I could run and give her a huge hug. "Start getting them to the ship," I called, and she nodded, gathering them into the two remaining boats, and using her magic to send the boats rocking past the marsh and out into the sea.

Boys continued running, and more still emerged from the depths of the jungle, staying in the sun and waiting for their turn to get onto a boat.

"I think I've got all my boys!" Lochlan yelled.

"Think?" I echoed, looking for mine, mentally tallying. Everyone but two.

The pixies were getting closer, and Bastian grabbed my arm. "We don't have time to count, love. We've got to get these boys out."

"Go, go, go!" I yelled at the boys running out into the marsh, the sun still shining down.

I looked up, praying the clouds wouldn't cover the only thing keeping us safe right now. Shadows swooped down, but the crew lined along the edges of the sun ray that painted the jungle ground, jabbing at them with their swords and torches. Another rowboat returned to the marsh, Leoni commanding it with her magic as she piled more boys in.

I arched my neck, searching for the crocodiles, when the flash of a tail emerged from the water, shimmering and scaled. The mermaids were here. They were helping us, keeping the crocodiles at bay. My heart swelled, but I didn't have time to think about it as the final boys ran through the opening Driscoll created and out onto the bank, all of them huddled together, shaking and watching with wide eyes as the pixies flew toward us, so close now.

"Go," I yelled to the crew, and they began filing out.

Boys were now using their water magic to ride waves that took them to the ship, Leoni instructing them while using her own magic. Sweat dotted her brows, and pink flushed her round face as she concentrated on making waves that would ride as many as possible toward that ship.

"I'll stay and watch your brothers," Bastian whispered in my ear. "You go now."

"Absolutely not."

"Now is not the time to be stubborn."

The pixies flew closer, near enough that they could shoot their magic at us. A ball hit one of the crew members in the back, sending him sprawling onto the ground. Ollie.

"No!" Bastian yelled, running to him and checking the pulse on his neck.

Bastian's face twisted, and that was all the confirmation I needed that Ollie was dead, along with countless others.

Driscoll's brows furrowed. "You just killed one of my friends!" He shot out another hand, a huge tree toppling over and falling on a few of the pixies. Another tree tipped and blocked them from going farther.

The final crew members ran through, and Lochlan and Mal gestured for me to go. We didn't have time to argue. I ran through the tree line but paused at the edge, Bastian by my side, Lochlan and Mal right behind me.

"Gabby, let's go," Lochlan yelled.

I met Hammond's gaze, looked at all those brave boys who'd helped us. "We'll be back for you," I said, and he nodded.

I turned and ran onto the bank, Bastian, Mal, and Lochlan right behind me. Driscoll closed the trees, right as Lochlan squeezed through.

He let out a scream that stopped me in my tracks, his face stark and pale.

"What's going on?" I rushed to him, grappling at him.

"Driscoll!" I looked back at him. "Open the trees back up!"

Driscoll raised a shaky hand, falling to his knees, but all he could manage was to snap a branch.

Lochlan's face turned into a grimace as he yelled out, and shadow hands crept out over him, trying to pull him back in.

"No!" I screamed.

I grabbed his arm, and Bastian and Mal grabbed his other as we pulled and pulled, finally yanking him free. He stumbled out onto the bank, but unlike everyone else, his shadow had been left behind.

Chapter Fifty-Seven

"We have to go back!"

I struggled against Bastian, pounding at his chest.

"Let me go!" I snarled. "I'm getting his shadow back."

"Love, you know we can't."

Pixies still shot their magic through the tree line, balls flying toward us. Bastian whirled me out of the way, and Mal and Lochlan dove into the muddy sand.

I got up again and tried to run toward the trees, but Bastian grabbed me and hauled me toward the empty boat, where Leoni and Driscoll sat. The final batch of boys rode their wave toward Bastian's ship, but I couldn't leave, not without Lochlan's shadow.

"Stop!" I thrashed in his arms until a large hand landed on my arm.

"It's okay," Lochlan said.

"It's not okay." My voice wobbled. "Your shadow, you—"

I gasped. The blue lines had already appeared, faint dots at the top of his neck that would slowly stretch the longer he was away from the island, from where he was bound.

I broke into sobs as Lochlan gently pushed me toward the rowboat.

I stepped into the boat, numb, despite what we'd accomplished. We had gotten the boys and most of Bastian's crew out. We'd gotten their shadows, and yet the losses weighed on me. Multiple crew members dead. Multiple of the older boys dead. Goji dead. Lochlan was as good as dead.

Bastian grabbed the oars and began to row.

The boat rocked underneath us, and my gaze snapped to the murky green water.

"What was that?" Mal asked.

A chill skittered down my back.

"My guess is a crocodile," Driscoll said, swallowing. "Something was helping us, keeping the crocodiles away, but now . . ." His eyes darted nervously to the water.

"What do we do?" Mal asked.

Leoni slumped forward, her limbs likely as tired as mine were after all that use of magic.

"Use your magic," I said, "to get our boat the bloody waters away from the marsh."

I peered down, looking for signs of the mermaids. I'd seen them—I was sure of it. Maybe their magic was growing weak, too, all of us depleted after using so much.

I thought about mentioning the mermaids, but Mal hadn't seen his sea princess in months, and I didn't want to get his hopes up that she was here.

A large, green body leapt out of the water, its huge jaws opening, sharp teeth snapping right at Mal's face. He threw up a water shield, stopping the crocodile.

"I can't use my magic to help," Lochlan said quietly.

Right. Without his shadow, he wouldn't be able to use water magic.

"It's okay." I reached across the boat and laid a hand on his arm as Bastian stood and jabbed a sword into the water.

Mal directed the boat through the marsh as crocodile heads slowly popped up, Bastian using his sword to slice at any creature that came near. Leoni grabbed her sword and stood, doing the same. Between them and Mal, we were able to get out of the marsh and into the open sea, the ship so close now. Another crisis averted.

Mal steered us in silence as we approached the ship, and Kara threw a rope ladder down for us. Driscoll went first, then Leoni, then Lochlan, and then Mal. I turned to Bastian, and he gestured for me to get on the ship.

I could barely believe we'd made it. I grabbed onto the rope ladder, my heart finally starting to beat in a normal rhythm.

Just then the rowboat cracked in the middle, splitting apart as a crocodile pushed up through the bottom. I screamed, grappling for the rope, my fingers grasping tighter onto it as our little vessel splintered, wood flying everywhere. Bastian flying back with it.

My body slammed against the side of the boat, while Mal, Lochlan, and Leoni screamed to get me pulled up.

"No," I yelled. "Don't you dare! Not without Bastian."

My eyes swept down as I hung from the ladder, and there Bastian was, on the edge of a piece of the boat, the crocodile's mouth clamped down onto his hand. I reached out.

"Grab my hand," I said with a shaky voice.

Pain lanced his face, but he stretched out his other arm and grabbed onto my hand.

I yanked him, but he yelled out in pain, the crocodile still latched onto him, unmoving.

He slowly looked up at me and swallowed. "I love you," he said.

"No. This is not goodbye." My voice came out raw and ragged. "This is not the end. I fought and fought for you, and now it's your turn to fight for me. For us. For our future. Bastian Lore, don't you dare leave me now. Don't you dare let go."

A low rumble left the crocodile's throat, and he tugged at Bastian. I gripped Bastian's hand tighter in mine.

"He'll take us both down," Bastian warned.

"No." My voice shook. "Bastian, no. Don't let go. Please." My voice broke on that last word.

He blinked, then his hand slipped from mine, and just like that he disappeared below the water. A scream wrenched from me as the crocodile pulled him deeper under. Crimson spiraled up, then coated the surface of the water.

The crew let out gasps, screams.

"Gabby," Lochlan said softly. "We need to go. If the clouds cover the sun, the shadows, they could come after us."

I shook my head, searching the water wildly. "No, no."

"Just pull her up," Kara said quietly as Mia sobbed.

It was my fault. This was all my fault.

The water was blood red, and a ragged cry tore through my throat. "Just let me try," I pleaded, hanging there on the side of the ship. "I'll use my magic. I'll get him back."

"You're too weak—" Mal started.

"No," I said, feeling inside of me for that thread, tugging at it, begging the water.

Bring him back. Bring him back to me. But Mal was right: I was too weak.

I couldn't move, and the world melted away as I stared, willing Bastian to come back.

My heart leapt to my throat as the water bubbled around me. I braced myself for the crocodile to come for me. I'd kill it. I'd kill it for what it had done.

The seawater exploded, wood flying as Bastian broke the surface, gasping, blood everywhere. I grappled for him, using one hand to grasp his jacket tight and pull him to me. His eyes rolled back in his head.

I arched my neck. "Get us up. Now!"

I wound my arm around him as we were pulled up, hands reaching for us and yanking us safely on deck, where we both sprawled out.

I didn't even take a breath before rolling to my knees, patting Bastian down, looking for the source of the blood.

"Where is the blood coming from?" I murmured. "Where?"

Everyone crowded around us.

"There," Mia said with a shaky voice, and I followed the line of her pointing finger to Bastian's hand. His missing hand.

Blood poured from the wound, his mangled flesh hanging down, and bile rose in my throat.

He coughed, and I cupped his cheeks. "It's okay. It's going to be okay."

One of the crew members knelt down, the doctor they kept on board, tying off the wound and stopping the flow of blood.

"So that's what it takes, huh?" Bastian said weakly.

I jolted, not realizing he was conscious. "What?" I said.

"To get you to touch me? Just need to lose my hand."

I let out a half laugh, half cry and hugged him tight as the tears came.

"I'm so sorry the crocodile did that to you."

Bastian gasped in pain, his face twisting. "I did it . . . to myself. Sliced off my hand and swam as fast as I could toward you."

My hand floated to my mouth.

"You said no more sacrificing myself." He swallowed. "You said to fight for us. So that's what I did."

I leaned down and pressed kisses all over his face. "You did good, pirate lord."

We were safe, and we were together. For now, that was all that mattered.

Chapter Fifty-Eight

The moon shone bright overhead, stars strewn across the sky, sparkling with a brilliant intensity. The crew lay across the main deck, everyone sleeping, exhausted after our excursion. Bastian lay with them. He'd given up his cabin to some of the boys, while most of the others slept belowdecks in the bunks. I tried to sleep, but no matter how tired I was, I couldn't shake the images of Goji, of the crew members we'd lost, of Lochlan's shadow getting ripped from him. Bastian's mangled arm.

I looked behind me. The pirate lord grimaced in his sleep, in immense pain. We'd stopped the blood loss, and sewed him up, but his life would be so different going forward with only one hand to use.

I leaned against the railing but stiffened when the water started bubbling below. Were the shadows coming after us? I couldn't handle more conflict. We'd spent all day sailing as far from Sorrengard as possible, but that didn't mean the shadow king wouldn't send out his shadows in retribution. Especially now that they had the cover of night.

I held my breath until a head emerged from the water: fire-red hair cascading down pale shoulders, huge purple eyes gazing at me as the water lifted her higher until she was level with me.

"Marian." I stepped back in surprise. "Have you come to see Mal?"

She reached for me. "No, please don't tell him I'm here." She arched her neck to look over my shoulder and her gaze instantly found him as he lay on his side, sleeping.

"I did what I could to help you escape, but I fear it wasn't enough." She tipped her head toward Bastian. "I used my magic to keep the crocodiles trapped underwater as long as I could, but one of them escaped. I'm so sorry."

"We owe you a debt," I said. "One I'm not sure we can ever repay."

"No." She shook her head. "I owe you for saving him."

I looked between her and Mal. "So why don't you want to see him? He misses you."

"My father doesn't know I'm here." Marian wrung her hands together. "He would never have allowed me to do something so foolish like save the prince. Let alone marry the prince."

I grasped her hands, and her eyes flashed with surprise. "So convince him. Fight for Mal. Fight for your love. It's worth it."

I thought of Bastian and all we'd been through, and I wondered if he'd agree.

"I know." She squeezed her eyes closed for a moment. "You're right. I just . . . it's hard to stand up to the king."

I remembered that feeling, how I'd planned to run away with Bastian rather than face my father, remembered all the heartache I could've saved everyone if I'd fought for what I wanted.

"Standing up for ourselves can be hard," I said. "But sometimes it's the hardest things that bring us the most peace. You deserve that peace. You deserve not to be at war with what you want versus what everyone else wants for you. Mal is good. He is kind. He is brave. And he will make you so happy."

Tears filled her eyes, turning them a lighter shade of lavender. "I'll think about it." Her voice shook. She sniffled and wiped the tears away, straightening. "I have to get back now. I just wanted to say thank you for being so brave, for going against all the odds and succeeding."

I thought of those we lost. "I don't know if I could call it a success, but we did save our boys."

"You did good, Princess Gabrielle," she said.

Behind us, someone moaned in his sleep, and I turned to see that it was Lochlan. He mumbled, "I'm coming. I'm coming for you." His body twitched, sweat trickling down the sides of his face. "I'll find you. I promise."

My heart twisted. "He must be having dreams about his shadow. We couldn't escape with it," I said to Marian.

Her mouth dropped open. "I'm so sorry." She peered at Lochlan as he turned to his side, still mumbling those same words. She tilted her head. "But I don't think he's talking about his shadow."

"What do you mean?" I asked.

She tapped a long red nail against her chin. "Mal mentioned these dreams to me a few times. Lochlan always said the same thing: 'I'm coming for you.' Mal could never get him to talk about it, though."

I blinked a few times, not sure what else these dreams could possibly be about, but Lochlan quieted, his body growing still.

"I really must go now." The wave pushed Marian back and lowered her down into the sea.

"Promise you'll think about what I said?" I asked. "Your father doesn't get to tell you who to love. Just remember that you have power, Marian. You have your voice back. So use it."

She bit her lip, looking unsure, but nodded. "I promise." Then she disappeared under the water.

I glanced at the sky above.

"You know, for someone who preaches so much about standing up for yourself, you don't really follow your own advice." Leoni joined my side.

I hugged her tight. "I missed you so much. I'm so sorry we fought."

"No." She sighed. "I'm sorry. I was lashing out at you, and it wasn't fair." She looked up at the stars. "The truth is sometimes I don't know who I am, who I can be, without you."

My brows furrowed. "You're the captain of my guard. You're my fiercest protector."

"And what happens when you don't need me anymore?" she asked.

I put my hands on her shoulders. "I'll always need you."

"But not to protect you."

"When I'm queen—"

"Gabrielle," she said, cocking a brow. "Think about what you just said to Marian. Is that what you really want? To be queen? For Bastian to be king?"

My brows furrowed. "Well, no, but it doesn't matter."

"Yes it does. Why do your dreams matter less than others? Talk to your brothers, talk to your mother. Don't accept a fate that you'll only be living in with half your heart."

Her words stunned me. "You're saying I should tell them I don't want to be queen and that I . . . what? Want to be what?"

She looked at me like I was an idiot. "What do you want to be?"

I glanced behind me at Bastian. His. I wanted to be his. But I wanted more than that too.

"Oh, come on." Leoni planted her hands on her hips. "You volunteered us to work on the ship. To rig sails and repair canvas and swab the deck. Who does that? I mean, really, who does that?" She gave me a pointed stare. "So I'll ask you again, what do you want to be, Gabrielle Aster?"

"A pirate," I said, surprising myself when the answer came so easily. Blood and water. That's what I wanted to be. A pirate. I wanted to sail the seas and be free. I stared at the ocean in shock. "Do you think I can do it?"

"Yes," Leoni said. "I do. But you can't run away this time. You can't do it in secret. You need to speak your truth. Stop asking for permission from those who won't grant it. Apolis will be okay. We'll all be okay. Go live your life."

My mouth dropped open. "I—I—" I said weakly. "When did you get so smart?"

She rolled her eyes. "I've always been the smart one, Princess."

I laughed and shoved her.

Leoni clapped her hand on my shoulder. "Now get some sleep. We arrive in Apolis tomorrow." She walked away and left me alone with my thoughts.

Tomorrow. Tomorrow would decide my fate. I thought about Leoni's words. No. I would decide my fate, and this time, I wouldn't run.

Chapter Fifty-Nine

The ship sailed toward the docks of Apolis, my home rising in the distance. Homes dotted the rocky hills, the glittering river cutting through and circling the court. From the main deck, I could see our bustling market, our castle gleaming under the sun.

I frowned when I noticed all the guards standing on the boardwalk, some with water spears in their hands, others with balls of water they were ready to launch like cannons.

My mother pushed through the guards, her gaze hard as stone.

Mal and Lochlan appeared at my side, and her hand floated to her mouth as she crumpled into one of the guard's chests. We came closer, and the guards shot each other unsure looks, spears beginning to falter. Then the boys began running to the railing, shouting out and whooping at seeing their home, and chaos broke loose on the boardwalk.

Weapons forgotten, everyone rushed to the docks, looking for familiar faces as the boys shouted for their mothers and fathers. Those would be hard conversations to have, since most of their fathers were gone. But we'd get through it.

The ship sailed closer, and Bastian shouted out orders as it slowed, allowing the crew to dock it while boys reached down and mothers reached up.

More and more people began streaming in from the markets, from their homes, curious about the commotion, then realizing exactly what was happening. Soon, it felt like the entire population of Apolis was crowded on the boardwalk and beach as boys jumped from the side and down onto the dock. Others used their magic and rode onto the beach on waves.

Everyone was crying, hugging, laughing.

"You did it," Leoni said from next to me.

"We did it," I said.

"Damnit, I'm crying." Driscoll wiped a tear from his eye, and I just laughed.

"You know that it's okay to cry?" I asked him as cheers rang out along our shore.

"Not when it makes my face all puffy and red." He frowned down to me. "Your complexion is puffy and red all the time, so you don't understand how devastating that can be to someone like me who has skin as smooth as a baby's bottom."

Leoni leaned over. "Everything that we've been through and still not a drop of humility. Truly amazing."

My mother recovered and ran the length of the dock as Lochlan and Mal climbed down the rope ladder. She crashed into them, sobbing.

They brought their arms around her, and I stretched a leg over the side of the ship, glancing back at Bastian as he stared at me and gave a nod. I nodded back and climbed down the side of the ship, joining my family and savoring this moment of happiness before we had to break my mother's heart all over again.

Hours later, I finished telling my mother everything that had happened on our journey to the shadow court, Mal, Lochlan, and Bastian interjecting when necessary, while Leoni and Driscoll mostly stayed silent.

My mother sat back, hands steepled, brows furrowed.

We sat at a large round table in our great hall, where we often held important meetings with other court leaders or our priestesses and council members.

Bastian squeezed my hand under the table, while Leoni and Driscoll kept shooting nervous glances from me to my mother, who sat across from us, Mal and Lochlan on either side of her.

She'd teared up at the news that my father and all the men he took were dead but remained composed. I guessed she'd already grieved him so much that there wasn't a lot left to mourn.

The crown gleamed on her head in the sun that shone through the windows.

"That's . . . unbelievable," my mother said. "Everything. All those poor boys still stuck there."

"We're going to work on a plan to save them," I said, squeezing Bastian's hand back.

My mother frowned. "Save some human boys?" She shook her head. "I feel sorry for them, I do, but we have much more to focus on than their well-being." She placed her hand on Lochlan's shoulder. "We need to get your brother's shadow back first and foremost. That is the priority."

"I agree, Mother," I said.

Her lips flattened when her gaze landed on Bastian. "And I appreciate the pirate lord's help. I am sorry for everything he's gone through, and he will be handsomely rewarded for his efforts, but it's time to move on, Gabrielle. You will be crowned queen and we'll find you a suitable husband that will bolster our reputation and give our people hope. That you can have strong heirs with to lead our people into the future."

Leoni looked over to me, and I bit my lip, knowing I could no longer run from this. I'd told Bastian my plan early this morning, and even though he was in pain and exhausted, he said he'd support me in whatever decision I made. Now, he tensed beside me, realizing what I was about to do.

I took a deep breath as everyone waited for my response. "Actually, Mother, there's something I need to say."

"Maybe now's not the right time, love," Bastian whispered, but I shook him off and stood.

"I'm relinquishing my right to the crown."

My mother gasped, opening her mouth to speak, but I cut her off.

"I'm not made to be queen. I don't want to rule, and our people deserve better. They deserve someone whose heart doesn't belong elsewhere." I looked down at Bastian, and he lifted my hand to his lips and pressed a kiss to it. My mother's lip curled. "My entire life I tried to do the right thing, to train to be queen, even though I didn't want to be." My heart pounded as I spoke. "I planned to run away from all of this because I was so afraid to face the truth. But after all I've been through, I'm not afraid anymore. Our boys are back. Our princes are back. We don't need to be strong again. We're already strong. We will rise from the ashes of those lost and show our continent, our world, who we really are. I will be there every step of the way, cheering Apolis on. I will do everything in my power to aid Apolis and find out what's stirring in the shadow court, what this shadow king is planning. But I will not do it as queen."

My mother's cheeks reddened, and she looked away from me. "You disappoint me, daughter," she said.

"For that, I'm sorry." I raised my chin. "Actually, I'm not. I'm doing what's best for me, and in doing so, I'm doing what's best for our people."

"And who will rule?" my mother asked.

I locked eyes with Mal. His eyes widened in return, as if it was just hitting him that he might be perfect for this role. That he was born to be a leader, a king.

He cleared his throat. "I can do it. I can be king."

Our mother slowly turned toward him. "But our traditions—"

"What about them?" he asked. "Is that what truly matters here? Because I think making sure the right person is on the throne is what's for the best. I think putting our happiness above duty is what matters."

"So you're going to become king and marry the sea princess?" my mother asked. "While Gabrielle is off gallivanting with a pirate."

His lips curved into a smile. "That's exactly what I'm going to do. And that's exactly what she's going to do."

He nodded at Bastian, approval in his gaze.

I sat down, proud of my brother. He and the sea princess would make a wonderful king and queen.

"King Salazar will never allow his daughter to marry an elemental," my mother said. "We have a very fragile peace with the seafolk, and they only tolerate us because we share the same type of magic. Don't make us new enemies, not when we already have the shadow court to contend with."

Mal placed his hand on my mother's arm. "Mother, I can do this. I can bring us together and forge a new alliance. I'll also be calling a conclave."

My body stiffened at that. The last conclave between the courts hadn't been called since before the Shadow War. That conclave was when the courts decided they had to go to war against Sorrengard. I wondered if this conclave would come to the same conclusion. If we'd be going to war again.

Mal straightened. "We cannot ignore this threat. So I will summon all the courts together, and we will figure this out."

My mother's shoulders slumped. "Fine. I suppose I have no say anymore." She looked over to Lochlan. "We're going to put all of our effort into helping you."

"Yes," I said, and Mal nodded.

Lochlan's face tightened, and he stood now, fists balled at his sides. "Actually, that's a journey I'm going to have to take on my own."

My mother threw up her arms. "What has gotten into all of you? Did the shadow court addle your brains?"

"You're not going back to the shadow court alone," I said. "No way."

Lochlan shot me a charming smile. "You're right. I'm not."

My mother just harrumphed. "Why will you not let us help you, son?"

"Because I think the person who can help me is trapped, and I need to rescue her."

I started at that, Bastian and I exchanging confused glances.

Leoni leaned forward, and Driscoll tilted his head, all of us waiting for Lochlan to explain.

He pushed a hand through his thick auburn curls. "I've been having dreams about a woman trapped in a tower. It's real. I know it is, and I think it has something to do with my shadow, but I can't piece it all together without finding her."

"A woman . . . trapped in . . . a tower?" my mother asked like she couldn't have possibly heard him right.

"What are you talking about, Loch?" I said.

He started pacing. "I know it sounds crazy, okay? I feel crazy. But I hear her voice. At first I ignored it, thinking it was that damn island. But every night I see her and I hear her, and she's crying out for help."

"But where is she? Who is she?" I asked. "How will you even find her?"

Lochlan stopped pacing and shrugged his huge shoulders helplessly. "I wish I knew. I see flashes of a tower that's surrounded by thick clouds. I see a woman staring out the window, crying for help, saying something about a magic bean . . ." He shook his head as I straightened.

"A magic bean?" Driscoll's brows furrowed.

Lochlan let out a frustrated sigh. "I know how it sounds."

"That's the sky court," Bastian said, and all our heads whipped in his direction. He cleared his throat. "I've seen that very magic bean you speak of. It was one that I sold to someone from the sky court. It was created in Sorrengard."

"Perfect," my mother muttered.

"Who did you sell it to?" I asked.

"That I don't know. The deal was done through third parties. But I'm sure of the bean's location. It's the sky court. It's in Valoris."

We all turned wide gazes on Lochlan, who stared at Bastian, a new determination settling in my brother's eyes.

The isles of Valoris sat at the top of tall mountains that were almost impossible to scale, making it hard for other elementals to visit the sky court. I'd made the harrowing journey with my father once and didn't care to repeat it. Going that high up had made my stomach turn, my head spin.

"That's it." Lochlan snapped his fingers. "She's in the sky court. She must be, and I have to go to her. Immediately."

"Lochlan, wait!" I held out my hand. "You can't just leave. We need to help you, get your shadow back and then go find this girl."

If she was even real. But I didn't say that part out loud.

Bastian cleared his throat and put a hand on my arm. "Your brother clearly needs to do this. Just like you needed to seek me out against everyone's advice. No one thought you could save a pirate, not even me, but you proved us all wrong." He gazed at me, and my heart stuttered. "You saved me, love. Now your brother needs to save himself. Let him."

I tore my gaze from Bastian to look at Lochlan. Tears welled in my eyes at the thought of saying goodbye after we'd just been reunited.

"Do what you need to do," I said quietly.

Mal nodded. "We'll be here when you return."

My mother looked around at us like we were crazy. "Did the shadow court steal your brains along with your shadows?"

Lochlan smirked. "Does it really surprise you, Mother? We've always been as wild as the sea."

Mal and I grinned at him, a laugh escaping me.

"So you're just going to head off on some dangerous journey alone?" My mother's voice wobbled.

"He won't be alone." Driscoll stood.

I nearly fell out of my chair at that.

"What?" Driscoll flicked a piece of lint off his shirt. "No offense, but the pirate life isn't for me. I'm still trying to figure out my place in this world, so might as well join another adventure. One where I'll probably almost die a million times, and maybe then, when death is staring at me right in the face, I'll figure out what I'm meant to do. Then I'll save the day, just like I did in Sorrengard." He looked around the circle and wrinkled his nose. "You all are welcome for that, by the way."

"You're an idiot," Leoni said, then stood. "I'll go with him too." She looked down at me. "You don't need me anymore, but he might. I know what I'm meant to do, and I need to keep doing it. I need to guard, to protect."

"Uh." Lochlan scratched his head. "I was kind of hoping to do this alone . . ."

"Once their minds are made up, you won't change them," I said.

"Lucky you," Bastian muttered, and I elbowed him.

"Well, I guess this meeting is adjourned," my mother said with a shaky voice. "I think all three of you have lost your minds." She looked from me to Mal to Lochlan.

We smiled at each other.

"I think we're finally becoming who we're meant to be," I said. "A king, a pirate, and . . ." I looked at Lochlan. "A hero, maybe? We'll find out."

Everyone, save for my mother, nodded in agreement, all of us smiling like fools despite the circumstances.

Bastian leaned over and kissed me on the cheek. "I'm proud of you, love," he whispered.

One thing was for certain: whatever I did, whoever I became, I'd do it with him by my side.

Epilogue

The sea rolled out in front of us as the ship bobbed next to the dock.

Mal, my mother, and other members of the water court stood on the boardwalk, looking out at us. Tears slipped down my mother's cheeks, and Mal put an arm around her, bringing her to him. Bartholomew stood behind them. He'd decided to finally put his bard skills to the test on Arathia, see if he could find that untapped audience he was so eager to impress. He waved, and I gave a small wave in return.

Bastian came to stand by my side. "Are you sure you won't regret this?" he asked, staring out over Apolis.

I turned to him. "Trying to get rid of me already?"

He wound his arms around me and crushed me to him. "Never," he said fiercely.

The ship left the dock, sails billowing above us as I watched everyone grow smaller and smaller, little pinpricks in the distance.

"Good." I turned my head and pressed a quick kiss to his lips. "Because you're stuck with me forever, pirate."

"Forever is a long time," he murmured into my mouth. "Which is good because there are still so many things I plan to do with you in my cabin—"

"Get a room," Kara yelled from across the main deck.

I smiled into Bastian's lips. If it wasn't Driscoll or Leoni shouting at us, of course it would be one of his sisters.

I turned and leaned my head into Bastian's chest, his arms wrapped tighter around me as the wind fluttered my hair, the scent of salt and sea wafting through the air, the sun on my face. It was a perfect day at sea.

"I'm worried about them," I said.

"Who?" Bastian asked.

"Mal, Lochlan, Driscoll, Leoni. All of them."

"Mal is going to be a most excellent king. We already promised your mother we'd come back for the coronation. And Lochlan, well, you did the right thing letting him go. I have a feeling he needs this. Needs to find this woman plaguing his dreams."

"What about the blue lines?" I thought about when Bastian first arrived in Apolis, how those blue lines had stretched so dangerously close to his heart until he'd gotten back to his ship that he'd been bound to. "How long do you think he has?" I asked.

Bastian's chest rose as he sighed. "I'm not sure, love. When I finally made my way back to Apolis, I'd been separated from my ship for eight months. But we don't know enough about any of this to be sure. Maybe it depends how old a person is, whether they're human or elemental, how strong they are. It might be longer for your brother."

"Or not," I said, saying what we were both thinking.

"He's going to find this mysterious woman trapped in a tower, and he's going to get his shadow back. And if he needs our aid, we'll give it. Plus, Leoni and Driscoll will keep him company."

"Or drive him mad," I said.

"Well, that's a very good possibility as well," Bastian agreed, and I laughed.

We fell into silence as we gazed out at the open sea.

"So what's next for us?" Bastian finally asked. "The princess and the pirate."

"Mm, has a good ring to it, doesn't it?"

In the distance, water sprayed from a whale's spout, dusting the air.

"Aye, it does, but you didn't answer my question."

"Well," I said. "You're not the villain anymore, and you don't have to be. I promised some boys we're going to create a new home for them and rescue them, so that's exactly what we're going to do."

Bastian chuckled. "You just love inviting danger, don't you? You'd go back to that island after everything we went through?"

"I would." I stared out at the endless sea before us, thinking of those boys and the lives they had ahead of them.

"So where could we possibly put them?"

I gently pushed myself out of his arms.

"What are we going to do?" He spread his arms out wide, one of them still bandaged and healing. "Are we going to find undiscovered land somehow? No court, no city, is going to welcome a bunch of lost boys."

"No," I agreed, "but a pirate ship will."

He cocked a brow and brushed a wisp of hair from my eyes. "What is going on in that mind of yours?"

"We can buy ships for them. They can use the ships however they'd like: to become merchants, to be mercenaries for hire, to sail the seas and be free. They don't need land. They need a place to call home, and what better place than a ship where they can create their own communities?"

Bastian stared at me for a moment, a look in his eyes I didn't recognize. "I think I fall more in love with you every day."

I crossed my arms. "Even when I tried to drown you? Or tricked you with the pixie dust? Or wrecked your ship—"

"Shut. Up." He pulled me to him, lips capturing mine and drowning out my next words.

He leaned me back against the railing, one hand sliding around to my waist, his tongue slipping into my mouth. I let out a moan, and he kissed me harder.

"I liked you better when you were fighting," Kara shouted. "We have a ship to sail, and you haven't even told us where to go yet, Captain. So if you could remove your tongue from the princess's mouth for a moment and give us some damn orders, I'd really appreciate it."

He let go of me, leaving me breathless.

"Are you sure we can't just find an abandoned island somewhere and live out the rest of our lives alone?" he asked, then cut a look at his sister, who was glaring at him. "Because right about now, that sounds rather preferable to this."

I laughed. "You'd miss it. Now go. You have a job to do, my pirate lord."

"And you're going to help me do it, my pirate queen."

"Now that I like," I said, grabbing his hand as we walked toward the middle of the deck. Bastian began telling the crew our new plan while I stood by his side.

This was the me I'd always dreamed of being, and now I had my entire future ahead of me. Maybe not as the queen of Apolis. But as the queen of pirates. As the queen of the sea.

WANT MORE of the pirate lord? Check out this spicy bonus chapter from his point of view.

TO FIND out if the playboy prince ever finds the woman trapped in the tower, read Tower of Tempest now—and keep reading for a sneak peek!

Sneak Peek: Tower of Tempest

POPPY

Gran's cough was getting worse.

She sat on the stone floor, huddled by a crackling fire in the hearth. I stood from my small bed that lay next to hers and padded across the floor of the tower. She hacked again, her frail body shaking. I crouched down next to her and grabbed a ladle from the simmering pot that hung over the fire. Smoke curled from the pot, twisting upward, and I tightened my wings to my back, avoiding any embers catching the black feathers. I'd caught fire once when I was little and didn't have any desire to repeat that experience. I blew until the liquid cooled, then brought it to Gran's lips. Her normally russet skin looked ashen, sweat dotting her forehead.

"Here," I said.

She sipped it. "You're fussing again. Go do something else, girl."

The words might have been harsh, but they had no bite.

I hesitated. "Gran, let me go . . . outside. I'll gather more herbs and maybe, I can even visit a healer's shop and buy a tincture—"

"No." Her sharp eyes snapped to me, dark and assessing as ever, even in her weakened state. A shawl covered her thin shoulders, flowing down over an oversized linen dress that hung to her ankles. We'd always lived humbly, but despite that, Gran managed to look as regal as ever as she straightened her shoulders, head held high. She grabbed her silk bonnet and draped it over her short white hair. "You will not leave this tower," she rasped, another cough rattling her chest.

"But Gran—"

She held up her hand, silencing me. "I won't hear any more of this." I wanted to argue, but she didn't need any more stressors, not in her current state.

She pressed her hand against the stone wall and slowly stood, walking toward her bed and sinking onto the end of it. "Sing me a song, hm? Your favorite?"

It was a song I knew well, one Gran had sung since she took me in as a baby and brought me to this tower. We might not have been related by blood, but Gran was my family. The only person in this world that I had, and if she wanted me to sing her a song, then I would.

I sat on a stool next to her bed, readying myself to sing, but Gran's eyes were already fluttering closed, so I began humming softly instead until her breathing deepened and she was drifting off.

I stood, my blue linen dress hanging to my ankles—mine with laces up the front that made it easier to remove given the wings sprouting from my back.

I needed to while away the time until Gran awakened. A book, perhaps. My gaze drifted to the bookshelves we'd spent months building. They stood on either side of our beds, and the shelves stretched overhead, connecting. We'd even built a little ladder that stood between our beds so we could reach the higher shelves. My gaze drifted to the easel and array of paints arranged on a little table next to the bookshelves. Or maybe I should do some painting, something to cheer Gran when she woke up. Maybe one of her home. Though I'd already done dozens of those.

Gran often brought paint, canvases, and books from the closest village, helping me explore new worlds since I couldn't exactly venture out on my own.

My mouth twisted as I thought about getting out all the paints, the paint brushes, having to clean them afterward. Reading it was.

I ventured over to the ladder and climbed it, letting my fingers run over the spines of the books. There was no organization to any of it. Books were stuffed wherever we could fit them, some sticking out farther than others, some piled on their sides. Yet, somehow, despite the chaos of it all, Gran and I knew the place of every single text here.

I stretched up onto my tiptoes and reached for the one I wanted, then plucked it off the shelf. Dust covered the spine, and I blew it off, watching as it poofed up into the air. Little motes danced in the last sunrays of the day that shone through the single window in our home. Outside, the sky had turned a hazy purple as the sun disappeared over the horizon. I meandered to the little bench Gran and I built that sat underneath the window, sinking down and opening the book.

I loved this one. Gran had found it on the side of the road after making a trip to the nearest village. The cover was green with a gold embossing around it. The story was about a woman from the earth court who loved to garden, and every day she'd tend to her flowers, fruits, and vegetables. One day, a man was waiting for her, holding a sickly plant in his arms. He wanted her to save it. It wasn't easy, but she worked to bring that plant back to life, and as she nurtured it, she nurtured him as well, and they fell in love. In the end, he revealed it was never actually about the plant. He'd just wanted an excuse to get to know her. It was everything I loved in a story: a strong heroine, heart-pounding romance, and a woman who fought for the things that mattered to her.

I set down the book, glancing up at Gran, who let out another harrowing cough. Gran had saved me when I was a baby, was the reason I was even alive today. Maybe it was my turn to rescue her. I couldn't let her wither away like that flower in the book. I needed to fight for her, to nurture her back to health and take care of her like she'd done for me over the years.

Sometimes that care had been misguided, but she'd done her best. Now it was time to do mine. Mind made up, I strode across the room to grab my cloak from a little hook on the wall, then shoved my feet into boots that had worn far too thin. I'd need new ones soon. Like all my clothes, the cloak had slits in the back so I could slide my wings through. Nerves fluttered in my stomach as I gazed out the window. The view of

Valoris stretched out before me, everything so small, a tiny world living beneath me and my tall tower. Puffy white clouds gathered around the outside of the window, and trees dotted the hilly terrain beyond the meadow that surrounded our home. Green mountains rose in the distance, tall and stark under the waning sun.

I snuck a glance behind me. Gran still slept, coughs wracking her body. She was too weak to use magic to leave like she normally did, and even if she was strong enough to use her magic, she certainly didn't have the strength to go foraging or to walk to the nearest village. So I'd have to do it for her, even if I wasn't supposed to.

With darkness pushing away the light, this would be the best time to go unnoticed.

I tiptoed past her sleeping form and knelt to the ground, slowly removing a loose stone from the floor. Gran thought she was being clever putting it here, but I knew where she hid the magic bean. I'd found the loose stone long ago while sweeping. The broom had snagged over the edges, and when I'd lifted the stone, it revealed a little chest. I reached down and lifted out the chest, which contained gold, a few maps, a necklace, and a small green pod, unassuming but powerful.

Gran had never used it, didn't have to when she had shadow magic, could bend shadows to her will, make them pluck her from the tower and bring her to the bottom. My wings twitched. I didn't have the same magic as her, but it didn't matter . . . I couldn't use the magic I did possess. Had never been able to. Though it would make my life much easier if I could flap my wings and leave this tower. Though she hadn't told me about the bean, I always assumed it was to be used in case of an emergency. Gran had told me about this kind of magic, powerful and not easy to acquire. I pinched the bean, rolling it between my fingers, feeling its power jolt through me.

I stood and straightened my shoulders as I walked toward the window and tossed the bean to the ground far, far below before I could change my mind. It disappeared from sight as it dropped.

With bated breath, I waited, silent, watching, until a beanstalk shot up past my window, thick and ropey, twisted and knotted. I bit the inside of my cheek, doubt freezing me in place. Another cough fought its way from Gran's lungs, harsh and throttled. I turned back to the window, determined to see this through.

The beanstalk swayed in the wind, and I climbed through the little window and latched onto it, arms wrapping around the massive stalk. It would be a simple trip to get Gran the herbs she needed. She'd understand. She had to—because there was no turning back now.

READ NOW!

www.ingramcontent.com/pod-product-compliance
Lightning Source LLC
Chambersburg PA
CBHW031115160726
47991CB00004B/1392